PRAISE FOR "EATING BULL" BY CARRIE RUBIN

"A solid thriller that manages to infuse one boy's coming-of-age with a whole lot of murder."

— *Kirkus Reviews*

"A deftly crafted novel of suspense and a compelling read from beginning to end ...Very highly recommended."

— *Midwest Book Review*

"Each of Rubin's characters is carefully developed and believable."

— *Akron Beacon Journal*

"Rubin is a masterful storyteller who weaves her medical knowledge into a gripping thriller, diving head-first into a meaty subject that has been ignored for far too long."

— *Dianne Gray, award-winning Australian author of Soul's Child and The Everything Theory*

PRAISE FOR "THE BONE HUNGER" BY CARRIE RUBIN

"The reveal is a real shocker, and Rubin's winning lead is well-suited to sustain a series. This is just the ticket for Robin Cook fans."

— *Publishers Weekly*

"The author's prose is sleek and organic, regarding both descriptions and punchy dialogue. ... An aptly crafted, riveting, and often unnerving mystery."

— *Kirkus Reviews*

"Rubin's ability to blend the investigative and medical thriller components into a wider-ranging exploration of Ben's psyche and his career and family challenges lends to a story that is gripping, involving, and hard to put down."

— D. Donovan, Senior Reviewer, *Midwest Book Review*

"*The Bone Hunger* has more twists and turns than the Iditarod Race. It'll keep you guessing until the end and hollering for more from Carrie Rubin"

— *Mysterious Book Report*

PRAISE FOR "THE BONE CURSE" BY CARRIE RUBIN

"*The Bone Curse* is a strong medical thriller — inclusive, skillfully written, and inviting."

— *Foreword Reviews*

"A tense, perceptive tale of an investigation into a terrifying threat."

— *Kirkus Reviews*

"Take note medical thriller fans, the genre has a new contender, and her name is Carrie Rubin."

— Larry Brooks, *USA Today* bestselling author

"A teeth-grinding story of ancient curses and mystical remedies ... The Bone Curse will keep even the most skeptical reader awake long past midnight."

— Andra Watkins, *New York Times* bestselling author
of *Not Without My Father*

PRAISE FOR "THE SENECA SCOURGE" BY CARRIE RUBIN

"fun, fast, original, and won't strain your emotions."

— *ScienceThrillers*

"*The Seneca Scourge* by Carrie Rubin was impossible to put down."

— Trudi LoPreto for *Readers Favorite*

"I love, love, love, LOVED this book. 4 out of 4 stars ... well written, well thought out, well planned, and just a great book altogether."

— *Online Book Club*

"Rubin masterfully blends medical thriller, mystery, and sci-fi into a thoroughly enjoyable read."

— Audrey Kalman, author of *Tiny Shoes Dancing*

EATING BULL

EATING BULL

CARRIE RUBIN

Science Thrillers Media

First edition, 2015

Library of Congress Control Number 2015950698

FIC031080 FICTION / Thrillers / Psychological
FIC031040 FICTION / Thrillers / Medical
FIC043000 FICTION / Coming of Age

ISBN 978-1-7328541-1-6 (trade paperback)
ISBN 978-1-7328541-0-9 (ebook)

Cover design by Lance Buckley Design

To my mother for surviving a difficult year, and to my stepfather for getting her through it

1

JEREMY

Pain made people do horrible things: kick their cats, beat their kids, swallow a fistful of pills. But whether it was physical or emotional pain that made Jeremy Harjo Barton want to snatch the gun from his grandpa's hands and blow the ex-soldier away, he couldn't say. On that afternoon, he had plenty of both.

A bullet would shut the guy up, no doubt. Stop the fat-bashing once and for all, not to mention leave a gaping hole in his hangdog face, a face far narrower than Jeremy's own moon-pie mug and one that hadn't seen sunlight in five years, other than from a window.

Do you think I like being fat, Grandpa? Don't you think I'd lose weight if I could?

From the plaid sofa, Jeremy watched his grandfather polish the gun, the cleaning cloth twisting and flapping around the barrel. It was Wednesday's ritual. First the old service revolver, then the Beretta, and finally the Bowie knife. Richard "Dick" Barton cleaned each piece while seated in his ratty recliner, a nearby side table holding the waiting munitions.

Who am I kidding? Jeremy thought.

He was no more likely to handle a weapon than he was to climb Key Tower in downtown Cleveland. Rescuing overturned beetles and petting stray dogs was more his style.

A smile crossed his lips when he pictured the sniffing mutt who'd wandered into their yard the day before, its matted fur the same dull brown as the summer grass. Despite a throbbing, walnut-sized boil near his groin, Jeremy had shuffled outside to pet the dog, the cool licks on his face worth the pain in his thigh.

A bellow from his grandfather broke his reverie, and the pleasant image faded. "What the hell are you smiling about? If you'd get off your butt and exercise, your mom wouldn't have to race home to take you to the ER. How the hell did you get that thing, anyway? It's not like you're slogging through the jungles of Nam. Like you kids today would know anything about that."

Jeremy considered telling the recluse that present-day soldiers were as competent as GI Dick had been four decades ago, but he didn't have the energy. Nor did he have the energy to get off the couch and go to his room, although he wanted nothing more than to return to his online game. His mom was on her way though, and the effort of waddling up the stairs, combined with the pain in his infected groin, kept him glued to the sofa.

"Huh? You listening to me? I asked why you let it get so big? You think your mom's got time to haul your ass to the ER every month? Your asthma wouldn't act up if you lost weight, and you wouldn't get a dirty boil either." His grandpa coughed and cleared mucus from his throat.

Jeremy poked a cuticle-bitten finger through a hole in the cushion fabric. His eyes teared. He blinked the moisture away, hoping his grandfather hadn't noticed.

"Oh, I don't know." GI Dick's tone thawed a degree. "Maybe this clinic thing she took you to last month will help. You think?"

The chewed finger found its way back to Jeremy's mouth. "I hope so," he said softly, but he didn't believe it. According to his grandfather, Jeremy was born fat, and one way or another, he knew he would die fat.

The front door banged open, and his mother, Connie, rushed in.

"Hey, kiddo," she said, crossing the small living room to give Jeremy a peck on the head. When she stepped back, her leg struck the coffee table, sending an empty bag of potato chips wafting to the floor where it joined two cola cans and a torn gaming magazine. "Sorry it took so long. I didn't get done until three thirty and missed my bus. Did Rex get here yet?"

Jeremy shook his head but held back a comment. He didn't care for his mom's boyfriend any more than his grandpa did, but he didn't like giving her grief about it. His grandpa and Rex hassled her enough.

Dick put the gun and cleaning cloth on the end table and picked up the smaller pistol, peering at it through his reading glasses. "You counting on that ass to drive you?"

After rubbing the sting out of her shin, Connie pulled a cardboard container and some napkins from her bag and handed them to Jeremy. The scent of baked crust filled the air. "Here, sweetie, it's all I had time to grab. We'll get something else for you later. How's your thigh? You doing okay?"

Jeremy's mood lifted the moment he saw three slices of pepperoni pizza from Sandy's Italian Eatery nestled in the grease-stained box, and despite having a hot poker near his left testicle, he nodded.

To her father, Connie said, "Come on, Dad, how else am I going to get there?"

"If you'd kept up the maintenance on my Buick, you wouldn't have to rely on that crap boyfriend for his car."

Connie stepped behind her dad and rubbed his shoulders. "I took care of your car just fine. It was old. It died."

Dick grunted but said nothing, his face going slack from the short massage.

"I'll run and freshen up." Connie abandoned the back rub and sprinted up the stairs to her bedroom, brassy blond ponytail swaying back and forth over her blue cashier's smock.

She and Jeremy each had a bedroom upstairs along with a small bathroom they shared. Dick slept in the master bedroom on the main floor. A green Formica kitchen, cluttered living room, and layers of dust completed the small Cleveland home.

The neighborhood was crappy, too. Rundown houses, abandoned buildings, neglected yards. But it was less than a mile to school, and Mr. and Mrs. Duong, the old couple next door, were pretty nice. They paid Jeremy to mow their tiny lawn and shovel their sidewalk, which required at least two puffs of his inhaler to complete.

As Jeremy polished off the last of the pizza slices, the doorbell rang. Before either he or Dick could respond, Rex burst in, dressed in his usual snug T-shirt and low-slung jeans.

"Hey, Eating Bull. Dick. How's life?"

Jeremy balled up the greasy napkins in his hand and squeezed. Not only did he hate the nickname (*thanks for that, Grandpa*), he hated that Rex spewed it, though the guy was careful not to say it around Connie.

"Why don't you let my daughter use one of your cars?" Dick asked, forgoing all pleasantries, his grip tightening on the pistol.

"Not mine to give. Belongs to the company." Rex eyed the threadbare chair next to Dick as if it were covered in turds and took a seat on the edge.

"Hmmm, seems to be available whenever you want something from my daughter."

Awkward silence cloaked the room, broken only by the air conditioner kicking in. Despite the cool blast from the window unit, Jeremy's pits felt moist and sticky. He shifted his position on the couch, triggering an involuntary gasp of pain.

"Connie, hurry up now. Jeremy's hurtin'." Dick turned to look over his shoulder at the stairwell behind him. Soon Connie came flying down. Though she was overweight, Jeremy would take her mild plumpness over his whale body any day.

Rex bolted up when he saw her. "Let's get moving. I gotta be somewhere in a half hour."

"You're not waiting there with us?" Connie smoothed a loose-fitting blouse over her jean shorts, sending a whiff of drugstore musk Jeremy's way. He could hear the disappointment in her voice.

"No can do, but call me when you're done, and I'll pick you up."

"Yeah, right, just like last time," Jeremy mumbled.

"What was that?" Rex's smile twitched.

"Nothing." The last thing Jeremy wanted was to get Rex worked up. If the guy stormed off, they'd have to take a bus to the ER, and Jeremy wasn't up for that. He pushed off the flattened cushion, grimacing as he stood.

Connie rushed forward and grabbed his arm.

"I'm okay, Mom," he said.

But he wasn't okay. His groin pulsed and burned, the pain of the red lesion second only to his mounting fear over its treatment. He didn't like needles. Especially needles near his junk.

The three headed out to a red Camaro, Connie's arm around a limping Jeremy, and Rex sighing in impatience behind them. Dick remained housebound as always.

Jeremy hoped the wait wouldn't be long. He wanted the thing done with. He wanted the pain gone. He wanted to get back to his room. Back to his game. Back to disappearing.

———

An hour later, Jeremy sat on a puke-green chair in the ER waiting room, his trepidation mounting. His mom perched on a yellow seat, its plastic base mottled by a brown stain the shape of Florida. Jeremy worried about its origin and hoped it had nothing to do with the dirty-diaper smell permeating the muggy air.

The room was packed, kids all over, coughing, sneezing, retching. Every time the door to the main unit buzzed, a nurse darted out to yell the next name, and everyone hushed and straightened in anticipation.

After a few cycles of patient-in, patient-out, each seemingly longer than the last, heavy sighs surfaced behind Jeremy. He turned and watched a woman he knew approach the triage window. A teenage girl with a cradled arm trailed behind.

"I'm Sue Fort, Kayla's mother. This is ridiculous."

With her nearly shaved head, impressive stature, and ear full of studs and tiny hoops, Jeremy would have recognized the woman even if she hadn't identified herself. She looked like an African warrior from his online game. Strong biceps underneath a purple V-neck tee only strengthened the comparison.

Jeremy shrank down in his seat, praying his fat-clinic nurse wouldn't see him. Considering his girth, the attempt was laughable.

"We've been waiting for almost forty-five minutes. My daughter clearly has a broken arm. It doesn't take a doctor to diagnose that."

The young secretary maintained a blank face, as though she'd heard it all before. Her goth vibe clashed with the pediatric-themed setting. "We'll get to you and your daughter as soon as we can. As you can see, it's very busy in here."

"Well, as you can see, a broken bone is very busy in *here*." The fat-clinic nurse pointed to the lump in her daughter's arm. "One that can lead to neurovascular compromise."

At that, goth woman raised her heavy-lined brows. Her gaze traveled to the daughter, a thin, pretty girl with a complexion far clearer than Jeremy's own pasty skin. Rows of beaded braids wrapped around her skull.

Way out of my league, Jeremy thought.

"So tell me," Sue said to the ER secretary, "do you have your testimony ready for when you're sitting on the stand explaining why you let my daughter's arm turn gangrenous in the waiting room?"

Though Jeremy wasn't a doctor, and unlike English, biology wasn't his best subject, even he knew the warrior's words were extreme, but it worked. Goth secretary stood, took a few steps backward, and reached for the arm of a passing guy in scrubs. Jeremy wasn't so sure Supermom would be happy with what appeared to be a sleepy resident, but after a short whispered exchange, goth woman pushed a button and buzzed in the warrior and her floor-gazing daughter.

Jeremy glanced at his mom. She raised her eyebrows in response and gave his shoulder a squeeze.

Behind them, the outside door whooshed open, and the smell of nearby fast food walloped him. His mouth watered. He was about to ask his mother for a buck or two for the vending machine when the buzzer to the main unit sounded, and a scrubs-clad, elf-sized nurse popped out and barked, "Jeremy Barton!"

Jeremy nearly jumped off the seat at the sound of his name. Pain blasted his upper thigh, and between the boil and his sweaty bulk, it took a few seconds to propel out of his chair. He could feel the silent stares.

Once inside the main ER hub, he saw a central work station surrounded by four counters. Textbooks, computers, boxes of gloves, beverage containers, and other debris littered the surfaces. Some staff members sat at the counters. Others whizzed around, in and out of curtained-off examination rooms. Some carried papers and clipboards, others medical equipment, and one big guy carried a vial of blood.

Jeremy's knees buckled. His pace slowed.

"Hmm, this scale should work for you." The waifish nurse pressed her lips together and gazed at Jeremy's belly. The top of her head was level with his chin, and he could see dark roots in her frosty, cropped hair. "It's a high-capacity scale, goes up to five hundred pounds."

Neither Jeremy nor Connie spoke.

"Go ahead. Step on it. We need your weight and height to add to the triage vitals." She offered a transient smile. "I'm Gloria. I normally work in the ICU but got pulled to the emergency department tonight."

The way she said the word *pulled* made Jeremy think the move hadn't thrilled her. He imagined she preferred cooperative kids in comas to fat teens wielding pus-filled boils.

Jeremy stepped on the scale, heat shooting through his groin.

"Three hundred and ten pounds." Tinker Bell slid the adjustable measuring rod down over his head. "At a height of five-nine." The nurse tsked her tongue and shook her head as she jotted the numbers on a form attached to her clipboard. Before Jeremy even stepped off the scale, she spun down the hall like a skinny tornado. She touched down at the second curtain from the end and held open a pale blue drape, waiting for them to catch up. "Go ahead and have a seat on the bed."

Jeremy gritted his teeth and hoisted himself onto the exam table, sweat beading his forehead. His chest tightened when he pictured the needle coming his way, and he checked his pocket for his inhaler.

"You okay, hon?" Connie rubbed his back a few times.

"Yeah, I'm—"

"Here. I'm not sure this will fit, but it's the only one that will come close." Gloria tossed a speckled gray gown on the exam table. "You'll at least need to take your pants off so the doctor can see your leg, and if you have any bandage covering the boil, you'll need to remove it."

With that, the tiny nurse was gone, leaving nothing in her wake but the tinging of curtain hooks over a thin metal rod.

"Well, she's certainly efficient," Connie said. She lowered her voice and added, "But kind of a b-i-t-c-h." Her giggling did little to ease Jeremy's nerves. "Pretend I didn't say that. Here, let me help you get those pants off."

Normally a fifteen-year-old would rather die than hear those words come from his mom, but by then Jeremy's pulse outpaced even the beeping machines down the hall, and he allowed his mother to help him remove the XXXL black sweatpants. His sweaty boxers hugged his crotch like a Speedo. He hated needles. He knew everyone said that, but he really hated them. He looked up on WebMD what they did with boils, and he was damn sure he wasn't going to like it.

Each moment Jeremy's mouth got a little drier, palms a little moister, throat a little tighter. He passed the minutes listening to wailing alarms and crying kids, neither of which inspired confidence.

He heard the warrior woman walk by with her daughter. "I knew that arm was broken."

Finally, the doctor entered.

"Jeremy? My name's Dr. Sneeker. Nice to meet you."

Despite his anxiety, Jeremy smirked, prompting the doctor to add, "Yeah, not the coolest of names, is it?" Dr. Sneeker's dark hair plastered his forehead, and stains soiled the pits of his scrubs. Silver-rimmed glasses rested on a linear nose. "So, I understand you've got a nasty boil."

Indicating with a gesture that Jeremy lean back on the table, the doctor snapped on a pair of gloves. Jeremy jumped.

God, please make this go quick.

For the next few minutes — *hours?* — Dr. Sneeker tended to the festering wound, Gloria assisting him, the Vanna White of pus. All the while, Dr. Sneeker chatted merrily, distracting Jeremy with school and video game talk. When he inquired about Jeremy's favorite game, Jeremy's answer of *War of the Wilderness* made Dr. Sneeker's head shoot up. "Hey, I just started that one. What level are you?"

"Forty-nine."

"No kidding. I'm only at level seven. I'm new to this massive multiplayer online stuff, but man, I love it. I like any kind of puzzle or game. What's your character?"

"A shaman. Kajika is his name."

"A healer, huh? My kind of guy." Dr. Sneeker winked at Connie. "Plus, those guys are lucky. They don't have to worry about getting sued." He paused and a shadow crossed his face. After a moment, he asked, "What does the name Kajika mean?"

Jeremy hesitated. He picked at a loose thread on the gown. "Walks without sound. It means one who walks without sound."

Dr. Sneeker half-smiled, half-frowned, then resumed his procedure. When he finished, he capped a big Q-tip wand saturated with pus and handed it to Tinker Bell.

Happy birthday, Jeremy thought.

Leaving Gloria to bandage the wound, Dr. Sneeker donned a serious expression and pulled up a stool. Jeremy wondered if he was about to tell him his leg would turn green and fall off.

"I'd like to talk about your weight. I know this is the ER and I don't have much time." As if on cue, his pager trilled. Dr. Sneeker read the message and frowned. His speech quickened. "Look, you and I both know you need to lose weight, am I right?"

Jeremy saw Gloria give a sharp nod as she finished wrapping the wound, as if the question had been addressed to her.

"I probably don't need to tell you that extra weight you're carrying around puts you at risk for chronic disease. Your blood pressure's a little high, not terrible, but it's in the at-risk zone. Plus, your arteries are probably already thickening, and that's only going to get worse as you get older. I know you've been seen here before for your asthma too. And the friction from your skin rubbing together? Well, that's a setup for infection."

He finally took a breath, and Connie jumped in, her lips trembling. "I know he needs to lose weight, Doctor. *I* need to lose weight. It's just so hard, you know?"

Judging by the doctor's fit body, he didn't. Jeremy put on his pants as his mother continued.

"I work two jobs, I'm a single mom and, well, there isn't a lot of time to cook for Jeremy. I end up bringing food home. But I did take him to a weight management clinic last month."

"Excellent. Glad to hear it. There are always things we can blame, but it's ultimately on us." Dr. Sneeker stood, ready to leave.

"That's right. Time to make some better choices." Gloria opened the curtain and moved out of the way to let Dr. Sneeker by.

Jeremy sat on the table, head down, gaze on his tennis shoes, the laces wide and loose to accommodate his feet. He barely heard as Gloria gave Connie the discharge instructions and antibiotic. He wanted to go home. Tuck himself into his room. Eat.

He wondered if the Dr. Sneekers and the Glorias of the world knew what it was like to lie on an exam table, looking every bit a beached whale with a red, angry boil, and hear someone talk about making better choices. Choices they themselves never had to worry about. He doubted Gloria, in all her petite pixie-ness, knew the feeling of craving food so badly all other thoughts ceased. Or the feeling of not being able to stop eating, being so out of control that it was as though the food ate the person rather than the other way around. Or hearing bullies toss out names like "lard-ass" and "fat-ass" like they were confetti.

Jeremy bet Tinker Bell had never experienced any of those things, so who was she to talk about choices?

"Let's go, honey," Connie said.

Jeremy inched off the table, relieved to feel much less pressure and pain in his groin since the pus was gone. As he and his mother exited the curtained space, he spotted the girl with the broken arm. A bright pink cast covered her limb. She and her mom were in the room across from Jeremy's. Judging by the way the warrior woman looked at him, he knew she'd heard the recent exchange. He turned away from her pity smile and headed out with his mother.

"Wait," the warrior called out. "Ms. Barton, Jeremy, can I talk to you? I'm Sue, the nurse from the public health weight management clinic."

She caught them as they were about to exit the main unit and motioned them to step away from the door, into the corner of an unoccupied room.

"We remember you." Connie fidgeted with the strap of her knock-off purse. "I'm sorry we didn't keep our follow-up appointment. Between work and not having a car, well, it's tricky, and we don't have insurance."

Sue waved her hand as if dismissing the matter. "I know. I understand. Please call the clinic and reschedule. Our social worker can meet with you. Remember, we're open 'til seven on Thursday, so that should work better for you." Sue shifted her gaze to Jeremy. "I want you to know, I heard how that nurse treated you, and I don't like it one bit. She has no idea the obstacles you face."

The warrior stared at Jeremy, hands on her hips, jaw set. He shuffled his feet, not sure what to say.

"I work with kids like you all the time. I know how hard it can be, both from my work and from my own past experience." Her voice rose in volume, and she leaned forward. "Everyone blames the individual. 'Eat less,' they say, or 'take more stairs.' Yes, those are important things to do, but what these people don't understand is how hard society makes it."

The warrior's stance was wide, feet planted, and with the way her nostrils flared, Jeremy feared smoke would shoot out of them.

"Tempt us with sugar, fat, and salt. Tell us to eat this product and that. Tell us to visit this restaurant or that ice cream shop. All the while, they make money while we as a nation grow fat. Plus, overweight people are belittled and ridiculed. That's not okay."

Jeremy was relieved that for once people weren't staring at him.

Kayla approached her mother and pulled her to the door. "Come on, Mom, let's go."

Sue blinked a few times and then nodded. To Connie, she said, "Please, schedule Jeremy's follow-up. We'll talk more. It's time someone did something about this. In fact, I have a proposal for you."

And with that, Sue and Kayla left the ER, leaving Jeremy to wonder what exactly that proposal was.

2

DARWIN

Killing a fat man was hard work, especially when severing the neck. Or maybe it was the fault of the crude weapon.

Jagged ends of the broken glass slashed and sawed, fouling the air with a yeasty fusion of beer and blood. The long neck of the bottle slipped in his hand, and he sliced the man's triple chin instead.

(You must do better.)

The killer secured his grip around the glutton's girth and trapped him between the restroom sink and his own fit body. The man's enormous belly heaved and spasmed in protest but with less strength than before. More sawing. Back and forth. In and out. Over and under the sticky tissue. The victim gurgled and sputtered. He flailed his hands at the weapon but failed to snatch the glass.

(He's too weak. Can you feel his life slipping away? Can you feel his futility?)

The killer answered the inner voice. "But he almost escaped. It's so messy. Should be quicker. Must..."

He hushed. The bottle met resistance, something hard and grisly like cartilage. The man's fight ceased, and when the serrated bottle finally punctured and severed the windpipe, hissing air marked the only protest. Once the bottle scraped the cervical vertebrae, the killer knew the man was dead. Yet he kept thrusting. Thrusting and sawing at bone, displaying a disciplined intensity only he could possess.

(It's over. Your first kill. Survival of the fittest, Darwin. That's what we'll call you from now on.)

Darwin. He liked that. Given his superior condition, the name suited him, even if it wasn't what Charles Darwin had in mind.

Letting the new name percolate, Darwin stepped back and dropped the obese man to the floor, the wide-eyed skull smacking the metal sink before landing. In the mirror, blood and sweat dripped from an angular face onto a muscular chest. Red clots blended with the sports logo on a gray sweatshirt, making its tiny embroidered athlete a sanguineous inkblot. Bits of yellow fat clung to hair. Bone flecks glistened on skin.

Bile rose in Darwin's throat. He leaned against the wall and squeezed his eyes shut.

Must shower. Now.

For Darwin, a day at work called for a ten-minute shower and three soap-downs, not counting dozens of hand washes. A few hours at the gym netted fifteen minutes and four to five soap-downs, depending on the equipment used. Sex required twenty minutes and five soap-downs, seven in the genital region, sometimes as many as ten. But killing? Killing was unprecedented. Who knew what germs the man carried?

Darwin stumbled to the toilet, nearly tripping over the bloody heap on the floor. He vomited. Stringy, gastric fluid coated his mouth, and he retched again, spraying acidic saliva down his chin.

A shaky hand wiped it away. More shower time. More soap-downs. How much cleansing would he need?

His body swayed in the small bathroom, woozy from the heaving and disgusted by the grime. Gasoline fumes from the outside pumps heightened his nausea. July heat bathed him in sweat.

Avoiding the dead lump on the dirt-streaked tiles, he walked from one end of the room to the other. Four steps.

Is that right?

He paced the cramped area again. Then again. Four steps each direction.

He counted his trips. "One, two, three, four. Two, two, three, four. Three, two, three, four. Four, two, three, four. Five, two, three—"

(Stop.)

Darwin froze and then sagged in relief. He'd worried The Voice had abandoned him. Got him into this mess and left him on his own to resolve it.

(You are embarrassing yourself. Where's your focus? Your discipline?)

The Voice was right. He had to get a grip. A man who could run ten miles as if it were a stroll to the corner store and bench press two hundred and fifty pounds could overcome blood. A man who could refrain from plying his body with unhealthy food could tolerate bone bits. A man who'd survived a four-hour bus ride after his alternator had died could surmount oily fat.

(Yes, you can.)

Darwin straightened. His strong shoulders returned to full posture. Glancing at the beefy mound on the floor, he stepped over the body and back to the sink.

His first kill. Spontaneous and unpolished, but successful nonetheless.

Power and pride replaced weakness and disgust. He lifted the chrome tap and rotated it to the hottest setting.

Discipline.

Into his palm, he pumped soap from a wall dispenser. With the same vigor he used to sever half the man's neck, he sudsed the liquid into a lather.

Discipline.

For several minutes Darwin scrubbed, stopping only to remove his sweatshirt, grateful for the T-shirt underneath. Like a gritty strawberry-banana smoothie, blood, fat, and bone bits swirled down the drain.

Discipline.

When he finished, he skipped drying his hair with the hand-dryer, eager to exit the bathroom before someone knocked on the door. Still, he couldn't resist addressing the dead man one last time.

"You shouldn't have sat next to me on the bus. You shouldn't have pressed your sticky flesh into my space, making me breathe your stench. And you should've waited for the bus station bathroom to finish being cleaned before crossing the street to this shithole."

Darwin kicked the dead man's prominent buttocks with his thick boot and laughed.

"Shoulda, coulda, woulda."

3

SUE

Sue Fort plucked dried cranberries from her salad, annoyed the Green Globe Café had messed up her lunch order yet again. In the second-floor break room, she listened to her colleagues discuss Juney Andrews, a six-year-old girl removed from her home for morbid obesity. Sue had agonized over the decision for weeks. Foster care was the last resort, but it had to be done.

Too bad not everyone could see that.

Still, many co-workers were on Sue's side, or at least they pretended to be. They understood employees of the public health department, especially an urban health department like the Cuyahoga County Public Health Center, or CCPHC, made enemies easier than they made friends.

"The media's painting you out to be some sort of monster, as if you did this all on your own," Shelly Gunther said.

Shelly was the prototype exercise physiologist. Trim, fit, blonde, unwavering in determination. She worked the pediatric weight management clinic at the health center, along with Sue and Gabrielle Esposito, a registered dietitian. Every health department varied in its low-income and indigent clinic offerings. In addition to the pediatric weight management clinic, CCPHC also housed a women's clinic, a travel clinic, and a general adult clinic, the latter of which Sue staffed on Tuesdays.

Gabrielle piped in. "That's what you and the social workers get for being on the front lines. More risk of crazy psychos."

"Well, someone had to be," Sue said.

"Yeah, because the endocrinologist was too chicken-shit to do it himself. Threw you to the wolves, a.k.a. the press."

Sue cringed at Shelly's choice of words. "In his defense, the doctor was filling in for another endocrinologist the day we removed Juney. He didn't even know the family." Although Sue wouldn't admit it, her blood still steamed over the man's disappearing act.

"Tough. He's the doctor. It's his name on the removal form whether he likes it or not." Shelly reached across the table and squeezed Sue's hand. "You had to do it. That child was eating herself to death, and her parents did nothing to stop it."

Sue had no doubt of that, but when a child got tossed into foster care because of morbid obesity, the public had questions. Sue would forever be the face tied to those questions.

But she could live with that. It wasn't the first family or patient she'd angered, and it wouldn't be the last.

The wooden chair legs creaked when she slid the seat back. Like most everything else in the building, the table was old, its cheap wood more etched and marked than a high school lovers' tree. The break room itself was small, and other than a worn couch and a kitchenette, the table was its main occupant. Because most of the clinical staff preferred bringing their own lunch or getting takeout, it was either the break room or their desks. Some days the desk was as far as Sue got. Too many phone calls and reams of paperwork.

Gabrielle scrunched her sandwich wrapper into a ball and tossed it into the trash can by the door.

"Three-pointer," Dr. Green, the new psychologist to the clinic, called out.

He had been quietly eating his lunch until then, but Sue knew he supported the group's decision to remove Juney Andrews from her family. Sue respected his opinion, and the pediatric patients seemed to like him. He was "dope" according to her daughter, Kayla, who had met him at a department picnic a couple months back. Kayla had also said his dreadlocks put the rest of their sorry styles to shame.

"Is Tucker Andrews still leaving you nasty phone calls?" Gabrielle asked.

"Well, he's certainly not happy," Sue said. "I don't blame him. If someone took my daughter from me, I'd be kicking and screaming and scratching people's eyes out."

Shelly capped her water bottle. "We saved her life."

Sue stared at a poster on the wall. The words *The Ten Great Public Health Achievements of the Twentieth Century* were followed by a list of the various advancements. The lower right corner showed a child receiving a vaccine. The little girl looked none too pleased about her advancement.

"They'll get her back. Mrs. Andrews has shown promise in her understanding of the situation. It's only temporary." Dr. Green stood and packed up his plastic lunch set. "Not to change the subject, but did you guys hear about that murder? Some guy got hacked to death in a gas station bathroom."

Sue straightened and felt her tension over Juney ease. "Yes, horrible wasn't it?"

Dr. Green dumped his unsweetened tea can into the recyclable bin. "Does Al know anything about it, Sue? I know your husband's not a homicide detective, but as a police officer, he must have some inside scoop."

"Al works for the Cleveland Heights Department. The murder happened by the bus station in the third district, but he's heard talk."

"Do they have a suspect?" Shelly asked.

"Not that I know of. It was tragic. The man apparently bled to death from a neck wound, though the police haven't mentioned a weapon." Sue left it at that. She'd learned from her husband that a jagged instrument had been used to cut through the man's throat, a bottle most likely based on the bits of glass embedded in his tissue.

"From what I saw on the news, the man was morbidly obese," Shelly said. "Only a few burgers away from a heart attack."

Though Sue would have put it more eloquently, she knew Shelly was right.

And the issue made her blood boil all over again.

Back in her office, Sue had a few minutes to answer phone calls before the Monday afternoon clinic. Her office consisted of a cubicle in a room of six other such cubicles, all divided by gray-paneled partitions. What the dividers offered in visual privacy they lacked in auditory privacy. Or olfactory, for that matter. The lithe nurse from the travel clinic and her irritable bowel syndrome made that all too clear.

If only she wouldn't eat so much processed food, Sue thought. *Thin doesn't mean healthy.*

Kayla's voice pinged in her head. "God, Mom, you don't have to be so judgmental all the time." And when Sue would tell her not to swear, Kayla would say, "God, Mom, I'm not swearing. Why are you so weird?"

Thoughts of Kayla darkened Sue's mood. Her third and final child caused her much more angst than the two older ones had. Jeanette, twenty-three and pursuing a master's degree in urban planning at the University of Chicago, had been a breeze. McCabe, twenty and a pre-med student at Ohio State, flew through his teenage years so uneventfully, Sue had convinced herself she was the greatest mother in the world.

And then there was Kayla.

At sixteen, she'd already tried Sue's patience a number of times, and lately things seemed to be getting worse. First, the broken arm from planking, a silly fad where kids suspended their prone bodies from a structure with minimal support, and more recently, a change in eating habits.

Is she getting too thin?

"Stubborn like her mother," Al would say. Then he'd squeeze Sue's backside and add, "My wife is stubborn and strong, but thank God she's still got some cushion for the pushin'."

That she did. Even though Sue exercised regularly and shed fifty pounds years ago, pounds that had crept on after that horrible night in college, her hips chose to stay put.

Thinking of that night deepened her funk. She tried to push memories of the man from her mind. Tried not to feel the weight of his body or smell the stink of his breath. Instead, she distracted herself with voicemail.

The first call was from a neighbor with terminal ovarian cancer, thanking Sue for the fresh berry fruit salad. Sue was pleased the woman had liked it and made a note to come up with other dishes her ailing friend might tolerate.

The next message prompted a groan, and as she leaned back in her chair, its support soft from years of wear, she listened to Brent Johnson plead his latest case.

"I know what I did was wrong. Having sex with those women when I knew ... well ... it was wrong, I see that now, but I don't think I need to keep coming in for weekly visits. I promise I'll take the cocktail you gave me. I don't need a babysitter anymore."

Wrong, Mr. Johnson, you most certainly still need weekly observation.

Like the endocrinologist having the misfortune of being on the case when Juney Andrews had strolled in, Sue had the misfortune of being on the clock when Brent Johnson was dragged in. The man was HIV positive but failed to take his meds regularly or use protection during sex. Because of the gravity of the case, the health department had been forced to go public with his information in order to protect the health of the women caught in his web of promiscuity, especially since he hadn't disclosed his infection to them. Didn't matter if he looked like Brad Pitt or not. Putting the public's health at risk was where she and her colleagues stepped in.

When Sue started for the clinic, her phone rang. She debated answering but then sat back down.

One less task for later.

As soon as Angie Leonard's voice flooded the line, Sue winced.

"Listen, Mrs. Fort, I told you I was takin' my little Toby to Children's, and you went and called the police anyway. And now Jackson is pissed off because when they come by to talk to me, they caught him smoking weed which, I'll have you know, is for medicinal purposes. He's angrier than shit at you. You know my boyfriend works for the health department, don't you? He helps check out those old buildings. Why'd you have to go and do that?"

Sue inhaled before speaking. As calmly as she could, she reminded Angie that as a public health nurse, her obligation was to Toby, and when the boy hadn't returned for his follow-up appointments nor been seen at the children's hospital for his dangerously high blood pressure, it was Sue's job to track the family down to make sure Toby was all right. Given they hadn't returned her phone calls or letters, she was required to call the police.

"You're a bitch, you know that? Jackson says everyone hates you and I believe it. You're a fu—"

Sue slammed the phone in its cradle, hands shaking. One more patient angered.

Terrific.

The rest of the afternoon fostered more unpleasantness. Children gaining weight instead of losing. Parents disinterested in their child's progress or making endless excuses for why it was impossible. Frustration after frustration. Failure after failure.

Sue understood. Losing weight was tough. Anyone who claimed it was as easy as eating less and exercising more was a fool. So many other factors made up that equation.

Something needed to be done. Someone needed to take action. Needed to scream and shout and threaten the only possession the powerful treasured: the almighty pocketbook. And if that sweet, apathetic Jeremy Barton showed up for his appointment on Thursday, Sue knew who she'd bring to her shout-fest.

After the clinic closed and the rest of the staff departed, Sue completed her electronic charting, having been delayed by a phone call with a community physician. She felt discouraged and drained. The quiet unnerved her, and each click of the keyboard echoed in the silent space. When she finally finished, she turned off the computer, grabbed her stethoscope, and stood to exit the staff room.

Before she got there, a shadow darkened the doorway. A large man filled its frame.

Sue inhaled sharply, and her hand flew to her chest.

Tucker Andrews. Juney's father.

"What? How? Why are you here?" Sue's other hand tightened around her stethoscope. "Have you been in the waiting room this whole time?" She wondered why the staff hadn't seen him when they'd locked the patient entrance. Once locked, people could exit but not enter. Had he been hiding? The thought made her heart thump harder.

Mr. Andrews ignored her question. "I want some answers, lady, and I want them now. When are we getting our daughter back? We're doing everything you asked. How come you won't return my phone calls?"

"I told you, I'm not supposed to talk to you directly. You're supposed to call the social worker or our lawyer."

"Screw the lawyers. Screw your social workers. And screw you. I want my daughter back. You had no right to take her. She was doing fine. She's only six for Christ's sake. Still plenty of time to outgrow her baby fat."

Sue stepped backward, ashamed to let the man intimidate her, but his words bullied as much as his bulk, and his face flushed brightly beneath his auburn stubble.

She tried to maintain full posture, tried to exude confidence, tried to be the Sue she'd long since become. "Mr. Andrews, you need to leave. I'm going to call security if you don't."

Tucker Andrews sprang forward, his nose inches from her own. Every instinct told her to run. Hadn't she learned anything from that night long ago? Coppery fear soured her mouth.

"This isn't over. If we don't get our daughter back soon, you'll be sorry." He spun around and stormed out to the waiting room. Shortly after, Sue heard the clinic's front door whip open with such force, the hinges rattled.

After he exited and the quiet returned, she wondered how sorry she'd be.

4

DARWIN

The weight of the bar almost crushed his chest, and his shaky arms were seconds from collapsing. One more rep would make ten. He had to succeed. No reward until then.

(Discipline. Remember what you're capable of.)

The Voice's sudden presence empowered Darwin. Ignoring the tremor in his arms and the heat of his hands inside the lifting gloves, he gripped the smooth metal rod more tightly. His heart drummed and his vision clouded. He hadn't eaten in hours, compelled as always to get his workout in before dinner.

(No reward before punishment.)

He emitted a primitive cry and pushed the weighted bar into the air one last time. Steel plates quivered and clanked, signaling his success.

Seconds later, the bar crashed onto the support base above his head. His elbows locked in protest and required a few rounds of extension to restore circulation. Once able, he folded the wobbly limbs over his chest and tried to steady his pounding heart with deep breaths.

Finally he stood, slowly, hoping to avoid a woozy rush. Despite his fatigue and hunger, he smiled. A six-mile run after work followed by thirty minutes of circuit training, twenty minutes of core, and an hour of heavy weightlifting. All in his own home. Forget those bastards at the gym. They may have kicked him out, but they hadn't slowed him down.

Weaving his way around a room packed with fitness equipment instead of furniture, he staggered to the bathroom. He'd already done a ten-minute, three soap-down shower after work, just as he did every day. One more set of the same and he would be allowed nourishment.

In the partial-length mirror, Darwin's naked body glistened and rippled. His abs pleased him. As such, he allowed hot water in the shower.

Once clean and pure, he prepared his meal and dined at the counter. Dinner consisted of four ounces of grilled chicken breast (its weight confirmed by the scale next to the refrigerator), a cup of steamed broccoli, and a half cup of brown rice. Because of his workout success and his sculpted abdominal muscles, he allowed four apple slices with a tiny dab of caramel.

He would enjoy the treat. Tomorrow could be different.

Once finished, he moved onto the final reward. After putting on precision glasses and applying two coats of hand sanitizer, Darwin lifted the white sheet covering his worktable and folded it as precisely as if it were a flag.

Beneath the protective linen lay his current masterpiece, a six-thousand-piece, human-anatomy jigsaw puzzle. Front and back poses of a man's skinless body were bordered by images of individual organs. Heart, lungs, brain, liver, kidneys. When completed, the product would measure over five by three feet.

Dozens of other puzzles decorated his space. Exotic lands dotted the walls. Sports-themed collections peppered the weight room. Three-dimensional projects lined a dresser and desk, including the Eiffel Tower, the Leaning Tower of Pisa, and the Taj Mahal. A model of the Washington Monument had once enjoyed similar placement but, due to a flaw, Darwin had to destroy it. All because of the fat kid at the hobby store, the one whose girly yellow smock stretched taut over his gluttonous gut.

"Sorry we're out of your preferred brand, sir, but this glue will work equally well."

But the adhesive had not worked equally well. It had streaked in three places. As a result, two months of work had to be destroyed.

Fat idiot.

Recalling the incident delivered Darwin to a different, sadder place. He dropped the jigsaw piece containing the temporalis muscle and closed his eyes.

He visualized the one puzzle his sanctuary lacked, the one he hadn't found despite years of searching. A young boy riding in the sidecar of a motorcycle with his father at the helm.

The two-thousand-piece puzzle had been a gift from his dad when Darwin was six years old. Day after day, piece by piece, they worked together, until only one small section remained. A young, eager Darwin, perched on his stool by the window in winter or out on the curb in spring, waited daily for his father to return from work so they could continue their project. He knew right away where he'd hang the finished puzzle. Above his bed.

But one day his father didn't come home. Never made it out of a four-car pile-up on the highway.

And Darwin never saw that puzzle again.

"There was so much going on, I don't know what happened to it," his mother had said. "Now quit your whining or I'll give you a slap."

Darwin hadn't believed her. Who could believe a useless, fat stump? One who'd gained more than a hundred pounds after his daddy died, plying herself and Darwin with food rather than comfort. She hadn't cared about his daddy. Marrying that loser only a year after the funeral had confirmed Darwin's suspicions.

"It's for the best. Your momma doesn't have any skills. We need someone to take care of us. Now you mind your tongue or you'll go to the basement."

What kind of twisted man married an obese sloth? A chain-smoking pencil and a grapefruit — together, that was what they were. And it wasn't long before his mother grew into an immobile melon.

Disgusting.

Shaking off the memory, Darwin pinched the skin on his upper arm, squeezing less and less tissue each time until the pain became intolerable.

Fat people. Fat people all around him. Invading his space, slowing him down, skyrocketing the cost of his health insurance. His whale of a co-worker, claiming she needed a special ergonomic chair to accommo-date her girth. Miss Fat Witch had even complained to their rotund boss that Darwin's attitude frightened her and she worried her weak heart could not sustain such harshness.

He would show her harshness.

Darwin stopped pinching and sat motionless. He imagined the fillet knife from the wooden block in his hands, or better yet, the puntilla blade, a superior tool for slaughtering a large animal. He imagined it slicing through Miss Fat Witch's blubber and burying it into her organs. Organs far more fat-coated than those on the puzzle before him.

Or maybe the worthless hobby-shop blimp. Slice him into pieces and then glue him back together with his shitty adhesive.

Lightness enveloped Darwin, a lightness he hadn't fully enjoyed since the gas station kill ten days before.

(Soon. You'll find your peace again soon.)

Darwin nodded. He reclaimed the temporalis muscle piece and connected it to the rest of the puzzle, just as he would connect the murders to their motive for the ignorant cops.

(You'll make them see soon enough, Darwin. You'll make the whole world see.)

5

JEREMY

Eight days after his ER visit, Jeremy arrived for a Thursday evening appointment at his fat clinic. Or weight management clinic as his mother had told him to call it. He and Connie sat opposite the nutritionist, Gabrielle Esposito, in a room that looked like every other clinic room he'd seen, only in worse shape. Worn medical instruments on the wall, stained sink, exam table with a torn cushion.

After scrolling through Jeremy's nutrition calendar for the previous month — the one he was supposed to use to track every morsel that landed in his cakehole but he'd actually only used to document the first four days — the raven-haired dietitian paused, left the room, and returned with a glob of fat and a collection of sugar tubes.

"This is what five pounds of fat looks like," she said, waving the lumpy mass in front of Jeremy's face. Like a big yellow turd, the plastic model measured a foot long and at least six inches wide. She dumped it in his hands. "Here, feel it. See how heavy it is? Think of how many of those are inside you. And those sodas you've been drinking? Look at how much sugar is in them."

Gabrielle held up a glass test tube filled with granulated sugar. The juice, chocolate milk, and fruit-punch sugar tubes followed. "That's how much sugar is in the fluids you've been drinking. Empty calories of sugar."

After creating a dietary goal they both agreed on — Jeremy would drink only an occasional diet soda, limit juice to an eight- to twelve-ounce serving per day, and eat fast food only twice a week instead of near daily — she handed him off to Shelly Gunther, the exercise physiologist, but not before giving his shoulder a squeeze and reminding him that starting with small goals instead of unreasonable ones would yield the most success. "Baby steps, Jeremy. Baby steps."

After a few minutes with the exercise physiologist, Jeremy decided he preferred the dietitian's sugar tubes and repulsive fat blobs. The moves Shelly demonstrated within the confines of the examination room seemed more like giant steps than baby steps. Between the exam table and the sink, the fit woman leaped through the air, first in a series of jumping jacks and then a sequence of tuck jumps, drawing her skinny knees up to her slim belly. Then she dropped to the ground, kicked her feet out, jumped them back in, and shot up into the air. Burpees, apparently.

Right. More like barfies.

The blond jumping bean burst up into an air jack. Jeremy almost laughed out loud, and he suspected his mother was similarly amused. He'd look like Shamu having a seizure if he tried that.

Finally, Shelly stopped the exercise demonstration. Barely out of breath, she said, "Ten of each move separated by thirty seconds of jogging in place. Or walk if you need to, but try to push yourself. And use your asthma controller med every day. Don't let your asthma be an excuse. Start slow, modify the moves if you need to, then work your way up to three sets. You'll be surprised by the progress you make if you don't give up, but this is in addition to the increased walking you promised me you'd do. To and from summer school, right?"

His mom shifted in her seat. Jeremy knew what she was thinking. She didn't like him walking to school, even though it was only four-fifths of a mile away. She preferred he rode the bus, because a couple blocks of the journey near Mason High School were drive-by shooting worthy, but the stretch on Clark Avenue wasn't as bad, and they both knew kids walked the route every day. They also knew walking to and from school was more realistic than going to a gym, given there were no fitness facilities nearby. And hell if he was going to use the high school's weight room. He saw enough of that bully, Calvin Swanson, already. He didn't need to offer himself up for more abuse.

"Right," Jeremy said.

After his sessions with the Fat Slayers ended, he moved onto the psychologist. The Fat Slayer name had come to Jeremy when he'd realized the dietitian and the exercise freak were not unlike the Rafkin Slayers in his online *War of the Wilderness* game, two sisters who killed evil Rafkin demons. Only in this case, the demons were fat cells.

Jeremy hadn't met the psychologist at his initial appointment the previous month. His image of a balding, bug-eyed priss burst apart when a fit, dreadlocked man entered instead. Jeremy's eyes widened at the guy's jeans and Cleveland Browns T-shirt. Reading glasses dangled on a black cord around his neck.

I can work with this, Jeremy thought.

After introductions and small talk, Dr. Green sat on a stool opposite Jeremy and Connie who remained seated against the wall. He dived into a thirty-minute question-and-answer period targeting Jeremy's past history, family history, and social history. When he asked how Jeremy felt about having to attend summer school for math, Jeremy shrugged and said, "Better than repeating freshman algebra."

That answer would have to do. He wasn't about to tell Dr. Green — or his mother — that the reason for his lousy math grade was probably because he'd refused further tutoring from the pudgy teacher. True, he couldn't be sure the dude's close contact and weird leg rub had meant anything, but he'd been too disturbed to find out.

"You mentioned you live with your mother and grandfather and that your grandmother died of cancer. What about your father?" The psychologist's posture was relaxed with one leg positioned on the other. An electronic tablet for note taking rested in his lap.

"Um, he died before I was born." Jeremy studied a poster on the wall depicting a properly proportioned plate of food. To him, it looked like an appetizer. "Car accident. Drunk driver killed him."

"Oh, I'm sorry." To Connie, Dr. Green said, "That must have been difficult for you."

Connie fiddled with the metal clasp on her purse. "Well, we weren't exactly a couple. Clayton Harjo was a boy I ... um ... a boy I knew for a short time."

Jeremy's mother avoided talk of his father like a bad case of herpes, so their conversations on the subject had been scant. Jeremy took her silence to mean she was embarrassed she'd hooked up so casually and, as such, had little knowledge about the man.

Dr. Green slid the stool back and leaned against the exam table. His fingers stopped typing. "Harjo. Your middle name. That's Native American, I take it?"

Jeremy straightened and his customary monotone assumed a spirited cadence. "Creek. Of the Muskogee tribe. My dad was one-eighth Creek Indian. Well, at least that's what he told you, right, Mom?"

Connie nodded but said nothing, her eyes and fingers still focused on her purse clasp.

"Which would make you one-sixteenth. Not many Native Americans around Cleveland," Dr. Green said.

Jeremy leaned forward, his stomach rolls multiplying. "The way I figure it? His grandpa, or maybe even his great grandpa, came this way from Oklahoma. Or who knows? Maybe my dad came to Ohio on his own. See, in the 1800s, the Creeks were forced by the U.S. Army to leave their land in the Southeast. They had to head to the Indian Territory of Oklahoma."

The psychologist clasped his hands behind his head, the tablet resting precariously on his folded knee. "Wow, I'm impressed. Pretty interested in the subject, huh?"

As if caught knitting a pink scarf, Jeremy leaned back and resumed his slouched position. "Yeah, I guess."

"Oh, don't get me wrong, I think that's fantastic. We should all be so interested in our heritage." Dr. Green shifted his attention to Connie. "You gave your son a nice gift by making Clayton's surname Jeremy's middle name. A piece of his father, so to speak."

Connie offered the psychologist a quick smile and nod. "Not to change the subject, but I was ... well, I was worried about how to pay for all this. I mean, it's great Jeremy gets to meet with so many of you and you've all been helpful, but they want us to come back in a couple weeks and then every month. I'm not sure I can afford that, even with a sliding scale. I don't have insurance. Neither of my jobs is actually full time, so I don't get benefits, and I make just over the limit to qualify for Medicaid."

Dr. Green held up his hands. "I hear you. You're not alone. You can meet with our case worker. She'll get you sorted out, and she'll tell you what to expect with the new healthcare law too."

After a few more minutes of exchange, Dr. Green sent Connie out of the room so he could talk to Jeremy one on one. Jeremy wasn't an idiot. He knew where Dr. Green was headed. The psychologist wanted to uncover the myriad of crap that made Jeremy stuff his face, but

Jeremy was hungry, tired, and sick of answering questions, so he simply shrugged at the right times and said things like "not really," and "I don't know," and "it's no big deal."

Some uncomfortable moments of silence came from Jeremy's indifference, but Dr. Green smiled as if he had all night to wait. Finally, apparently realizing he'd reached the limits of their interaction, the psychologist crouched, looked Jeremy in the eye, and said, "I believe in you, Jeremy. You might not, but I do. You can do this. One year from now, you'll be walking through that door a new man — physically, mentally, and maybe even spiritually."

With that he was gone, his encouraging words allowing Jeremy an imperceptible sparkle of hope.

Thirty minutes later, Sue the Warrior peered at his neck, her fingertips prodding the skin as if searching for embedded jewels. Up close, Jeremy noticed the nurse's eyes were brown, and inside the irises, tiny flecks of coal shimmered, an effect that made her all the more imposing.

"This velvety, blackish stain here?" Sue ran two fingers around the base of Jeremy's neck. "This is called acanthosis nigricans. It's from insulin resistance, a sign your body isn't using insulin as well as it should."

He knew the area she was talking about. He first noticed it more than a year ago. He thought the stains were stubborn dirt.

"Don't you know how to wash yourself, boy?" his grandpa had asked, gripping Jeremy's collar and yanking it backward to expose his neck. "You need to get in there with a washcloth and scrub, for Christ's sake. Ain't no one gonna do it for you."

So Jeremy had scrubbed. Scrubbed so hard he nearly ripped off a layer of skin. Yet the black stains remained and he realized it was a part of him, not understanding its significance until months later during an ER visit for his asthma. A hurried doc had pointed it out.

"Does that mean he has diabetes?" Connie asked Sue. Her eyes were wide, mascara smeared beneath the lower lashes.

The warrior shook her head. "Not diabetes, but it's a sign of pre-diabetes. Remember the blood we drew at Jeremy's first visit?"

Jeremy remembered. He hated needles. He hated the sight of

blood. Especially his own. He'd worried he would pass out, but when the needle poked through his buried vein, he'd concentrated his gaze on the stupid cat poster hanging on the phlebotomist's wall instead of the burgundy juice filling her tube.

Sue continued. "It showed his blood sugar was normal, meaning he doesn't have active diabetes, but his insulin level was high, and his hemoglobin A1c was borderline. We tried to notify you of the lab results but you never called back."

Connie smoothed loose strands of hair behind her ear, strands that never stayed put in her ponytail. "Sorry, so busy, you know..."

Sue waved the apology away. "I would have kept calling had the labs been more abnormal, but aside from the pre-diabetes red flags, everything was good, including his liver enzymes. Fatty livers are common nowadays. Kids as young as Jeremy are getting liver disease from their obesity." The nurse's sharp gaze found its way back to Jeremy. "But you're not off scot-free. Your blood pressure is still borderline high, and you told me you've been using your rescue inhaler several times a week, which means you need to do a better job of using your controller inhaler. I'm glad your boil healed, but you're at risk for getting more. Hypertension, sleep apnea, asthma, diabetes, liver disease, skin problems — these are all complications of obesity. With a body mass index of almost forty-six, which is extreme or morbid obesity, you're on your way to getting all of them. In fact, I'm surprised your labs look as good as they do, though I suspect the doctor will start you on metformin for the high insulin. Do you understand all that?"

Her blunt words struck like an ax. For a moment, nobody spoke. Then, to Jeremy's surprise, his mother started to cry, not all-out weeping, but a slow trickle of tears.

Jeremy swallowed. He blinked his own eyes. He lifted a hand, wanting to pat his mom's arm, but she was too far away. His chubby fist plopped back onto the exam table.

Sue stepped forward and settled onto the chair next to Connie. She grabbed her hand. "Hey, it's okay. I know how hard it can be. I used to lug an extra fifty pounds around, and with as many times as I lost and regained it, you'd think I'd be all stretched out by now, but I finally kept it off. It's not about dieting. It's not about eating lettuce or grapefruits all day, or running until your shins splinter and crack. It's about changing your lifestyle. The family's lifestyle."

Connie wiped away tears with her free hand, smearing mascara even more.

"But our world doesn't make it easy, does it? You work your tail off to make ends meet. You barely have time to see your son let alone stop and cook a meal, right?"

Connie nodded, sniffed, and nodded again. Sue reached over her and plucked a tissue from the box on the counter near the sink. She handed it to Connie.

"So you bring home food after work, either from the Gourmand's Buffet on the nights you work there or from Jeremy's favorite, Burgers and Buns, or Sandy's Italian Eatery near your other job at Home Solutions. I'm not blaming you. Many families do the same, sometimes every night. Of course it's up to you and Jeremy to decide what goes into your mouths and what doesn't, but the act is like pushing an enormous rock up a hill, isn't it? Temptation at every corner, neighborhood sidewalks not safe for strolling, no steady means of transportation, endless convenience stores and fast-food joints but rarely a legitimate grocery store."

Sue quieted. Muffled voices from the hallway grew and then softened as people passed by.

Finally, the warrior woman stood, planted her hands on her hips, and scowled. "That's why I'm going to do something, something to put a dent in this insanity." Another pause. "And I want you and Jeremy to help me."

Connie stopped crying and glanced at Jeremy. He shrugged.

"What do you mean?" Connie asked. "What can we do?"

"First of all, you can take care of yourselves. Treat your bodies the way they deserve. We will help you do that. No judgment. No punishments. Only guidance and support as you meet your goals. Jeremy, you can do this. Trust your gut, literally and figuratively."

With the number of cheerleaders Jeremy was gaining, he figured he could start his own squad. "Um, okay."

"But while you're helping yourselves, I want you to help me help others. Lots of others. In fact, the whole country."

Jeremy stared at the warrior as if the word *crazy* were tattooed on her forehead. "Uh, how are we supposed to do that?"

Sue's face lit up, her grin rivaling the Joker's. "You and me? We're going to sue the food industry."

Jeremy's mind spun as Sue led them through the gray-floored health department halls toward the parking garage. She'd offered to drive them home since Jeremy was the last patient in clinic.

Sue.

Sue wanted to sue.

And she wanted them to help her.

"Junk-filled restaurants, food and beverage industries, fast-food joints. You name it, we'll sue it," she said as Jeremy and Connie struggled to maintain the pace behind her. "Sure, it might prove futile. We might barely get off the ground before we get shut down, but it's a start. We'll make some noise, at least. We'll do some shouting."

She paused at the stairwell to let Jeremy catch his breath. He resisted digging his inhaler out of his sweatpants.

"People don't realize the time and money the food industry invests to find that perfect combination of fat, sugar, and salt to keep us mindlessly munching. That right amount of sweetness to trigger our bliss point. Not to be evil, mind you, but to maximize profit. You don't see anyone stuffing themselves on carrot sticks or broccoli sprigs, do you? But a bag full of chips? Can't stop 'til they're gone."

"Well, that's true, but—"

Sue cut Connie off. "It's a lot to take in, I know, but promise you'll think about it."

At that moment, the stairwell door flew open and a man exited.

"Oh, hi, George," Sue said. "Working late, I see."

The man looked up, glanced at Jeremy's belly, then Sue. "You too, I guess."

He said goodbye and continued on his way. Connie stared after his dark hair and slim waist.

"Who's that?" she asked, the playful lilt in her voice making Jeremy's cheeks redden.

"That's George Koster. He's one of our statisticians, though I don't work with him much. A rather serious guy, but yes, he's quite a looker."

"Certainly gives a gal incentive to lose a few pounds, doesn't he?"

Sue and Connie laughed. Jeremy shook his head. He ignored their chatter about husbands and boyfriends and instead focused on surviving two flights in the concrete stairwell. With each step, his breaths quickened, and his chest tightened. He buried his hand in his pocket and grasped the inhaler.

Still there.

On the third floor, they crossed one more hallway, bathed in the same white walls as the floors below. Brown doors with security keypads broke the monotony every fifteen feet or so. At the end of the hall lay their final destination, the exit into the muggy parking garage.

In the back seat of Sue's Ford Focus, Jeremy sucked two puffs from his inhaler. He planted his head against the seat and nodded in response when Connie asked if he was okay.

He tuned out all external stimulation and let the motion of the car calm him. His breathing steadied. His airways opened. He closed his eyes and pictured his round face smeared all over the tabloids: "Obese teenager sues Burgers and Buns for making him fat."

He could hear his grandfather already. "What in the hell kind of crap is that? Suing other people for your fatness? That's horseshit. Christ, what's this world coming to? A bunch of pussies."

And Rex? He'd side with GI Dick. The only things Rex and Dick seemed to agree on were their hatred of fat people and Jeremy's nickname. His grandpa had once spouted it after witnessing Jeremy devour a stuffed-crust pizza three years earlier. "You're supposed to eat the thing, not snort it. You sound like a goddamn bull. Ha, Eating Bull, that's what you are." Dick had used the nickname ever since, despite Connie's objection.

Jeremy wondered what Kajika, his online shaman, would think about Sue's plan. Or his father if he were alive. A gnawing ache gripped his belly, and he quickly brushed the thought away.

Stupid.

Just as well his dad had died. Jeremy would never want him to see how obese he'd become. He imagined the shame his son's moon face plastered over the newspapers would bring.

The boy behind the lawsuit.

The poster boy of fat.

6

SUE

The best part about having hair no longer than a dusting of sand was the speed of getting ready in the morning. Within ten minutes, Sue showered, moisturized, dressed in dark slacks and a summer blouse, applied a coat of lavender eye shadow and mascara, and brushed on a sprinkle of blush. After breakfast, a swipe of her trademark rose lipstick would finish the ritual and, voilà, a not-bad-for-her-age, forty-eight-year-old woman emerged. To her, age was only a number. She'd never felt so strong and healthy. Some days, though, the stress one-upped her, and she felt every bit her five decades.

She hoped the day ahead would not be one of those days.

As she dug through her jewelry stand for a trio of silver necklaces, she thought about Jeremy and Connie Barton. Clasping the first of the chains around her neck, she wondered if they would bite. It had been almost two weeks since she'd proposed the lawsuit idea, and she had yet to hear back. She hoped she hadn't come on too strong.

"Did you do the Sue stampede?" Al would say.

But Sue had learned long ago a wimpy approach netted wimpy results.

Al remained in the dark about her litigation plans. She knew she needed to tell him. With or without the Bartons, she would move ahead, but one hurdle at a time.

She had, however, told Al about Jeremy.

"You should see him. On the outside there's this apathetic kid with monosyllabic responses and a face as unmoving as a rock, but on the inside, a spirit is begging to come out. Sometimes he lets it, and it's beautiful to see the animation. And the vocabulary on that kid? Impressive."

She left it at that, patient confidentiality and all, but over the past couple weeks, Sue's thoughts had traveled to Jeremy often. She worried about his home life: a passive mother who was frequently absent, an agoraphobic grandpa, a dead father, no friends, a sketchy maternal boyfriend. Dex or Rex or something like that. She'd seen the name in Dr. Green's notes somewhere.

Sue wanted all her overweight patients to succeed, but something about Jeremy made her feel a special kinship. She wanted him to know there was hope. She wanted him to know he didn't have to continue down the same weight-gaining path.

And she needed a plaintiff to make the lawsuit work.

Al popped into her head again. "Don't manipulate them, honey."

Sue brushed the fictitious warning away. *Nonsense.*

She secured the last of the silver necklaces and headed downstairs to the kitchen, by far her favorite room in their four-bedroom, three-story Cleveland Heights home. Though neutral tones dominated the house, a rainbow of colorful accessories splashed every nook and cranny. Pillows, artwork, vases, lamps.

The yellow kitchen boasted a wide-open space with a large center island whose tan and brown quartz meshed with the living room's cream-colored sofas. The kitchen bay window welcomed bountiful light, and the clean, white appliances sparkled in the sun's rays.

When Sue entered, Al looked up from a dismantled toaster and grinned. A screwdriver poked from his hand. "There's my lovely lady." He stepped forward and planted a loud smack on her lips.

Reaching for a coffee mug from the cabinet above Al's head, Sue frowned. "What have you done to our toaster? It worked fine yesterday morning."

"The damn thing was toasting too light."

"That's what the dial is for."

Al shook his head. "Wasn't set right, but don't worry. It'll be good as new."

At over six feet, Al complemented Sue's tall stature. Though his hair showed more gray and his skin more lines, he still possessed the same strong physique as when they married.

"Yeah, like the microwave you fixed last month and the television in the basement still missing its insides. I refuse to enter your house of horrors down there."

"Hobbies, baby, house of hobbies. These things take time, but don't you worry, they don't call me Al the Fixer for nothin'."

"Well, Fixer, sit and have some coffee with me. I have a few minutes before I need to leave." Sue mixed berries and yogurt into a bowl, the red and black juices from the fruit bleeding into the vanilla cream. On top, she sprinkled granola.

As they sipped the hazelnut blend, she asked about Al's work. After a few minutes of the latest police politics, she asked about the murder in the gas station bathroom. "Any new leads?"

"None. Do you believe it? A gas station bathroom makes for a diffi-cult crime scene. All sorts of footprints, fingerprints, and buttprints around that place."

"The guy have any enemies?"

"Don't we all? But no, nothing stood out. Homicide's taking the heat on this one, and I hear they're frustrated as heck. Guess the attack was brutal. The guy was huge, obese. Must have taken a strong man to do the job."

Sue sighed and sipped her coffee. She wondered about the nature of humankind.

"Speaking of enemies, what's going on with that Andrews case? That guy hasn't contacted you again, has he?" Al's tone assumed a hard edge. He gripped the Cleveland Indians mug in his hands, burying the ugly mascot completely.

Sue had told Al about her frightening encounter with Tucker Andrews in the clinic two weeks before. As she knew he would, her husband had erupted in anger. He wanted to personally deal with the guy, but after she'd calmed him down, both of them agreed reporting it to the police was the best course of action. She'd also notified the social worker on the case as well as the health department's lawyer. She hadn't heard a peep from the man since. Last she was told, Juney continued to lose weight in the care of her temporary foster family.

"You know I don't like that whole thing. I don't like you in the lime-light so much. Makes you an easy target. Especially after that mess with the HIV guy. What was his name again?"

Sue felt her face heat. "Someone had to speak up for Juney. At the rate she was going, that poor child would have died before she was thirty. And as for Brent Johnson, that man infected a woman with HIV, and he exposed several more. We had to go to the authorities. Sometimes the greater good trumps personal rights. He's lucky he didn't face criminal charges. I explained that to Brent when he came for his required visit yesterday, but he still blames me for his problems. 'I work in sales. You're hurting my job. It's too inconvenient to come here every week.' Boo hoo, sob sob. What about those women?"

Al raised his hands in defense. "Hey, hey, I know that. I'm not saying it wasn't right. I just wish it didn't have to be you. You have enough enemies from your job as it is."

Any thoughts of sharing her intention to sue the food industry disappeared more quickly than the last bite of yogurt.

She glanced at the microwave clock. "I have to get going."

Al stood too. Winking, he said, "Try not to make anyone mad today, okay?"

Before Sue could answer, Kayla entered the room. "God, Mom, who have you crossed now? Why do you always have to put yourself in everyone else's business?"

Although accustomed to her teenage daughter's tone, the sting was no less sharp.

"Watch how you speak to your mother." Al peered at Kayla from over his shoulder as he cleared the mugs from the counter.

Sue considered reprimanding Kayla, Al's rebuke tepid as usual, but figured she'd bite her tongue and save the battle for something else. "What are you doing up so early? And all made up too."

"I'm walking to Tammy's. We're going to Beachwood Mall and then Legacy Village as soon as they open. Huge sales today."

Sue and Al exchanged glances. Al remained silent. Sue inhaled, channeling calm. "Summer vacation or not, you know you're supposed to tell us beforehand of your plans. When we're at work, we need to know where you are. You may be sixteen, but you still have to follow the rules."

Kayla crossed her arms in front of her. "Weeelll, it's beforehand, and I'm telling you, so I think that meets your criteria."

Sue stepped forward. Her finger waved inches in front of Kayla's pretty face. "This is the last warning you'll get. Speak like that to me again and watch yourself get grounded."

Al sighed. "Kayla, apologize to your mother."

Kayla muttered a "sorry," clutched her tiny gold purse, its tassels longer than the actual case, and stomped toward the front door.

"Hey, what about breakfast?" Sue called out.

"I'll eat at Tammy's." Kayla's voice faded, the door slamming behind her.

Silence enveloped the kitchen. Sue searched her memory for the last time she saw Kayla consume a full meal. Lately, it seemed the girl had either already eaten or lacked an appetite. When she did dine with them, she played with the food on her plate.

Given that Sue had left the health department after dark the night before, she asked Al about Kayla's dinner.

"I don't know. When I got home, she told me she ate an early meal," he said.

Sue leaned a shoulder against the wall. A painting of an outdoor cafe swayed from the impact. She remembered buying it two years before at the annual starving artists' sale at a local hotel. Kayla had gone with her, and together they had oohed and aahed over the inexpensive paintings, struggling to limit themselves to just two or three. A huge stack of artwork had ended up in the trunk and backseat of Sue's car, and the two hooted at their indulgence. When they got home, Al was incredulous. "Seven paintings? You bought seven paintings?" Mother and daughter had erupted in laughter all over again.

Where has that little girl gone?

"Al, do you think we should be worried about Kayla's eating? It seems her appetite has been off the past couple weeks. She's awfully thin."

"She's always been thin."

With her tongue, Sue dislodged a blackberry seed from her back molar. She made a mental note to monitor Kayla's eating more closely. Although Sue dealt with overeating disorders every day, the opposite spectrum exceeded her comfort zone.

Al approached and gave her a hug. "Kayla's fine. She's sixteen. This is what teenagers do. We got lucky with our older two."

Sue hugged her husband back, a long, hard hug that prompted surprise from him. She blinked and looked away. "I have to go. I should be home at a decent time."

"I'll walk you out. Just promise me you won't annoy anyone today."

Together they walked out to her car, hidden in the driveway by a huge oak tree. The sun's unobstructed rays already heated the day, and Sue was appreciative for the tree's shade, but when she reached her baby-blue Ford Focus, she froze. Al did too.

Spanning driver seat to back seat in red spray-painted letters screamed a vile word. A word Sue detested. A word that harkened back to a painful night when a terrified, powerless college girl had suffered a brutal man's despicable act.

Scream and I'll kill you, bitch.

That single spray-painted word released a torrent of memories Sue fought to submerge daily, memories she swore would keep her from ever being powerless again.

BITCH.

7

DARWIN

It was almost too easy. Almost as if the fat bastard wanted to die.

Darwin had trailed the man for the past week, the itinerary never varying. Stop one, where Darwin had first encountered the pathetic sheep: an after-work coffee run, waffling and ruminating over which pastry to pair with his venti iced java. Stop two: home to devour his snack. Stop three, one hour later: a drive to a take-out hellhole *du jour*. Stop four: back to the empty house to inhale the several thousand calorie meal. From his car across the street, Darwin witnessed the nightly feeding frenzy through the townhome's living room window, his innards churning in disgust at the sight.

Every time the fat moron departed, he left the garage door open. When he took off to fetch his last supper, Darwin stepped out of his car.

What a wonderful Friday night this will be.

He entered the garage and slid behind a stack of boxes near the townhome's side door. While he waited, he donned gloves, booties, a plastic gown, and a hood to spare his hair.

Standing in a confined space came easy to Darwin. He ignored the sweat dripping down his chest, his tolerance of the August air and the heat-trapping garment a sign of his disciplined nature.

(*Discipline is the root of success.*)

The Voice had chosen the victim and guided the planning, but it was Darwin who would see the kill to fruition. No jagged bottle. No vomiting. No panic this time around.

Cardboard fibers tickled his nose. Gasoline fumes, musty blankets, and trash cans scented the air.

He waited.

Discipline.

His thoughts drifted back to another period of confinement. Or rather, periods. A cold, dark basement, its tiny closet punishment for fruit-punch stains on the carpet, or a torn romance novel, or waking Mommy from her nap. Shivering, crying, skin raw from her pinches, Darwin's chubby body clothed in nothing but underpants. Oh, how he had pined for his father. How he had dreamed of their escape.

If only he'd had The Voice for guidance back then, but he hadn't appeared until college, and even then only sporadically. Not until recently did The Voice fully enter Darwin's life.

A vehicle rolled up the driveway. Darwin's breath caught. The knife's razor-sharp blade hid in the shadow of the boxes. He crouched lower.

Once inside the garage, the car's engine shut off, its refractory tinkling blending with Darwin's accelerated breaths. Although he could not see the glutton, he heard him exit the vehicle with his plastic take-out bags. The man hummed an old seventies tune as he climbed the entrance's short staircase.

Darwin clutched the knife. He inhaled, catching the sickening scent of deep-fried food.

(*You can do this.*)

As soon as he heard the key turn the lock and the door push open, Darwin stepped out from behind the boxes. He watched the enor-mous man waddle into the house, the food sacks by his side stuffed and weighted. Darwin's disgust extinguished any last-minute hesitation.

With the keenness of a wolf, he pounced. He toppled the man to the kitchen floor. With his right foot, he kicked the door shut.

For a moment, he lay on the wiggling, squealing man. Plastic bags shot out over the linoleum, and a pink bakery box flew into an adjoining room. A pie popped out, splattering globs of cherries across tan carpeting.

"What in the...? Who the hell are...?"

The fat prey bucked and writhed, attempting to knock Darwin off, but the man's flabby bulk was no match for Darwin's fit physique.

Darwin assessed the surroundings. The home's neatness surprised him. He expected a gluttonous pig to have a dirty, disgusting trough.

"Get off me. I have money. I..."

Darwin ignored the pleas. He loosened his hold just enough to allow the man to flip over. With muscular thighs, he re-pinned the blimp's waist. Once face to face with his captor, the sheep's eyes widened in fear. They focused on the knife clasped in Darwin's hands.

"What are you—?"

Before the man could finish, Darwin raised the knife high above his head. With a grunt, he buried the long blade deep inside the thick chest, right into the heart. The force of Darwin's entire body accompanied the blow, and when he withdrew the blade, blood gushed like a geyser.

The man's flabby arms flailed and flopped, and his rolls jerked beneath Darwin's thighs. Darwin plunged the knife in again.

"This is what happens to gluttonous sheep. The undisciplined. The weak."

Each word timed with another thrust of the knife. Blood poured over the tile in crimson rivulets, reaching then blending with the cherry pie in the adjoining room.

"You worthless sheep. You disgust me. You..." Darwin's words were rushed, breathless, incoherent even to himself.

Thwack. Knife in, knife out. Over and over again, stabbing a body that had long since stilled.

Finally, he stopped, his hands shaky, his forearms weak. Below him, wide, vacant eyes pleaded even in death.

Blood bathed the floor. The cabinets. The refrigerator. Sticky fluid dripped from Darwin's gloves, his gown, even trickled down his face, and for a few seconds, his composure teetered.

He stared at the man beneath him, the carnage around him.

(Calm yourself. You conquered the sheep. You're just starting, but you're one step closer.)

"Closer to what? What if—?" The sound of his own tremulous speech hushed him to silence.

(No second thoughts. It is what must be.)

Darwin nodded. He understood. And as soon as he did, the sought-after calm returned, just as before.

A moment of weakness, he thought. *Forgive me.*

He would have to pay for that feeble lapse. At home, he would endure his punishment, but at the moment, he had to get out. Had to make sure no sign of him was left behind.

The Voice was right.

They had only just begun.

8

JEREMY

The abandoned building with its boarded-up windows and peeling brown paint beckoned, but Jeremy kept going. He didn't need to catch his breath yet, not like when he had first started walking to and from school last month. During the first couple weeks, he had to lean against the old laundromat for a good ten minutes before he could go on. Five blocks had been enough to empty the air from his lungs.

Over the last week, his endurance had improved, and despite the near ninety-degree heat that Monday afternoon, Jeremy figured he might be able to make it all the way to his next resting point, a gas station another quarter mile down. After that, he would have only two blocks left until he reached his crappy house.

A ladybug flitted in front of his face and then landed on his forearm. He scooped the insect up in his hand, careful not to squish it. Hoisting his backpack farther over his shoulder, grateful it contained only a math book and binder, he squatted as best as his thick limbs would allow and released the ladybug to the ground.

When we show our respect for other living things, they respond with respect to us.

Kajika's words surfaced in Jeremy's mind. His online avatar often quoted the Arapaho, along with many other Native American tribes. Of course, Jeremy wasn't sure how a ladybug would show him respect, but he'd always liked the saying and kept the words nearby whenever he was tempted to squash a spider or trample an anthill.

He resumed walking along the four-lane avenue. Although the busy street offered more security, it also invited horn honks and fat-bashing catcalls.

"Hey, lard-ass, can you find your cock in that wad of fat?"

"Squeal like a pig, piggy, squeal like a pig."

"Is that an earthquake or just your ass shaking?"

He'd heard it all.

Summer school ran a total of six weeks, from July eighth to August sixteenth, one to three thirty in the afternoon. Although at the fat-clinic appointment two and a half weeks earlier Jeremy had played nonchalant with Dr. Green, in truth, he hated taking the summer course. He'd never been a strong math student — English was more his thing — but had Mr. Pottage actually helped him instead of feeling him up, Jeremy would have received the extra tutelage and wouldn't have failed the class. Well, not failed, but a D-minus was pretty close.

Maybe he had misinterpreted Mr. Pottage's actions. After all, it was nice to have a teacher take interest in him, especially one whose waistline matched Jeremy's. Maybe the hand on Jeremy's knee during the second after-school session had been merely an innocent gesture to accompany the teacher's assurance of, "I'm always here if you need me."

But what about that crap on the third visit? The man had rubbed his thigh, Jeremy was sure of it. Right after Jeremy's excitement at having solved a complex equation.

Jeremy shook his head. Maybe he should have told his mom, but he hadn't wanted to worry her. She had enough going on. And no way in shitsville would he mention it to GI Dick or pencil-pecker Rex. They would call Jeremy a fag, or a prick tease, or teacher's bitch, or some other slam. So Jeremy had simply quit going to Mr. Pottage's tutoring sessions, making up some excuse about needing to help his mom after school. As a result, his homework and quiz scores nosedived, as did his eventual grade, more than Jeremy had expected. No matter how hard he tried, the red pen marks seemed to multiply more than the algebraic equations themselves. It appeared Mr. Pottage had chosen tough grading as a means of communication.

Under the blazing sun, Jeremy shifted his backpack to the other shoulder. A river of sweat dripped down his spine, and his T-shirt stuck to his chest and belly. He wiped moisture from his forehead and reconsidered taking a rest.

The Fat Slayers encouraging faces and slim waists bobbed before him. "Baby steps, Jeremy. Use the small victories to fuel more."

None of those small victories included mastering Shelly's circuit workout. Jeremy had tried two jumping jacks and one burpee and said, "Forget this." But at least he was walking.

A whiff of fresh bread hit him.

Burgers and Buns.

He stopped and stared in the restaurant's direction. He dug in his right pocket and found both his inhaler and the five-dollar bill he had tucked there. Just in case.

Images of hot, salty fries danced through his brain and teased his taste buds. Four days since his last splurge. No one would know.

A commotion behind him broke his reverie.

Half a block down, on the sidewalk he'd already covered, were four kids.

Shit.

He recognized Calvin Swanson straight away. No mistaking that height, muscular build, and red hair. If Jeremy had a dollar for every time the idiot junior — the only junior in freshman-level summer school — had called him *lard-ass* or *fat fuck*, Jeremy would have enough dough to buy the whole Burgers and Buns chain.

With Calvin were two of his cronies, almost as mean and equally ugly. The fourth kid was Tito Harris, a skinny little guy with vitiligo patches speckling his black skin. Although the same grade as Jeremy, the two had never shared any classes, probably because Tito took only advanced-level courses. During summer school, the mini-Einstein had been tutoring the other kids.

Jeremy had never seen Tito walk home from school before. Given the scene unfolding, he understood why.

In front of a convenience mart, Jeremy watched Calvin Swanson and his two sidekicks, one Hispanic, one white, begin to work over Tito Harris. The group had advanced enough for Jeremy to overhear their conversation, though the people in passing cars seemed indifferent to the impending drama on the rundown street.

"Tell you what, zebra boy, you get me the answers to the test and I might let you breathe another day."

Jeremy watched as Tito pushed up his glasses and looked at the sidewalk. "You know I can't do that. Mrs. Connor doesn't show me the test."

"Well, you better find a way to make her."

Tito tried to walk away, but Calvin tripped him, knocking the kid to the ground. The small boy slid on the concrete, splitting open the skin of his knee. Blood beaded the area. The sidekicks snickered.

Jeremy remained rooted to the ground, not sure how to proceed. He could turn around, head into Burgers and Buns, and pretend he never saw anything. But what about Tito? That kid was no match for the three of them.

His airways tightened. Swallowing, he longed for a cold drink.

He took a step forward, then stopped. Wheezy breaths begged for his inhaler. Diesel from a passing, rumbling truck sealed the deal.

But it was too late.

Before he could raise the medication vial to his lips, one of the cronies noticed him. The kid tapped Calvin on the shoulder and pointed Jeremy's way. Jeremy's windpipe narrowed to the size of a straw. His hand clutching the inhaler froze.

"Well, if it isn't the biggest fat fuck of them all." Calvin moved away from Tito and sauntered toward Jeremy. His sweaty, rust-colored hair glistened in the sun, and lines of moisture dripped from his scalp onto his pimply face.

Jeremy wheezed. He squeezed the inhaler in his closed palm, still too paralyzed to use it.

"What's in your hand, fatso? Extra snacks for later?"

The sidekicks laughed, and the shortest one of the pack, still a good five inches taller than Tito, said, "Probably a pizza and a couple burgers."

Calvin crinkled his upturned nose and sniffed. "I don't know, maybe some shit too, because I sure as hell smell shit in the air. Fat shit and zebra shit. And believe me, with an old man who inspects sewage systems for the health department, I know what shit smells like."

Tito picked himself up off the ground and stepped forward, blood trickling down his leg. "Cut it out, Calvin. We want to go home. I'll help you study for the test, but that's the best I can do."

Jeremy studied Tito, barely five feet tall, his spindly dark arms covered with white patches, the pigment completely gone. The largest patch on his right arm resembled a small rat. A few circles covered his knees symmetrically, and maybe even his thighs, though the jean shorts covered those. Below his brown-framed eyeglasses, dime-sized spots dotted the middle of his cheeks, and a few larger patches occupied both sides of his neck.

And yet, Tito had stepped forward.

Jeremy shifted his gaze to the sidewalk. A large crack fractured it diagonally, and he wished he could flatten himself and dive in.

"Leave us be," Tito said again.

With a grunt, Calvin ripped the glasses off Tito's face and tossed them into the weedy grass of the berm. He wadded the skinny kid's striped polo shirt into his left hand and made a thick fist with his right.

Jeremy's gut swirled. Sweat dripped in his eyes. Without knowing what he was doing, he advanced another step, and although he had to lean forward and lift his chin to form any words through his wheezing, he said, "Leave him alone."

Calvin wasn't listening. To Tito, he said, "Look here you little spotted shit, I already told—"

A thunderous bellow shattered the air. "Calvin!"

A truck door slammed, and a brawny man dressed in a white collared shirt, khakis, and heavy black boots rushed toward them. He grabbed Calvin's arm with a ferocity that stunned them all.

Dragging Calvin to the truck, he said, "Goddamn it, kid, what the fuck are you doing? You're supposed to be staining the deck at your mother's place." He shoved Calvin into the passenger seat and rounded the truck to his own door. The cronies hustled away.

The man, who Jeremy assumed was Calvin's dad given the matching tomato mane, looked at Jeremy and Tito with an expression of disgust. To Calvin, he said, "You hanging out with the fatties and the freaks now? God knows what you'll catch from them." He climbed into the truck and drove away.

For a moment, Jeremy and Tito said nothing, both as motionless as the fire hydrant next to them. Finally, Tito cleared his throat. "Um, you okay? You look a bit rough and you sound even worse."

Jeremy blinked. "Yeah, I'm okay."

The inhaler, sticky and warm from being clutched in his hand, finally served its purpose. Jeremy took two puffs and waited for his airways to open. He took two puffs more. Once relief trickled in, he wandered over to the long grass and helped Tito look for his glasses.

Tito snorted. "Watch, I'll step right on them."

No sooner had he said it than they both heard a snap.

"Crap." Tito bent over and retrieved his glasses, which were now minus one arm.

The boys studied the glasses. Together they burst out laughing. When Tito attempted to don the broken glasses, the plastic dangled from one ear, and the two laughed even harder.

Soon Tito was clutching his side. "Please, make it stop."

Jeremy's hysterics prevented him from doing anything of the sort, and he plopped to the grass, unable to support his overtaxed body any longer.

When they finally collected themselves, Tito held out a hand to assist Jeremy up off the ground. "Thanks for your help. Calvin is a jerk."

Embarrassed, Jeremy didn't take Tito's proffered hand. He worried he'd pull the tiny kid right on top of him. Instead, he wiggled his way to an upright position. "I didn't do anything. Just stood there."

"Nah, I could tell you were gonna help. Guess his crazy old man saved us both."

As they crossed the street, they exchanged introductory words. Tito confirmed he didn't usually walk home. "My mom picks me up around four o'clock, but she couldn't today. She doesn't like me walking. Not since my brother ... well, she just doesn't like it."

They chatted a little more, and at the next corner, Tito indicated his street. When he learned Jeremy's house was only a couple blocks north, he suggested they get together sometime. Before waiting for an answer, or perhaps realizing nothing was forthcoming from Jeremy's wide-open mouth, Tito spun around on his spindly legs and trotted toward home.

Jeremy, not understanding what had just happened but not sure he minded, considering he couldn't remember the last time he'd laughed so hard, trudged the rest of the way home, even bypassing his second rest spot, the gas station with fresh doughnuts and ninety-nine-cent sodas. He longed for a cold drink and a seat on the couch next to the air conditioner. And a half dozen of those doughnuts.

But then he thought of the clinic. He thought of the progress he'd made, small as it was.

Tugging at his slightly looser sweatpants, the waistband drenched with sweat, he pondered the warrior woman's proposition. At first he thought her idea was ridiculous. Suing people for making him fat? How dumb was that?

But then he realized hardly a moment went by that he didn't think about food. Didn't those fast-food joints call to him every single day? Something had to make him crave food like that. He sure as hell didn't crave green beans.

Flipping the inhaler in his pocket, he replayed Calvin's words in his mind. *Well, if it isn't the biggest fat fuck of them all.* He imagined all the other Calvins of the world. No shortage of jerks like him. He then thought of all the junk food that screamed his name.

Could Sue be right? Were others to blame, at least in part? Did they make it that much harder for him to succeed? He knew he'd never be skinny like Tito, but didn't he at least deserve a chance?

For the first time since that crazy nurse's scheme had been proposed, Jeremy didn't dismiss the idea.

9

SUE

Human arteries immediately narrowed in response to a fatty meal. As such, after scanning the lunch crowd, Sue figured Burgers and Buns ought to have an ambulance nearby.

Behind a string of bustling employees working the cash registers, the restaurant's huge menu board beckoned, a color-coded gateway to fat. Singles, doubles, triples, even quadruple-patty burgers, should a patron be so brave, all served on homemade bread rolls or buns. Upon the red meat, one could heap cheese, chili, bacon, ham, potato chips, and French fries. Vegetables, too, though Sue supposed at that point any attempt at nutrition was long lost. For those with a sweet tooth, cookies the size of an infant's head completed the meal.

To the franchise's credit, a veggie burger and chicken patty were among the choices, along with a few salads, though none were of the green leafy variety.

So this is Jeremy's favorite restaurant, Sue thought. *No surprise there.* She wondered about his diet and exercise progress since his appointment three weeks before.

The line to order stretched nearly to the door. While Sue waited, the aroma of cooking grease and baked bread accosted her. Despite years of smart food choices, even she had trouble resisting their seduction. There was no denying the burgers looked tasty. Their visual appeal on the menu board far exceeded that of the iceberg-lettuce choices tucked in the bottom right corner, but when it came her turn to order, she selected a Greek salad and bottled water, raising her voice in order to be heard above the din.

With her meal in hand, she weaved through a collection of occupied tables. She found an empty padded booth against the far wall. A framed photograph of an overweight man wearing an apron and stuffing a four-patty hamburger into his mouth hung above it. Behind him in the picture, a crowd rooted and cheered. Though the photo disturbed her, the booth offered more room to display her notes for Sammy.

Sammy Sanchez was a lawyer Sue knew from his interactions with the health department. Their most recent encounter involved an apartment landlord with cockroach-infested rentals whose low-income residents had experienced excessive rates of asthma attacks. The health department had been involved with inspecting the buildings, and Sue's fellow nurses had seen some of the patients in the health center's clinic. Sammy filed lawsuits on their behalf. Sue suspected the lawyer made minimal income from that type of work, but his willingness to defend the little guy earned her respect.

She figured between the two of them, they could do some effective shouting.

She uncapped her bottled water and took a sip. At the same time, she saw Sammy enter the restaurant, easily recognizing his fancy suit, well-coiffed salt-and-pepper hair, and precise posture. She waved to signal him. He nodded and pointed to the menu board.

Ten minutes later he joined her. They made small talk while she forked lettuce leaves and he chewed a chicken patty. After Sammy updated Sue on some of his most recent pro-bono cases, Sue pushed her salad aside, rested her hands on the table, and leaned forward.

"Have I got something for you," she said.

Sammy raised one eyebrow. "Oh?"

"Yes. And be ready to become a household name."

Sammy laughed, but when he listened to Sue relay her plan, his expression went from surprise to amusement to scorn, and finally, to skepticism.

"Let me get this straight. You want to sue companies for making people obese? That's a bit far-fetched, don't you think?"

"Not just companies. Industries and organizations as well."

"Such as?"

"Well, we'll have to keep it in the state, right? We could target specific Ohio restaurant chains, starting with the one we're in now." Sue made a sweeping motion with her arms. "My patient eats at Burgers and Buns all the time, not this location but the one near Clark Avenue. There are several others around the state. The owner makes lots of money off people's poor habits and health."

"No one's forcing them to eat here."

Sue blanketed the table with the articles she'd brought. "We could also target a couple of the big Ohio food companies, such as Bilko's Snacks and Brover's Industries. Those two produce enough crap to give every Ohioan a heart attack. Worse, they dress up their junk food with names like Snacks on the Go, Energy in a Bar, Fuel for the Soul. You've seen their garbage. Their snacks contain so many chemicals, expiration dates aren't necessary. Those things could survive an apocalypse."

Sammy leaned back and placed an index finger over his lips. "Go on."

"What about cities and their poor built-environments? Not to sue, but to raise awareness. All over the country, urban areas have food deserts, one-mile areas packed with fast-food restaurants, convenience stores, and liquor stores, but little healthy food. In rural areas, the distance is ten miles. There are also unsafe neighborhoods that prohibit walking."

Sammy flipped through a report outlining food industries' efforts to create the right combination of ingredients to keep human fingers reaching for more. His silence boosted Sue's confidence, and her pitch sped up.

"We could sue television stations for advertising unhealthy food and drinks, especially during children's viewing hours, though I guess that's a federal suit. And how about restaurant associations, those in Ohio since that's within our legal jurisdiction? Maybe, after our case takes off, we could think about a class-action suit, getting multiple clients involved from multiple states. Think about—"

Sammy dropped the paper and held up a hand. "Whoa, whoa there, Erin Brockovich. Slow down. You've already got me organizing a class-action lawsuit?" He let out a snort. "That's a little out of my league."

"I know, I know. Sorry. I'm just excited." Sue twirled the bracelets on her arm and steadied her breath.

Sammy leaned forward. "Look, your heart is in the right place. I've read these kinds of studies too. You know Jonathan and I are into fitness and nutrition." At that he laughed. "Can you imagine Jonathan's reaction if I said I was suing these industries? His dislike of frivolous lawsuits is bad enough. Add to that his belief overweight people lack willpower, and we're headed for a virtual shitstorm."

Sue didn't much like Sammy's boyfriend. One would think the assistant manager of a home-improvement store wouldn't flaunt such superior airs. "People like Jonathan are exactly the type we need to convince. Make them see it isn't as simple as putting down the fork and going out for a jog. Not really, anyway."

"But why me? Why not a lawyer better equipped for something like this? You know lawsuits like these are bound to go nowhere."

Sue drained the rest of her water. "Because you care. I've seen what you've done for those low-income families, and you do it behind the scenes with no recognition. Here's your chance to do something in front of the scenes. In fact, the attention could benefit your firm, especially in these economic times."

Sammy scoffed. "Well, that part's certainly true."

"I'm not naive. I know the lawsuit likely won't amount to anything beyond a litigation hassle for the parties involved. I don't expect to see a courtroom. It's the attention I want. It's the attention we *need*. This country is making itself sick by its sheer inability to stop eating. We can't expect individuals alone to change. They need incentive. They need help. Just like what was done with the tobacco industry."

Sammy exhaled slowly. "Well, do you at least have a plaintiff in mind?"

Sue balled up her napkin and nodded. "I'm working on it. I found a kid who'd be perfect. He faces risks from all the determinants: genetics, low socioeconomic status, single mother, poor support system, physical complications of obesity."

"And he and his mother have agreed?"

"Don't worry. I'll have the plaintiff for you. And I'll get the word out too. I know a local reporter."

Sammy smiled. "Yes, making noise has never been your problem. Not to mention making enemies."

The word *BITCH* flashed in Sue's mind, the slur on her car since painted over and the vandalism reported. Was it Tucker Andrews, payback for his daughter's removal? Or Brent Johnson, revenge for publicizing his HIV status? Or maybe even Angie Leonard, more worried about her boyfriend's drug arrest than her son's health. Was one of them finally carrying through with their threats?

Scream and I'll kill you, bitch.

She fingered the row of jewelry on her left ear. "Yes, I seem to be quite gifted in that department."

"What does Al think?"

Sue remembered how enraged her husband had been when he saw her car. How he had demanded the scouring of the parking garage's security cameras. Unfortunately, her car had not been within camera range.

"From now on," he had said, dragging her around the department's ramp, "you park within these areas. Under no circumstances are you to park away from the camera. I don't care if you end up on the highest level. And if it's late, you call a security guard to escort you."

How would Al take the lawsuit?

"Al will be fine. Don't worry. Just promise you'll consider my proposal. Any action's first step is thought."

Sammy accepted the papers Sue handed him. He barked a laugh. "Sure. Why not? What could possibly go wrong?"

After lunch, back in her office, Sue had five minutes to make a couple phone calls. Since it was Tuesday, she staffed the adult community clinic, not her favorite place to be, especially since she'd have to face Brent Johnson for his weekly HIV check-in. She much preferred the pediatric weight management clinic. In fact, when she'd first accepted the position as a clinical nurse for the health department five years prior, she had made that clear.

Before taking the job, she worked as a health educator in the community, having gone back to school in her thirties for a master's degree in public health. Prior to that, she was employed as a hospital nurse practitioner. She enjoyed the position, but the evening shifts made raising a family difficult. Plus, she had clashed with some of the physicians. Dr. Arrogant Heart Surgeon had called her controlling. That was right before she reminded him that M.D. stood for medical doctor, not God.

Bygones, she thought.

The first call was to Connie Barton to remind her of Jeremy's upcoming appointment in two days.

You know that's not the only reason, Sue...

A man answered and told her Connie wasn't home.

"Is this Jeremy?"

"No. This is Connie's father. What do you want?"

After a minute of unhelpful communication, Sue asked the surly man to remind Connie and Jeremy of the appointment on Thursday.

"You from the fat clinic?"

"It's the weight management clinic, yes, and it's important Jeremy keep his follow-up." Sue paused. "And please remind her I was hoping for an answer about the issue we discussed. She'll know what I mean."

"You mean about suing them places for making Eating Bull fat? That's the dumbest idea I ever heard."

Eating Bull?

So Connie had discussed it with her father.

And he was their first opposition.

After completing the call, Sue dialed Tony Farr, a reporter from the *Cleveland Times* with whom she frequently interacted. She liked the awkward, large-nosed man and had to suppress a smile when Kayla compared him to a proboscis monkey. Though Sue admonished her daughter for the hurtful analogy, she had to admit, the description was apt. Tony had served Sue well in the past, including writing an objective story about Juney Andrews's removal from the home and Brent Johnson's HIV-spreading ways.

He answered on the third ring, and after small talk, Sue announced her intention. She kept it brief, mentioning only that she would soon have a big story for him, one involving the food industry and obesity. "Are you in?" she asked.

After a few beats of silence, Tony said, "Wow, Susie, you don't mess around. Don't have enough people mad at you yet?"

"Look, I have to go, but I wanted to give you a heads up."

"Well, of course I'm interested. You bring me nothing but excitement. Speaking of, has your husband said anything about those two murders?"

"He doesn't work homicide."

"Yeah, but he must've heard something."

"I don't know anything more than you. Two men were murdered in the last three weeks, and there's no suspect in either case."

"But weren't they both obese?"

Tony's excitement was obvious, but Sue didn't much like the direction he was taking. "Over two-thirds of Americans are overweight. If that's your angle, you better look for something else."

Sue wrapped up by telling Tony she'd be in touch. Then she pulled a compact from her purse, powdered her face, popped two mints into her mouth, and hustled to clinic, where she discovered her first patient was Brent Johnson.

The look on his face suggested he was no happier to see her than she him. It also suggested he was fed up with his court-ordered visits.

But how fed up?

Sue wasn't sure she wanted to find out.

10

DARWIN

With meaty hands resting on a cluttered desk, Mr. Gut, Darwin's blubber-faced superior, pressed his lips together and nodded, as if what Miss Fat Witch had to say actually merited his time and attention that Tuesday afternoon.

He's either an idiot or a good actor, Darwin thought, wishing he was anywhere but that office, parked next to his insufferable co-worker and facing his patronizing boss. A sniff of the pastrami-scented air and a glance at the disheveled space told Darwin all he needed to know about Mr. Gut's discipline. How he'd risen to the top of the food chain was a mystery. Perhaps he'd eaten everyone in his path.

The image made Darwin snicker.

"Something funny about your colleague's complaint?" Mr. Gut's faux-concerned gaze targeted Darwin while his sausage fingers twiddled a pen.

"See? I told you. He always acts like he's better than the rest of us."

Miss Fat Witch's whining grated like metal against metal, and Darwin almost covered his ears. He parted his clenched jaw, but before he could retort, The Voice cut him off.

(*Play the game. You can't risk suspicion.*)

Darwin bit back his words, lowered his head, and apologized.

"Oh, sure, you say you're sorry now, but what about the next time you belittle me or make fun of my glandular problem?"

Darwin's temples twitched. "I merely hinted you wouldn't need a special chair if you took better care of yourself." The folds of female flesh bursting from the confines of her current chair confirmed Darwin's assumption.

"Not everyone can move around in their job like you. I need that ergonomic chair. I have a bad back and arthritis in my neck. I can't help if I need..."

What you need is a shiny blade in your belly. Twisting and turning. Cutting and carving.

"...and sir, one time when I took a file he needed, he gave me such a menacing look, I developed chest pain out of fright. I have a genetically weak heart and high blood pressure. I've purchased a treadmill and I'm trying to make improvements, but I can't handle sudden scares."

A genetically weak heart? Nothing a sharp knife can't cure.

For the next few minutes, Darwin listened to examples of workplace sensitivity while he pictured images of butchered tissue.

(Not her. Not now, anyway. She's too close.)

When the charade ended and Darwin agreed to be more sensitive to Miss Fat Witch's needs, he stood and exited the pigsty, leaving the two human hogs behind. In the nearest bathroom, he scrubbed his hands using five applications of soap. Before returning to work, he entered the stairwell and began his afternoon climb. His muscles tensed and his pulse quickened even before the exertion. Thanks to the trip to the principal's office, he was behind schedule. How dare she throw off his timetable? Tuesdays demanded ten trips from top to bottom, three times a shift. At least it wasn't hump day. Wednesdays called for fifteen.

As he sprinted up the steps, moisture beading his forehead and wetting his armpits, he planned out the evening. After work, he'd stop at the grocery store. He preferred the fresh food market in the suburb, where the clientele cared more about what they consumed, but once a month he braved the larger chain to stock up on long-term items. Pushing past the gluttonous masses, their fat children clinging to carts packed with snack cakes and ice cream and whining for the latest sugar-laden shit, Darwin would gather his needed supplies as quickly as possible. The children were like young geese, waiting to become foie gras at the hands of their oversized parents. They should be removed from their homes, every last one of them, like that girl on the news.

To make the shopping experience more tolerable, Darwin would calculate his calorie burn for the day. That would help distract him.

Three stair rounds done, seven to go. Sweat now sprinkled his shirt.

After unloading his supermarket purchases, he'd complete thirty minutes of cardio and twenty minutes of core, but that was all he'd have time for. He had to be at the gym before nine or he would miss her. And that would be unacceptable.

He needed to study her. Needed to scope out the parking lot. Needed to determine the best angle for his rented vehicle, the best position to block any wandering eyes.

The Voice had chosen her two days before. Because of her, Darwin could no longer use the gym. Talk about injustice. He wouldn't have lashed out if she hadn't hogged the machines and messed up his circuit work.

Regrettably, at first Darwin had questioned The Voice's decision. "But she's losing weight. She's working on improvement. Is she really our best—"

The Voice had cut him off with such fury Darwin had recoiled in shock, both from fear and from a searing pain in his brain. In penance for his defiance, Darwin had been forced to forgo all sustenance that evening and exercise so strenuously he nearly passed out. He then endured a twenty-minute cold shower with metal clips pinching his nipples since starvation had not been enough. Months before, when he'd first applied clips to his sensitive parts, he'd felt foolish, but he'd soon learned pain kept obsessive thoughts at bay, thoughts that made him as weak as the sheep around him.

(*Only through pain and discipline can pleasure and purity be had.*)

The following day, Darwin had adjusted his thinking and no longer questioned The Voice.

His third kill had been chosen. The next piece of their mission found.

And soon the world would fit those pieces together.

11

JEREMY

For Jeremy, refusing cookies was like refusing a suitcase full of cash — it simply didn't happen — and yet there he was, saying, "No, thanks," when Tito's spindly, spotted arm held out the plate. Had Tito himself grabbed a handful of the baked goods, Jeremy would have followed suit, but snarfing down chocolate-chip cookies while Tito gnawed an apple, his apparent after-school snack of choice (*was that even possible?*), seemed wrong.

"Suit yourself," Tito said, returning the cookies to the counter. Jeremy's gaze followed their path. His taste buds tingled in protest.

Still thinking of the cookies, he followed Tito out of the pine-scented kitchen and up a narrow staircase, its steps creaking beneath even his friend's small frame.

"This house is so old, drives me crazy. It burps and farts with every freakin' movement." Tito directed Jeremy into his room, the last door on the left. Dozens of family photographs lined the wallpapered hallway, including a huge portrait of the Harris family on the end. Mother, father, and two sons. Jeremy wondered where Tito's brother was.

"I still can't believe my parents let me walk home. I didn't think they'd go for it at first." Tito flipped on the bedroom light. "But I told them you were a big guy — no offense — and reminded my mom she wouldn't have to leave work to pick me up. It's all about the spin, Jer." He smiled, and the white spots on his cheeks shifted to higher planes.

Jeremy pointed to Tito's chrome frames. "I see you got new glasses. Did you tell your parents what happened with Calvin?"

The thin boy plopped down on a chair in front of his computer. "Nah. No need to give them extra worry. These are my old glasses." Tito opened the top desk drawer and pulled out a fistful of broken eyewear. "When you look like me, glasses don't last long. My parents think I'm clumsy."

Jeremy took a seat on the twin bed. In addition to the desk and bed, the room contained a dresser and two bookcases, each loaded with books and games. And bridges, lots and lots of bridges — on the shelves, the walls, everywhere the eye traveled. Models, posters, puzzles, and photographs. All bridges.

"Guess you're into bridges, huh?"

"Oh, man, I love them. See that framed photograph of the Golden Gate Bridge? I took that picture when we were in San Francisco. When I was little, my parents were worried about me. Thought I was obsessed, like Rain Man or something, but it's cool now."

As Jeremy listened to Tito ramble on about suspensions, trusses, and supports, he wondered if Rain Man was gone after all. But he didn't mind. He leaned against the headboard, content just to listen. Tito talked about becoming an engineer. In between breaths, he took another bite of apple, and Jeremy was reminded of the cookies he weirdly no longer craved.

Eventually, the conversation steered back to Calvin. Even though only one week of summer school remained, Jeremy wouldn't be rid of the guy. The two would be in the same math class, a fact the bully had reminded Jeremy about earlier that day. "You and me, lard-ass. We're gonna get to know each other real well."

At that point, pimple face had turned to his cronies and said, "Hey, what do you get when you cross a whale with a spotted zebra?" When the cronies shrugged, Calvin said, "I don't know, but let's super glue these two fuckers together and find out."

"You know," Tito said, breaking Jeremy's unpleasant thoughts, "we can get Calvin back. Have a little fun at his expense."

Jeremy righted himself on the bed, tugging his T-shirt down. "How?"

Tito turned and faced the computer. With a click of the mouse, he opened his Facebook account. "The skinny nerd way, that's how."

Tito laid out his plan. "A fake Facebook account. We'll call her

Courtney. Courtney Kline." Tito was already searching for images of girls and stopped on a blonde. "Perfect. Cute, but not too cute, so he doesn't get suspicious. She looks about our age, don't you think?"

Jeremy rubbed the back of his neck. "I don't know. That's catfishing, isn't it? We could get in trouble."

"Who's gonna know? We won't do anything bad. Just mess with him a little. The jerk deserves it. He's an asshole of the largest diameter."

Jeremy could not dispute that.

Tito's fingers flew over the keyboard. "It's the safest prank we can do. When my mom checks my browser history, she'll only see I was on Facebook. She knows I have an account."

Jeremy said nothing. Connie rarely used his computer except for the few times she needed to search something. She always said, "Who has time for the virtual life when I can hardly keep up with the real one?"

Thank God for the Duongs and their WiFi or Jeremy wouldn't have any Internet access at all. It wasn't like he was stealing. Mrs. Duong had given Jeremy their password one day when she asked him how school was going and found out he couldn't search the web for his classes. She shook her head and wrote down their password. Jeremy took extra care mowing their lawn that week.

But Facebook fraud made him nervous. They might regret it.

"Regret is for pussies," his grandfather would say.

Jeremy doubted that was true, but he didn't want to risk Tito thinking him lame. His new friend might never invite him over again. Plus, getting Calvin back would feel good, even if the revenge was not of the noble warrior kind.

With Tito at the helm, Courtney Kline came to life. She loved movies, shopping, and horses, and when Jeremy worried that was too stereotypical, Tito laughed and said stereotypical was exactly what the ugly ape needed. "He'll never believe a smart chick is friending him."

After they created the fake profile, they sent out friend requests to random people and then to Calvin.

"Now we wait and see if he bites," Tito said.

The next hour and a half flew by. Jeremy never wanted the afternoon to end. He learned Tito's brother, Derek, was killed two years prior by a stray bullet in a drive-by shooting not far from their school route. He was seventeen.

"Ever since then," Tito said, fiddling with a remote control for a draw bridge, "my parents haven't let me out of their sight."

Tito learned of Jeremy's small dose of Native American blood. "Cool," he said. "But they have it tough, don't they? Higher rates of alcoholism and drug use. Higher rates of obesity too."

Jeremy stiffened.

"I'm sorry. I didn't mean anything. I just figured that might make it harder for you."

As if Tito were the fat whisperer, Jeremy found himself spilling details about the weight management clinic and the bossy nurse who worked there. He even blabbed about the lawsuit proposal but immediately regretted it. *That's because you're a pussy*, he could hear his grandfather say.

Tito stroked his chin with his thumb and index finger, his gaze on the Brooklyn Bridge poster covering his closet door.

Probably thinking what an idiot I am, Jeremy thought.

Finally, Tito nodded. "Sounds like a good idea. Look what happened with smoking. Those tobacco settlements involved some major dough. My mom struggled for years to quit. Losing Derek made her take it up again for a while. It used to be cigarettes were everywhere, tempting people. Now it's crappy food that's tempting them. Why shouldn't some of these food companies pay for their part in the mess?"

A flutter rolled through Jeremy's insides and for once not from hunger.

Does Tito really believe that? Would anyone else?

A knock on the door broke Jeremy's thoughts. A woman with Tito's petite frame but none of his blotchy skin entered. Jeremy blushed when she embraced his pudgy paw in her own warm hands.

"So nice to meet you, Jeremy. I appreciate you walking Tito home."

Jeremy nodded. A mouth-watering scent of herbs and garlic had followed Mrs. Harris up from the kitchen.

"Mom, I'm not a child."

Mrs. Harris released Jeremy's hand and turned to Tito. She assumed a breathy tone. "Did you come right home after school? You didn't dawdle, did you? Were you careful by ... that street?" The woman's fingers found her apron string, its yellow fabric dotted by red stains.

Spaghetti, thought Jeremy, as he inhaled the intoxicating air. *Or maybe lasagna.*

"Yeeees, Mom."

"Okay. Good." Mrs. Harris's restless hands moved onto her shiny, straight hair. "Dinner's almost ready. Would you like to stay, Jeremy? I'm making baked rigatoni."

At the words, Jeremy's salivary glands kicked into overdrive. The pasta scent nearly knocked him into a coma. At his house, a home-cooked meal was rarer than a jock at Comic Con.

But what if he ate too much? What if conversation stalled while Tito's family struggled to ignore the almost literal elephant in the room? What if he disgusted them?

"Uh, I better not. I have to get home." Jeremy lowered his head and hunched his shoulders, thanking Mrs. Harris for the offer.

"Another time then. You're always welcome."

Jeremy felt his eyes sting at her warmth, and in embarrassment he retrieved his backpack from Tito's bed and followed his new friend out. In the driveway, he met Mr. Harris, a fit-looking man and equally attractive as his wife. His skin showed no marks of depigmentation either. Jeremy wondered if Tito was alone in his disorder.

Tito made Jeremy promise he'd come back Friday. "To, you know, finish what we were working on."

Jeremy said he would and then started for home. Between Tito's approval of the lawsuit and Mrs. Harris's pasta, Jeremy's concerns about the Facebook prank temporarily faded. Maybe next time he'd have the nerve to stay for dinner.

It dawned on him he hadn't eaten since the giant candy bar he'd devoured in the school bathroom during afternoon break. He always kept a stash in his backpack.

Almost four hours.

Might be a record.

Later that night, up in his room playing *War of the Wilderness,* Jeremy heard the front door slam, announcing the arrival of his mother along with their late dinner. He had blasted through level fifty-one where Kajika took out a band of roving robbers and murderers. He navigated Kajika through one more battle, collecting a magical arrow for his effort, and closed the game. Although Kajika's gold and ivory bow had mystical powers, the skilled shaman rarely needed to invoke them.

For a moment, he imagined himself in Kajika's world, braided hair flapping in the wind, muscular body leaping and sprinting over gullies and gorges as he took out bullies and scumballs with his powerful bow. He pictured Calvin holding women and children hostage. With unprecedented stealth, Jeremy would sneak up behind him and let his golden-tipped arrow fly.

Jeremy's own daydream betrayed him though. In his mind, the red-headed bully turned toward him and sneered. "You don't stand a chance, fat boy."

A roar from his grandfather shattered Jeremy's reverie.

"Hey, kid, get your ass down here. Your mom's got your dinner."

Jeremy struggled to stand. His desk chair, a cheap office-store product with a busted back, squealed its protest.

After he'd returned from Tito's, a snack of cold cereal and toast had held Jeremy over. He'd wanted more, but he resisted. Although sugar sodas remained in the fridge for his grandpa ("Just because the kid's got a weight problem doesn't mean I can't enjoy a soda every goddamn once in a while"), Jeremy had refrained and chose a diet cola instead. He'd even attempted one set of Shelly's circuit workout but quit when his grandfather bellowed that the "damn roof would cave in."

As the Fat Slayers had urged, he'd been taking baby steps and hoped he'd be down a few pounds at his follow-up the next day. He made a promise to himself to go easy on Connie's takeout.

In the kitchen, GI Dick was still blowing hot air, and to Jeremy's disappointment, Rex was there too. Must have found time in his precious schedule to give Connie a ride home.

"How's the kid supposed to lose any weight if you bring this crap home so late?"

"Not tonight, Dad, please. I'm tired." Connie puffed away her troublesome tuft of hair and tossed plates and forks on the table, their stoneware and stainless-steel collision an auditory assault.

"Look at this junk," Dick said. "Barbecued ribs, fried chicken, mashed potatoes. We're all going to get fat."

Rex finished sanitizing his hands and sat at the table. "He's right. Maybe you should bring the kid home a salad or something. No offense, Jeremy. Then again, The Gourmand's Buffet isn't known for its healthy choices." Rex didn't take any of the confiscated buffet food. As usual, he'd brought his own stash and laid out grilled chicken, a tomato, and an empty whole-wheat pita pocket.

"If she'd gone to college instead of getting knocked up, she'd have a decent job." Dick threw a fried chicken breast on his plate.

Jeremy sat at the end of the table, eyes cast downward. He was suddenly starving.

"Bet those folks at the fat clinic wouldn't look too fondly on this crap. Then again, their solution is to sue."

"What are you talking about?" Rex sliced perfectly proportioned chicken and tomato wedges into his pita pocket.

Dick summed up Sue's proposal, flush with his negative commentary.

Rex barked a strange noise. "Perfect. Help the fat folks blame everyone else."

Three pieces of fried chicken, a slab of ribs, macaroni and cheese, and a mountain of mashed potatoes smothered Jeremy's plate. He thought about taking his food upstairs but feared leaving Connie alone with Dick and the Prick.

"I'll tell you what makes people fat. Eating this kind of shit." Dick spat out a wad of chicken skin. "You should be cooking dinner at a normal time, not giving us late-night leftovers. Quit stacking the cupboards with crap. And make Eating Bull get off his ass. You need to—"

"Stop it," Connie cried. A tear plopped into a pool of gravy on her plate. "Just stop it. And quit calling Jeremy that awful name. God, I'm doing the best I can. I'm so tired." Connie buried her head in her hands and massaged her temples. Then she shot up and ran from the room.

Silence swallowed the table. Jeremy shoveled in food at an exponential rate, tasting nothing of the choking mass yet needing it more than ever.

After a few seconds of silverware clicking against teeth, Rex said, "What's her problem? Other people manage to work two jobs without making their family fat. It's not like she's curing cancer."

Dick pointed his fork at Rex and gave it a vigorous air thrust. "Hey, that's my daughter you're talking about. She works hard. She's sensitive like her mother." Dick dropped the silverware weaponry, and his jaw went slack. He studied his plate. "She's a good girl. Just like her mother was."

Rex poked a wandering piece of chicken back into the pita bread. "I didn't mean anything. You're right. She's a hard worker. Tough being a single mom."

Dick's gaze shifted to Jeremy, and instead of a fork, he jabbed a knobby finger. "You need to help your mother out. What do you do? You sit at your computer and play goddamn video games. You eat everything in this house and dip into my shit when you run out. You don't lift one finger to help your mother. It's you who's wearing her out. You."

Jeremy didn't answer. Just kept eating and swallowing. Chicken, ribs, potatoes, roll. Fork, chew, swallow, repeat. But no matter how much he shoved into his mouth, he couldn't satisfy the ache in his gut.

He thought about the warrior woman. He thought about taking on the Dicks and the Rexes of the world, only instead of fat-hating agoraphobics and miserable boyfriends, he'd take on companies and organizations.

More cheesy macaroni. More buttered bread.

Could he do it?

Did he have the guts?

12

———————

SUE

I n epidemiology, a point existed beyond which an infectious disease could no longer be easily contained. The point of no return. The tipping point.

The same could be said for many situations. An initial thought led to planning. Planning led to preparation. Preparation led to implementation. And once the gun triggered the first leap out of the starting block, turning back proved impossible. Perhaps the race would never be completed, but the dust was disturbed nonetheless.

Electricity coursed through Sue's veins. She had just reached her tipping point.

"You're sure about this?" In the center of the room, she hovered on the edge of her stool, eyes on Jeremy. The boy slouched on the exam table, its paper covering scrunched and torn beneath him. Connie sat opposite him, her chair against the wall, fingers fiddling with a tiny cross on her necklace. Even though it was Connie who had spoken the critical words first, Sue needed to hear them from Jeremy.

Jeremy chewed his lower lip and stared at the floor. "Yes. I think we should do it."

Sue exhaled slowly, restraining herself from a boisterous *hallelujah*. "You understand we may not get anywhere beyond the first steps. A judge might throw out any lawsuit we file, but that doesn't mean it's not worth proceeding. It's the attention we seek. To make people wake up and take notice there's more to America's weight problem than the individual alone."

"Do you think there's any chance a lawsuit would succeed?" Connie asked.

"Too early to say. At first, Sammy Sanchez thought no, but after looking through the information I gave him, information on how food manufacturers manipulate ingredients to keep us eating, he's wondering if maybe we might have something."

Sue paused and slowed her speech from Porsche to Smart Car. "It's called product optimization, the testing of food until the right combination of sugar, fat, and salt is found to virtually addict us. Junk food releases feel-good hormones in our brains. Like I said before, it's not broccoli we can't get enough of."

Connie slipped her restless hands beneath her thighs. "When Jeremy told me last night he wanted to do this, I wasn't so sure. I don't want to see him get hurt."

"We'll ruffle feathers. Or become laughingstocks. Maybe even get threats." Connie's chin darted up in alarm, and Sue quickly added, "But don't worry, I'm the feather-ruffling champion. My shell's thicker than a turtle's. Since Jeremy's a minor, I'll be the main face and spokesperson alongside Mr. Sanchez."

The lines on Connie's forehead smoothed, and her posture relaxed.

Sue swiveled to Jeremy. "What made you decide to go along with this?" When Jeremy said nothing, his eyes back on the floor and his body corpse-like in stillness, Sue shifted to Connie.

Connie's lips twitched, as if searching for the proper response. "Well, last night wasn't so good at home. You know, Jeremy's been trying hard. He's walking to summer school and everything, but he's only lost three pounds. I know you'd like to see at least two pounds a week." Connie turned her head toward the opposite wall. "It's my fault. I'm a horrible mother. I don't cook dinner for him. I bring food home from work, often late at night. I tried to do better after our last appointment, really I did, but it only lasted a few days. I don't have a car to go to the market to get fresh food whenever we need, and before long, all the fruit and vegetables are gone. Soon we're back to how we always were. It's not his fault, it's mine."

Jeremy pushed himself off the exam table, pulling a long sheet of wrinkled paper with him. He stood like an awkward Weeble, and Sue longed to wrap her arms around him. She watched his Adam's apple bob up and down.

"Don't. It's not your fault, Mom."

Sue suspected Jeremy wanted to say more, but though his lips moved and his hands clenched, no words followed. When Sue was about to break the awkward silence for him, Jeremy surprised her by lifting his head and zeroing in on her gaze.

His face flushed, and his jaw muscles tensed. "Let's do this," he said. "It might be stupid, but it's worth a shot, right?"

After a brief hesitation, the three of them looking from one to the other, Sue stood and enveloped as much of Jeremy in her arms as she could. He stiffened, but she maintained her grip, and soon his body relaxed.

Sue was barely able to complete the appointment. The excitement, but also trepidation, over what they were about to do overshadowed her clinical duties. She managed to congratulate Jeremy on his miniscule weight loss. She also recommended he see his primary-care physician for an asthma check-up.

"Um, he doesn't have a primary doctor," Connie said. "We need to find him one. Dr. Sneeker said the same thing last time we went to the ER. He and Jeremy kind of hit it off, didn't you, Jeremy?"

Jeremy was kicking the exam table with the heels of his over-stretched shoes. "I guess. He's into games and puzzles like me."

The doctor's name surprised Sue, and Connie must have spotted the recognition on her face. "Do you know him?" she asked.

Sue picked up the blood pressure cuff, smoothing out the trapped air. "Yes, we've had interactions over some of the other children in the clinic. He's not always the most sens... Well, let's just say he's not big on sharing the blame when it comes to obesity. I wouldn't mention the lawsuit to him if you see him again."

She left it at that. If Jeremy had bonded with the man, no need to taint his impression.

By the time Sue finished her clinical assessment, it was already half-past seven. She escorted Connie and Jeremy back to the conference room inside her office suite. The space was windowless and gray, and other than a coffee stand in the corner and a central table littered with papers, it was furniture-free. On the wall hung two posters: a "Keep It Simple" message related to public communication and an incident command system flowchart.

Sue motioned them to have a seat at the table. "I'll be right back. I have information on obesity research to give you. Then we'll talk about the lawsuit."

When Sue stepped out of the room, she nearly collided with the department's statistician.

"Oh, George, you startled me. Not used to seeing you in this part of the building, especially at this hour." She invited him into the conference room and introduced him to Connie and Jeremy.

"We saw you in the hall the last time we were here," Connie said, lowering her eyes and smoothing her hair.

George exchanged pleasantries and handed Sue a report. "I have those frequency distributions you asked for. I figured you might still be up here after the evening clinic."

Sue flipped through pages of colorful tables and pie charts containing statistics she needed for a grant proposal to an outside funder. She thanked him and said, "Hold on a sec. I made my special granola. Let me give you some as a thank you."

She left the trio to make small talk while she retrieved the obesity resources and homemade snack from her desk. *You can thank me later,* Connie, she thought with a smile. From what Jeremy had mentioned to the psychologist about Connie's current boyfriend, the woman was due for an upgrade.

Sue weaved around the desks and workspaces of her colleagues, each one accented with personal touches. A collection of sugar-filled test tubes and lumpy fat models for Gabrielle. A stability ball and two fitness bands, one red, one blue, for Shelly Gunther. And a back and neck massager for their suite partner with irritable bowel syndrome.

At her own desk, Sue found the litigation primer and obesity resources she'd printed for the Bartons in the event they went along with her plan. She grabbed the pamphlets, along with a tin of granola for George. Before she could return to the conference room, her work phone rang. A private number.

When she picked it up, her stomach flipped. Tucker Andrews was on the line. Their last active communication was three and a half weeks prior when he'd cornered and intimidated her in the clinic waiting room.

Sue sank to her chair and gripped the phone receiver. "Mr. Andrews, you know you're not to contact me directly. You need to go through the social worker or the—"

"That woman hasn't returned my calls for over a week. This is bullshit. I have a right to know how my daughter's doing. She should be at home, not in some foster place. Who knows what they're doing with her there?"

"They're helping your child lose weight. They're getting her off blood pressure and diabetes drugs." Sue was glad Tucker Andrews couldn't see the tremor in her hands or her shivering arms. She wouldn't want to grant him the satisfaction.

"Don't give me your clinical crap. What about attention? What about love? Are they giving her that? Huh, are they?"

"You need to lower your voice. I will not speak to you when you're verbally abusive." Sue wondered about the wisdom of her next question but asked anyway. "Did you spray paint a slur on my car recently? To threaten me?"

Silence traversed the line, but whether from confusion or admission of guilt, Sue didn't know.

Finally, Mr. Andrews said, "I don't know what you're talking about, but believe me, you'll know when I threaten you."

Sue wiped a moist palm on her slacks. "That's a threat in and of itself. I have no choice but to report this phone call to the police, and it will be added to your growing file. Juney is in the custody of the state. I'm sorry it came to this, but your daughter's life was at risk. Her mother was given every chance. You, too, though last I heard, you weren't living with your wife and daughter. So, if you really want your child back, I suggest you stop acting like a Neanderthal buffoon and start proving you're capable of being a decent father."

As soon as the words left her mouth, Sue wished they hadn't, but she refused to let anyone, especially a bullying man, diminish her.

"That's it. I've had it with you guys. All of you." His words hissed with such hatred Sue half expected saliva to fly through the receiver and spatter her cheek. "I'd like to know what you'd do if it was your kid? How'd you like it if someone took your daughter away?"

Sue slammed the phone down and grabbed George's tin of granola, but her hands shook so badly she dropped it again.

Her scattered thoughts sought out Kayla. Her breaths grew tight and suffocating when she imagined a life without her. Without any of her children.

Her mind flitted to Brent Johnson. His hatred was less overt than Mr. Andrews, but their last clinic encounter had been equally tense. As if his mandated HIV drug checks were Sue's fault alone. And then there was Jackson Weber, her pot-smoking colleague (though she couldn't remember ever meeting him), who'd shot her an angry e-mail a few days back for sending the cops to his girlfriend's house.

Three angry men in one week.

A record, even for Sue.

She could only imagine what the proposed lawsuit might bring.

13

DARWIN

A white cargo van suggested sinister happenings, so Darwin had opted for a minivan rental instead. With the seats flattened, it would suit his purpose.

At nine p.m. on August sixteenth, he drove into the Lifestyle Gym's parking lot and looked for a black Saturn, the one with an orange stuffed kitten hugging the rear window. He knew she would be there. She exercised every night, Fridays included.

He spied the car in its usual spot, far from the door. Given the majority of cars huddled near the front entrance, parking next to Rosa's Saturn proved easy.

"Seems silly to work so hard inside and then not take advantage of extra steps in the parking lot, don't you think?" the bubbly woman had once asked Darwin as she walked toward the entrance alongside him, eager to socialize. Although he'd found her presence presumptuous and annoying, he could not fault her reasoning. All extra steps paid off.

Is it really meant to be her? She's—

The Voice shut him down with a harsh confirmation. Pain seized Darwin's temples, and his hands flew to the spasming muscles so he could knead out the tightness.

(*If it weren't for that fat social monkey, you'd still have access to the gym.*)

Darwin made no further protest. He still hadn't recouped the money invested in home exercise equipment, and though plentiful, the machines and free weights fell short of his needs. A new gym would only invite more fleshy chatterboxes though, not to mention endless shower time.

Leaving the engine running, Darwin peered over his shoulder to ensure the plastic lining was in place over the flattened seats. The covering was difficult to see in the darkening sky. Only a distant street-lamp illuminated the van's interior, but turning on the overhead light would be risky. Rosa would exit the gym any moment. He would have to trust he laid out the lining properly.

A part of him knew he had, but a nagging cerebral tug compelled him to check, the same tug that at home had compelled him to repeatedly sharpen the butcher's knife he now clutched in his gloved hand. He had replaced its sheath only to immediately remove the leather casing and sharpen the blade yet again. Only after ten cycles at the honing steel had he been able to leave the weapon alone.

Next to him in the passenger seat, a vinyl bag with a change of clothes awaited. On top rested a ski mask, though Darwin thought the concealment overkill, given the secluded location.

He conducted another surveillance: Immediately to the north and west sides of the van, a field of weeds and overgrown grass abutted the parking lot. On the east side sat the Saturn and beyond that, a frontage road with minimal traffic. Behind the van to the south lay the expansive parking lot with no nearby cars.

Perfectly secluded.

And yet, Darwin's insides swirled.

(*Relax. You've planned everything perfectly. The only thing left is your prey.*)

The prey. Rosa. In the gym, the woman had seemed to be everywhere: on the adjacent treadmill; waiting her turn at the weight bench; clutching her empty water bottle behind him at the fountain, a wide grin on her heart-shaped face. Every time she'd babbled and percolated, her silly words of weather and reality television had distracted Darwin from his sets, forcing him to repeat the reps all over again. He couldn't deny her dark eyes and full lips held a certain allure, but the jabbering monkey was fat and fleshy. Thus, repulsive.

She's trying.

Confusion clouded his brain.

The Voice redirected him.

(*You should be in there, bench pressing, cycling, using the elliptical. Not her.*)

Darwin had never encouraged her. He tuned out her prattle, and if that failed, he switched machines. His workouts required discipline and concentration. And yet, she would always find him.

Finally, he had snapped. After three repetitions of the same circuit thanks to her blather, he said, "Can't you see I'm focusing? Bother someone else with your goddamn ceaseless talk."

Rosa, a look of horror on her face, took the hint and never bothered him again.

Until the incident on the treadmill.

Darwin felt his body tense at the memory. He licked his lips, the minty toothpaste from a five-minute scrub still tingling his tongue.

The gym had been particularly crowded that June evening. All the treadmills were occupied. Darwin waited his turn, filling the minutes with push-ups, squats, and crunches, but as his routine fell out of sequence, his agitation grew. Bike, weights, treadmill, core. Bike, weights, treadmill, core. That was how his circuit was supposed to go, but he was forced into a bike-weights-core cycle instead, and every time he lunged for a vacated treadmill, some yoga-panted woman or quick-footed man beat him to it. All the while, Rosa hogged a machine, jabbering to the woman on her left, trotting at a tortoise's pace.

That day had already challenged Darwin enough. Miss Fat Witch was whining at work, a flat tire stalled his car, and — worst of all — before leaving for the gym, he had paused to add a few pieces to his almost-finished jigsaw puzzle, a complex structure of antique apothecary bottles, all an agonizingly similar shade of brown. As he reached for a piece, his sleeve had tagged a corner of the puzzle, and a large chunk of the jigsaw went sailing to the floor. Darwin had been distraught, and immediate punishment was necessary. As such, he was only allowed a fat-free cheese stick and six almonds pre-workout.

Later that same evening, waiting for a treadmill, Darwin had paced and hovered. He looked at his watch and counted his heart rate, the increased pulse more a result of low blood sugar and stress from the circuit alteration than the exercise itself. He listened to Rosa chatting away with her companion, an overweight toad of a woman in pink spandex, her wide ass an egg crate of dimples.

Finally, Darwin cracked. With eyes full of fury, he leapt toward Rosa. "Either speed-walk or run, or get your fat ass off the treadmill."

Unable to stop himself, he grabbed Rosa's wrist. The dark-eyed woman howled and stumbled on the treadmill. Before Darwin could claim the machine for himself, three red-faced and sweaty men tackled him to the floor, the tallest of whom had given Darwin an approving, come-on look only moments before.

After that, the gym had banned him. All four area locations.

His gym, not hers.

Replaying the incident reignited his humility and rage, but a flicker in the rearview mirror transported him back to the evening's agenda. A figure was approaching. Quickly, he donned the ski mask and secured the knife.

He'd almost blown it. Punishment would surely follow. But first, payback.

With the stealth of a prowling cat, Darwin slunk into the van's back compartment and opened the side door closest to Rosa's Saturn. He tipped his masked head out to watch her.

As she approached, he faltered. Even in the dark he could see the Rosa of this evening was slimmer than the Rosa of two months before. As she walked, she released her hair from its ponytail and shook the dark locks loose.

(*Don't let her fool you. She's still polluting the earth with unhealthy habits.*)

Rosa was almost upon him, but still Darwin hesitated.

(*She robbed you of the gym. She presumed you were equals. Such a foolish woman. Discipline, Darwin. Only sheep show weakness.*)

Darwin gripped the knife. Indecision put him on par with those he had to eliminate.

No more weakness.

As his thinking cleared, the cerebral ache lessened.

Darwin waited a few more seconds. Rosa, singing a nineties pop tune under her breath, clicked the door lock's release. He anticipated the tensing of her body, the surprise in her eyes, the scent of her fear. He would grab her before she was aware of his presence, shove her in the van, and slit her belly from navel to chest with a blade sharper than a surgeon's scalpel.

With her ear buds still in place, an oblivious Rosa reached for the Saturn's door. Darwin pounced. He grabbed her around the waist and pushed her toward the van, but she didn't tumble in as planned. Instead, she screamed and kicked, landing a solid blow to Darwin's left knee. Pain immobilized his leg, and he almost buckled to the ground. His grip on the woman slackened but held.

(*Go for the neck. Incapacitate her.*)

As Darwin thrust the knife toward his squirming prey, she smashed her boulder of a skull against his forehead. He yelped in shock and pain. Bursts of light blinded his eyes, and before he could react, Rosa spun around and kicked him in the groin. A sickening nausea joined the orbital stars, and Darwin's grip gave way. She took flight. Rosa the slow walker, Rosa the ingratiating talker, Rosa the tub fled into the night, screaming and hollering for help.

Darwin had no choice but to ignore his pain. It wasn't the first time he'd had to overcome near incapacitation. He hopped into the van and shifted into reverse. Tires peeled out of the parking lot. He ripped the face mask from his head, blinking away hurt and dismay.

How could this happen? This was my chance to take the mission to the next level.

He failed. He failed miserably.

And now he would be punished.

14

———————

JEREMY

Teenagers specialized in tuning out adults, and Jeremy put his talents to good use that Monday afternoon. With Sue at the wheel, Connie in the front passenger seat, and Jeremy behind her, they were en route to the lawyer's office, having just picked up Connie early from Home Solutions.

As the warrior woman droned on about society's responsibility for obesity, Jeremy let his mind wander to the back-and-forth Facebooking between Calvin and "Courtney." Things were heating up between the bully and the fictitious hottie. When Calvin had messaged Courtney about chiseling his six-pack abs, Jeremy and Tito had snorted in laughter. They were both hoping a picture would follow, because although summer school had ended three days before, Jeremy knew he'd face the chiseled idiot again. He and Tito would need an ace up their sleeves.

Jeremy tuned back in when he heard Connie mention her boss's reaction to her early departure.

"I know you want us to keep the lawsuit idea quiet for now, so I told him it was a family thing. He said okay, as long as I found someone to work for me, but he made sure to point out he wouldn't be around to cover my backside."

"Sounds like a peach." Sue slid the car onto I-90 East. "Sammy's office is on Prospect."

Connie's boss was anything but a peach, unless it was a putrid peach. The few times Jeremy had met the über-fit dude, the guy had looked at Jeremy as if fatness were contagious. The assistant manager crinkled his upturned nose at Connie, too, though she was merely plump. In fact, Jeremy wondered if his mother had lost a few pounds. Maybe the Fat Slayers had cast a spell. Weight loss by fat-clinic proxy.

Jeremy also noticed his mother had spruced up for the afternoon. Her shoulder-length hair was loose and brushed to a shine, and her highlights recently retouched from a do-it-yourself drugstore kit he'd spotted on the bathroom counter. Fancy makeup adorned her face, and an unfamiliar lavender dress hugged her body.

Sue fiddled with the collar of her blouse. "I haven't told my colleagues yet either. They'll find out soon enough." Steering with one hand, she overtook a reasonably paced Prius before jerking the Ford Focus back into the right lane. Jeremy wondered if she was preparing for the Indy 500. Then Sue's tone lightened. "Speaking of colleagues, I heard a certain statistician wants more Connie time. I hope it was okay I gave George your number."

Jeremy straightened, forgetting about Sue's driving for a moment. Although he couldn't see his mom's face, her giggle told him she was more than okay with it.

"It's fine. Thank you." Connie swept back her hair, and Jeremy could see her beaded earrings sway back and forth with Sue's abrupt lane changes. "We're getting together for coffee this weekend."

"Excellent. From what I've heard about your current man, he's a real pain, and my brief interaction with him at your house this after-noon confirmed it."

Both women laughed. At that point, Jeremy understood the fresh highlights and makeup. And the weight loss.

After a quantum leap from the interstate onto the Prospect Avenue exit, during which Jeremy grasped the hand grip and prayed for his life, Sue drove a few uninterrupted blocks to a red brick building on the right. A row of squat trees served as landscaping, and Sue chose the empty metered spot next to them. A sign near the building's entrance promised an insurance agency, a dentistry clinic, a real estate office, and Mr. Sanchez's law practice.

Inside the compound, a black letter board encased in glass and positioned between two chrome elevators directed them to the second floor, Suite 2B.

After a short elevator ride (the stairwell's temporary closure from fresh paint made Sue grumble), they entered Mr. Sanchez's office. The room contained a small reception area with an L-shaped desk. Behind the cherry-wood structure sat a gray-haired secretary, identified by her nameplate as Janine. Nestled among the expected office items — computer, phone, inbox, outbox — was a male doll with splayed limbs and a flat, wide-eyed face. Jeremy thought it looked like a voodoo doll.

Janine must have caught his expression. "Isn't he wonderful? I got him in New Orleans. Got this guy there too." She pointed to a bizarre laughing gargoyle pinned to the lapel of her plum suit. When she subsequently confessed to Jeremy that she, too, was a gamer, he scratched his head and wondered what world he'd just entered.

As they waited for Mr. Sanchez, the three guests seated in leather-upholstered chairs, Janine chattered on, skipping over the small talk and heading straight for the juice.

"Scary about that woman who was almost abducted outside her gym last Friday, isn't it? Some guy in a ski mask. They said on the news it might be linked to the murders of those..." Her voice trailed off when her gaze met Jeremy's.

"The two fat dudes, you mean?" Jeremy figured he might as well help her out. No need to mince words.

He was aware of the murders, not because he followed the head-lines — though GI Dick kept the news on practically nonstop — but because after the last one happened almost two weeks ago, Calvin had made sure to inform Jeremy during class that another "fat bastard got iced."

GI Dick talked about the murders, too, though he railed on the media for connecting the motive to weight. "There are fat people all over the country. Odds are two victims in a row will be lard-butts."

Jeremy thought about asking the killer to visit the agoraphobic old man to test the theory. He imagined the headlines: *This just in: The killer has struck again. A normal-weight, cantankerous ex-soldier this time around. Looks like there's no connection, folks.*

Janine cleared her throat. "Yes, the two overweight men. It sounds like the cases might be related."

Connie's fingers fluttered to her purse strap.

"Coincidence, I'm sure," Sue said, patting Connie on the thigh. In a tone that made Jeremy want to cover his crotch, she added, "Men who attack women should be strung up by their nuggets and whipped."

Finally, Mr. Sanchez called for them. After introductions were made all around, the trim, well-dressed lawyer looked Jeremy in the eye and gave him a firm handshake. "No need for formalities. Call me Sammy."

Sammy's office housed the same dark cherry furniture and beige walls as the reception area, but instead of voodoo dolls and gargoyles, his wall displayed an antique shotgun and pistol, along with two gold-plated daggers.

"You like them?" Sammy asked Jeremy. "They're part of my collection. I've got an old flintlock musket at home I've been meaning to bring in as well."

Jeremy offered what he hoped was a manly nod, while his mind wondered about the sanity of the inhabitants of the law office.

Sammy lined three chairs in front of his desk. Jeremy chose the seat closest to the window. Connie sat next to him, then Sue. When Jeremy slumped onto the seat, his thighs poured out from beneath the armrests like a fallen soufflé. He hated skinny-people chairs.

The lawyer folded his hands together and rested them on his desk. He, unlike his secretary, did not mince words. "Let me be frank. This lawsuit will likely go nowhere."

"Then why go through the trouble of filing it?" Connie said, her body perched tense and compact on the end of her chair, as if trying to take up the least space possible.

Sue beat Sammy to the response. "To get attention. To make people understand our cause. To finally be heard—"

The lawyer raised his hand, cutting Sue off. The warrior woman's brows rose, and her silenced mouth formed the letter O. She leaned back and picked fluff from her black pants. Jeremy bit the inside of his cheek, trying not to smile.

"Like Sue said, we'll get attention," Sammy told Connie and Jeremy. "Tobacco litigation had to start somewhere. I believe this does too, and who knows where it might lead? For both you and me." The lawyer paused, a mole under his chin catching Jeremy's eye. "But a lot of people will think it's ridiculous. They'll think blaming industries and organizations for the country's obesity is the easy way out, another way for Americans to shirk responsibility."

Sue chimed in again. "But society does play a—"

Another raised hand. Another bristle from Sue.

"We'll be laughed at and ridiculed. The papers will go crazy. Bloggers will have a field day. Do you understand that?"

Jeremy swallowed and shifted his gaze to Sammy's antique pistol. Although the lawyer treating Jeremy like a man pleased him, the words did not.

Connie's hand hovered over Jeremy's thigh, her fingertips barely a butterfly's touch on his sweatpants. "Um, how exactly does it work?" she asked.

"We start by filing our initial complaint with the court that the defendants' industries contribute to obesity and its complications. Then a summons is delivered to the defendants — actually, in a civil case they're called respondents, but we'll stick to the familiar — who have twenty-eight days to file an answer, usually a list of responses to each of our charges. Next, both sides request information pertaining to the case, including depositions where defendants and witnesses are formally questioned. Somewhere around here, a judge will request mediation and settlement, hoping to avoid a trial. Going to trial, of course, assumes our case isn't thrown out, which most likely it will be."

"But think of the attention we'll garner." Sue gave a single clap of her hands.

Not wanting to sound stupid but curious about the answer, Jeremy asked, "Who exactly are the defendants?"

"Since, at this point, we can only file suits against businesses within the state, we'll limit our initial charges to..." Sammy used his fingers to tick off each of the defendants, "Burgers and Buns, the restaurant chain you frequent; Bilko's and Brover's, two of Ohio's biggest processed food producers; and the Ohio branch of the restaurant alliance. That last one is a stretch though. It's more to raise awareness, as Sue has pointed out."

Connie rubbed her bare arms, the summer dress apparently no match for the office's central air or the stressful conversation. "This is all kind of overwhelming. I just ... I mean ... I think it's a good idea and all, but I don't want to see Jeremy get hurt."

"I understand." Sammy shifted his gaze to Jeremy and leaned back in his leather chair. A cloud of vanilla-scented mist sprayed from an automatic air-freshener on a shelf behind him. "When you sue, privacy rights of the plaintiff are waived, and since we're suing on behalf of you, Jeremy, the defendants will be privy to your personal information. We'll have Sue shoulder the public scrutiny though. She's an old pro at that." Sammy stared hard at Jeremy and Connie, as though making sure they understood what lay ahead. "Also, I don't want you to be expecting a big windfall from this. That's definitely the wrong attitude to have. Money should not be our motive, because you probably won't see any."

Jeremy looked at his mom, her expression as blank as his. The idea of money hadn't crossed his mind.

"Oh, no, I wasn't even thinking along those lines," Connie said.

Sue held out her hands, palms up. "But who knows? If we can take this thing far enough, there might be some interview opportunities, a chance for you to make some extra cash. That is, if you're willing to face the public, Connie."

Connie paled and hugged her arms.

Sammy drummed his fingers on the desk. "One step at a time. For now, just make sure you want to proceed, Jeremy, and I'll file as soon as Sue gives me the word."

The air went still. Jeremy thought about Calvin's endless taunts and GI Dick's badgering, as if by a snap of the fingers, Jeremy could make himself thin. He pictured the look of disdain and disgust on opinionated faces: his mom's boss, Rex, kids at school, teachers. He heard their whispers and witnessed their finger-pointing. He sensed the fast-food restaurants and the packaged junk food calling his name. *Jeremy. Jeremy.* Insistently, insanely, until the only way to squelch their addictive pleas was to shovel their garbage into his mouth. In the pit of his belly, he felt the fear of a walk home from school. It was better with Tito, but the threat was ever present.

Jeremy clutched the armrests of his chair, his redundant flesh pinched and sore from the wooden confinement. He studied the Persian rug under his soiled shoes.

With a boldness that surprised even himself, he interrupted Sammy's response to a question Connie had posed and said, "I want to proceed. I want to go ahead and sue."

A few minutes later, they were back in the reception area. Jeremy's head spun with the knowledge he had just become the poster boy of fat. In an attempt to lessen the vertigo, he homed his gaze onto Janine's ugly voodoo doll.

He was contemplating its effectiveness on Calvin when he heard his mother's surprised voice. "What are you doing here?"

"I could ask you the same thing. Thought you had a family matter."

Jeremy shifted toward the source of the comment.

What's my mom's boss doing here?

Sammy seemed equally startled. "You two know each other?"

Connie gripped the pamphlets Sammy had given her, knuckles white around the glossy paper. "Mr. Newman is my boss."

"Jonathan is your boss?"

Given the look on Sammy's face, Jeremy guessed the lawyer would have been less shocked to learn Jeremy had just taken a crap on the floor.

"Yes, at Home Solutions. He's the assistant manager."

Sue smacked the side of her head. "How did I not make the connection? I knew you worked at a home improvement store, Jonathan, but I never realized it was the same one as Connie."

Sammy finally closed his mouth. He tugged at his suit jacket and smoothed it into place. "Yes, well, Jonathan is my... He's my..."

"I'm Sammy's boyfriend." Jonathan's tone was as flat as his stomach. Then he smiled and added, "And sometimes his secret."

The awkwardness continued until Sammy dismissed them. "I think we're done here. I'll call Sue once I've made the first step, and of course—" A throat clearing and a glance to Jonathan. "Everything is confidential."

That suited Jeremy fine. Given Jonathan's tight-lipped expression when he looked Jeremy's way, Jeremy had a good idea where the man would land on the lawsuit debate.

As the three plaintiffs (Jeremy finally understood the meaning of the word) drove to meet Sue's reporter friend, Connie shared similar concerns.

"If Mr. Newman finds out about the lawsuit, he'll fire me."

"He can't fire you for that. At least I don't think so." Sue sped through a yellow light toward Superior Avenue. A man in a Cleveland Cavaliers jersey jumped back up on the curb, yelled something, and shook his fist at her. She seemed not to notice, nor did any members of an apathetic crowd waiting in a hot, sweaty huddle near the bus kiosk, paper fans batting like propellers. The tall buildings behind and across from them offered little shade from a cloudless sun.

"He won't say it's because of the lawsuit. He'll find some other excuse to get rid of me. He doesn't have a great view of obese people.

You should hear how he talks about our overweight manager. And he certainly wouldn't agree about suing food companies."

Jeremy wondered how his mother expected the lawsuit to remain quiet when it was the exact opposite they sought, but he kept his thoughts to himself and maintained his hold on the hand grip.

After a final lurching turn and some butt-bruising turbulence in the increasing traffic, Sue landed her Ford Focus on the runway of Superior Avenue. Grabbing an oven-sized purse splattered in polka-dots, she grinned like an evil mastermind and whipped open her car door. "Let's go meet Tony Farr, our attention spreader."

Tony's office turned out to be a table at a coffee shop near the *Cleveland Times* building. The reporter thanked them for meeting him there.

Sue made introductions. Although the thirtyish, jean-sporting, thick-haired Tony seemed polite and pleasant, the only things Jeremy could focus on were the size of the guy's schnoz and the way he looked at Connie, like a puppy enthralled with a butterfly.

After collecting coffees for the adults and a diet soda for Jeremy, to which the warrior nodded her approval, Sue got down to business.

"Remember when I told you I might have a great story for you? Well, the story is here."

"Uh-oh, who'd you piss off now?" Tony flashed a smile at Connie, his teeth at least prettier than his nose.

Sue's lips formed a tight line, parting only for a sip of her steaming latte. A braver Jeremy would have told her to lighten up. It's not like the dude said the f-word. Jeremy studied the inviting but off-limits cake pops lining the counter and fought back a smile.

Sue filled Tony in on the litigation plan. "So what do you think? You interested?"

Tony dumped a packet of artificial sweetener into his cup and rubbed a well-manicured hand over his chin. "Do I want the story? Of course I want the story. I'm a former big kid myself." To Jeremy, he said, "Used to weigh almost three hundred pounds. Finally able to do something about it, though it wasn't easy. Takes a lot of discipline."

"So you're unbiased then?" Connie said. Though Jeremy didn't think the question was a joke, Tony laughed anyway, a horsey whinny of a laugh.

Tony turned to Sue. "You're sure you're up for this? You haven't exactly made friends with the public in the Juney Andrews and Brent Johnson cases."

"Not everyone sided against us. There are plenty of supporters as well. People who know sometimes the rights of a few must be suppressed for the benefit of many."

After further discussion, the group agreed to a full interview with Tony the following Thursday. Sue made the reporter promise not to publish the story until Sammy filed the complaint. He argued against the delay, until a plea and a soft arm squeeze from Connie silenced him. His cheeks flamed pinker than the strawberry cake pops, and he nodded. He then proposed Jeremy's home for a location, but Connie gave a quick shake of her head. "My father, well, it's best to meet some-place else."

Instead, they agreed to meet at Sue's. When Tony asked if Al would be okay with that, Sue reached into her giant purse and pulled out a tissue. She gave a noncommittal nose blow in response.

The reporter squinted and cocked his head to the side. "You have told your husband, haven't you? Once this gets out, all hell could break loose."

Sue's uncharacteristic silence was answer enough. For the first time, Jeremy realized he wasn't the only one with something at stake.

No longer craving cake pops, a sense of dread engulfed him. He pushed the remainder of his soda away. He thought about his online avatar, the powerful shaman who tackled all the evil forces tossed his way. He tried to channel Kajika's courage.

Yeah, right. A fat-assed pussy like me.

15

SUE

The roomy kitchen was awash in yellow. Yellow paint, yellow window valances dotted with daisies, yellow place mats on the round table near the bay-window nook. According to a nurse educator at the health department, a woman who practiced chromotherapy and believed colors could be used to manage disease, yellow purified the body and stimulated the nerves. Two years before, when Sue had announced she and Al were redoing their kitchen in various shades of yellow, the chromotherapist had widened her eyes and waved her hands back and forth.

"Oh, no. You shouldn't make a room yellow. It seems cheery, but it actually creates frustration and anger. People are apt to lose their tempers in yellow rooms."

Although Sue had raised an eyebrow and exchanged glances with Gabrielle, the dietitian in the room at the time, Sue now wondered if Nurse Chromotherapy didn't have a point after all. With Al's plate banging and cupboard slamming that morning, the sunny kitchen seemed to be living up to her prediction.

Sue carried her hazelnut coffee and whole-grain cereal to the table, along with the lifestyle section of the paper. She normally breakfasted at the counter, but Al's violent buttering of a piece of toast on the center island scared her away. She wasn't entirely surprised. On August twenty-ninth, Sammy filed the legal complaint. On August thirtieth, the Friday before Labor Day, Tony published his article. In the eleven days since, Al and Sue had argued nonstop, almost more than they had in their twenty-five years of marriage.

Neither the lawsuit nor the article were a surprise to Al. Sue had come clean with her husband before Tony had conducted the interview at their home. But every day his anger over the litigation grew, deepening with each new understanding of what the act would mean and the attention it would garner. "Attention that my wife, who's already nose-deep in controversy, does not need."

The *Cleveland Times* article gave few specifics about the litigation, only that a suit was filed against various Ohio industries, charging them with contributing to obesity and its medical complications. The article also outlined food manufacturers and restaurants' responsibility in the obesity epidemic as well as the struggles faced by the plaintiff in the country's "obesogenic" environment.

Although Jeremy and Connie went unnamed, Sue did not. In fact, her name populated nearly every paragraph and, without reading over his shoulder, Sue had known precisely each time Al came across it, thanks to his intermittent jaw clenching.

She imagined the health director's mug would display similar displeasure. Dr. Chen had been on vacation before the article was published, spending Labor Day and the rest of the week at his lake home. Although he'd returned the day before, catch-up work had consumed him, and by the time he'd learned of the lawsuit and the increased number of calls to the health department it had generated, Sue had slipped out for the day.

She knew her luck wouldn't last.

Unable to take Al's silence any longer, she swallowed a spoonful of cereal and said, "It had to be done."

"Bullshit!"

Sue's spoon clattered to the bowl, splashing milk on her indigo blouse. She dabbed at the droplets with a napkin. "We all marvel at the increasing girth of our brothers and sisters, and yet we do nothing about it," she said quietly. "It's time someone does something."

Al stuffed half a piece of wheat toast into his mouth and chewed like an angry lion. Sue swore she could see the poorly masticated glob descend down his throat. "Why is it your job?" he said. "Why is it my job? It's not my fault the neighbor needs a scooter to fetch his mail. It's not my fault my big-bellied partner can't quit eating a double cheese-burger and large fries at lunch. And it's not your fault either. They have only themselves to blame."

"I don't think you really believe that."

"Well, apparently it doesn't matter what I believe. Sue does what Sue wants. To hell with everyone else. But it's me who's stuck dealing with the aftermath of an angry public."

Tucker Andrews, Brent Johnson, and Jackson Weber flashed in Sue's mind. "I can take care of myself."

Al started to respond, but a revving engine drowned out his words. Both of their gazes shot toward the living room, though neither could see the front window from the kitchen. A loud idling followed the final roar, and before Al or Sue had a chance to get up, Kayla bounded down the stairs. Ignoring her parents and skipping breakfast yet again, the girl disappeared into the living room.

Sue shot up and sprinted after her. She grabbed a handful of Kayla's gauzy shirt before her daughter could open the door. "Where do you think you're going?"

"Um, to school? Where do you think?"

Sue looked through the decorative stained glass flanking the door on either side. Out by the curb, in a haze of exhaust and booming rap music, a black car with tinted windows and tires three times its require-ment rocked and waited.

Sue shook her head and planted her hands on her hips. "Oh no, young lady, not in that you're not. Who is that?"

"He's my friend. God, Mom, why do you always have to make a big deal out of everything?"

Kayla whipped the door open with a newly cast-free arm and stepped out. Sue was right on her heels. Behind her Al said, "What in the hell?"

Near the pimped-out beast, Sue booted Kayla out of the way and opened the passenger door. A surprised kid greeted her, his neck weighted down with chains, one of which showcased a dangling gold letter T.

"Please step out of this car. Now." Sue could barely get the words out through her clenched jaw.

The driver exited and ambled toward Sue. His jeans hung low on skinny hips, revealing eight inches of striped boxers. "Hey, it's all good, Momma Fort. Chill. I'm Trey, but you can call me T."

Sue's cheeks flushed a purple rage. She stomped forward until only a foot of space separated T from her fury. An excess of men's body wash assaulted her nose, and she had to strain to keep from sneezing. Outranking him in height and muscle, but not in nonchalance, she fired question after question.

When Trey Devers announced he was nineteen years old — three years older than Kayla — Al grabbed Kayla's bicep and dragged her to his own car inside the garage.

Ignoring Kayla's protests, he turned to Trey. "You be on your way now, son. I'll drive my daughter to school. Next time you want to see Kayla, you need to come to the door like a man."

Despite her earlier irritation with Al, Sue was grateful. He tended to avoid the heavier parenting requirements, weighting Sue with the responsibility, but as angry as she was at that moment, he couldn't have picked a better time to step up. No telling what would have come out of her mouth.

Sue bid Trey a brisk good-bye. The young man shrugged and said, "Whatevs," before sauntering back to his car.

Another revving of the thunderous engine polluted the quiet neighborhood before Trey drove off. Birds flapped in a disordered panic, their squawks and screeches taking over where the muscle car left off.

Still shaking, Sue turned to thank Al, but her husband had already pulled out of the driveway, a fierce expression on his face alongside an equally vicious-looking teenage girl.

Not even a wave in Sue's direction.

Stepping back into the house, she cleaned her breakfast dishes and retrieved her purse from the coat rack. Motionless in the foyer, she stared at the bag's colorful polka-dots, the rainbow of circles blurring together beneath misty eyes. Maybe Kayla was right. Maybe the big tote was dumb.

Mini movie reels spun through Sue's mind: Kayla taking her first steps with her older brother and sister cheering her on, Kayla in the department store with her tiny fingers running the length of a silky blouse ("Is this one bright enough, Mama?"), grade-school Kayla surprising Sue with a beaded and glitter-glued Mother's Day card. "Best Mom Ever!" it shouted in a full spectrum of color.

Her phone ringing from inside her purse startled Sue out of her trance. She fished out the mobile and saw Connie's name on the caller ID. She barely had a chance to say hello.

"They have my name. They used my name," Connie said in a rush. "Not Jeremy's, thank God, but they used my name. And they showed my picture. A photo from work, for employee-of-the-month or something, I don't know. I can't—"

"Whoa, slow down. Who used your name?"

Sue listened as Connie sputtered about a television news station's morning report. They said a local woman, Connie Barton, was suing organizations in the food industry for making her son obese. Most of the information came from Tony's article, but instead of only Sue and Sammy's names being mentioned, the television reporter had discovered Connie.

Sue rushed to the television and flipped to the local channels. Blips about skinny jeans, avocados, and the weekend's box office numbers. Nothing about the lawsuit.

How did a TV reporter learn about Connie? Tony would never have said anything. Nor would Sammy or Al. Who else knew?

She scoured her brain. Jonathan Newman had come into Sammy's office when they were there. Had he connected the dots after seeing the newspaper article mentioning his boyfriend's intended litigation? What about Connie's father, Dick? He knew and, according to Connie, didn't approve. Rex, Connie's old boyfriend? Did he know? Did he want payback for Connie's new interest in George? Or maybe the reporter sought public records.

While Connie prattled on, another call pinged. Dr. Chen, the health director. Sue's boss.

Letting the call go to voicemail, she promised Connie everything would be fine. All their names would surface eventually, especially if Connie wanted to grant interviews should the lawsuit garner attention. The leak just happened earlier than they wanted.

Sue plodded to her car with leaded limbs and twisted insides. Though aware the unease was out of proportion to the minor set-back, she felt its prickly talons nonetheless.

―――

Later that morning, Sue stood in the third-floor stairwell of the health department. She exhaled deeply and tried to relax her muscles. The yellow sticky note suspended from her computer monitor had made clear the day's first task: SEE DR. CHEN ASAP.

Taking one last deep breath, she stepped into the hallway and collided with a man standing outside the stairwell door. His eyes gazed down the corridor as if looking for a particular office or department. After collecting herself and apologizing, she offered assistance, but he shook his head and entered the stairwell instead.

Sue lingered at the end of the hallway. Something about the man seemed familiar.

That face...

Or maybe she was stalling.

Rubbing her arm, massaging out the collision's sting, she walked three office doors down to Dr. Chen's suite, her sensible heels clicking on the gray tile. When she entered, she found Dr. Chen's secretary in the outer office, rummaging through a tiny refrigerator. She indicated with a nod that Sue go to the closed door behind the receptionist's desk. Given the speed with which the young woman averted her eyes, Sue knew word of Chen's displeasure had circulated.

Her knock on the director's door prompted an immediate, "Come in." Inside, the head of the health department paced his well-trodden carpet. His hands rubbed a protuberant belly as if feeling for upcoming contractions, and a pink flush spread from face to scalp, visible through thinning strands of hair.

As soon as Sue closed the door, Dr. Chen erupted. "How could you do something like this without telling me? What were you thinking? You had to know this would affect the department."

"This lawsuit has nothing to do with the health department."

"It has everything to do with the health department." Despite his droopy eyelids, Dr. Chen's orbits seemed to bulge. "You work here. The plaintiff is a patient here. Of course the public will make the connection to us, just as they did with Juney Andrews and Brent Johnson. Sure, our role was pivotal in those instances, but many other forces were at play including law enforcement and social services."

Sue felt her own fury rise. In her opinion, Dr. Chen used the words *our role* a little too liberally. His was not the face behind those cases. His was not the name uttered in households across Cleveland and beyond. Like the endocrinologist, Dr. Chen had been all too content to leave his reputation out of the stink pile, allowing Sue to suffer the public's ire.

"You have a knack for this kind of thing," he had said a few months back when the public demanded more than a polished public-relations response.

So it was Sue's face alongside the department's spokesperson. Her name. She bore the brunt of the anger, and she was willing to do so in order to benefit the greater good.

Dr. Chen finally sank into the chair behind his cluttered desk. "Look, the Juney Andrews case is just starting to die down. I understand her father has threatened you, and I'm sorry for that, but at least the media isn't chomping at our tails anymore. It would be nice to be the good guys for a while."

Sue took a seat as well, her hands buried under her trembling thighs, as if by immobilizing the limbs she might keep her hotheadedness in check. "I assure you, I am pursuing this on my own, not as a health department employee. That was already made clear in Tony's article. This will not get in the way of my job."

"It better not. We can't afford to lose you." Dr. Chen's tone became more conciliatory and his expression glum. "I respect your intention. Really I do. God knows losing weight has been a failed battle for me. But I'll be forced to insist on a leave of absence — or worse — if this litigation balloons out of control."

Remaining quiet, Sue squeezed her thighs with her hidden fingertips. The dread in her belly returned.

"It's bad timing too. I assume you've heard about those two men who were killed and the woman who was attacked outside her gym. There's talk someone might be targeting..." Dr. Chen cleared his throat and looked down at his own girth. "Well, targeting overweight people. Your case will only draw more attention to the psychopath."

Sue shook her head. "First of all, no connection exists between the murders and weight. Tongues are wagging in excitement despite no proof to support the gossip. And second of all, attention is exactly what we need from this lawsuit. We want the whole country talking about the issue. Only then will we make an impact. As a public health practitioner, you should know that."

Sue knew deep down Dr. Chen agreed. He preached many times about the multiple causes of obesity and insisted any successful solution would require targeting them all.

Dr. Chen sighed and rubbed his fingers over tired eyes, eyes that did not convey the calm of a recent vacation. "Just tread lightly. Please. It's not only the department's reputation I worry about. It's your safety too. I don't want to see you get hurt. Or anyone else for that matter."

Sue breathed for what seemed like the first time in days and granted her hands their freedom. "Don't worry. I'll be fine. I assure you, an imaginary serial killer targeting overweight people is the least of my, or anyone else's, worries."

16

DARWIN

High above the road where Darwin was running, a crow cawed, and within moments another carrion feeder joined the first. The bird cries broke the steady seesaw of his labored breaths. Undernourished and confused, he covered his head with sweaty forearms, convinced the dead-flesh eaters were about to swoop down and peck at his soul.

In his panic, he lost his balance. His legs, two linguine noodles from miles of running, stumbled, and he spilled to the ground. Twice he tried to right himself, but dizziness prevented it.

Fuel. Need more fuel.

(*Get up. You have half a mile left. It was your failure that brought you here.*)

Darwin tried once again, and this time, by pressing his hands first against the concrete and then against his thighs, he righted himself. The whoosh of a passing jogger almost knocked him back down.

"Sorry dude," the portly man said over his shoulder.

Darwin tensed his wobbly muscles and fisted his numb hands.

Who are you to address me? he thought. *You are nothing but a sheep.*

Slowly, the killer resumed his lifeless trot. At least The Voice was speaking to him again. After the Rosa disaster, he had turned his back on Darwin, but not before demanding punishment.

To make up for his miserable failure with Rosa, a failure that could have revealed his identity or landed him in jail, Darwin was forced to severely restrict his caloric intake. In addition, he had to run an extra one hundred and fifty miles before he could kill again. One hundred and fifty miles on top of his usual cardio routine.

To further repent, he had sliced small cuts into his upper arms with a razor blade and pinched his nipples and scrotum with metal clips. After over two weeks of such discipline, The Voice returned, and Darwin had sighed in relief.

Without The Voice to guide him, how would he find his next target? How would he carry on the mission? He had to make the police and the public see the connection once and for all. Only then would the operation succeed. Only then would others follow his lead.

That night's run would complete the punishment, allowing Darwin to refocus on the mission without distraction. Critical, given the ultimate conquest had recently been revealed.

Two days earlier, as Darwin was powering through ten cycles of pre-work push-ups and abdominal crunches, a news story on TV had caught his attention. There was that woman again. The woman who blamed the world for a teenage boy's gluttony.

As he replayed the news clip in his mind, the frivolous lawsuit once again generated such rage within him that he pushed his overtaxed body through the last half mile of his run with no further stumbles or setbacks.

Renewed energy fueled him. Sweat poured off his muscular flesh. Soon he would feel whole again. His penance had been paid.

Another kill would be his reward.

17

JEREMY

Jeremy was two and a half weeks into his sophomore year, and for the first time in a long time, he had a friend to eat lunch with.

Tito tossed the remainder of a pizza slice onto his cafeteria tray. Regarding Jeremy's hesitancy over the Facebook prank, he said, "Don't worry, we're only interacting. And when Calvin makes a fool of himself for Courtney, we'll spread it around. Let him suffer some humiliation for a change. He'll never know it's us." A bite of an oatmeal-raisin bar made Tito grimace. He dumped the dessert alongside the pizza and pushed the tray of uneaten food away. "Speaking of girls, when you gonna talk to her?"

Jeremy eyed the discarded pizza and oatmeal treat, wondering how anyone could so disinterestedly toss it aside. For him, choosing the turkey wrap over the pizza had been an act of colossal willpower, but bit by bit, his efforts seemed to be paying off. The day before, the fat-clinic scale boasted another five-pound weight loss. Two hundred and ninety-nine pounds.

The Fat Slayers had cooed and praised, the fitness freak of the duo even performing a celebratory tuck jump. Both women had outlined new goals.

"Let's get fast food down to three times per month, okay? And up your vegetable intake. You've still got a long way to go," Gabrielle had said.

Shelly had encouraged the addition of weights. Using five-pound dumbbells, the lithe bunny had bobbed up and down in a series of squats and biceps curls. "You see? By incorporating light weights, you'll burn more calories and get your heart rate up. Use heavier weights for isolated strength training. Muscle burns more calories than fat, you know. Who doesn't want that?"

Who indeed?

Although Jeremy hadn't had the nerve to tell Fat Slayer Shelly he still hadn't mastered her circuit workout, especially with GI Dick bellowing from one floor below about the pounding and thumping, he was pleased with his progress. Images of being plump rather than fat, images he had never before dared conjure, nudged their way into his head.

"Hey, earth to Jeremy. I asked when you were going to talk to Lacey." Tito snapped his fingers in front of Jeremy's face, dragging Jeremy back to the cafeteria.

At the mention of Lacey from history class, Jeremy felt his face flush. His gaze went back to Tito's oatmeal-raisin bar, and he sensed its invisible pull. "What do you mean?"

"She likes you. I've seen the way she looks at you, and she's always asking you for help."

"Asking what chapter we're supposed to read for homework is not the same as liking me."

"Well, you won't know until you talk to her, will you?"

Jeremy could count on one hand the number of friends he'd made over his lifetime. Garret, back when he was in kindergarten, until the kid got whisked away by social services. For what, Jeremy never knew. Then there was booger-eating Tim from the old apartment building, the scuzzy place Connie and Jeremy had shared until Jeremy was ten. After his grandma died of lung cancer though, and Mean Disability GI Dick became Crazy Mean Disability GI Dick and refused to leave the house, Jeremy and Connie had relocated to her parents' home and its increasingly crappy neighborhood, one Dick refused to leave. ("This was your mother's and my goddamn house for over thirty years. I'm not moving.")

Jeremy longed for their old apartment. Just him and his mom. And maybe a mouse or two.

Tito made three. Three friends in his lifetime. To think Lacey would be interested in Jeremy was as ridiculous as thinking Jeremy hated pizza and burgers.

Though Lacey was overweight, she was thin by Jeremy's standards, and her chestnut hair and perfect complexion out-leagued Jeremy's mud-colored shards and pimply chin.

Apparently sensing the conversation had reached a dead end, Tito changed the subject. "Any news on the lawsuit? Are the food giants quaking in their artificial preservatives yet?"

Jeremy's gaze darted to the kids at the tables on either side of them. He drained the last of his skim milk, wishing he had an oatmeal bar to make the watery liquid taste less barfy. So far, no one at school seemed aware of his extracurricular legal activity. Evidently, none of his peers watched the morning news.

Big surprise there.

And if they did, they hadn't linked the name Connie Barton to him. Why would they? He doubted anyone knew his last name. Or his first name for that matter. Ironic how he could be so fat and yet so invisible at the same time.

"Nah. We're waiting on the defendants' answer to the complaint. Or something like that." Jeremy tore tiny pieces from his napkin, balled each one up, and aimed the paper missiles at his open milk carton. Without looking at Tito, he asked, "Did you tell your parents about the lawsuit?"

"No."

Jeremy felt heat creep into his face again. Tito must have seen it, because he added, "But not for the reason you think. I've already told you, suing the companies is the right way to go."

Jeremy glanced up. "Yeah?"

Tito rubbed his left cheek, index finger hiding the white skin patch, as if aware of its exact location. "In fact, you're kind of a hero when you think about it. Wait and see, once this all comes out, you'll be the latest Avenger."

Jeremy snorted, and the exhaled air shot several napkin balls across the table, making both boys laugh. Tito flicked them onto the floor.

"The reason I didn't tell my parents is because, well, because they might get worried if they thought you were going to be all over the news. Like it might draw attention to me or some dumb shit like that."

Tito stared off for a bit. Then he stood and grabbed his tray, so

Jeremy did the same. After dumping their trash near the conveyor belt, they headed toward the cafeteria's double doors.

Within a few steps, Jeremy froze. His gut clenched, and his turkey wrap threatened to reappear, either from above or below.

Standing in front of him was Calvin and one of his minions.

"Hey, look. It's fat-ass and zebra boy." Calvin's words both sounded and smelled like sour cream.

Tito tried side-stepping the two bullies, but Calvin shifted to the left and blocked Tito's exit. All around the cafeteria, students quieted their chatter and turned toward the brewing spectacle.

"So, pudge-prick, I learned something interesting from the old man. Says you're suing people for making you fat. You and some pushy nurse he works with. She likes them young and porky, I guess." Calvin made thrusting motions with his pelvis and simulated masturbation with his right hand. He spoke in a falsetto. "Oh, Jeremy, harder, harder. I love how your fat pools around my ass."

"Come on, Jeremy." Tito once again tried to maneuver around the two kids, but Calvin still prevented them from passing.

Jeremy remained rooted to the ground, gaze focused on a ketchup-smeared hamburger bun near the trash can. The cafeteria was hushed save for a few chuckles and a, "Fuck yeah, Calv," from somewhere in the back.

Evidently bolstered by the cheer, Calvin stepped closer, so close his Metallica T-shirt grazed Jeremy's belly.

"What kind of idiot blames other people for being a heifer? They putting the food in your mouth? Huh?" Calvin's sour cream and onion breath blasted Jeremy with its nauseating warmth.

Yet Jeremy remained mute. He wanted to step back or step away or make any sort of motion at all, but he couldn't. All he could do was study the discarded hamburger bun, while hundreds of amused and curious gazes burned through him. He wondered if Lacey's was among them.

"Leave him alone." Tito again tried to create interference, making Jeremy feel even more pathetic.

A single swipe of Calvin's arm sent Tito stumbling backward, as if he were no more than an annoying fly. A few laughs sprinkled the room. From downcast eyes, Jeremy saw feet shuffling out the doors, probably the few students who wished to avoid witnessing what was about to unfold.

Calvin grabbed Jeremy's T-shirt and yanked it up. A pale mound of bouncing flesh popped out. Calvin smacked the rolling mound once, then again, harder.

"You disgust me, you chubby fuck. Talk about a useless waste of space." Calvin grabbed two handfuls of fat and squeezed until the skin grew pink from pressure. "Wait until more people find out what you're doing. Better watch your back. You never know what—"

Before Calvin could finish, Mr. Mendoza, the beefy gym teacher, seized the pimply, red-headed bully and yanked him off Jeremy. The instructor matched Calvin in height and exceeded him in brawn, but whatever he said to Calvin as he dragged him away, Jeremy couldn't hear. His ears were too full of the sound of his beating heart and air-starved breaths, breaths that even two puffs of his inhaler didn't immediately tame.

The rest of the school day passed by in a sea of taunts, whispers, and finger-pointing as news of the lawsuit spread. The sudden attention chafed, far more than Calvin's physical fat pinching, and Jeremy longed to return to invisibility. To make matters worse, a student had tracked down the news clip from Tuesday morning, and in a game of virtual tag, the story bounced from phone to phone faster than Jeremy could register the sneers it generated.

"If you can't lose weight, blame someone else, right lard-ass?"

"What's the matter, chubs? Momma got tired of turning tricks for cash?"

"Hey, hippo, why don't you sue your parents for making you butt-ass ugly too?"

A few kids approached Jeremy in support. Other fatties mostly and, to Jeremy's surprise, Lacey too. If not for their encouragement and Lacey's smile, Jeremy doubted he would have lasted the day.

After a walk home punctuated by fat-bashing taunts from other ambling students, Jeremy's first surprise was finding Connie at the house on a Friday afternoon. Normally she took the bus straight from Home Solutions to The Gourmand's Buffet to work the dinner shift.

The second surprise came in the form of Rex. Jeremy hadn't seen the dickwad for a few weeks, a sweet gift as far as he was concerned. When Jeremy entered the house, the front door slamming behind him as always, Connie and Rex stood in a face-off in the living room. Rex's hands were thrust deep in his pockets. Connie's were flexed into fists by her side, knuckles white against her navy chinos.

"Thanks to you, I lost my job. I can't believe you called the TV station. What am I supposed to do now?" Connie's venomous tone and fire-red face shocked Jeremy as much as the contents of the words themselves.

He halted inside the linoleum-tiled entryway, gripping his backpack strap. In addition to books, the bag overflowed with candy bars and chips he'd purchased from the gas station on the way home, though he had to push aside mental images of the Fat Slayers shaking their heads and tsking their tongues in order to do so. He needed a little something to drown out the day's abuse.

"Wasn't me. Not my fault the restaurant fired your ass." Rex's gaze was on the sofa's torn afghan, not Connie, making Jeremy question the validity of his statement.

"You're an asshole." Spittle sprayed Rex's face.

"Jesus Christ, woman."

Rex wiped his cheek and chin free of Connie's saliva with one hand and thrust the other into his pocket to retrieve his sanitizer. He squeezed out a small lake and rubbed his hands back and forth creating enough friction to spark a fire. Airborne molecules of alcohol stung Jeremy's nose and watered his eyes.

"You should've done your homework. It wouldn't have taken too much effort to learn that Burgers and Buns and The Gourmand's Buffet are owned by the same family. Then again, I always knew you were stupid." Rex laughed. "Dumb blonde but a damn good lay, I'll give you that."

Two obstacles impeded Jeremy's race to his bedroom, where both Kajika and chocolate-coated caramel awaited: Connie blocking the stairwell, her uncharacteristic lioness stance suggesting interruption was not an option, and Jeremy's hesitance to leave his mother alone with a douchebag.

Connie appeared unaware of Jeremy's presence, which to him seemed as unlikely as not spotting an orca in a kiddie pool.

Shaking her head in exasperation, she said, "How would I know that? Even my lawyer didn't catch it. And who are you to suddenly offer advice? You who's done nothing but use me to your advantage."

Jeremy wondered where GI Dick was lurking. Not in the kitchen, apparently. Always under their feet until the one time he might prove useful. *Figures.* But he must have heard them fighting. He was agoraphobic, not deaf.

"Me use you? Ha. That's a good one. Didn't hear you complaining when you needed my car."

"Yeah, but I had to whore myself out to get it, you jackass."

Like a snake about to strike, Rex slithered closer to Connie. Jeremy instinctively took a step forward, his feet finally free from their tether. "Once a whore, always a whore." Rex waved a hand in front of Connie. "And if you think this little makeover of yours — weight loss, touched-up hair, nicer clothes — is going to change you from trailer trash to lady, you're sadly mistaken. Even your pretty new boyfriend sees you for the tramp you are."

"At least George treats me with respect. You're a... a..." Connie's voice cracked, and tears sprouted in her eyes. "You're a loser piece of shit, that's what you are."

Rex grabbed both of Connie's arms and pushed her backward. She stumbled before regaining her balance, and her white blouse caught and ripped on the stair's thin, metal railing.

Jeremy rushed forward. "Leave her alone," he said, forehead vein throbbing in fear as much as anger.

Rex flung his arm back as if to punch Jeremy. Jeremy flinched and stepped back alongside his mother. Rex barked out a laugh. "Ooh, such a tough guy you are. Fatty to the rescue." Rex quickly lost interest in Jeremy. He narrowed his eyes and grabbed Connie's wrist, blanching the surrounding tissue. "We're not done here. You think you can dump me for the next guy dense enough to look your way? No one treats me that way, especially not a stupid slut. Believe me, you'll regret it. You'll—"

An ex-soldier's thunderous voice cracked the air. "If you don't get your goddamn ass out of here, you'll be the one with regrets."

All three cranked their necks to the kitchen where Dick had materialized, presumably from the musty basement. His right hand clutched his Beretta, and there was no sign of a tremor in the flannel-sleeved arm that aimed the barrel at Rex's head.

Jeremy's bowels hitched, and he worried he'd crap his pants.

Apparently Rex was equally stunned, because his eyes widened and he leaped backward, stumbling as Connie had only moments before.

Then, as if reclaiming his cool, he tugged on the hem of his snug shirt, glared a final silent warning to Connie, and shuffled out of the house. As expected, the door slammed behind him.

For a moment, there was only silence. Then Connie shook her head and waved her arms as if trying to shake off the whole encounter. She bolted for the backyard.

GI Dick lowered the gun. Just as Jeremy was about to thank him, or congratulate him, or whatever the hell it was someone did at a time like that, his grandfather scowled. He looked as if Jeremy *had* crapped himself.

"Time to man up, Eating Bull. Jesus, you'd think the bastard child of an Injun would be less of a pussy." GI Dick hocked a loogie from his throat and spit it into a napkin he grabbed from the table. He turned and trotted back down the basement stairs.

Jeremy blinked at the discarded wad of snot balled up on the table. He might have remained there indefinitely if the weight of his backpack hadn't reminded him of its contents. He mounted the stairs. Didn't sprint. Didn't climb them two at a time as Fat Slayer Shelly would have liked. He trudged them. As if each of his unlaced, stretched-out shoes were encased in cement.

Once in his room, one hand powered on the computer while the other ripped open the backpack. Before the monitor even requested a password, a king-sized candy bar was stuffed in his mouth.

A bag of potato chips and a chocolate nut bar impatiently waited their turn.

18

Being a frequent flyer of controversy, Sue was used to unwanted news, but unwanted surprises, like the call she got from Sammy the night before, left her agitated and antsy. How else to explain the scorched tongue from overheated tea at breakfast or the shattered mug that followed?

In the morning air, humid for late September, she exited the Ford Focus, its new blue paint a shade darker than the original hue. Though the hurtful letters were physically gone, in her mind's eye, the word still glowed like a neon sign.

BITCH.

She adjusted her yellow V-neck sweater and marched up to Sammy's office building. No time to worry about car vandalism. New headaches awaited.

As promised, the exterior door was unlocked. Sue bypassed the elevator and climbed the single flight of stairs to the second floor. Repositioning the polka-dot purse over her shoulder, she hoped the newest development wouldn't send the lawyer packing in frustration. Setbacks were inevitable.

Sammy opened the office-suite door before Sue had even reached for the handle. His Saturday morning attire of polo shirt and chinos was more casual than his usual garb. She wondered once again if his boyfriend, Jonathan, was behind the most recent leak. Not sure whether or not she should broach the subject with him, she followed him into his office where Connie waited.

After Sammy had called Sue the night before with the news, his voice tight and tense over the phone, Sue had immediately phoned Connie about Sammy's request for a meeting. Sue offered to drive, but Connie had rung Sue earlier that morning and told her a ride would no longer be necessary. George would drop Connie off. Whether that meant George and Connie had spent the night together, Sue wasn't sure.

What ever happened to taking it slow? she wondered.

Sue sat next to Connie. Sammy parked his perfectly postured frame behind the desk and thanked them for coming on such short notice.

Connie crossed her legs under a long skirt and bounced her foot up and down, anxiety etching her face. "I would normally be working the restaurant's breakfast buffet, but you probably heard what happened."

Sammy nodded. "Yes, I'm sorry about that. I should have been more astute. I hadn't realized Chad Hawkins, the owner of Burgers and Buns, has a brother-in-law who owns The Gourmand's Buffet. Different last name." Sammy pushed a stack of folders off the desk blotter and rested his elbows on its foamed surface. "They can't fire you for filing a lawsuit against another business. Do you want me to fight it?"

"Of course you should fight it." Sue edged forward, her anger over Connie's dismissal growing by the minute.

"No," Connie said. "They didn't fire me for that. At least that's what they said. They fired me for taking food home." She shot a pleading look at Sue, then Sammy. "But everybody does that, not only me. I brought dinner home for Jeremy. It was easier that way, but it's against the rules, so there's no point in fighting. I have no defense. And now I don't know what I'm going to do for money." Connie's feet went back to bouncing, her entire lower limbs on a joyride.

"Well, maybe it's your turn to get paid for an interview. Like somebody else already did," Sue said.

"Yes, let's talk about the latest snafu, the reason we're here. Who do you think talked to the tabloid?" Given his pensive expression, Sammy's question seemed more rhetorical than direct.

The tabloid was *The Friday Inquirer*, a tawdry national publication full of celebrity cellulite, unsubstantiated news, and shocking revelations from everyday people. Sue supposed the unfavorable article on their lawsuit fit the latter category.

"Can I see it please?"

"You haven't read it yet?" Sammy asked Connie.

Connie shook her head. "Sue called late last night, and I didn't have a car available to go buy a copy. All I know is what Sue told me. An article came out about the lawsuit and you wanted to meet this morning."

So George didn't spend the night, Sue thought. She was oddly relieved though not sure why. Aloud, she said, "I didn't want you to fret about it overnight. This is nothing we can't handle."

Sammy leaned over and retrieved a copy of the tabloid from his leather briefcase. The angle afforded Sue a view of a tiny bald spot emerging in the man's hair.

He plopped the magazine onto the desk, his heavy sigh ruffling the thin, colorful pages. "Of course we can handle it, but I won't deny it's a blow." He gave Connie a doleful expression. "And I'm sorry to tell you, Jeremy is no longer anonymous."

Five minutes later, Connie closed the tabloid. She reached into her purse, withdrew a tissue, and dabbed at her nose. Though Sue could see no tears in the woman's eyes, the act suggested they might soon follow. Sue reached over and squeezed the younger woman's arm.

Outside Sammy's office window, cars rushed by, their rhythm broken by an occasional horn honk, but inside the room was still. Connie leaned forward and reopened the magazine to the article, as if hoping the words might not still be there. Nurse, lawyer, and mother once again studied the title which was spelled out in big, block letters as if to spotlight its offensiveness.

EATING BULL SCALPS THE FOOD INDUSTRY

Beneath the headline blazed a photo of Jeremy outside Burgers and Buns, stuffing his face with a handful of fries. Given the backpack slung over his shoulder, Sue suspected the fast-food restaurant was the one near his home.

The angle of the picture was far from flattering, causing Jeremy to look shorter and more overweight than he actually was. To make matters worse, the backpack strap trapped and lifted the side of his T-shirt, displaying a mound of meaty flesh rolled over his sweatpants. Ketchup stained his chin, and another blob sullied the shoulder of his gray shirt.

Although the implication of the picture was clear, who took it and when were not.

Jeremy was not the only one with an unappealing glamour shot. A third of the way down, a narrowed-eye, snarling Sue exited the health department. Judging by the microphones thrust in her face, the image was snapped during the height of the Juney Andrews case, right after social services had removed the child from the home.

Sue remembered the day well. Exhausted and frustrated from endless meetings and phone calls, she had been upset to find more reporters waiting outside the building. Her anger had been aimed less at the press and more at those who'd left her to shoulder the onslaught alone.

A photo of Sammy followed, looking stern but handsome despite a gaping mouth. He stood behind a podium at a Cleveland university. He explained to Sue and Connie the picture appeared to have come from a lecture he had given law students about the rewards of pro-bono work.

Sue said nothing, imagining the lawyer was probably regretting his latest free offering to Sue and the Bartons, but she also knew Sammy was no fool. Whether the case ever granted him riches or not, the attention would certainly grant him fame.

And finally, Connie graced the page, standing behind her checkout line at Home Solutions with ponytailed hair, blue smock, rushed expression, and a collection of paint brushes and stencils in her hands. Given her thinner appearance, Sue figured the photo was taken recently, but by whom, once again, was the question.

As was often the case with photographs, words were hardly needed, but the article flooded the text with them regardless. Identifying all four parties by name, including Jeremy, the author of the piece spelled out the basics of the litigation plan. Burgers and Buns was the only defendant named, suggesting to Sue that whoever leaked the information lacked the full details. A few short sentences mentioned the temptation wrought by the food industry, but no supporting science of its role in contributing to obesity followed. Instead, the bulk of the unsupportive article addressed the lack of willpower of obese individuals and their desire to place blame elsewhere.

The magazine's lost opportunity to educate the public on the complex nature of obesity, including the genetic, biologic, social, and environmental forces behind it, infuriated Sue, almost as much as the personal information that followed. The writer noted where Jeremy attended school and the food he most enjoyed, suggesting the confidential source knew the family, at least peripherally.

"Why would someone do this? Jeremy's only fifteen." Connie's eyes moistened, and she blinked repeatedly.

"Do you have any idea who leaked it?" Sammy asked.

Sue pointed to the title. "Who knows of this nickname? The loose lips must belong to someone close to you. My money's on Rex."

Sue filled Sammy in on the former boyfriend. She wanted to toss Jonathan's name into the hat as well, given his disdain for the overweight, but his knowledge of the nickname seemed less likely. Plus, Sue wasn't keen on antagonizing Sammy by suggesting his boyfriend might be sabotaging the lawsuit.

Connie slumped in her chair. "It was Rex, without a doubt. We had a bad argument the last time I saw him, and he warned me I'd regret it. I bet he was also the one to call the television reporter after the first newspaper article came out."

"Do you think his motive was revenge or money?" Sammy's tone was gentle.

"Probably both."

The next ten minutes covered damage control, Sammy doing most of the talking, cutting Sue off whenever she offered suggestions. Though not used to playing co-pilot, Sue would accept the second-in-command position if it meant getting their litigation through its first steps.

"It's time to get the word out there. I wanted it to be on our time, but now our hand's been forced so we're on the defense." Sammy plucked a legal pad from a drawer and started a list. "Newspapers, television, radio, magazines, social media, whoever you can get to speak to you. We need to set the story straight. We need to get public support or our efforts will go nowhere. This article portrays the food industry as the victim. We need to prove the opposite."

Both women nodded. Sue started to speak, but Sammy continued. "I received the final defendant's formal response yesterday, in which, of course, they deny all charges. Next step is discovery."

While Sammy outlined their press response, his cell phone rang. He checked the number. "It's Jonathan. Please excuse me."

As he stepped into the reception area to take the call, Sue caught snippets of conversation. Sounded like reporters were calling Sammy's home, and Jonathan didn't know what to tell them. Sammy lived alone. Perhaps Jonathan had stayed the night. Perhaps Jonathan had snooped. Had run across their case file in Sammy's briefcase. The photos would not have been difficult to obtain, either for Jonathan or Rex.

A cold hand on Sue's arm broke her reverie. "I have to tell you something," Connie said, eyes wide, gaze darting between Sue and Sammy in the outer room.

Sue responded with a tentative, "Yes?"

Connie exhaled a puff of air. "Jeremy's father is alive. I know I said he was dead, and that's what Jeremy believes, but he's alive."

Sue had been reaching into her bag for a mint, but her hand froze midway. "What?"

"Terry Harjo — or Clayton Harjo as Jeremy thinks he's named — was a mistake. We only hooked up once when I was eighteen. He was a friend of a friend sort of thing, and I was drunk and not thinking clearly."

Sue let Connie continue, too shocked to do otherwise.

"But he was also a mean drug addict, practically homeless, no family, abandoned as a teenager. Worked his way to Ohio, but from where I don't remember. I was going through a rebel phase. Figured it would piss my father off to go out with the guy. By the time I found out I was pregnant, Terry was long gone. In prison."

"Prison?" *Talk about a discovery*, Sue thought.

"He beat a guy up, nearly killed him. Left him in a coma, I guess. I don't know if the guy ever woke up or not, and I don't know how much time Terry got. I only heard he ended up in prison. Once I found out I was pregnant with his child — there was no one else's it could've been — I was relieved he was gone. I never told Terry he had a son. Never spoke to him again after our night together."

"Why in the world did you make Jeremy's middle name Harjo?" Sue regretted her tone, especially after seeing Connie's face crumple like a fallen cake.

"I don't know. I was young, naive. I wanted my son to have some knowledge of his background. I wanted him to have something he could be proud of. You can't really tell he has Native American ancestry, but he's got that same roundish face Terry had. So I lied and told him his father's name was Clayton and that he had been killed by a drunk driver. I admitted to not knowing his father well but said he was a noble guy and he would have been proud of Jeremy. We've never talked about it since. The last thing I wanted was for Jeremy to know the truth, and I definitely don't want Terry in his life."

Connie blinked and turned away, but the tears finally fell, and although Sue questioned Connie's actions — and, God forgive her, the woman's intelligence — her heart ached for the mother. To be pregnant so young, to be a single mom, to have to abandon any hope of college, to have a dead mother and an agoraphobic father.

Sue gave Connie's back a gentle rub. "I'm sorry you're going through this, but you don't need to worry about it now. If you decide to come clean with Jeremy later, fine, but you have enough going on. Besides, the man's in prison."

Connie bolted upright, her body tense and her legs bobbing once again. "But is he? What if he's out now? What if he sees this article?" Connie jabbed at the tabloid with such force Sue worried the woman would sprain her finger. "He'll recognize me, or at least my name. And what if he recognizes himself in Jeremy? What if he suspects Jeremy is his son?"

Connie took a breath, and Sue finally connected the dots. Reluctantly, she finished what Connie had left unsaid. "And what if he tries to find you?"

19

DARWIN

Trips to the hobby store with its fat employees and even fatter patrons sickened Darwin, especially on a Sunday evening when he should be allowed peace. His work schedule was often hectic, so he was grateful for any respite he had, but he had run out of jigsaw glue for his latest creation, a 3-D model of the human brain. It complemented the two-dimensional body he'd completed during the summer.

Inside the expansive store, row upon row of scrapbook paper, sketching pencils, paints, and other craft supplies bombarded him until he finally reached the aisle he needed.

He scanned the area for the beefy, yellow-smocked kid who had sold him the worthless alternative brand in the past, the adhesive he'd promised wouldn't streak. But streak it had, and Darwin still seethed over the necessary destruction of his labored work.

All the whale's fault.

He flexed his biceps and rapid-fired his pecs. He inhaled deeply. He needed to maintain discipline. Unfortunately, a hacking, over-tanned, leather-faced breadstick of a woman blocked the small section of jigsaw glue he needed. To Darwin, her damaged skin and lingering haze of tobacco stench made her as vile and weak as any of the rotund sheep trolling the aisles.

He wrinkled his nose in disgust, and when a violent, frothy cough ensued from the woman, a fine mist of pulmonary fluid sprayed the very adhesive bottles he sought. Darwin cringed and lifted his hoodie over his nose. For a moment, he feared he'd vomit, or worse, flee, lacking the discipline to remain in the shop to get what he'd come for.

Just as he was about to bolt, the human matchstick looked at him and said, "Screw you, buddy." Then she turned and walked away.

If not for his strictly groomed fingernails, the force with which Darwin fisted his hands would have drawn blood. His taut neck muscles flexed and strained until the protective sweatshirt fell from his face, and a crazed animal emerged.

(*How dare she speak to you like that? As if she were above you.*)

Darwin stepped forward, imagining his hands around the woman's scrawny, weathered neck. No knife necessary.

(*Not her. She doesn't fit the mission. Find your discipline.*)

He breathed in and out of flared nostrils. He forced himself to remember the visit's purpose. The thought of having to return to the sheep-ridden store the next day if he didn't buy what he came for moved him to action. He grabbed three bottles of the adhesive farthest from the woman's bronchial spray. At least ten extra minutes of shower time and two additional soap-downs would be needed. His jaw clenched again.

Armed with the puzzle glue, Darwin hustled down the aisle toward the checkout, but in his haste to escape the human cesspool, he rounded the corner too quickly. A huge-bellied man powering a motorized cart rammed into Darwin's legs. Darwin sprawled backward, arms and legs flailing for balance like a spastic court jester.

Instead of apologizing, the bastard tugged on his fraying T-shirt, its cotton fibers stretched far beyond capacity, and said, "Watch where you're going, buddy." He advanced the cart forward and departed, nearly driving over Darwin's foot as he whirred by.

Darwin half-ran, half-stumbled to the checkout. The aisles of merchandise were nothing more than a sea of red fury. One trembling hand grazed his face as the other one dumped its contents onto the counter. He instantly regretted touching his face and imagined viral particles from the cough-contaminated adhesive replicating on his skin.

Vaguely aware of the clerk's alarm over the disjointed man before her, Darwin struggled to find the correct change. The whale in the motorized cart whizzed by and exited the store, but not before mumbling "asshole" beneath his breath.

Darwin snatched his bag of merchandise from the clerk and

stepped outside to a gray and overcast sky. Through a raging haze, he watched the obese man motor over to the store's cart corral, stand, and waddle back to a silver sedan in the handicapped space. Darwin squeezed the plastic bag with a chokehold strong enough to strangle a horse. Except for mounds of fatty flesh, the prick's walk was no more disabled than Darwin's own.

(*Seize the moment. This is an opportunity. A sign.*)

Darwin blinked, trying to clear the fog. *Did he mean…?*

(*Kill him. Follow him and kill him.*)

For the next ten minutes, breathing more calmly than he had since he'd entered the hobby store, Darwin followed the gluttonous animal's car through a series of winding roads, each leading farther and farther into heavily wooded properties.

Seclusion. A sign indeed.

As Darwin tailed the man through expansive lots with homes tucked deep within sheltering trees, he understood his next act had been as preordained as the clouds that finally wept their moisture, a splattering drizzle at first but within minutes, a pelting downpour. He turned the wipers to high, paradoxically calmed by their frenetic energy.

This is the mission's next deed.

His vehicle contained all the required tools: knife, cover gown, gloves, plastic sheeting for the car's seat, change of clothes if necessary. No trace of him would be left behind. He was as prepared as he was disciplined, and when Darwin followed the sedan into a long, wooded driveway, he thanked his guiding power for the gift. Envisioning what would happen soothed his angst even more. He could almost feel the firm hilt of the knife, the thrusting of the blade, the warm ooze of blood between his gloved fingers.

With one hand he pulled the hood of his sweatshirt onto his head and yanked the strings to tighten it, thereby securing his hair. Then he readied himself for impact. Pressing down on the accelerator, he rammed the sedan's bumper with his own, their automobiles too far away from both the road behind them and the split-level home up ahead to attract any unwanted attention.

(*Perfect.*)

The sedan slammed its brakes. Tires scraped gravel. While Darwin donned gloves and cover gown, the obese man flopped out of his vehicle. His holler shrieked two octaves higher than it had in the store. "What the hell are you doing? Christ, this is private property."

Darwin stepped out, hiding the knife and his gloved hands behind him. He surveyed the surroundings one final time: dense blocks of trees on either side, no other humans in sight, rain thick enough to obscure visibility, its pelting drops showering Darwin's face and lips, wiping away traces of the woman's spewed coughing. As if signaling her approval, Nature had given him the perfect setting in which to purify her world.

And in the name of purification, Darwin pounced on the fuming whale. The man's arrogant ranting quickly shifted to shock, and upon the first pierce of abdominal flesh, pathetic pleas of mercy took over. The knife buried deeper into the sheep's fleshy folds.

(*That's it. Rid the world of the weak and undisciplined.*)

Thrust after thrust, stab after stab, bits of black T-shirt, feculent intestines, skin, and blood meshed together. With each powerful plunge of the blade, Darwin's peace, calm, and control grew, all necessary attributes for continued interaction in the real world, attributes he needed in order to go on fooling the people around him.

When he finished, he used his blood-soaked gloves to inscribe the word GLUTTON on the sedan's inside back window, so that the rain would not wash the letters away.

With that, the public would have no choice but to make the connection.

And then a fat teenager, his mother, and a nurse would get their due.

20

JEREMY

Considering the narrow dimensions of his three-foot-high locker, Jeremy realized one benefit of obesity: he would never get stuffed inside one. Unlike Tito who'd spent ten minutes in a similarly compact compartment back in middle school. Tito had relayed the tale nonchalantly, as if describing a ride in an elevator, but Jeremy's throat had constricted at the thought.

Taking only what he needed for homework, he left the rest of the textbooks and notebooks at school. Come December, covers would be torn and spirals unraveled, but five weeks into the year they were still intact. The extra backpack space allowed for a convenience store reload. All he wanted was escape from the building, followed by food and his online game. Kajika was one level closer to earning a new gate key.

"How do you think you did on the essay question?"

The female voice startled Jeremy. He slammed his locker door harder than intended. It popped back open, banging back and forth on its hinges. "Oh, hi, Lacey. Um, I think I did all right. I wasn't expecting a pop quiz though."

"None of us were. It's totally unfair."

Jeremy nodded, additional words failing him. Tortoise barrettes restrained Lacey's hair, though loose strands swept her face. Her pastel blouse fanned the waist of her jeans, and Jeremy liked that she didn't try to hide her body in loose-fitting fabric. He tugged the hem of his own shirt, hoping it wasn't riding up like it sometimes did. Together they studied passing students.

Finally, Lacey said, "Hey, how is the lawsuit going? Is the other side taking it seriously?"

"Not sure yet. Some people support us. Others think the whole thing is stupid."

"Well, there are always going to be buttheads."

Jeremy laughed, the act making him feel lighter. Humor had been in short supply the last couple weeks. "Yeah, plenty of those. I'm on my way home now for an interview with *US Life Magazine*. The lawyer wants us to get our side of the story out to help gain support. There's been a lot of stuff in the papers and online, some of it pretty brutal, and this should help—"

"Look guys, it's the world-famous Eating Bull. And he's talking to a cow."

The sound of Calvin's jeer sank Jeremy's momentary lightness. His face flushed in anger and embarrassment. Unable to make eye contact, he stared at Calvin's T-shirt, where a snake slithered through the eyes of a giant skull.

I am so sick of this shit.

"Whoa, big guy, what're you gonna do? Charge me? Guess that's what bulls do, right?"

Calvin searched the gray-lockered corridor, still congested with students collecting their belongings. He spotted a girl carrying a red cardigan sweater.

"Give me that," he said, his face a constipated scowl.

When the hesitant girl relinquished it, Calvin held it out in front of him and started waving it back and forth like a matador.

"Come on, Eating Bull. Show us what you got."

Jeremy watched the sweater flick back and forth. In his mind, he withdrew an arrow from Kajika's beaded quiver, loaded the gold and ivory bow, and released a poison-dipped arrow into the red-headed prick.

In reality, he stood motionless.

"Oh, come on, kind of a pussy for a bull, aren't you?"

Kids shuffled by, headed for home or extracurricular activities. Some hurried, heads bowed. Others sauntered by, smiling and pointing.

A few stopped, placed bets, and watched the fun. A sea of black, brown, and white faces.

Calvin stepped closer. The sweater waving intensified.

"Cut it out, Calvin. Don't be such a jerk," Lacey said.

The pimpled matador froze. He slowly lowered his arms along with the cardigan. His rat-like gaze fixated on Lacey.

"Ooh, looks like the cow has more spunk than the bull." Behind Calvin, a few kids snickered.

Calvin started to moo, first slow and low, then louder and more drawn out, his lips pooching like plump, pink slugs.

Jeremy wanted to say something, anything, but managed only a low grunt.

Calvin kept at it. "Hey cow, why don't you join the bull in blaming the world for the size of your ass?"

Lacey's expectant gaze burned through Jeremy. Yet his immobility and mutism persisted.

He heard a sigh from Lacey, followed by, "Screw you, Calvin." She spun around and walked away, leaving a spate of mooing catcalls behind her.

The departure signaled an apparent end to the festivities, and the rest of the small crowd dispersed, but not before a faceless voice mumbled, "Pussy."

Someone yelled Calvin's name. The bully sneered at Jeremy, then tossed the sweater back to its gum-chomping owner and strolled down the hall, as if the recent five-minute exchange had been nothing more than a fart in a windstorm.

Jeremy secured his locker and trekked to the school's exit, studying the floor along the way. Bits of candy wrappers, tissues, and torn notebook paper littered the walkway, and as he opened the door and stepped outside, a piece of paper wafted up in the air, carried away by the early October breeze. He watched it float by, wishing he, too, could drift away.

Except for the usual fat calls and taunts from passing cars, his walk home was quiet. Tito had not accompanied him for the past week, something about Mrs. Harris having to pick him up for one thing or another. Jeremy hadn't been to Tito's house, either, not since the Monday prior when they'd posted more crap on fake Courtney's Facebook page. They'd laughed at Calvin's attempts to impress the fictitious girl with how many pounds he could bench press and how many hours he worked out, even more than his dad who'd once been a bodybuilder. Hopefully, Jeremy had only imagined the tightness in Mrs. Harris's greeting that night or the way she'd averted her gaze.

Kicking a rock on the sidewalk, he watched it roll over the berm and onto the pavement. He thought of his weakness in front of Lacey, and as if on cue, the hole in his belly grumbled. Up ahead, near Clark Avenue, Burgers and Buns beckoned. He smelled the grease. He visualized the burger's juice dripping off his fingers. He tasted the salty sting of the fries.

The tantalizing sensations overpowered him, stomping out competing images of his new ability to walk home without using his inhaler or his almost two-week stretch of ditching fast food in favor of the meals his mother had cooked. Connie no longer had an evening job, and, thanks to the upcoming interview payment, no longer needed one.

But while Connie continued on a healthy trajectory, looking better and happier than Jeremy had ever seen her, especially given their recent used-car purchase, Jeremy could feel himself stumbling down the all-too-familiar wrong path. A path he had hoped to never wander again.

He doubted the Fat Slayers would be pleased when he mounted their scale, yet he couldn't resist the restaurant's call. Before he was able to cross Clark Avenue, Burgers and Buns reeled him in.

Inside, under the restaurant's bright lights and tantalizing photographs of succulent food, he ordered two burgers with extra cheese. While he chewed in a corner booth, he strategized his next level in *War of the Wilderness*, anything to steer his mind from the guilt of his self-sabotage. He wondered what level Dr. Sneeker was on. He remembered what Sue had said about not telling the ER doc about the lawsuit, that he wasn't a fan of finger-pointing, but unless Dr. Sneeker never listened to the news or read the paper or surfed the Internet, Jeremy suspected he'd already found out. Would he treat Jeremy differently the next time he saw him?

Why not? Everyone else has.

When he finished at Burgers and Buns, he stopped at the gas station to load up on candy and chips, using money he'd mooched from his mother for a fictitious school project (he didn't want to dig into his meager savings). He walked the last few blocks home, preparing himself for the onslaught of the magazine interview.

But when he entered the uncharacteristically tidy house, he saw he had underestimated the chaos. The small, outdated living room overflowed with people. Some he recognized; some he didn't. Barely had he looked up when a flash of camera lights blinded him. He blinked a few times to accommodate, and when his vision cleared, he noticed his mother and Sue perched on the sofa, his grandmother's ratty afghan absent, as if not worthy of photography. Apparently the wall wasn't either, because instead of the usual scuffed surface that separated the living room from the kitchen, Jeremy stared at a two-dimensional, coffee-brown wall boasting two large windows, beyond which flourished a vast, flowering meadow.

Nothing like a fake backdrop to class up the joint.

In addition to the clicking photographer, four other people Jeremy didn't recognize huddled together near Sammy. Surprisingly, Jonathan was also present, fussing with the lawyer's already muss-free hair.

Leaning against the wall near the staircase were Tony, the big-nosed reporter from the *Cleveland Times* who'd interviewed them at the onset, and George, Connie's new boyfriend. Both were staring at Connie as the photographer snapped photos, Tony's expression that of an admiring fan and George's flat and unreadable, save for a pitying glance Jeremy's way. GI Dick, who stood under the arched kitchen entry, wore a mask of irritation, and despite the photographer's verbal cues and the scattered conversations, Jeremy heard his grandfather gripe about the state of his home. "Jesus Christ, it's like a circus in here. Goddamn vultures."

No one paid the old Army man any attention, and Jeremy hoped he might be similarly blessed. Perhaps he could pull a Tito and slink up to his room unnoticed.

"Hi. You must be Jeremy." An androgynous individual stepped forward and thrust a slim arm toward him. "I'm Tar. The reporter."

Tar?

Thanks to an ill-cut blazer, Jeremy could not say with certainty whether Tar was of the penis- or vagina-toting variety, though he leaned toward the latter. Before he had time to ponder, more hands greeted him, other reporters or assistants or something or other, and in the next breath, Jeremy was led to the couch where he assumed the spot Sue had just vacated. Sue talking, his mother talking, Tar talking, Jonathan primping his boyfriend, the lawyer pushing the meddling hands away, GI Dick cussing, Tony still staring at Connie, George still corpse-like. And then the questions came.

"What made you decide to do this?"

"Have you always been overweight?"

"What's a typical day's diet for you?"

"What do your friends think?"

Friends?

Questions pelted Sue, too, and though she seemed happy to answer, some made the warrior stiffen, her nose sniffing at the air like a huntress, especially when Tar asked, "After instigating Juney Andrews's removal from the home, aren't you afraid of making more enemies?"

Every so often, Sammy piped in, redirecting a question or asking Tar to pose it differently, and once Tony chimed in when he thought the reporter too harsh on Connie.

All the while, Jeremy craved the king-sized chocolate bar stuffed in his backpack's front pocket.

Sue rambled on about the website she'd created with the help of George to promote their cause. The camera kept flashing. Voices grew louder. Soon the cacophony became so great, Jeremy felt himself shrink, a not entirely unpleasant sensation. In fact, a few minutes later, he wondered if he had vanished completely.

An elephant in the room that nobody saw.

21

SUE

Sue believed any task requiring less than five minutes was best tackled right away, so despite her reservations, she returned Brent Johnson's phone call as soon as she reached her office at seven thirty. Though the *US Life Magazine* interview at Connie's house had gone well that afternoon, Sue's nerves were frayed. After taking half the day off, she had piles of work to catch up on.

"Mr. Johnson, we've had this conversation a dozen times. You do realize that it's not me alone who requires your weekly check-ins, don't you? That was a court-ordered decision. I'm only helping to enforce it."

She flipped through a stack of messages and notes on her desk. One of the notes included an update on the Juney Andrews case. Given the six-year-old's notable weight loss and health improvements, the child would remain in foster care for the time being.

Mr. Andrews will not be pleased.

Sue tuned back into Brent Johnson, aware of the strain in his voice. He said, "I understand that, but your recommendation led to the court order, and I'm hoping another one from you will lead to its removal. I've done everything you asked. I'm taking my HIV meds. I'm using condoms. I'm relaying my condition to my sexual partners. I'm being very good. Please let me drop these visits and get back to my life."

Sue gave him virtually the same answer she'd given him numerous times before. "If all you say is true, then your behavior will be taken into consideration at your next case review which comes up next month. Have a nice evening."

Sue hung up the phone, and before tackling anything else, decided to visit the break room for something to eat, having only snacked on a few light appetizers at Connie's two hours earlier. She imagined Al stewing at home, upset by her absence at dinner yet again, a dinner that would be similar to all their dinners over the past few weeks: silence from a sullen husband and food rearranging by an increasingly thin daughter, whom Sue had not seen eat a solid meal in months.

She had talked to Al about Kayla's food aversion and had even tried to get Kayla to see a doctor, but both efforts were met with resistance. And frankly, Sue's own reserves to fight yet another battle ran low. She knew she could not avoid the needed confrontations much longer, but, unlike her diminishing daughter, she had too much on her plate. At least Kayla had given up nineteen-year-old Trey. Or so she claimed.

The hike to the break room felt like a trudge through molasses. The high of the interview combined with the weight of the work on her desk and her family problems had exhausted her.

If Al muttered one more time that Kayla needed her mother, Sue would scream. She had never shirked her maternal duties, but after years of birthing, molding, and nagging; after years of assuring good grades, good manners, and good citizenship; after years of cooking, tutoring, and guiding, did she not deserve a respite herself? Could Al not step up for a few months while she made her contribution to the world?

She sighed. Self-pity had never been her guide.

No need to let it be now.

In a short time, the three of them would have it out. No more mumbling, silent treatment, or avoidance. Only solutions.

When Sue entered the break room, she was startled to find Gabrielle Esposito, the dietitian, performing a headstand against the wall.

Without losing her balance, Gabrielle smiled and explained she was working late to complete a lecture for dietary students. "But I was due for a yoga break."

"Keep that up and you'll be due for a chiropractor."

Sue scoured the fridge and grabbed a blueberry yogurt from her leftover stash. Finding a container of her homemade granola in the cupboard, she poured out a handful and sprinkled it on the yogurt. When she turned around, Gabrielle had moved from headstand to downward dog. The dietitian asked about the lawsuit and then swung into an upward dog and looked at Sue. "You're doing the right thing. Don't let anyone tell you differently. Everybody hates the messenger, but they need the message regardless. Thank God for people like you."

Sue stared at her snack, its contents blurring through teary eyes. Gabrielle's words could not have come at a better time. She swallowed a gritty lump and, buoyed, said, "Things are going okay. It was rocky at first, especially after that tabloid leak blindsided us. We found out it was Connie's ex-boyfriend. He all but admitted it, but maybe it was a blessing in disguise. Sammy and I have worked hard to get the message out, and as you've seen, our story has popped up in blogs and newspapers, mostly local, but some far-reaching. Snippets have even been on morning news shows. Not the big ones yet, but we're getting there, and we have more hits on our website every day."

"Not always the nicest of comments, though, are they?" Gabrielle moved on to triangle pose.

"I knew there'd be outrage when I started rolling this snowball. Nothing I can't handle. At least people are talking on both sides." Sue put her yogurt down and looked up at the ceiling. "But I still need something bigger. We did an interview for *US Life Magazine* and that's big, but I need bigger. And now that the cat's out of the bag, I want to get Jeremy out there more."

Sue left it at that, not revealing the show she had in mind, one that would garner all the attention they needed. She remembered what Connie had told her. Terry Harjo was still alive. Would such visibility put Connie and Jeremy at risk? Was the man still in prison? Maybe Al could find out. He would be angry to learn of yet another potential danger, but so be it.

"Do you think that's wise?" the flexible dietitian asked. "Do you think all that attention might backfire and cause Jeremy to lose the progress he's made?"

Sue leaned back against the counter. She twirled a tiny earring hoop. "I guess that's a possibility. We'll find out where he's at this

Thursday in terms of weight loss, but Connie has gotten her act together. She's not working as much since she lost her restaurant job, she's cooking meals, she's bringing in money from interviews. And she's dating George."

Gabrielle bolted up from a right-angle pose. "Our George? The statistician?"

"Yep." Sue smiled. "At least something fun has come out of this." She sobered again and added, "I worry Jeremy is getting picked on at school. He hasn't said much about it, but I've drawn a few conclusions."

As Sue tossed her yogurt container in the trash, Mark Swanson, the health department's sanitarian, entered the break room. He wore his typical khaki pants and short-sleeved shirt embossed with the health department's logo. "Whoa. Guess a bunch of us are working late. The bastards don't pay us enough for this."

Sue forced a tight smile. She murmured goodbye to Gabrielle and was about to leave when Mark said, "Hey, you hear about that murder a couple weeks ago? A third obese man met his maker."

Sue and Gabrielle exchanged looks. Sue had indeed heard about the murder. Al had made sure of that. Part of his reticence about the lawsuit was his belief that a killer was targeting the obese. He worried the litigation would draw Sue into the fray. Sue had tried to convince him of the absurdity in that assumption to no avail.

"The police haven't made any connections," she said to Mark, her spine stiffening.

"Well, the guy wrote the word *glutton* on the rear window. That's awfully specific."

Sue examined her watch. Twisted it. She had not heard that detail. *Does Al know about it?* She opted to change the subject. "Say, I'm worried your son — Calvin is it? — may be giving Jeremy a hard time in school."

"Jeremy? You mean the fat kid you recruited?"

The cauldron in Sue's belly boiled. Her instinct was to bite back, but she tamed the beast within. "If you could talk to your son, that would be great."

She nodded to Gabrielle, who was quietly rolling up her yoga mat, no doubt wishing she could teleport out of the tense surroundings.

Before Sue exited the room, she heard Mark say, "From what I hear, your boy's a real pussy."

With a satisfied pull on the door, Sue left the office suite at nine forty-five that evening and made her way to the parking garage. Completing so much work eased her burden, and with a renewed sense of peace, she wondered if Al would be interested in a beer and a discussion. No terse words or tension, just discussion.

She'd even managed to put the ugly exchange with Mark Swanson out of her mind. Perhaps she'd overreacted. Although she and Mark had never been close — their paths didn't often intersect — they had always been civil colleagues. Like her, he probably had a long day, and they had taken their fatigue out on each other, both oversensitive to their own causes. Accusing his son of bullying when the only proof she had was Jeremy's vague questioning ("Is there a dude named Swanson who works with you as a sanitarian or something?") was a stretch. When Sue had tried to glean more from Jeremy at the time, he merely shrugged and said, "His son goes to my school. Kind of an a-hole, that's all."

Mark didn't have it easy, Sue supposed. Being divorced and living away from your child had to be difficult.

Darkness had fallen, and though the ramp was decently lit, Sue did not enjoy strolling it at night. She'd promised Al she would park in the vicinity of a security camera, and she had, even though the location was not convenient.

Something rippled to the left. Tensing, her gaze darted in that direction.

Nothing.

Picking up the pace, she spotted the Ford Focus ahead. Her newfound peace from moments before vanished. She wanted to get home.

Clicking the key fob to unlock the car's door, she hurried the last few feet. Her rigid torso started to relax.

A bath would feel good.

When she reached the side of her vehicle, a figure in a black ski mask popped out.

Sue yelped and reached for the car door, but before she could open it, an arm encircled her chest and immobilized her. A firm object pressed into her back.

Terror consumed her. She couldn't think. She couldn't scream.

Trembling with fear, visions of another dark night flashed before her. A man in her college apartment. With a knife. Pinning her to the ratty carpet. Pulling her plaid skirt up and her pink underwear down, threatening to stab her if she fought. Fetid breath on her face, a horrible, endless pain between her legs. The raw thrusting.

Sickening memories paralyzed her. She knew she needed to do something, needed to struggle free, but her arms and legs abandoned her. Her self-defense training was gone.

Fabric brushed her cheek, the covered face pressing against her own. The scent of musty wool teased her nostrils, and the unidentified object probed deeper into her back.

"You need to quit meddling in people's lives. If you don't, you'll regret it. Your family will too. Got that?" The raspy threat was barely a whisper.

Sue said nothing, limbs still useless noodles. She willed herself to fight back. Find out whose face wore the mask. She was no longer that scared little girl.

And yet she stood there like a trapped animal, heart thudding in her chest, lungs heaving for breath within the firm embrace.

"I said do you got that?" The hard object jabbed painfully into her spine.

Sue nodded. "Yes," she whispered.

The man's grip suddenly released, and as if submerged under water for too long, Sue gulped in the cool, evening air. When she turned around, the shadowy figure was gone.

She leaned against her car, steadying her respirations and willing her heart to slow down. She rubbed her hands together to make the trembling stop. Then she did something she rarely did.

She cursed.

"Goddamn it, Sue. God. Damn. It."

Long ago and ever since, she had promised herself she would never again lose control to another. Ever. Never would she allow her power to be wrestled away, no matter how terrified she might be.

And yet she had. Like a frightened little college girl, she had.

You are not *that girl anymore. Far from it.*

She stood to full height, straightened her shoulders, and relocked the car. She marched back inside the building toward the security office on the main floor, dialing 9-1-1 on the way.

He thought he could scare her away. From what, she wasn't sure. No shortage of enemies for Sue Fort.

She tightened her jaw and put the phone to her ear.

Yeah, screw that, buddy.

22

DARWIN

Back in the Middle Ages, the Coffin Torture was an open metal cage in the shape of a human body. Suspended from a tree or a gallows, the device restrained and compressed its victim beneath the scorching sun for hours. Animals feasted on the captive's blistering flesh until death prevailed. The chamber was particularly cruel for over-weight prisoners, its steel confines crushing and cleaving both skin and muscle.

Inside his quiet home on a Friday evening, Darwin studied the image on the jigsaw box propped up on the table. He imagined if the device were in use today, a plus-sized option would be required.

Like a man tasting rotten meat, he grimaced. Fat was all around him.

The steel coffin occupied the right corner of the puzzle, a four-thousand-piece rendition of medieval torture devices. For fifteen minutes, Darwin paced the lengths of the table, scouring the spread-out project for the last piece of the section, the bleeding thigh of a dying man, his face etched in agony and despair.

He rustled a gloved hand through the cardboard jigsaw bits, all varying shades of brown, black, red, and gray. Despite hand cleansing and sanitizing, the gloves were a recent addition, an added security against skin oil and debris damaging his work. The stepped-up home protections had become increasingly necessary to combat the inability to do so at work and around others. They would not understand. He would look odd. He could not afford unwanted attention.

But restraint was proving more and more difficult.

(*Do not despair. You are strong enough to continue the deception.*)

Another kill would bolster his strength. Nothing calmed as much as the act of dominating the sheep, confiscating their power, stealing their life force as his own, a force far more deserving of his exceptional physical body than their flabby, undisciplined forms. If only he had been chosen sooner. Who knew how powerful he would be?

Nineteen days since his last acquisition. The pathetic hobby shop patron.

Darwin's hand shook as it surveyed the pieces, and a periodic dizziness blurred his vision. Hunger pains rumbled in his empty belly.

He needed another kill. It was already the eleventh of October.

(*Not yet. Soon. Haste leads to mistakes, and mistakes lead to capture. There is still so much to accomplish.*)

He wiped drool from his lower lip. Realizing what he'd done, he cursed, ripped off the contaminated glove, and retrieved another from the box on the table.

Once regloved, he refocused on the puzzle, maintaining an upright position, never wanting to sit for too long.

He examined the box again. His eyes were drawn to the Judas Cradle, where an emaciated, nude man was slowly being impaled by a triangular tip inserted into his anus. Darwin longed to get started on that section. Or the Flaying Torture, where an old man's skin was ripped from his body piece-by-piece, his wrists and ankles bound to a pole, no hope for escape. The executioner's small knife seemed well suited to its function.

Instead, Darwin maintained his search for the missing Coffin Torture piece.

A lesser man would have given up by now, he thought, but like his mission, finished results required systematic completion.

When Darwin finally found the piece with the bleeding thigh, however, his joy failed to meet his expectations. Something about the mission troubled him, though he did not dare think it into thought.

But The Voice heard anyway.

(*It does not matter he is a boy. He will become a gluttonous man.*)

Despite Darwin's best efforts, another nagging rumination surfaced, and he feared the repercussions.

(*Why do you question me?*)

The booming reverberations of The Voice pierced Darwin's gray matter, and a bolt of pain ignited. He gripped his head and cried out in alarm.

(*It means nothing that the mother has lost weight or the nurse who helps him is not obese. Their actions contribute to the weakness of the nation. You must follow the mission in all its parts. And when the boy's name is known by millions, all three will get their due. And you will be a leader of many.*)

More agony ripped through Darwin's brain, as if he were the man in the Head Crusher at the bottom of the puzzle.

"Make it stop. Please make it stop." His begging turned to sobs, a response he knew would only heighten his punishment.

(*You know what you must do.*)

Darwin nodded and replied "yes" over and over again. Though not resolved, the pain reduced. Darwin looked up. He blinked. He shuffled to his weights and hefted the heaviest dumbbells he owned. Then he spied the razor blades and nipple clips on the shelf.

He knew what he had to do.

23

JEREMY

While waiting for the light to turn green, Jeremy watched yellow and orange leaves swirl in a sudden wind gust outside the passenger window of his mom's new Jetta. Well, new to her, anyway. Even though it was a Wednesday morning and he should be in school, he and his mom were headed to Sammy's office for a deposition.

Most of the fall leaves dispersed and moved on, but one plopped to the ground while another remained airborne, as if held by an invisible string. Jeremy imagined himself the first leaf, big and heavy, while Tito was the second, so weightless the wind could carry him forever.

Given his new notoriety, he worried Mr. and Mrs. Harris would never allow Tito to see him outside of school again, a possibility that had encouraged three fast-food stops in the past week alone. But the day before, Tito had invited Jeremy for a sleepover the following Friday, and though his friend was still vague on the subject of his parents' hesitation over their friendship, Jeremy had eagerly accepted. He only wished their get-together was sooner.

"You're sure you're okay with being here?" Connie's question broke Jeremy's reverie, and he realized they'd already pulled into a metered spot in front of Sammy's building.

"Hey, it got me out of school, didn't it?"

Connie gave him a sad smile. "I'm sorry your grandfather was so mean to you."

"What, the hundred times he called me a 'pussy' or last night when he said if I show up at this deposition, they'll laugh me 'out on my fat ass'?"

Connie examined the steering wheel, hands still poised at ten and two o'clock, even though the vehicle idled against the curb. Her newly sleek body modeled dark pants and a teal sweater. A matching barrette clasped her hair, the strands no longer stringy or brassy. When she spoke, her voice hitched. She paused and tried again. "I'm sorry, Jeremy."

Jeremy shifted his gaze to his tan chinos, purchased specifically for the deposition and already bunching at his crotch. "For what?"

His mother let out a staccato laugh and shut off the engine. She laid her head back and looked through the sunroof. "For everything. I haven't done right by you. Our house. Your grandfather. Letting him talk to you like that. It's not right. But for so long I've felt trapped, ever since Grandma died and Grandpa developed, well, you know. It was better when it was you and me alone. Remember that stinky little apartment?"

Jeremy did. He missed it terribly.

"But so many responsibilities. I was always exhausted, and I felt like I had no options. Oh, I don't know what I'm trying to say. I'm babbling. I'm going to try harder though. I think ... I *feel* I'm in a better place now. You know?"

Jeremy pulled a thread from the new black sweater. "It's okay, Mom."

"No. It's not. I know I need to do something about your grandfather. It's just, you know, one thing at a time, right?"

Jeremy nodded. "We should probably get in there."

"Yes, but one more thing. I'm really proud of you." Connie rotated in her seat and tilted Jeremy's face toward her own. "I know this isn't easy for you, and honestly, I still don't know if we're doing the right thing. I hope the kids at school aren't—"

Jeremy pulled away and grabbed the door's release. "School's fine."

"Oh, okay, but I know the lawsuit and the attention it's drawing can't be fun for you. I'm hoping it'll be worth it. In fact, I think only good things are in our future."

Jeremy's new pants strangled his thighs, and the sweater irritated his flesh. Like a cat at a scratching post, his stubby nails clawed at his neck. He crawled out of the car as quickly as his bulk would allow and headed toward Sammy's office.

He hoped his mother was right.

***

Reality television had never been Jeremy's thing. He would rather play *War of the Wilderness* and enter Kajika's world than view whiny, skinny, over-tanned wannabes. But if there was a show that dumped Sammy Sanchez's deposition members on a deserted island, forcing them to duke it out for survival, Jeremy would tune in with a tub of popcorn and bated breath.

At ten thirty that morning, the eligible contestants were parked around a large table in a conference room whose interior matched the rest of Sammy's practice, with cherry-wood paneling, beige walls, and plush carpeting. Unlike Sammy's office, no antique armament adorned the walls. None of his secretary's voodoo dolls terrorized the table, either. Only a silver water pitcher sweating beads of condensation, a collection of crystal drinking glasses, and a wooden bowl holding plastic-wrapped peppermints.

To Jeremy's left sat Sue and to his right, Connie. Sammy, in all his posture-perfect rigidity, flanked Sue, and next to him was Reggie Clifton, Sammy's likable paralegal whom Jeremy had only recently met.

Perched on the last chair on their side was Sammy's secretary, Janine. Gone was the gargoyle lapel pin, replaced by an ugly troll. Jeremy wondered what other creepy creatures the woman's jewelry box had spawned.

On the opposite side of the table was Chad Hawkins, the owner of Burgers and Buns, or the deponent, as Jeremy had learned from Sammy. The man's Buddha belly inside his tieless suit suggested he enjoyed a number of his own restaurant's delights, and the reddish hue of his face and pate beneath the goatee and thinning hair hinted a blood pressure pill might be in order. Sandwiching Mr. Hawkins were two lawyers named Valerie Munch and Anand Amin. Both names forced Jeremy to suppress a snicker.

The restaurateur wore a look of disdain. He parted and resealed his lips as if a bad taste swam inside. Jeremy thought about tossing him some mints. His lawyers assumed more professional expressions, though what simmered beneath their surfaces, Jeremy had no idea. Scorn for his mom and him? Respect? Indifference?

Finally, at the end of the table perched a court reporter, a bland woman whose name Jeremy didn't catch, and for that he felt shame, given he, too, knew the ache of invisibility.

Or at least he had.

He listened with interest as Sammy led the discussion. The lawyer had previously told Jeremy neither he nor his mom or Sue needed to be at the deposition — only the lawyers, the deponent, and a court reporter had to attend — but Jeremy's presence, along with his mother's and Sue's, might prove useful so they could get a feel of things to come.

Although Connie had been hesitant over Jeremy's participation, Sue had been gung-ho, and Jeremy, too, had wanted to attend. More and more, law research had trumped *War of the Wilderness*, surprising even himself. In the past, thoughts of college had barely materialized. Surviving high school was the goal. His school's graduation rates stank. But lately, new daydreams had reared their timid heads. Graduating pre-law. Mock trials in law school.

Yeah right, fatty. Tell that to the eight pounds you regained at your follow-up last week. The Fat Slayers' disappointment rivaled your own.

Although the requirements of high school would probably not allow attending the depositions of the two Ohio-based food manufacturers, Broker's Industries and Bilko's Snacks, Jeremy intended to learn everything he could from the one that morning.

He tuned in to Mr. Amin who gestured with his hands and spoke through prissy lips.

"You can spin your words of 'social determinants,' and 'product optimization,' and 'feel-good dopamine release' all you want, but no judge is going to hear a case that blames my client's restaurant for making this young man obese." Mr. Amin's gaze flickered briefly to Jeremy as if he were a booger in his line of vision.

So much for respecting us, Jeremy thought.

"Did my client force Mr. Barton to eat at his restaurant? Did he force Mr. Barton to select a quadruple-patty burger over a salad? Did he shove food into Mr. Barton's mouth? No."

The court reporter tapped away. Though her face was as expressive as a turnip, Jeremy wondered whose side she was on.

Sammy whispered something to Reggie who jotted a note on his legal pad. He let Mr. Amin continue.

"I'm sorry Mr. Barton struggles with obesity. I'm sorry he suffers complications of asthma, borderline hypertension, and — if I remember correctly — hyperinsulinemia. I'm sure the pressures on him are enormous."

Ms. Munch joined Mr. Amin in the donning of an empathetic expression while Mr. Amin carried on, flipping a fancy pen between his long fingers. "But to say my client is responsible is ludicrous, and you know any judge or jury would think the same. Frankly, I'm surprised by you, Sammy."

Sammy lifted his silk tie and flicked at a piece of lint. "I bet that's precisely what the tobacco-company lawyers said before their clients paid billions of dollars to the Tobacco Master Settlement."

Temporary silence.

Score one for salt-and-pepper Sammy, thought Jeremy.

Mr. Amin leaned forward and took a sip of water from a glass he'd poured earlier. Ms. Munch did the same. Finally, she said, "That's an entirely different situation."

"Is it?" Sammy asked, pushing one manila folder aside and opening another. "I trust you've reviewed the studies I sent you. The ones that show foods high in fat, sugar, and salt cause the brain to surge with dopamine, leaving the person feeling good and craving more. Simply *seeing* pictures of the food can trigger the brain's response, much like white powder triggers a cocaine addict's craving. The food industry knows this. That's why they spend money on product optimization. Therefore, like tobacco companies, they should take some responsibility for what their products are doing. Restaurants too."

Chad Hawkins burst up, his rounded belly bumping the table. Water swished inside the glasses. "Don't spew your fancy science on me. I'm not the one forcing food in that fat kid's mouth. It's not my fault he can't shut his pie-hole."

Jeremy could hardly believe the big-bellied guy's hypocrisy.

Mr. Amin put a hand on the burger king's arm at the same time the warrior woman raised hers and said, "His name is Jeremy. Don't you dare refer to him that way again."

Jeremy shifted in his chair. The room sparked with tension. Even the court reporter glanced up, offering Jeremy a small smile.

"Let's all calm—" Sammy didn't get far before Sue was at it again.

Jeremy worried they'd kick her out, given her presence was a generous courtesy granted by the opposing team.

"No. I won't stand for it. This is exactly the mindset we have to fight. Mr. Hawkins here proudly displays addictive, fattening junk on his menu. He offers free food to those who can devour the most. He even posts signs calling vegetable eaters 'losers' and claiming those who order salads are 'yellow bellies.' He knows exactly what he's doing."

"Sue, please." Sammy tapped Sue's hand with two fingers, and she fell silent, but her nostrils flared and her temples throbbed. Jeremy decided right then and there he'd name his next female game fighter Sue.

Sammy got the meeting under control, and the rest of the deposition proceeded in a calm but nonetheless interesting fashion. Jeremy got so caught up in the process, he almost forgot he was the plaintiff to whom they referred. Words like *pre-diabetes* and *food addicted* in reference to him were drowned out by the new legalese he was learning. He dared picture himself in the future working side-by-side with Sammy, fighting for other fat kids.

"Wasn't that the guy who started it all?" they'd ask, and Sammy would nod and pat Jeremy on the back.

Sammy concluded by saying, "As you can see, my client has become rather well-known, and his platform will grow even more with future public appearances and news stories. We have plenty of supporters. Don't kid yourselves into thinking the publicity will only help your restaurant. I recommend you take us seriously."

His words had their desired effect, and Jeremy could see the fear and anger on Mr. Hawkins's face. Jeremy suspected he could also hear the man's thoughts.

You'll be sorry, kid.

24

SUE

In Sue's mission to tackle the country's obesity problem, a mission that did not ignore the importance of individual responsibility but ponied up society's role as well, she hoped the news Al had just relayed about Jeremy's father being out of prison would not result in another setback. She had an exciting update to share with Sammy and the others at dinner that night. She didn't want anything to spoil it.

She pulled the final plate from the dishwasher, shelved it, and moved onto the silverware. "Are you sure it's the same Terry Harjo?"

"Well, how many can there be?" Al sat at the kitchen island, eyeing a small nick in the yellow paint near the bay window. Sue imagined him adding the touch-up task to his list. Most men despised honey-do lists. Al made his own.

"Maybe it's best I don't tell Connie yet. There's enough going on."

If Al thought it a mistake to remain silent on the issue of Jeremy's father, a father the boy presumed dead, he didn't say. In fact, Al and Sue's entire conversation for the past fifteen minutes had consisted of sentence exchanges but no real connection, which suited Sue fine. The two of them had reached a tentative truce, and she did not want to upset the balance.

Al had initially been supportive after Sue's scare in the parking lot two and a half weeks earlier. She'd refused to label the encounter an attack. She believed the man had only intended to frighten her, not cause physical harm. Unfortunately, only the man's ski-masked head was caught on tape, so no identity was made.

Once the issue had settled down, Al's anger returned, as did his demand she back off the lawsuit, but twenty-five years of marriage did not happen without compromise, and after intense conversation, Al had relented. He'd been further buoyed by the public support Sue's actions generated, a higher percentage than anticipated, though still the minority. As such, Sue thought it best to keep quiet about the amount of hate mail she received.

With Kayla, Al had agreed to step up, and although the girl still sassed ("God, you guys never let me do anything"), still pushed food around her plate, and still fell behind in her grades, Al's increased focus kept her in line.

Furthermore, Sue had scheduled an annual physical for Kayla, and from there, she would seek an appointment with a therapist if necessary, one who had experience with adolescent eating disorders.

Sue closed the dishwasher. She scooted to Al, kissed the top of his head, and said she had to go. "The reservation is at seven thirty. I shouldn't be too late. Just have to catch everyone up on some things."

Al pulled a notebook from his back pocket and walked over to the chipped wall paint. With a pen from the counter, he jotted something down. "I'll take care of that spot this weekend."

At seven fifteen, spruced up in an outfit of dark pants and a red- and white-striped turtleneck that Kayla had said made Sue look like a candy cane, Sue navigated her car out of the driveway and onto East Overlook Road. She only had to drive a few blocks south to Cedar Road and then head east toward Beachwood Place Mall.

Passing her neighbor's colonial-style home, she noticed a black truck idling near the curb. A man hunkered behind the wheel, head lowered, baseball hat hiding his face.

Her shoulders tensed, and she strained to make the guy out in her rearview mirror. No luck. She exhaled. Ever since the parking garage incident, paranoia had gotten the best of her. She reminded herself that all the other nasty sentiments she'd received had come via e-mail, phone, or letters to the health department. No one knew where she lived.

Still, a darkness dampened her previous joy, a joy generated by the good news she was about to share with the others.

Another glance in the mirror prompted a tighter grip on the steering wheel. The same truck was cruising behind her.

Calm down. Black trucks are common.

Yet, when she turned left onto Cedar Road, the truck did too. As she proceeded to pass residential, then business-lined blocks, the truck did the same. She shifted to the right lane. The black truck followed, only a leather-clad motorcyclist between them. Sue feigned a right turn by flipping on the blinker. The truck's blinker soon flickered. Despite their reasonable proximity and the illumination of streetlights, the driver remained unidentifiable in the darkening sky.

Sue's mouth went dry, and a metallic taste coated her tongue. She reached for a mint from the container resting in the spare cup holder. A Mini Cooper settled in behind her, making the distance between the Focus and the truck even greater.

Yet he still followed.

She fumbled for the cell phone in her purse. Wanted it handy should the need to dial her husband arise. Or 9-1-1.

You're overreacting.

The Tell Tale Tavern beckoned ahead. Sue made a right turn onto Richmond Road.

The black truck did, too.

Gripping the phone, Sue accessed the keypad while trying to maneuver the last block of traffic before the restaurant's entry.

It could mean anything. Maybe he's eating at the same place. It wouldn't be that unusual.

But the truck had started out near her home. An unlikely coincidence.

She took the final left turn, held her breath, and readied herself to dial for help. The black truck continued off on Richmond Road, not following her after all.

Pulling into a vacant spot in the crowded restaurant lot, Sue dropped the phone and exhaled loudly. She needed to get a grip. Not everyone was out to get her. What if in her paranoid fear she had caused an accident?

She swallowed the remains of the mint, nothing but a soggy mass on the back of her tongue. The radio crooned a snappy pop tune, and she turned it up in order to calm down. By the time she opened her car

door and headed into the Tell Tale Tavern, her breathing had returned
to normal, and her mood lightened considerably.

She focused on the excitement ahead.

By fifteen minutes to eight, a larger group than Sue had planned was
seated at the table. Although expecting Sammy, Jeremy, Connie, and
Tony (she'd hoped the newspaper reporter would publish the big news),
she had not expected Jonathan and George. It *was* a Saturday night
though. Perhaps she should have invited Al and Kayla. Then again, she
was not yet ready to share her news with them.

Al might not reciprocate her enthusiasm.

After receiving their beverages from a waitress in a clingy sweater-
dress, Sammy asked Sue for her big news. She insisted they order
first. Sammy, George, and Jonathan simultaneously donned reading
glasses to examine the menu's small print. A round of laughter
followed.

"Old people," Jeremy said, prompting more chuckles.

"If Al was here, he'd have done the same thing. The lighting's too
dim for him." Sue sipped her Chablis, feeling more guilt at her
husband's absence.

Tony dug in the front pocket of his checkered shirt. "Guess I
should've brought mine to complete the quartet."

By then the laughter had died down, leaving an awkward pause.
Sue gave Tony a courtesy smile. He cleared his throat, drank some
water, and cleared it again.

Sue glanced at Jeremy. Judging by the boy's expression, the entrée
choices displeased him. Words like *organic, free-range,* and *vegetable-based*
populated the menu. Everyone else marveled at the selections, and
given the men's penchants for healthier fare, Sue was relieved she had
chosen the place, especially after having learned Jonathan shunned red
meat. Luckily, the menu contained a variety of poultry and fish
options.

To Jeremy, Sue said, "Try the black-bean burger. I think you'll like
it. It's Kayla's favorite." *Or at least it used to be.* Back when her daughter
consumed more than thimble-sized meals.

"Will they at least bring a bread basket?" Jeremy asked, and
although Sue doubted he was making a joke, the others laughed.

"Careful, Eating Bull. White carbs are probably not on your diet plan."

Although Sue suspected Jonathan was trying to be funny, and she noted a smile on George's face, silence fell at the table. She saw Sammy nudge Jonathan. If he hadn't, she would have. Calling Jeremy that unflattering name, a name the media had pounced on and tossed about like a tiny craft on a stormy sea, was uncouth. Connie, seated between George and Tony, appeared uncomfortable as well, although Sue knew the woman would not stand up to her boss.

After they placed their orders, Sammy begged Sue not to keep them in suspense any longer.

She took another sip of wine and smoothed the fold of her candy-cane turtleneck. "As you know, we've received a decent amount of publicity, and thanks to the article in *US Life Magazine* — and yes, I suppose that dreadful tabloid story too — we're now getting more national attention. Snippets about our cause have appeared on news programs, in newspapers, and on social media, though the latter strays off topic. For example, despite our efforts to keep the debate on individual versus societal responsibilities for obesity, the Juney Andrews case keeps popping up."

Sue paused, unsure whether to share her concerns over the other issue polluting their cause. The waitress arrived with salads and soups. Once everyone had napkins in their laps and utensils in hand, she decided to go on.

"Another unfortunate link, well, gruesome really, is that some people think the recent Cleveland murders are connected to our litigation." Sue sprinkled pepper on her salad, and once she had collected her thoughts, she continued. "They're saying our lawsuit has triggered a madman to kill obese people. Which is ludicrous. The murders started before we filed. Plus, there's no proof a killer is targeting the overweight. It may be a coincidence all three victims were heavy."

"Seems like a rather big coincidence." Jonathan blew on a spoonful of vegetable broth.

"Jonathan's right. Didn't the last victim have the word *glutton* written on his car window?" George said.

Sue glanced at the statistician, not wanting to confirm his statement but knowing it was true. Al had told her the police initially wanted to keep that information from the public, but as so often happened in an interconnected world, the detail had slipped out.

"Can we not talk about this right now?" Connie asked, her gaze on Jeremy, who, other than his brief jokes and ordering his meal, had remained silent, poking away at some electronic game.

Then again, silence remained Jeremy's usual MO. Sue hoped the publicity would not overwhelm him. She'd been disheartened over his recent weight gain, but she'd also been encouraged by his interest in the case. Around Sammy and legal talk, the boy came alive, and she wished he would find the courage to maintain that confidence in other areas.

She realized the others were waiting for her to speak. Silverware clinked against bowls and plates, filling the conversation void. She got back to business. "We're getting attention, but we need more. We need a chance to tell our story beyond a one-minute sound bite, a different platform, so to speak. A place to get people focused on the issues, not sidetracked by Juney Andrews or murderers." She flashed the group a victorious smile. "And I've found it. Or rather, I've landed it."

All eyes focused on Sue. Even Jeremy looked up from his game.

"Tell us. Don't keep us in suspense any longer." Sammy twirled his beer bottle, his expression suggesting he didn't like being on the receiving end of case-related news.

"I got us a spot on the Dr. John Show."

Silence swallowed the table. Then, three beats later, everyone started talking at once.

"Dr. John? In Dallas? That's huge." Connie's eyes were wide. She reached across the table and squeezed Jeremy's hand, his plump fist gripping a slice of bread. His blank face didn't share Connie's enthusiasm.

Before Sue could elaborate, the entrées arrived. While they ate, she answered a flurry of questions, her brain on rapid fire.

***

Later, after the group had dispersed and Sue made her way home, she considered what she knew about Dr. John.

As a well-known psychologist, he hosted a variety of guests on a daily, syndicated TV show. Watched by millions around the country — the world, even — an hour-long spot guaranteed an enormous audience. Jeremy would be a household name, along with Sammy, Sue, and Connie, a fact that made Sue reluctant to share the news with Al. If the four of them expected the lawsuit to succeed, however, they would need the weight of the masses behind them. A show like Dr. John's could deliver that support.

The psychologist filmed his show in a home on a huge estate outside of Dallas. The audience watched on closed-circuit TV from a renovated barn a quarter mile from the house. Dr. John felt the arrangement allowed the feel of a live audience while maintaining the privacy of the guests, which made them more comfortable in sharing their stories.

Knowing his show would be the perfect venue, Sue had submitted her request two weeks back. She never expected to receive a response so quickly, let alone in the affirmative.

Furthermore, Dr. John had assured Sue he would be protective of Jeremy. He would not sensationalize the boy for ratings. To Sue, that was as important as the lawsuit itself, because what they were doing was big. Huge. There could be no backing out. No amount of threats or hate mail or perceived car-followings would deter her. The good that would come from their efforts was too great.

Besides, individual sacrifice was the price one paid to change the world, and Sue was willing to accept that.

She hoped the others were too.

25

DARWIN

From his workspace on the fourth Tuesday of October, Darwin stared out the window, his thoughts a disjointed mess. Rain pelted the glass. A lightning bolt electrified the sky, and thunder cracked moments after. Darwin's father had once told him lightning's distance could be calculated by using the number of seconds between flash and thunder. With every storm, father and son had done the math, curled up on Darwin's bed, a puzzle book open between them. After his dad died, young Darwin wondered how to calculate the distance between father and son.

Tearing his gaze from the window, he returned to work, his concentration poor. A colleague whizzed by, nodding in Darwin's direction.

If only his elephant of a mother had been the one to die, spending eternity within a cramped coffin. Much like the cold, tiny closet she'd made Darwin endure.

"Sometimes punishment is necessary," she had said, closing the door and turning the key, the click's echo in the quiet basement reverberating in his vacant heart.

Alone he would sit. Alone in that cold, dark, dungeon-like closet where he could feel the dirt cling to his pores and stain his nails as he tried to claw his way out. Sometimes a cockroach crawled over his pudgy, bare thigh, and he would shiver from both fear and cold, his little-boy underpants an insufficient shield against the elements.

Darwin squeezed his eyes shut. When he opened them, he tried to focus on work, but his mind did not cooperate, taking him back to that shivering child in the closet to the even fatter kid he'd later become. The shame. The embarrassment. The weakness.

Then The Voice had found him. Had guided him to a life of discipline, and Darwin had managed to overcome.

Maybe the boy could, too...

No, he could not go there. His defiance had already netted hours of painful punishment. Darwin pressed his temples with both palms, the action quelling the mounting ache behind his orbits.

The Voice had been erratic lately, sometimes absent for days, sometimes relentlessly present. Normally, work prevented his visits, too many other tasks requiring Darwin's attention, but lately The Voice visited him during his work shift and staying on task proved difficult, prompting odd looks from co-workers.

If only he could kill again. That would sort things out. That would quiet his mind.

(Soon, Darwin, soon.)

A loud thump, followed by a female cry, snapped Darwin to attention.

He stood and peered around the corner. Before he could stop himself, he laughed out loud. He barely recognized the laugh as his own, its tone sharp and malevolent, and he realized it must be The Voice's. The fact The Voice had materialized into actual sound rather than mere thought both fascinated and terrified Darwin.

"Don't stand there and laugh, help me up. My weak heart." Miss Fat Witch's plea came out between sobs. She lay sprawled backward on the floor, enormous ass still stuck in the seat of her precious ergonomic chair.

Guess the new treadmill hasn't paid off, Darwin thought.

His laughter stopped as abruptly as it had started. He blinked. He fisted and unfisted his hands. So much noise in his brain. He looked around, but the two of them were momentarily alone in the area.

He strolled forward until he hovered above her, her cranberry lips still shrieking for help. Her arms alternately flailed at the air and squeezed the chair's armrest in an attempt to push herself out of its confines.

As she lay trapped like a bloated bug, Darwin imagined grabbing the pencil from the counter and thrusting it deep inside her fleshy chest, bits of fat and blood sailing through the air and splattering the rain-dripped window.

(*No. Not yet. You can have her but not yet.*)

Darwin realized the woman had shut her screaming mouth and was staring at him oddly. Had The Voice spoken out loud?

Finally, he held out his hand. Miss Fat Witch grabbed it, though not before Darwin noted the look of disgust on her face. Her? Disgusted by him? He hated to think of the extended shower time and extra soap-downs their physical contact would require, and yet she was the one to express disgust.

Ungrateful, fat witch.

After a little maneuvering and a lot of muscle, Darwin pulled the woman up from her ergonomic trap, the chair itself squeaking and creaking in the struggle. Once upright, Miss Fat Witch splayed both hands, one on top of the other, over her left chest. Her breaths were labored and her face pale, and for a moment, Darwin worried he would have to perform CPR.

Save her only to subsequently kill her.

He smiled at the irony, and as he did, the perfect way to kill her materialized.

(*But it will have to look like an accident. She's too close to you.*)

Darwin assured The Voice it would.

Once Miss Fat Witch caught her breath, she shot Darwin a withering look and practically hissed. "You are a cold-hearted prick. Don't think I won't report this."

You do that, Darwin thought. *It will probably be the last thing you do.*

For the first time that day, through all the literal and figurative rainy haze, Darwin's mind was clear. He needed a kill. He had waited patiently. He was due. He relished the opportunity to plan his strategy.

Another kill would sharpen his focus. His need for strength and discipline had never been greater. The pinnacle of the mission drew near.

Because next month, Eating Bull would enjoy his last meal.

26

JEREMY

Lying on Tito's bed the Friday afternoon of his sleepover, Jeremy remembered something he'd read about social media: eighty percent of teenagers used it. Of those, almost ninety-five percent had Facebook profiles.

"Goddamn teenagers don't know how to interact with people," GI Dick had said, after hearing one of his news pundits preach about the subject. Jeremy had considered pointing out the hypocrisy of such a squawk from an agoraphobic man, but then the old guy added, "Thank God your beautiful grandmother isn't around to see the shit-pool this world has become."

The retort had dissolved in Jeremy's throat, but the conversation resurfaced that afternoon when Tito opened fake Courtney's Facebook account to check for new updates from Calvin. Up until their extracurricular stalking, Jeremy was one of the twenty percent of teens who shunned social media. He preferred to pass time with Kajika. After earning the latest level, Jeremy's avatar had advanced to the highest ranked shaman. As a result, the chief had emblazoned the tribe's golden crest upon Kajika's powerful bow, a sign of the healer's ability to bridge the natural world with the spiritual. As he often did, Jeremy wondered if his father would have liked the game.

"Oh, crap, check this out." Tito bounced up and down in front of his computer desk, almost crushing his latest bridge model with a fist-pumping arm. He righted the structure and punched Jeremy's thigh.

Jeremy was sprawled on the bed. He rolled a few times to right himself. When he saw the screen, he burst out laughing. A smug Calvin performing biceps curls wearing nothing but boxer briefs.

"The dude looks like Howdy Doody on steroids," Jeremy said, but despite Calvin's shock of red hair and pale skin, Jeremy had to admit the guy had impressive muscle tone. Too bad he had to be such a douche. "Is that on his own page?"

"Yeah, but looks like he set it so only she — or us, ha — can see it."

"You can do that?"

"Sure. You can make your updates private, friends-only, or set it so only a few specific people see it."

Jeremy decided he'd stick with shooting arrows at Jackaloids and Impites instead.

"What are you doing?" A knot formed in the pit of his stomach as he watched Tito copy the image.

"I'm making sure that lots of people get to enjoy this muscle-pumping pic." Tito had a sly grin on his face, and he pushed his glasses up higher.

The lump in Jeremy's gut grew. He sat up straighter. "Wh-what do you mean?"

Tito reached for his cell phone. "What's the point of having all the popular kids' phone numbers from tutoring if I can't share a little photo love?"

Jeremy stared at the rat-shaped spot of vitiligo on his friend's right arm. He wondered if the patch could spread. Like an image going viral could spread.

"Um, do you think we should do that?"

Tito looked at Jeremy from above his eyeglasses. "Seriously?"

Jeremy leaned back on the bed again and exhaled. His sweatpants pulled tight against his tree-trunk thighs, probably from the extra fast food he'd eaten the past week, his mom none the wiser.

Calvin was an ass, no doubt. He never wasted an opportunity to call Jeremy "Eating Bull," and he'd been texting other kids links to online articles and blog posts about the lawsuit, picking the most malicious and obscene rants from haters of their cause. As usual, Jeremy had done nothing to intervene. Just took it like the wuss he was.

But what had inactivity netted him? Jeers and stares from even more kids and a shroud of silence from Lacey whenever he walked past.

Mean father or not, Calvin was a dick, and he deserved something constituting payback. Still, Jeremy couldn't shake the feeling that what Tito proposed was wrong. Or his fear of getting caught.

"Everyone will know you sent it," Jeremy finally said, licking his chapped lips. He craved a soda from the Harrises' refrigerator, sodas he had vowed to avoid for the duration of the sleepover. His eating had been good that day, food choices the Fat Slayers would cheer. The excitement of hanging out with Tito mercifully dampened his appetite, though judging by Mr. and Mrs. Harrises' tight-lipped smiles, Jeremy suspected Tito had to cajole and plead to make the night happen.

"Not so, my friend." Tito opened a desk drawer and withdrew something from the back corner. "It's a prepaid phone. Hey, you gotta be crafty when your parents watch you like a hawk."

Jeremy rubbed a hand over his mouth. "But that's not a smartphone. You can't—"

"It will take longer, but I'll send each kid the URL to Courtney's Facebook page where I'll make the photo public. We don't even need that many kids. The picture will spread faster than gonorrhea."

Jeremy closed his eyes. In his mind, he saw an irate Calvin beating the crap out of him. Then he saw Kajika shoot an arrow into the bully's ass.

He reopened his eyes. "You sure we won't get caught?"

"You worry too much, big guy."

Tito's fingers started flying their way to payback. When he finished, he must have sensed Jeremy's unease, because he put down the phone and asked about Dallas and the Dr. John Show. "It's just over a month from now, right?"

Jeremy told him what he knew and then mentioned a huge powwow he'd discovered online. "It's in Dorner, Oklahoma, which isn't far from Dallas, the day before the show's taping. No way we could go, though. The warrior woman is too focused on the mission. There's no point even asking her or my mom."

Tito raised his eyebrows and shifted back to the computer keyboard. His fingers once again worked their magic, and in no time, Jeremy's hands held printed materials of the powwow and a map from Dallas to Dorner. Tito even produced a bus schedule thanks to a pop-up ad.

"Jer, it's barely over a two-hour bus ride. You've got money saved," he said. "Can't hurt to at least have the information."

Two hours later, on the way to a movie, Tito and Jeremy watched a YouTube clip of a dog mewing like a cat on Tito's smartphone — the one his parents knew about — in the backseat of Mr. Harris's Honda Accord. Earlier in the kitchen, Tito's father had tried to persuade them to stay home and watch a DVD instead. "You know what the theater's like on a Friday night," he'd said, picking up the same plate he'd already dried and swishing the dishtowel back and forth in a feverish rhythm.

Tito was relentless though, pushing on until his parents gave in. His power of persuasion impressed Jeremy. What the little guy wanted, the little guy got.

Mr. Harris pulled up to the fourteen-plex movie theater, its front exterior lit up like a football stadium. He confirmed a pick-up time before slowly driving away from the crowded curb, affording him the opportunity to eye the police officer roaming the ticket lines inside. Jeremy also noticed Tito's dad check the rearview mirror in their direction three times before finally driving away.

As the two boys, one tiny and lithe, the other large and heavy-footed, headed through throngs of people leaving or entering the movie complex, a red Camaro approached the curb.

"Well, if it isn't Eating Bull himself." Rex leaned over and lowered his head to make eye contact with Jeremy through the passenger window. His smile was its usual scowl. "No missing *you* out here. How goes it?"

Jeremy said nothing. Rex laughed and shot back up in his seat. Before he drove away, he added, "Tell your slut mom I said 'hi'."

Asshole, Jeremy thought but didn't have the nerve to say.

Inside the red- and gold-accented movie theater, new-release posters featuring beautiful people with beautiful bodies lined the walls. The scent of freshly popped corn nearly brought Jeremy to his knees, and if it wasn't for Tito bypassing the concession stand and beelining to theater number four, Jeremy would have caved in to its machine-gun popping, the sound nearly as tantalizing as the scent.

Before entering the theater, a second unpleasant jerk-sighting soured Jeremy's appetite. Calvin and a group of his friends entered auditorium eight down the hall. Not a big coincidence for a Friday night, but certainly a lousy one. Jeremy hoped Calvin hadn't spotted them.

After two hours of thunderous surround sound, smashed cars, and endless gun battle, Jeremy and Tito exited the movie, sharing opinions and rehashing scenes. Jeremy's nonstop talking and excited rants were as unfamiliar to him as they would have been to those who knew him, but he couldn't remember the last time he'd felt so pumped up and happy. He had never been to a movie with someone other than his mother, a fact he'd never admit out loud.

Outside, the air was ear-nipping crisp, but like the other loitering kids, Jeremy left his sweatshirt unzipped. The cold breeze prickled his airways, and his chest constricted. He reflexively reached into his pocket for his inhaler but found the space empty.

Left it in my overnight bag at Tito's, he thought. He'd be okay until they got back. He wasn't wheezing yet.

Waiting for Mr. Harris, Tito and Jeremy continued to debate the ability of a robot to mate with a human, Tito arguing the movie was unrealistic in that regard.

Jeremy disagreed and was about to say so, when the cigarette smoke from a nearby bald-headed man produced coughs instead of words.

"You want to wait inside?" Tito asked. "That smoke can't be good for your asthma."

Jeremy held up a hand and finished another round of hacking. When he recovered, he said, "Let's head over to the side of the building. We'll still be able to see your dad from there."

Bad move.

Not only did the side of the brick complex offer less lighting, it sheltered Calvin and his boys. By the time Jeremy and Tito recognized the hooded bullies, escape was too late.

Calvin sauntered forward. His cronies moved behind Jeremy and Tito, ensuring imprisonment. "I knew that was you, fat-ass. Saw you when you went into your movie. Waiting for daddy to pick you up, zebra boy?" Though the question was directed to Tito, Calvin's gaze never left Jeremy.

"Come on, Jer, let's go." Tito started dragging Jeremy away, but Calvin cut him off and shoved him out of the way. Tito's featherweight body flew into the other boys, who tossed him back and forth like a Beanie Baby.

Jeremy's chest seized into an airless fist. Tobacco fumes still drifted his way, and when he attempted speech, more coughing ensued.

Before he could catch his breath, Calvin slammed him against the brick wall. More coughing followed by wheezing.

Oh God, has he already discovered the photo?

The bully's pimply face hovered near Jeremy's, his hoodie pulled so low his rat-like eyes almost disappeared. "You really are a big fat pussy, aren't you?" Stale popcorn breath soured what little oxygen Jeremy could inhale, and his narrowed airways whistled like forced air through a straw.

Desperate for his inhaler, Jeremy tried to push Calvin away, but Calvin's muscular bulk was an immovable boulder. Jeremy dumped his remaining energy into fighting for each breath. Everything else muted and blurred, his lungs as empty as his courage. With each second his panic grew, and he worried he might die.

"Hey, what are you kids doing?" a man cried out.

Sagging in relief, Jeremy saw Mr. Harris barreling toward them. By the time Tito's father got there, Calvin and his cronies had taken off, laughing and slinging a few final fat slurs.

The next twenty minutes were blurry, Jeremy sucking air like an emphysemic, chest heaving and huffing. Mr. Harris's Accord sped toward the children's hospital, hands gripping the steering wheel so tightly his knuckles seemed to break through his skin.

The next thing Jeremy knew, he was on an exam table in the treatment pod, a nurse barking for albuterol. Within seconds, she slapped a blood pressure cuff on his arm and a pulse oximeter probe on his finger. An oxygen mask followed. Moments later, Gloria, the elf-sized ICU nurse Jeremy had encountered on his last trip to the ER, hustled over with a nebulizer. Jeremy was so desperate for the breathing treatment, he didn't care who delivered it. Gloria, probably unhappy to be working the ER again, wore her usual scrunch of disapproval as she maneuvered around his body.

After two back-to-back treatments, Dr. Sneeker popped in to listen to Jeremy's lungs. In his haste, he mumbled something incoherent and took off again.

Jeremy felt his airways go from pixie sticks to straws, and though he still had a ways to go, he no longer felt like a member of the Blue

Man group. Gloria voiced her approval at his improved oxygen saturation.

"Dr. Sneeker will be back, and the man who brought you in said your mom is on her way." Gloria started Jeremy's third treatment. Then she crossed her arms and raised her tiny head. "You know, your weight is not helping these asthma attacks. You have to get that under control."

Just had to get that in, didn't you? Jeremy thought as Tinker Bell flitted away to another patient.

Before the third treatment was halfway through, its sweet, gurgling vapors expanding Jeremy's airways from straws to pipes, Dr. Sneeker returned.

"How's my favorite gamer doing?" he asked. Before Jeremy could answer, the doctor put his stethoscope on Jeremy's chest. "Much, much better. You're moving air now. You were tighter than a drum when you came in."

"Where are your glasses?" Jeremy managed to ask while the medicine still aerosolized into his lungs.

"Oh, I don't always need them. Mostly for detailed work." Dr. Sneeker turned to Gloria who seemed to materialize on a wave of fairy dust. "Give him sixty of prednisone and a treatment with Atrovent please." The physician then reviewed Jeremy's adherence to his asthma medications, and Jeremy promised he'd been compliant. He insisted it was excitement over the movie, cold air, and tobacco smoke that had set him off. He left out Calvin's contribution.

After a few more treatment recommendations, information Jeremy had heard dozens of times before, Dr. Sneeker surprised Jeremy by shifting the conversation to the lawsuit.

"Oh, don't look so shocked. Of course, I know about it. It's all over the news. You're quite the celebrity. I've heard you even landed a spot on the Dr. John Show." Dr. Sneeker removed the breathing treatment paraphernalia and listened once again to Jeremy's lungs, giving a contented nod when he finished. He squirted hand sanitizer into his palms and scrubbed.

Jeremy hadn't realized the show appearance had become common knowledge. As always, everyone was a step ahead of him.

Doctor and patient briefly discussed details of the Dallas trip. Dr. Sneeker's interest pleased Jeremy. After Sue's warning, Jeremy wasn't sure how the physician would take the news.

Gripping the ends of the stethoscope hanging around his neck, Dr. Sneeker's expression sobered. "Just watch yourself, okay? Lawsuits take a long time, and people can get hurt along the way."

Jeremy was about to say he would when the physician cut him off. "Ah, there's your mother. I'll go review your care with her before we get you ready for discharge. You know me, I like to dot my Is and cross my Ts."

Dr. Sneeker shuffled off to a distraught Connie, George by her side.

27

SUE

Perhaps Sue should have listened to the chromotherapist after all. In the past six weeks, a great deal of hostility — both verbal and nonverbal — had been unleashed within the Fort's yellow kitchen. Maybe Al the Fixer could go down to his dungeon basement, scrounge up some brushes amidst all his weight-lifting equipment and other assorted debris, and paint the room a tranquil blue instead. At least then they might get somewhere, because recently they seemed stuck between a restrained truce and outright war.

This Sunday's been a war day.

Al washed the frying pan with such quiet precision that Sue's shoulders tensed and her stomach knotted, impeding her lemon chicken's digestion. She would have preferred screaming and hollering, even pan throwing, to the rigid muteness he displayed. She wiped up droplets of spattered oil from the white stove top and returned to the center island, tapping its beige-speckled quartz with her fingers while she waited for her husband to say something. Anything.

Finally, after toweling off the pan to a level of desert dryness, he turned around and faced her, resting his palms on the rim of the sink behind him. Above his head ticked the kitchen clock, its arms a smiling fork and spoon positioned at seven thirty-three.

"Do you know how many people watch that show?" Al's voice was chillier than the ice cubes in his water glass.

"That's the point, honey." Warm tea to his ice water.

"How long have you known about this?"

"Almost two weeks."

Al's face twisted into unstable storm patterns. Sue knew the tidal wave was about to hit.

"Two goddamn weeks? The taping is less than a month away and you've known about it for two weeks?" Her husband's muscular frame shook as he started to pace the room.

"I wanted to wait until the time was right. There's so much—"

"Two weeks? Christ, Sue, what in the hell is happening to us?"

Sue had not heard Al swear so much in years, not since a crook got off on a technicality due to a small error on Al's part during the guy's arrest. She could no longer remember the trivial infraction, but it was enough to let the man walk.

"Nothing is happening to us, honey. There's just a lot going on." She stood, grabbed Al's hands, and placed them over her heart, a gesture she'd done for years, a gesture that had come to represent her passion of right versus wrong. "I have to do this. I feel it in my core. To me, it's as right as you refusing a bribe to look the other way. In my heart, I know I'm right."

She led Al to the family room, needing to escape the yellow anxiety of the kitchen, and pulled him to the cream-colored couch with its burgundy pillows. He sighed, but she felt his body soften as he sat next to her. She glanced at the upstairs balcony leading to the three bedrooms, one of which harbored Kayla, her daughter's ear buds no doubt in place, thumbs texting friends about the injustice of her most recent grounding.

The last teenage tirade was during dinner when Kayla had asked for a reprieve from her punishment for the evening to go study with friends. Both Al and Sue had denied the request, reminding Kayla that the grounding was for two weeks, and two weeks exactly, the price she had to pay for missing her curfew the weekend before. That was followed by a string of, "You never let me do anything. You're so controlling." She ended with, "Maybe if I was one of your fat kids, you'd treat me more like a person."

Kayla had taken her plate, which Sue noted contained nearly the same amount of food as when they'd started dinner, slammed it in the dishwasher, and stormed up to her room. They had not heard from her thereafter, at which point, Sue had relayed the news of the Dr. John Show to Al.

Placing a hand on his thigh now, she took a breath and continued. "Look. I know all you see are threats and negative press, but you're missing everything else. I've received letters of support from people all over the country, people who've tried everything in their power to lose weight, but that's just it. It's not entirely in their power. You know that. Think about those snack crackers you love so much, the ones you've told me never to allow in this house again, so help you God."

At this, Al released a soft chuckle, which bolstered Sue on.

"And although there are plenty of hate comments floating around, there are also a surprising number of supportive ones, people who are thrilled someone is finally taking on the big companies. Our website is getting lots of traffic." Sue fluffed one of the pillows by her side. "Oh, and Sammy said the last two depositions with the Ohio food giants went well. The lawyers were not quite as smug this time around, not when Sammy showed them our latest support numbers. But..." Sue paused and placed her hands on Al's cheeks. Her lips brushed his, and she looked him in the eye. "But it's not enough. That's where the Dr. John Show comes in. Next month. November twenty-second and twenty-third."

Al leaned back and ran a hand over his thinning crop. "I get that. I do. And despite everything, you know I'm proud of you. You're tough. You make things happen. That's a big part of why I married you."

Though relieved by his praise, Sue knew she wasn't off the hook.

"But I worry about you. What if someone takes a threat too far? And what about these murders? Somebody is murdering fat people. What if it has anything to do with—"

"It doesn't." Sue brushed a few clinging crumbs from her pants with brisk, efficient swipes. "The murders started well before the lawsuit. Bad timing, that's all."

"Well, bad timing or not, let's hope the lawsuit doesn't draw the wacko's attention to you."

"I'm not overweight. Haven't been for a long time."

"Jeremy is."

His words halted Sue's grooming, and for a moment her hands hovered above her thighs. She thought nothing Al could say could veer her off course.

She was wrong.

She reflected on the phone call she'd received from Connie the day before. Jeremy had apparently been rushed to the emergency room for a severe asthma attack triggered by cigarette smoke, though Connie told her the father of Jeremy's friend mentioned some boys were harassing him, and Connie worried their taunts played more of a role than Jeremy let on. Although the teen would not confide in Sue, she suspected the lawsuit only increased his bullying. Nor had he disclosed anything to Dr. Green at his last clinic follow-up. She wondered if he'd discussed the issue with Connie. She wondered if he would confide in his father if he knew the man was alive.

Sue sighed. That was another important morsel she had neglected to relay to the necessary party, but Connie was so happy of late. Sue hated to burden her with heavy news. She would tell her before Dallas. No, she would tell her after the taping but before the show aired. Then Connie could tell Jeremy.

Oh, Jeremy. Sweet, quiet Jeremy.

In a soft voice, Sue said, "I do this for Jeremy, and all the others like him."

Al must have realized he'd struck a nerve, because he scooped Sue up in a hug for which she was long overdue. "Just promise me you'll be careful. There have been three murders so far, all of the victims obese and killed in a brutal fashion." Al released her and rubbed his stubbled chin. "It's been five weeks since the last murder, so who knows? Maybe the guy is done."

Sue rubbed her arms. "Dear God, let's hope so."

Sue and Al talked for another half hour, working their way back to the kitchen where Sue splurged on a bowl of vanilla ice cream with choco-late syrup and caramel topping. It felt good to discuss issues unrelated to lawsuits, difficult teenage daughters, and murders. They discussed plans for Christmas, hoping to get their two older children home for the holidays. A phone call on Sue's mobile interrupted them. She retrieved the cell from its charger on the counter, next to the kitchen scale.

Surprised to see Sammy's number on the caller ID, she worried something was wrong, but she needn't have. With an animation the stoic lawyer rarely displayed, Sammy told her about calls he received from law practices in Cleveland, Columbus, and Cincinnati, voicing interest in starting a class-action lawsuit against the two Ohio food manufacturing giants.

"The Cleveland practice has experience in class-action suits. We could rely on their expertise. Nothing is for certain, and I haven't met with any key players yet, but I wanted to make sure this is something Jeremy would want. A class-action suit might pull even more states in and then more industries. It could be huge. Huge like the tobacco litigation."

Sue suspected Sammy was getting ahead of himself — as he'd told her before, cases like theirs hadn't been successful in the past — but her enthusiasm must have been obvious, because Al saddled up on the kitchen stool next to her, eyebrows raised, hand rubbing her back.

Sue smiled and nodded. To Sammy, she said, "Of course, it's Jeremy's decision, but bringing other plaintiffs in, people whose health has been compromised by these industries, will not only raise more awareness for our mission, but it will also take some of the focus off the four of us, especially Jeremy. He won't have to carry the burden alone."

And neither will I, she thought.

After disconnecting with Sammy, Sue told Al the good news. At first, he didn't seem to share her zeal, perhaps worried additional litigation would snowball more grief his wife's way, but when she reiterated the safety in numbers, he offered an encouraging shrug.

"Let's go tell Kayla," she said, face flushed, energy soaring. "She'll be relieved to know the spotlight might ease up on me."

My God, this is really happening. This is going above and beyond what I hoped for.

Sue ran upstairs, taking the steps two at a time, something she hadn't done in years. She burst into Kayla's room, knowing she should knock first but too excited to do so.

She looked around, her expression going from glee to confusion. She checked the other rooms upstairs. Al checked on the main floor and even his basement lair. Sue looked in the garage. She called for Kayla outside, in the backyard and front.

Her confusion shifted to fear.

Kayla was gone.

28

DARWIN

The pecking of a woodpecker outside Miss Fat Witch's bedroom window grew tedious. Through the parted, red-velvet drapes, Darwin watched the bird flit from branch to branch of a nearby tree. He wondered if woodpeckers flew south for the winter. If so, they better hurry. It was already November first.

It was also five thirty on a Friday afternoon, which meant Darwin shouldn't have to wait much longer.

The feminine curtains sickened him. The entire mahogany-hued bedroom sickened him, even if the tidiness of the home was a pleasant, albeit confusing, find. As with his second victim, the well-kept surroundings rattled Darwin's assumptions and shook his equilibrium.

Still, the space repulsed him. Velvet bedspread smothered by a dozen maroon pillows of all shapes and sizes. Unblinking dolls nestled together on a shelf above the bed, dresses made of lace and silk. Bottles of perfume on the dresser top, some with fancy crystal dispensers. It was as if Miss Fat Witch deemed herself a princess and the bedroom her royal boudoir.

The only thing missing was a pile of romance novels like the trash his mother read. Darwin swished his tongue against his teeth, the image of the maternal whale leaving a nasty aftertaste.

Running gloved hands over the one object in the bedroom that pleased him, Darwin studied the treadmill's control panel. Simple enough to operate and sturdy enough to deliver. Miss Fat Witch's choice of exercise equipment was better than her choice of ergonomic chairs.

Darwin's lips curled into a smile. Between the closet and the ridiculous fluffy bed, Miss Fat Witch would take her last breath.

Dropping to the plastic sheet he'd spread out over the plush carpet to prevent DNA incrimination (the sheet would also collect blood should things get messy), Darwin pumped out thirty push-ups followed by a hundred sit-ups. Next came a series of triceps push-ups and triceps dips, sweat pooling inside the form-fitting gloves and cover gown. The dermal heat irritated and burned. Sitting up on his knees, he snapped at the gloves. He repositioned them. He couldn't get the fit right, so he repositioned them again. And again. The inability to find comfort distressed him, and soon his whole body felt on fire. The moisture inside the suffocating material drove him mad. He couldn't stand it a moment longer. He started to rip off the gloves but then stopped. What if she came home and he wasn't prepared? What if he—

(*Enough. Find your discipline.*)

Darwin closed his eyes and exhaled. *Thank God.* The Voice was calm when Darwin was anxious. Aggressive when Darwin was weak. Passive when Darwin was destructive.

Another round of sit-ups eased his torment.

(*Focus on the target.*)

Gaining access to Miss Fat Witch's home had been simple. Almost to the hour, she took a morning crap break. A few days before, her extended absence had allowed procurement of keys from her purse. Over the lunch hour, at the drugstore, Darwin had made copies of all six keys on the "It's Five O'Clock Somewhere!" keychain. He'd replaced the jangling set before she returned from lunch, thereafter trotting directly to the restroom to scrub his contaminated hands.

A key clicked in the door. Midway through an abdominal crunch, Darwin stiffened like a foxhound. The prey had arrived.

Gathering the protective sheet, he reassessed his supplies lined up on the dresser. He'd been forced to reposition the perfume bottles to accommodate his materials, and the asymmetry distressed him. He closed his eyes and refocused.

According to his research, between one hundred and fifty and two hundred milligrams of caffeine per kilogram of body weight could kill. Given Miss Fat Witch easily topped three hundred and fifty pounds, equal to one hundred and fifty-nine kilograms, a high dose would be required.

He'd brought twelve cans of extra-strength energy drink and one large bottle of extra-strength caffeine pills. Each pill packed two hundred milligrams of caffeine, and each can of energy drink contained two hundred and forty milligrams.

Enough to kill a horse, but if Miss Fat Witch vomited, additional administrations would be required.

Darwin gripped the treadmill bar, legs almost failing him. How many soap-downs would her puking involve?

(*Discipline.*)

He sharpened his concentration. By forcing the twat to consume an excessive amount of energy drinks and caffeine pills, he'd strain her "genetically weak heart." Toss in a strenuous jog on the treadmill and Miss Fat Witch would say hello to a myocardial infarction, probably well before she reached the lethal dose of caffeine.

But just in case, he had his knife.

Commotion in the kitchen was followed by Miss Fat Witch humming like a big-assed warbler. Darwin heard the microwave open, something clunk against its glass plate, and the slamming shut of the door. Uncorking of a wine bottle followed.

"Well, hello Mr. Riesling," the stupid whale sang.

Back to more humming. When the warbling approached the bedroom, Darwin seized the knife from the dresser and checked to make sure his protective gown and gloves were properly positioned.

Miss Fat Witch entered the room. Upon seeing him, she shrieked. Her hands flew to her heart, and a pile of mail shot from her arms and skittered across the carpet. The wine glass and its contents shattered against a jewelry stand near the door.

"What are you doing here?" she asked, her face pinched in confusion and shock.

She took a step back, but before she could escape, Darwin scurried over. One arm encircled her mountain of flesh and the other pressed the knife against her throbbing neck. He could feel the indentation of the skin under the blade, and he longed to draw blood from its surface, but he understood the need for discretion.

It had to look like an accident.

From there, The Voice took over, ceasing all worries of shower time, soap-downs, and capture, leaving only the thoughts necessary for mission completion.

Over the next fifteen minutes, Darwin poisoned Miss Fat Witch with two rounds of his calculated concoction, pumping her blood with eight thousand milligrams of caffeine. Like the pitiful sheep she was, she took it, a knife the only alternative. Then, dressed in the leggings and T-shirt Darwin had forced her to don, sheep became hamster and climbed on the treadmill. The frantic animal fought collapse, dimpled legs peddling the machine, mounds of flesh jiggling and shaking. Darwin almost admired her discipline, but The Voice cut him down with a burst of bitemporal pain.

Overall the task proved easier than planned and required less caffeine than anticipated. Such was the power of Darwin's own discipline, discipline that allowed him to ignore the breathless pleas, the wheezy sobs, the constant, "Why are you doing this?"

The treadmill sped faster and faster per Darwin's command. Mucus dripped from the sheep's nose, into her mouth, mixing with the tears and sweat already pooled there. Yet even that Darwin ignored, his revulsion held at bay, The Voice fueling him on.

(*Survival of the fittest.*)

Survival of the fittest, indeed, Darwin thought.

Every minute Miss Fat Witch grew weaker, Darwin grew stronger. When his colleague finally collapsed, her poisoned flesh bouncing off the treadmill and head smacking the base of the running deck, he listened to her gurgle her final breath.

A pulse check confirmed success. The Voice praised his efficiency.

(*You are a dominant wolf. You're ready for Dallas.*)

Pleased, Darwin collected his items, leaving no evidence of his presence. By the time someone discovered the gluttonous mound sprawled in front of the spinning treadmill, he'd be long gone, and a heart attack during exercise would be the obvious conclusion.

"Genetically weak heart and hypertension," the coroner's report would say. Maybe Miss Fat Witch had been right all along.

Darwin departed. Time to create his manifesto.

29

JEREMY

One of the many physical attributes Jeremy had missed out on was straight teeth. Back in middle school, while other kids got braces and retainers, Jeremy got a crooked smile. Then again, considering Mason High School's demographics, fine dentition was the exception.

Picking caramel from his molars in the stall of the school bathroom, a task made infinitely easier by the lack of oral metal, Jeremy stuffed the empty candy wrapper into his backpack and plucked out a package of chocolate, peanut-butter clusters. The lingering scent of piss and cigarette smoke in the vacant crapper did little to squash his hunger.

He had the hour free on Tuesday afternoons. After that, only fifty minutes of history class separated him from ditching the educational hellhole. He longed to stop at Burgers and Buns on the way home, but his newfound notoriety made those excursions unpleasant. The best he could do were quick trips to the convenience store, and as such, his backpack overflowed more than usual. The choices in the school vending machine sucked. Granola bars and flavorless baked chips. Nothing for him to pilfer at home either. Connie had seen to that, much to GI Dick's grumbling.

"I should be able to have a goddamn snack in my own home for Christ's sake."

To which Connie had surprised both father and son by shooting back, "Then go to the store yourself and buy what you need. Just keep it away from Jeremy."

Standing up to her father wasn't the only changing his mother had done. She continued to slim down toward a normal weight, reaping praise not only from Sue and the Fat Slayers but also from a local weight-loss facility that wanted to hire Connie as one of their spokespeople, not to represent the weight-loss journey, since Connie had already mastered that, but to represent the difficult process of weight maintenance. Connie had also earned some interview-generated paychecks, the most recent from a women's magazine extolling the challenges of a single mother fighting the system stacked against her. And she had a new beau.

Jeremy was happy to see his mother so happy. And when she asked questions like, "Are you sure you're okay, sweetie? You're not having second thoughts about the lawsuit, are you?" he would don his braces-free smile and lie. "Nope. Everything's good, Mom."

Connie deserved happiness. And even though George and Jeremy hardly exchanged words — the guy wasn't around all that much — Jeremy was happy his mother had someone new in her life.

Happy, happy, happy. Right?

Jeremy polished off the second treat in the king-sized triple pack. The mix of peanut butter and chocolate soothed the gnawing beast in his belly. He rested his head against the metal stall, foot propped up on the cigarette-burned toilet seat, its pock-marked porcelain a replica of Calvin's future face. Maybe Jeremy would be doubly blessed and the asshole would gain a hundred pounds, too.

It wasn't his intent to break into his emergency food stash. He was trying to save money for the Dallas trip which was only two and a half weeks away. His latest few dollars were gleaned from the Duongs for walking their new beagle after school. Earning extra dough was a plus, but the fact Jeremy *could* walk a dog without needing his inhaler was the real accomplishment. At least when he'd regained the weight, he hadn't lost the endurance he'd developed. But running into Mr. Pottage fifteen minutes earlier had sent Jeremy fleeing to the toilet, where only a mouthful of sweet and salty could tame his agitation.

Creepy, thigh-feeling math teacher.

Replaying the interaction, he sunk his teeth into the third peanut-butter offering. Mr. Pottage had called Jeremy into his empty classroom.

Jeremy didn't want to go. Not at all. But the guy was his former teacher. What could he do?

Mr. Pottage had pulled his chair up to an empty desk, indicating Jeremy have a seat. Jeremy moved the desk back a few inches and grudgingly squeezed into its confines.

Leaning forward, Mr. Pottage placed a hand on Jeremy's arm. "All this attention must be very difficult for you, isn't it?" A fleshy smile oozed onto the man's cabbage-patch-doll face.

The chair had edged closer to Jeremy's desk. The hand on Jeremy's arm remained.

"But I want you to know I'm here for you. If you ever need someone to talk to." Another shift closer, wood chair leg scraping across tile. "No one should have to face such stress alone."

Closer again, so much so that the teacher's pants rubbed against Jeremy's own.

At that point, Jeremy had shot up, mumbling, "Yeah, thanks, um, I gotta go." He'd fled to the bathroom, not only heeding the warrior woman's words of trusting his gut, but stuffing it as well.

As he savored the final bite of chocolaty peanut butter and contemplated digging for a nut bar, Jeremy hoped he hadn't misinterpreted the teacher's intention. He didn't know. Wasn't sure. Then again, the guy had rubbed Jeremy's thigh in the after-school meetings freshman year too. That was why Jeremy had ditched the tutoring sessions and ended up in summer school, but every time he played the encounter back, he construed it differently. What if it was nothing? He wished he could ask someone else's opinion, but he was far too embarrassed. Even with Tito.

His frustrating confusion tilted in favor of the nut bar, but as he grasped the bar from his backpack, someone entered the bathroom. Jeremy jumped, and his foot plopped from toilet seat to floor. At the same time the bell rang.

Jeremy kicked the toilet's flusher with his foot to mask the sound of crinkling candy wrappers being wadded up into his backpack. When he stepped out of the stall, one of the chocolate liners wafted to the floor.

He bent to retrieve it, face reddening from a combination of shame and exertion. The kid at the urinal, a junior basketball player Jeremy had seen around but never talked to, mumbled, "That candy bar someone else's fault too?"

Leaving the bathroom, the main compartment of his backpack still unzipped, Jeremy trudged toward history class. He tried to close the pocket on his way, but the zipper was stuck.

As he focused on the bag, his downward gaze caught a crowd of sneakers, and before he had a chance to look up, a throng of students knocked him over. He toddled backward and plopped onto the shoe-scuffed floor, his blubber softening the tailbone blow.

Calvin.

The backpack was less fortunate. It skidded across the floor, spilling the contents of the open compartment. Fruit-flavored candies, chocolate nut bars, and potato chips flew across the tile.

Calvin swept up the loot. "Whoa, Eating Bull, looks like you brought enough junk for everyone." With fists full of candy, he feigned confusion. "Oh, wait, my bad. Maybe this is all for you. Is fatty hungry? Fatty need a snack?"

Jeremy rose from the floor but not before wobbling a few times and having to yank his sweatshirt down over his belly. Laughter from the voyeuristic peanut gallery.

The backpack had landed next to a locker, but when Jeremy went to retrieve it and leave, thinking ignoring Calvin the best response (*how could he win?*), Calvin rushed him and shoved the nut bar into Jeremy's mouth, paper and all.

Kids laughed, and while Jeremy pushed at the hands that force-fed him, chants of, "Go Eating Bull go, go Eating Bull go," filled the hallway.

Held back by Calvin's cronies, Jeremy whipped his head from side to side to fend off the bag of chips Calvin now smashed against his face. He heard and felt the contents crunch against his skin.

"Go, Eating Bull, go. Go, Eating Bull, go..."

"Uh oh, watch out, he'll sue you."

"Cut it out, Calvin."

"Fatty want his chips?"

Voices all around, the sympathizers quashed by the assholes.

Finally, Jeremy batted the chips away, but not before tears sprang to his eyes.

Don't cry, you pussy. Don't cry.

A girl's command broke the fury. "Leave him alone or I'll get a teacher."

Lacey. Great. Rescued by the girl he liked. Just what Jeremy needed.

Further humiliation came in the form of Tito, calling for Calvin to back down.

"Oh, that's so sweet. The Freak Squad coming to fat-ass's defense. Talk about a great Dr. John show."

Bursts of laughter around him.

Where is that second bell when you need it?

Calvin started in on Tito's spots. Then he mooed at Lacey and rocked his pelvis back and forth. "Look," he said, pointing at Jeremy, his face a delighted sneer. "The fat fuck is crying."

Jeremy could not withstand another moment. Not one more second of the red-headed, douchebag prick. Something in him burst, an aneurysm storing a lifetime worth of abuse.

He yelled, "Nice Facebook undies, you pimply asshole. How's Courtney?"

The silence that followed curdled any additional comebacks from Jeremy. Tito darted off down the hall, shouting something about getting a teacher.

But then some kids behind Jeremy laughed, and a lanky student leaning against a locker said, "Good one, bro." Someone else said, "Yo, Calvin, you just got burned."

The bell rang, and the last of the lingering kids shuffled off, including Lacey, figuring the excitement over.

It wasn't over for Jeremy though. Calvin's face seemed to register something. He blinked a few times, his body blocking Jeremy's exit. His eyes narrowed, and his nostrils flared. He lunged at Jeremy and knocked him against a locker, the smashed metal echoing in the newly deserted hall. Calvin's knee dug into Jeremy's groin, igniting a wave of nausea. Jeremy thought he might puke.

Calvin pressed his full weight against Jeremy. "It was you, wasn't it? You sent that picture out. Made my life hell for a week."

Hell for a week? Try a lifetime. Jeremy said nothing, his legs trembling.

"I'll find out if you were behind this. You or your spotted friend. My old man's got a ton of connections in the police force. You're busted, lard-ass."

Calvin's upper torso leaned back while he scanned the hallway, but his knee dug deeper into Jeremy's groin. He released one hand and dug in his back pocket and pulled something out. A knife. The blade whipped open, its shine reflected by the overhead fluorescent light.

How he'd gotten the weapon past the metal detectors, Jeremy had no idea.

The switchblade scraped Jeremy's neck, and he understood how someone could piss themselves in fear.

"If I find out it was you, I swear to God, I'll cut you up into pieces, starting with your nuts and ending with your fat face."

Jeremy's airways collapsed, and he knew if he didn't get to his inhaler quickly, he'd end up back in the emergency room.

As Calvin started to say something else, the school's mousy, balding economics teacher fluttered down the hall. "Is there a problem here?"

With lightning speed, Calvin pocketed the knife. "No. No problem here, sir."

Jeremy could barely breathe let alone speak. He simply shook his head no. To do otherwise was to invite sure death.

Mr. Towner looked from Jeremy to Calvin and back to Jeremy. "Is that true, Jeremy?"

Jeremy could tell Mr. Towner longed for it to be true. Calvin towered over the diminutive teacher.

After a few failed attempts, sound materialized from Jeremy's mouth, a combination of wheezes and words. "Yeah, it's true. Lost track of time, that's all."

The trio went their separate ways, and Jeremy's next hour in history class passed in a heart-pounding blur. He dreaded the walk home. What if Calvin came after him? Jeremy would be alone since Mrs. Harris was still picking Tito up after school. Though Tito wouldn't admit it, Jeremy knew Mrs. Harris didn't want her son on the streets with his chubby friend. Too much risk. What if Mr. and Mrs. Harris discovered the Facebook fraud came from Tito's computer? They'd cut Jeremy out of their son's life for good.

Calvin's threat scared Jeremy, but not having a friend anymore?

That terrified him.

30

SUE

On the eighth of November, Sue and Kayla visited Dr. Riti Shah at the Pied Piper Pediatric Clinic. Posters of athletes, safe-driving guidelines, and an STD chart covered the exam room walls, but a balloon-wallpaper border hugging the paneled ceiling undermined the attempt at adolescent friendliness.

Sue knew the doctors' schedules were packed, so she'd requested an extra half-hour be tacked onto Kayla's general well visit that Friday afternoon. She hadn't wanted to surprise Dr. Shah with unplanned issues and cause the doctor to fall behind. The receptionist had obliged. In addition, the woman had shifted the appointment to the end of the day, thanks to a prior cancellation. "That way you'll have plenty of time to discuss the extra concerns."

Extra concerns. Plenty of those.

Sue suspected her blood pressure had risen five points in the last week alone. So much mother-daughter hostility.

Refocusing on Dr. Shah, Sue watched the woman add a final note to Kayla's electronic chart. "Sorry, we're switching to a new system. Haven't got the hang of it yet. Change is always difficult, don't you think, Kayla?"

The doctor's lilting accent soothed the tension in the room, at least enough to keep Kayla and Sue from stabbing each other with tongue depressors. Mother and daughter sat against the wall, opposite the pediatrician on her rolling stool.

"If you're referring to my mom's lawsuit against the world, that's not change. That's business as usual."

"I see." The doctor looked up from the laptop resting on the exam table beside her. She crossed a pair of plump legs beneath a flowing, flowery skirt and rested her hands on her thighs. "I suppose having a job as a public health nurse demands such involvement."

Kayla shrugged. "Whatever."

Long braided hair coiled around Kayla's head, secured in back by a silver barrette. Lavender eyeshadow colored her lids, and fake eyelashes plumped up nature's own design, an accessory to which Sue had first objected but eventually relented.

Choose your battles.

After a pause, Kayla added, "But that doesn't require taking fat kids out of their homes and suing restaurants on their behalf."

"Doesn't it?" the doctor asked, her body as still as the dead fly Sue spied under the woman's stool. "Sometimes we're forced into difficult situations because of our jobs."

Kayla gave another *whatever* look. Sue gripped the edge of her chair, willing herself to remain mute, the act akin to depriving a dehydrated man water.

"Unfortunately, what we have to do in our jobs can sometimes affect our home lives, as I imagine your mother's work has done to yours, but things smooth out over time, don't they? The last I read about the Juney Andrews case, the child has lost weight, and her health has improved. The paper said she may soon return to her family."

Sue nodded. The doctor was right. Life came in waves, and the Andrews wave seemed to be calming.

While the Jeremy wave swelled.

"I imagine a part of you is proud of your mother's accomplishments, yes?"

Although Sue anticipated another shrug or eye roll, Kayla surprised her by mumbling, "I suppose."

A velvety warmth enveloped Sue, and she fought the urge to give Kayla a hug. She knew her daughter was not ready for the affection, not after the icy stares, yelling, and name-calling that had erupted in the Fort home ever since Kayla had snuck out to be with Trey "T"

Devers. Sue had thought the chain-wearing dropout was out of the picture.

Having a missing daughter had invoked in Sue a pain like no other, even if only for a couple hours while Al tracked Kayla's cell phone to a party seventy minutes away, apparently at the home of Trey's friend. Sue's torturous thoughts had been all over the place, and she worried (incorrectly, as it turned out) her public actions had delivered her daughter into harm's way.

Dr. Shah brought Sue's ugly memory to a halt by standing up and clapping her hands together. "Now, how about I divide the two of you? I'll do Kayla's exam so she and I can chat, and then I'll meet alone with you, Mrs. Fort. Agreed?"

Directed back to the waiting room, Sue spent a few minutes responding to e-mails on her phone. Although Kayla's appointment was critical, Sue hated missing work. Interviews, depositions, and other public appearances related to the litigation already pulled her from the job, and she imagined Dr. Chen's patience had evaporated.

Bitterness over Al's absence from Kayla's appointment resurfaced.

"I can't possibly get away," he'd said, a phrase oft repeated in relation to doctor visits, teacher conferences, and school gatherings over the years.

Don't go there, Sue told herself, digging purple-painted nails into her palms while she watched a mother with a tear-streaked toddler check out at the counter. *This isn't Al's fault.*

Instead, Sue focused on what Kayla might be telling the doctor. "They're watching my every move. I'm a prisoner in my own home. My dad put a tracker on my phone, how crazy is that? They haven't even given T a chance."

Sue knew Kayla would say those things because Sue had listened to those words all week.

Twenty minutes later, Dr. Shah retrieved Sue from the waiting room. Mother and daughter exchanged places, Kayla taking up residence in the toy- and book-strewn area.

Back in the exam room and upon the doctor's prompting, Sue shared her concerns about Kayla's recent behaviors. "It's ironic, really. I spend my days helping children lose weight, yet I can't get my own daughter to eat. I'm worried she's developing a serious eating disorder."

Dr. Shah nodded in sympathy. "As you know, what Kayla and I

discussed is confidential, but she gave me permission to mention a few things to you. Her body mass index is seventeen point eight. That puts her at about the tenth percentile for her age, down from the twentieth where she used to fall. Not a dangerous zone, but we'll need to keep following it. I'll run some tests to make sure her nutritional status is okay."

Sue voiced her agreement.

Dr. Shah hesitated, rubbing her chin. "Mrs. Fort, what you're doing is great. You've managed to make people pay attention, which is no small feat in this inattentive world. Even if the lawsuit takes years or goes nowhere, you've at least got people talking. Believe me, I know how tempting food can be."

Sue flushed and thanked the woman. She hadn't expected the praise. Nor had she expected what followed.

"But I wonder if perhaps Kayla is feeling so out of control in her home life — having a mother who does so much for others — that she is exuding control the only way she can: through her eating."

Sue's natural inclination to fight kicked in. She started to protest, but Dr. Shah raised her hand. "Before you object, I am not blaming you. Fair or not, we both know mothers bear the brunt of their children's behavior, both in absorbing it and being held accountable for it."

Sue swallowed her planned words, their sting a choking glob in her throat. Instead, she said, "It will be better once the Dr. John Show is over. By then, a class-action suit might be on the table, and attention will shift from us. But I can't back away now. Not when we're gaining momentum."

"I'm not asking you to back away. Personally, I think you're a great role model for your daughter, and I suspect she does too. She's just not at an age to admit it. But I'm wondering if perhaps ... well, if perhaps in addition to Kayla seeing an eating-disorder therapist, some family counseling might be in order. At least until life calms down."

Family counseling.

The words cycled through Sue's mind in vicious repetition, leaving her disjointed and distracted while dropping Kayla off at home before heading back to the health department. Family counseling was for other people, not the Forts. Their name alone meant *strong* in French.

As in, the Forts can handle their own problems.

She idled at a red light at the corner of East Ninth and Superior, barely noticing the late afternoon traffic or the downtown pedestrians.

Family counseling.

When the light turned green, she tried to leave her self-pity at the intersection, but like her tires, her mind kept rolling, starting with Brent Johnson and their latest HIV-clinic encounter two days before.

"Well, if it isn't the queen of the buttinskies," he griped when she'd entered the room. Then he laughed, as if it was all in jest. "Oh, come on. You know I'm just messing with you. You can't help your busybody nature."

Sue had played tough at the time, repeating her practiced spiel. "Sometimes the individual must suffer at the hands of the greater good."

She might as well tattoo the phrase on her forehead.

Brent's ugly tone combined with the hate mail, the parking garage scare, Al's frustration with her, and Kayla's hatred of her, made the passing buildings and businesses of East Ninth Street blur into quivering masses.

A car horn startled her into awareness. Horrified, she discovered her Ford straddling the center line, cutting off a car in the left lane. She gave an apologetic wave, but when the man in the green Audi flipped her the bird, fresh tears fell, forcing a quick right turn into a bank parking lot.

After three nose-blowings and strategic eye-wiping to avoid smeared mascara (*thank God I'm not wearing Kayla's fake eyelashes*, Sue thought, barking a choked-off laugh, furious with herself for crying), her mobile rang. She checked the display. The health department's security office.

Unease twisted her belly. "Hello?"

"Yeah, Pete Michaels here. Wanted to let you know we just caught a guy lurking outside your office. Said he wanted to talk to you, but since it's after five and he seemed fishy to start with, we asked for his ID. Brent Johnson. He's one of the names you gave us after the parking lot incident, right?"

Sue confirmed he was, the knot in her stomach growing heavier than one of Shelly's weighted medicine balls.

"Didn't take much to make the guy squeal. He admits to scaring you in the parking lot but says he didn't have an actual gun. He also admitted to spray painting the slur on your car. The cops hauled him away. They'll hold him for a while for questioning. Should ease your mind a bit."

Sue thanked the guard and hung up.

Yes, Pete Michaels, it does ease my mind. More than you possibly know.

Exhaling heavily, she released a stale breath of anxiety, self-pity, and fear, cleansing her palate of all. Backing out of the bank, she drove the remaining few blocks to the health department.

Knowing the police had identified and arrested the man who had been threatening her would ease much of the burden in her life, including the tension with Al since her safety was his biggest concern. He no longer had to worry. And neither did she.

Her money had been on Tucker Andrews though. His anger had been so raw. Brent Johnson seemed more bark than bite.

Goes to show, you never really know the people around you.

Sue realized she should have asked Pete if Brent had tailed her car the night she had met the others for dinner at the Tell Tale Tavern. Probably just paranoia.

Back in her office, the partitioned suite empty, its staff gone for the day, Sue saw her voicemail light blinking. No surprise there.

A call from Mark Swanson dampened some of her earlier relief. The sanitarian, whose son Sue was convinced was bullying Jeremy, said he needed to speak with her. He sounded ticked-off. Sue put him in the he'll-call-back-if-he-needs-me file.

The next call nearly made her tumble out of her seat.

Terry Harjo.

Or so the man claimed. Saying he would like to speak with Sue and asking for a call back.

She rustled items on her desk, looking for a pen. With trembling fingers, she scribbled Terry's number on a sticky note as he recited the digits. His monotonous cadence was so eerily similar to Jeremy's it made the hair on her scalp tingle.

Frozen in her chair, pen still clutched in her fingers, Sue barely registered the next message: Dr. Chen requesting her in his office should she arrive before seven p.m.

Terry Harjo. Calling her.

According to Connie, she had never told him she was pregnant. He couldn't know about Jeremy. Had he recognized them on the news and contacted Sue, unable to reach Connie directly? (*Thank God for that.*)

Had he seen a resemblance? Was he doing some math and calculating dates?

Sue shook her head. No. She couldn't deal with it. One thing at a time, and if she wanted to keep her job, seeing her boss should be first. She replayed Dr. Chen's message. Like Mark Swanson, he did not sound happy.

Ascending one flight to the third level, she dragged herself down the deserted hallway to the director's office suite, low-heeled pumps clunking on the hard floor, mouth caking with every step.

Relax, Sue. He's not going to fire you.

When she reached the director's suite, she hesitated, surprised to see the door ajar. A keypad secured each of the offices, keeping the staff areas off limits to the public. A rule, not a suggestion. Why had Dr. Chen been lax?

Sue knocked. No answer. She pushed open the door and peeked inside. Given his office was behind another door beyond the secretary's desk, Sue couldn't tell if her boss was around or not.

She crossed the small space to his door.

"Dr. Chen? It's Sue. I got your message." She tapped a tentative knock, the door slightly ajar like the main entrance. No sound from behind it.

She slowly pushed the door open and stepped inside. "Dr. Chen? I—"

The words caught in her throat. She choked and almost vomited. She blinked, not believing — or understanding — the images her eyes sent her brain. Her hands flew to her mouth, and she stumbled back, falling against the wall, the light switch stabbing her flank.

There, seated at his desk, head lolled back and expression wide-eyed and full of shock, rested an eviscerated Dr. Chen, his intestines ripped from their cavity and piled grotesquely on top of an open pizza box. Around the bloody, yellow, fat-covered viscera coiled the crusts of the man's last meal.

Taped to the director's chest was a note, unreadable at that distance. Sue willed herself to step closer, her mind still shocked beyond comprehension. She squinted and read.

"Karmic justice not court justice will end your gluttonous hypocrisy."

For several seconds Sue couldn't move, couldn't react, couldn't breathe.

Oh, God. This is my fault. This is my doing. The killer knows about the lawsuit.

And then reality dawned. Brent Johnson. He killed Dr. Chen, and then he planned on killing her. That's why he'd been outside her office..

Oh God, dear God.

Sue bolted out of the room, knocking over a tall potted plant on her way. She burst out of the office suite and ran toward the stairwell and down to security.

She had to tell them. She had to tell them not to set the killer free.

31

DARWIN

Sleep eluded him. His internal clock told him Friday had become Saturday. One a.m.? Two a.m.? He flipped to one side, then the other. Just when he found comfort, an ill-defined ache jarred him awake. He hadn't intended to kill the man. At least not then, but the opportunity was there. His knife at the ready.

It was a good kill.

Was that him or The Voice? Darwin tried to discern, but the fog of near sleep muddled his attempt. So out of sorts. Everything coming together. So quickly. Perhaps too quickly. The manifesto was nearly complete. His message to the world. An invitation to like-minded citizens. Some would be followers. Others, leaders. A few elite souls might even share his discipline and replicate his actions.

Darwin kicked to loosen the thin blanket, his feet on fire.

So much clutter in his brain.

So many sheep in the world.

Gossiping about lawsuits when they should be reining in their lustful eating. Lustful eating that led to his knife.

Watch out foolish sheep, I am here.

The doctor had discovered what happened to a hypocrite, one surrounded by plaques and photos of good deeds done in the name of public health, all while sending conflicting messages with his weak and gluttonous ways.

Left side. Right side. Flat on his back. Comfort would not come. Only the comfort of knowing it was a good kill.

The director had opened the door to him as Darwin knew he would. Simply a concerned citizen wanting to bend the man's ear. The whale even offered a slice of the slimy pizza, as if Darwin would ever succumb to such filth.

Darwin had already donned the gloves before entering, hiding his hands in his pockets. The urge to kill was too great and the opportunity so readily available. From his long side pocket, he whipped out the knife, quick to unsheathe it, and like a stealth panther, he pounced across the room in one smooth motion. Such was his discipline. Such was his strength.

Darwin replayed the look of shock on the fat glutton's face when the shiny blade sliced his pendulous gut, knife burying deeper and deeper with each thrust. The slicing open. The stab to the heart to stop the man's fight. The withdrawal of the weeping intestines, slippery in his gloved hands as he dumped the fatty coils in the pizza box where they belonged.

Too soon for a kill.

His thoughts. Not The Voice. Where was he?

But it was a good kill. Relevant to their cause. There would be no further dispute of their mission, not by the police nor by the public.

As always, the kill had calmed him, though at the moment, his restless slumber argued otherwise.

They can't prove it was me. Can't make that connection.

If only The Voice would confirm, but he remained silent, the absent guidance creating the maelstrom Darwin's brain had become.

Surely he would approve. Surely everything would proceed as planned. He had to hold it together a bit longer. He could do that. He was a killer with a cause.

Dallas was only two weeks away.

32

JEREMY

There were two things Jeremy knew with certainty: he would never be skinny and his grandfather would never leave the house. It appeared that on one of those counts, he was about to be proved wrong.

"Admiring your guns does me little good," George said. "If you really want to show them off, let's go shoot."

George had stopped by that Saturday afternoon while Connie was out running errands. He was now coaxing GI Dick to the back door, just off the house's seventies-style kitchen where Jeremy was putting the finishing touches on a turkey sandwich. Whole-wheat bread, low-cal mustard, one tomato slice, two pickles, spinach leaves, hold the mayo and cheese. The Fat Slayers would be proud. Unlike at his clinic appointment two days prior where he'd lost an unimpressive two pounds thanks to his recent dietary sins.

"Jeremy, you have to get off this roller-coaster," Gabrielle, the dietitian, had said.

"She's right. The only up and down we want to see is you exercising." Shelly had mimicked biceps curls and marched in place to make her point.

Jeremy had merely nodded, not wanting to admit to Fat Slayer Shelly he still hadn't made it through her entire circuit workout, though he suspected she knew.

The scale doesn't lie.

But he would do better. He would. His mother had essentially renovated the kitchen from a fast-food grease pit to an organic hippy farm, and if he wanted to save more money for souvenirs from Dallas, he had to banish the after-school junk-food hauls.

George's foot held the back door open. "Come on. Imagine Connie's surprise when she gets home," he said.

GI Dick ran the back of a hairy hand across his mouth, face long, eyes hang dog. His other hand opened and closed into a fist by his side, and he rocked back and forth on his boots. "Oh, I don't know, Georgie Boy. It's been a lot of years now. Too many."

Over the last several weeks, George and Dick had become tight. They both liked attention to detail, and Jeremy had no doubt GI Dick thought George was far more of a man than his own fat pussy of a grandson. *But George would have to be God himself to get the old man outside,* Jeremy thought.

"If not your daughter, think of how happy it would make Karen. You think she would have wanted to see you suffer like this?"

Jeremy froze in his spot at the kitchen table, sandwich halted halfway to his lips. From his position, he had a perfect view of Dick and George at the door. He watched the blood drain from his grandfather's face, as if George were a vampire who'd just taken a bite.

Connie and Jeremy knew better than to mention his grandmother's name. George did not.

To Jeremy's continued amazement, however, GI Dick gave a shaky nod, regained some of his facial hue, and mumbled, "Yeah, suppose you're right."

The sandwich plopped to Jeremy's plate. He watched George open the door and help his grandfather step out onto the concrete steps. Once they were out of his view range, Jeremy leaped up, his large thigh banging the table, scraping the metal legs across the floor. He hustled to the window where he saw GI Dick at the top of the small stairwell, gripping the wrought-iron guardrail.

"Holy cow." Jeremy pressed a mustard-stained palm against the window.

Although his grandpa took no additional steps, the act rendered Jeremy incapable of further speech. The old man stood on the cement slab for five minutes, face turned toward the gray Cleveland sky, the fall breeze rustling the collar of his flannel shirt.

When they returned, Dick mounted the small step that landed him back in the kitchen and collapsed to the chair with the torn plastic upholstery. It made a farting noise when his bottom landed, but Jeremy was too stunned to laugh.

"You did it, Grandpa," he said, half of his sandwich still on his plate, a miracle in and of itself.

"I did it." Dick glanced Jeremy's way and gave a half smile. "I did it."

It didn't take long for the atmosphere to return to normal, but a feeling of "anything's possible" lingered within Jeremy nonetheless, even when George and Dick steered the conversation back to guns.

"I could take you out, show you my old service rifle. That baby's still got some kick. Got my service revolver, of course, and my Beretta semi-automatic .380 too."

"Now you're talking," George said, leaning against the window near Jeremy's mustard stain. "I want you to step outside every day. Maybe by next weekend, you and I will go out to the field not far from my place and take some practice shots."

Jeremy thought George was getting ahead of himself. Standing on the doorstep wasn't the same as going out for target practice, but apparently his grandpa disagreed.

"Damn right. A man's gotta protect himself, after all. Especially with some whack job on the loose. Killing fat people. Christ, what's next?" GI Dick's color returned to its ashen shade of normal.

"Tell me about it. The last man killed was the director of the health department." George went to the fridge and poured a glass of Connie's latest nutrient juice. He offered Jeremy a cup, but Jeremy shook his head. Green beverages crossed his no-can-do line. "It's a zoo over there with the crime scene. Shut down all non-essential services. Told us to stay away for the time being."

"That's some crazy shit, I tell ya," Dick said. "Shredded the guy to bits. Lot easier to take 'em out with a gun."

Jeremy chewed the last bite of his sandwich, the topic of conversation hardly inviting peaceful digestion. "I thought they caught the guy," he said, washing the dough down with a swig of skim milk. Given the killings, he was even more worried about having his chubby mug splattered all over the news.

The warrior woman had it worse though. In keeping her promise, she had deflected much of the heat from Jeremy and Connie by putting the spotlight on herself.

Then her boss got murdered. Cause and effect? Coincidence? Jeremy didn't know, but such a horrible find had to dent even the toughest warrior's resolve.

"They had a person of interest. Doesn't mean they caught the guy," Dick said, digging a finger in his ear.

"Tough time to be a celebrity, huh, Jeremy?" George offered a sympathetic look.

"Your lawsuit probably pisses the bastard off. Makes him want to polish off a few more fatties," Dick said.

Pushing his chair back with more force than intended, Jeremy stood and dumped his plate in the sink, his mind visualizing the king-sized chocolate bar hidden beneath his mattress.

"Connie said Sammy wants that reporter guy, Tony, to do another interview with you to get the facts straight, keep the case separate from the killings."

Jeremy nodded at George.

But were they separate?

"Tony, huh? That guy's got a crush on your mom." Dick spoke to Jeremy but smiled at George. "You got some competition, Georgie. Bet that guy can really sniff out a story. Ha. Get it? Cause his nose is so big?"

While Jeremy left the two of them laughing at Dick's dumb joke, he wondered, with a sinking feeling, what they said about him behind *his* back.

The best way to get his mind off food was to distract it with something else. So, after his grandfather's miraculous outdoor feat and the unsavory talk of killers, Jeremy decided to walk to Tito's house, thereby making both of the Fat Slayers happy by passing on his candy bars and getting some exercise.

Win win. Advance to the next level.

A cold wind whipped the air, slapping the blue windbreaker against his heft. Jeremy enjoyed its bite. Hands down, fall was his favorite season.

A call to the Harris home would have been wise, but lately, Tito rambled off all sorts of excuses why Jeremy couldn't come over. Facing his friend head on would prevent Mr. and Mrs. Harris from keeping Jeremy away.

Or so he thought.

Upon finding her son's friend on the doorstep in front of the mani-cured yard, Mrs. Harris pulled the side hems of her cardigan together. Whether fending off chilly air or hiding displeasure, Jeremy didn't know.

"Oh, Jeremy, hello. Was Tito expecting you?"

"Um, no, I was out walking and—"

"Mom, who is it?" Tito bolted down the stairs with a speed Jeremy could only imagine. "Jeremy! Good to see you."

Jeremy smiled. At least it wasn't Tito who didn't want him around.

As he remained outside, Mrs. Harris not yet inviting him in, lines of uncertainty etching her face, Mr. Harris came in from the kitchen, a cup of coffee in his hand.

After a brief hesitation, he said, "Jeremy. Come in. We need to have a chat."

Jeremy stepped inside, his legs two pillars of jelly.

"Dad, come on, don't—"

Mr. Harris held up a hand and cut Tito off. He directed Jeremy and Tito to the charcoal sofa. Mr. and Mrs. Harris took the matching love seat.

Jeremy wiped moist palms against his sweatpants. He watched Mr. Harris set his mug on the coffee table, remove his glasses, wipe them on his fleece sweater, and return them to their rightful roost.

Finally, the man said, "Jeremy, we recently learned Tito was involved in fraudulent Facebook activity. He then circulated embar-rassing photos of another boy. His mother and I are extremely disap-pointed, and Tito has been appropriately punished. He claims it was all his doing, that you weren't involved, but..."

Jeremy bit the inside of his lip and looked at Tito. His friend's expression was fierce, and a subtle shake of his head implied Jeremy was to keep his mouth shut.

Before Jeremy could admit any complicity, Tito belted out, "I told you, it was me and me alone. Jeremy had nothing to do with it. He's got enough going on. He's not about to tick off the school bully."

Jeremy kept his gaze on Tito. He couldn't let his friend take the blame. What kind of person did that? But Tito's nonverbal pleading spoke volumes. He wanted Jeremy to stay out of it.

"Were you involved, Jeremy?" Mr. Harris's question was firm, not accusatory.

"I, um..."

Tito jumped off the sofa. "I told you he wasn't! But if you keep pressuring him, he'll say he was in order to help me. 'Cause that's the kind of friend Jeremy is."

A quiver in Jeremy's jaw made him bite down until his chin ached. He knew he should speak up, but Tito was obviously protecting him. Probably worried about the fallout should the public discover Eating Bull was a cyberbully.

Jeremy. A bully. The irony was almost funny. Almost.

Mr. Harris pressed his hands together and brought them to his lips. He studied Jeremy as if he were a bug under a microscope. When Mr. Harris spoke, it was with a slight tremor. "Son, it's difficult for me to say this — you've been a good friend to Tito — but, well, we think it would be best if you two didn't see each other for a while. Not in person, not by phone, not by e-mail, not by anything."

Mrs. Harris nodded slightly, lifting her gaze from her slippers. She continued for her husband. "You have so much publicity around you right now, honey. We don't want Tito caught up in it. Not with all the negative attention, the threats against you, the ... the murders." Her voice hitched. "Tito is all we have left."

Jeremy barely registered anything after that. He wanted out of the house, out of its stifling atmosphere. His hand dived for his pocket. The inhaler was there.

Fighting tears, he mumbled something about understanding, said an inadequate goodbye to Tito, and stumbled his way out of their house. Both Tito and Mrs. Harris called after him.

His pace as he trotted home was one Fat Slayer Shelly would celebrate. Two blocks passed before he had to lean against a tree and use his inhaler. With his head resting against the bark, he waited for the medicine to take effect.

Fat Slayer Gabrielle was right. His life was a roller coaster. Up one minute, thinking he might be able to conquer the fat thing and make a difference for others. Down the next, thinking what a fool he was for even trying.

A big fat joke, that was what he was. Always buried by the same crap. Always the same hungry hole crying to be fed.

Anger and hurt welled within him as he pushed away from the tree and resumed the rest of the walk home. A soda can littered the sidewalk. He kicked the aluminum canister so hard it smacked the hood of a parked car across the street.

The more he walked the more frustrated he became. He started to run, chest heaving, airway tight. He didn't care. In his mind, he channeled Kajika, his powerful, braided shaman. If only he could be him. Sleek, strong, and brave, his muscled body navigating Nature's terrain like one of her children.

But he was only Jeremy. Fat, wheezing, fatherless Jeremy.

33

SUE

Pregnant clouds blackened the sky, giving the illusion of evening, but Sue knew many hours of strain and uncertainty stretched before her. Given the recent circumstances, howling wind and torrential rain seemed only natural.

Seated in Sammy's office on Tuesday morning, she waited for him to begin. The lawyer stood behind the cherry desk. Facing him were Sue, Connie, and Tony, while Jeremy slouched off to the side in a chair far too narrow for his hips. As usual, the teen wore sweatpants, and Sue longed for the day she would see him in a simple pair of jeans.

Sammy had summoned the group together. They needed to get things back on track, and Tony would help them do that. There was too much speculation on the public's part that the murder of the health director five days prior was a result of the litigation.

Thoughts of Dr. Chen made Sue's throat constrict and her stomach swirl. Her normally talkative hands rested on her tailored trousers.

Tony came prepared, notepad balanced on his right thigh and a recording device gripped in his left fist. Old school and focused. Sue liked that about him.

Still standing, Sammy said, "Thanks for coming. I realize you're missing work and/or school, but I felt it urgent we connect." He glanced at Connie and added, "I hope Jonathan didn't give you a hard time about missing work. I know he runs a tight ship."

That's putting it mildly, Sue thought.

Bringing up the media's response to the murder, Sammy moved on. "We had a bit of a lull yesterday, thanks to Veteran's Day, but today we'll get hit from all sides, much more than we did Saturday and Sunday when reporters were still scrambling for details. My phone has been ringing nonstop. Janine and Reggie can barely keep up."

As if to prove his point, a phone rang in the reception area, Janine's greeting muffled by the closed office door.

Sammy undid the lower button of his dark gray suit and sat behind the desk. His salt-and-pepper hair matched the sky outside the window. The damp climate triggered an ache in Sue's knees, an association Al balked at whenever she mentioned it.

Oh, Al, I think I've pushed you too far with this one. Her hands remained limp in her lap.

Sammy expressed his condolences to Sue one more time over the loss of her boss. She bit her lower lip to keep it from trembling.

As if reading her thoughts, Sammy said, "His death is not on you. It's only on the sick bastard who did this, pardon my French. The media is tying it all together though, and the health department is getting sucked into something it hadn't signed up for."

Sammy had that right. The CCPHC staff were jittery and anxious, a mood confirmed by the few personnel Sue had encountered at the mandatory gathering the day before, which included her, the health department's PR team, media spokesperson, attorney, security members, and interim health director, Dr. Nada Hasan, an internist who had never warmed to Sue in the past, and vice versa. Sue had felt the fingers pointed at her back, though none of her colleagues overtly blamed her.

Sammy's gaze zeroed in on Tony. "That's why we need you. As a reporter, I want you to make it clear this murdering psychopath is not tied to the lawsuit in any way."

Tony laughed. "I can't skew my story because you want me to. I'm all for getting the facts out, but I won't fudge any unknowns. How can you be sure the two are unrelated?"

A muscle clenched in Sammy's jaw. He straightened his desk blotter. Before he could respond, Connie said, "The murders started before Sue approached us with her litigation plans."

"True." Tony's stance softened as he looked at Connie. "But we can't say for sure the killer isn't fueled by the lawsuit. His hatred of overweight people is obvious."

Sue finally put her hands to use and massaged her temples. "I can't believe we're even having this conversation. It's so surreal." She glanced at Jeremy to make sure he was okay, but he just sat there, gaze on his laceless sneakers. She knew he was listening though. Teenagers heard much more than they let on.

"Well, we *are* having this conversation, and although I won't sensationalize the killings or insinuate there's a connection, I will report any facts." Tony still hadn't flipped on the recording device, and for that Sue was grateful.

Sammy extended his neck and stared at the ceiling. "Well, can you at least put the emphasis on the lawsuit? For example, three other law firms are joining our suit, all in Ohio. One in Chicago is close to jumping on board too." Sammy returned his gaze to midline. "That will make it a class-action suit, and once that takes off, more plaintiffs will join. Food and beverage manufacturers will feel the squeeze. I have the other lawyers' names and numbers. I'll give you the info when we're done."

"Are there other kids involved?" Jeremy asked, all heads turning to him.

"So far the other plaintiffs are adults," Sammy said.

"See? We won't be alone anymore, Jeremy." Connie smiled at her son.

The rain finally made its appearance, first in pattering droplets, then in a noisy downpour. The rhythmic hammering of the windows put Sue in a sleepy but restless state. She listened to Sammy drone on.

"Recent polls show the majority of respondents, sixty-three percent, think the lawsuit is baseless, but that leaves thirty-seven percent who think it's a good thing or aren't sure, a greater percentage than I ever expected." Sammy leaned forward, his distinguished face flushed. "We need to spotlight these numbers. We need to highlight the evidence of the addictive quality of food and the food manufacturers' role in it. Yes, the individual is ultimately responsible, no question about that, but society also has a role. That's what I want you to emphasize, Tony. I'm not asking you to skew a story. I'm asking you to quote me to get my point across, including my belief the recent murders have nothing to do with our litigation."

Sue saw Tony tense at Sammy's tone, and although she agreed with the attorney, she knew Tony would never spin a story on anyone's behalf.

Connie put a hand on the reporter's forearm. His expression eased. "If anything, these murders show how horribly our country treats overweight people. You can help get that point across. Please, don't make it harder for Jeremy. My boy has nothing to do with those poor people dying." Tony merely nodded, prompting Connie to add, "Besides, they caught the guy."

"They have a suspect, but they have no evidence he's the killer," Tony said. "He might have been in the right place at the wrong time. They've since released him."

"Brent Johnson." A crack of thunder swallowed Sue's words. She repeated the name. "He was a patient who had been threatening me for other reasons. Nothing to do with the litigation, and he'll be charged with that. But as much as I'd like to think the police have their man, after further thought, I think it's unlikely. Plus, the police didn't find a weapon on him or anything in his home to implicate him. So, unfortunately, I think the killer's still out there."

Rain pelted the window, drowning out even Janine's ringing phones. Despite the thick wool sweater, Sue could not shake her chill.

The rest of the discussion focused on specifics for the article, including the upcoming trip to Dallas for the Dr. John Show taping which was in eleven days.

Sue's mind wandered. She closed her eyes and sighed when she realized she still hadn't told Connie about Terry Harjo being out of jail. Or his phone call.

One mind-blowing thing at a time.

A text message disrupted Sue's rumination. Dr. Nada Hasan. "I'm sorry," she told the group. "It's nearly eleven, and I have to get back. The new boss wants to meet with me."

"Is she fat?" Jeremy asked.

Returning her phone to her purse, Sue looked at Jeremy in confusion. "No."

"Good," he said.

After a brief pause, Sue understood Jeremy's implication. His expression of relief mirrored her own.

Back at the health department, just before noon, Sue learned Dr. Hasan was in a meeting, so she caught up on work in her office while she waited. She assumed the interim director wanted to discuss the department's response to Dr. Chen's murder.

A call from the children's hospital interrupted her work on a grant proposal. To her surprise, Dr. Sneeker from the emergency room was on the line.

They greeted each other and made small talk, after which Dr. Sneeker said he wanted to know how things were going with Jeremy. He'd been worried about the boy since the last asthma attack and hoped the media attention and the recent murder weren't causing too much stress. "I stopped by the health department recently for another matter. I tried to see you, but you weren't in at the time."

"Sorry to have missed you, but as you know, my days have been a bit ... chaotic." Sue appreciated the doctor's concern. "Jeremy is good. He's much stronger than he first appears."

Dr. Sneeker agreed. He asked about the Dr. John Show, and as Sue relayed the taping details, relieved to have something upbeat to discuss, a shadow crossed her cubicle's partition. She looked up and saw Mark Swanson.

Super. How long has he been there?

After tying up the conversation with Dr. Sneeker, Sue disconnected and straightened some papers on her desk. Fidgeting with her row of earrings, she invited the sanitarian to sit down in one of her colleagues' chairs. He refused and got right to the point.

"Your fat boy is messing with my son. He and his little friend set up a fake Facebook account, drew out my boy, and got him to post embarrassing photos of himself. They sent those pictures out to a bunch of kids. Put my son through the wringer."

From what Sue had intuited from Jeremy, the only wringer that bully had been through was that of his father's. "I don't know what you're talking about. That doesn't sound like Jeremy. Did he admit to it?"

Mark, still standing, kicked a clump of mud from his boot to the carpet. "Nope. The friend said the fat turd had nothing to do with it, but I know he's lying."

"And what do you want me to do?" Sue asked, her voice a taut violin string. If indeed Jeremy had been involved, then she would do nothing but root for him.

"I don't want you to do a damn thing. Just keep that fat kid of yours from picking on my son. Otherwise he'll be sorry."

Sue bolted up, ignoring the climate-induced ache in her knees. "If you call Jeremy 'fat' one more time, I'll report you for harassment. Jeremy is a good kid, one who's had far too many obstacles in his way. I doubt he did anything to your son that your son didn't deserve."

Mark Swanson twitched his nose and gripped his belt on either side, making Sue wonder if he intended to pull the leather strap off and beat her with it. Instead of backing down, she stepped closer, her height almost equal to his. After her pathetic paralysis with Brent Johnson in the parking lot, she refused to be intimidated.

Finally, Mark fumed something about her and Jeremy needing to watch themselves and then left the office suite.

Sue retreated to her desk and leaned against its metal siding. Before she could make sense of her co-worker's hostility, her phone rang again. Dr. Hasan's secretary said the director was ready to see her. Sue exhaled and headed over.

Until the crime scene was cleared (and cleaned), a spare conference room served as Dr. Nada Hasan's office. Her desk consisted of a long table, on top of which rested a computer, a printer, and the usual papers, pens, and office supplies. Given its temporary status, no decorations or other furniture embellished the room, save for a gray file cabinet in the corner and a few framed black-and-white prints of Cleveland on the wall. Dr. Hasan, a woman with remarkably line-free skin for her early fifties, sat behind the computer.

The new boss dived right in. "This lawsuit of yours is drawing too much attention. Reporters from all over the country have called me, wanting to know if Dr. Chen was killed because of what the health department is doing. Convincing them it's not the health department suing the industries, but rather a lone culprit, has been difficult."

Culprit?

"And the crime scene has created a horrible spectacle, not to mention rampant anxiety among our colleagues." Dr. Hasan's speech pattern rose in both pitch and volume. "And then there's the public. We are a health department, for goodness' sake. People need to trust us."

The woman paused to catch her breath. She smoothed her dark, shoulder-length hair.

Sue jumped in. "I understand how difficult this is. Believe me, I'm sick about Dr. Chen's death. He was a good man." Her words hitched, but she continued. "The newspaper plans to publish a follow-up story on us so I can set the record straight, distance the litigation from the health department and these horrible killings. Make sure—"

"This has to stop, Sue."

Sue protested. "Surely as a public health practitioner you understand intervention has to happen at multiple levels to make any real change happen. Think about tobacco, lead toxicity, the drop in motor vehicle deaths after mandatory seatbelt laws. Individual behavior alone didn't solve those problems. It took—"

"Sue, please, stop. This lawsuit is keeping you from your duties, and the attention is too great." Dr. Hasan folded her hands together and rested them on the table. "We have to suspend you."

Sue stared at the woman, thinking she must have misheard. "What? I'm fired?"

"No, no. Not fired. Suspended. Until the situation calms down. No need to pack up your things. We'll reassess in a few weeks' time."

A few weeks' time?

Sue barely registered the woman's subsequent apologies and explanations. Something within her knew she should fight, but between Dr. Chen's death and Dr. Hasan's news, all her combat skills seemed to have vanished, the last of them used up on Mark Swanson. She left the interim director's makeshift office disoriented and trembling. She barely remembered getting into her car and driving home, thoughts vacillating between throwing in the towel and standing on her feet for another round.

Her hands gripped the steering wheel. Her world was crumbling. Maybe it was best to back down. Let someone else take over. Maybe Al was right.

A tiny voice welled within her. *Did Rosa Parks give in? Or Susan B. Anthony?*

Well-behaved women seldom make history. Isn't that what they said?

When Sue finally arrived home, a mass of reporters waited in her driveway, their vans blocking her access and forcing her to park in the street. As she made her way to the house, microphones besieged her, and eager faces peppered her with questions.

"Ms. Fort, is it true your boss was killed because you're suing the food industry?"

"Ms. Fort, do you feel responsible for Dr. Chen's death?"

"Do you think the Fat Killer will strike again?"

Sue stumbled her way to the door, fumbling for her house key, trying to drown out the escalating discord. If only Al was home. Then again, she hoped he and Kayla had not had to witness the mayhem.

Finally, she pushed her way in, slammed the door behind her, and leaned against its support.

Breathe. Just breathe.

She stood there motionless for several seconds before moving to the kitchen, her refuge, hoping to escape the circus noise from the front yard. She plopped her large purse on the center island and spotted a note on the table.

She walked to retrieve it.

Read it.

And dropped to the floor, a blinking mass of disbelief and despair.

The note said Al had taken Kayla to stay with his sister to get away from the mess. He would be back that night, but only out of his duty as a husband to protect his wife.

But if Sue didn't "let this crap go," she could consider herself a single woman.

34

DARWIN

There was no wind, no cold, no swooping birds, no smelly, polluted air. He easily tuned those elements out. Only his rhythmic breathing and steady heart rate registered, his cardiac chambers pumping at eighty percent of maximum for the past seven miles.

For running, Darwin preferred the Ohio Towpath to the city side-walks, especially in the evening or late in the season when there were fewer undisciplined sheep blocking his path. Pathetic, overweight masses walking at a snail's pace while thrusting salty fingers into bags of chips and gulping down twenty-ounce bottles of soda, as if nature must be accompanied by snacking.

The Towpath biking trail extended more than eighty miles from Cleveland on down, through parks and wooded habitats. Upon completion, the path would extend an extra twenty miles to New Philadelphia. For Darwin, its scenic trails made for an efficient running path.

On that Friday evening, save for a few cyclists braving the cold, the trail was deserted. To an undisciplined person, the dark sky and the isolation might prove frightening.

But not for Darwin.

With his thumb, he pressed the illumination button on the wrist band of his heart-rate monitor, the movement awkward with running limbs and sweaty fingers. Still on target. He checked it again to make sure. And then again.

He made himself stop looking. *Discipline*, he chanted in his mind.

He understood his intrusive, obsessive thoughts and compulsions were a test of his discipline. In others, such acts signaled weakness, illness even, but he knew his urges were a test to overcome, and he had performed well. His daily interactions with people required enormous discipline. He had to withhold all thoughts and impulses that might make those around him cast a wary gaze, or worse, approach him in concern. So far, his veneer had not cracked other than an occasional uninvited comment about his preoccupied demeanor.

He could not deny that until the killings, there were times he thought he would become trapped within his own head, unable to meet the daily requirements demanded in professional and social interactions. Then The Voice had directed him to a new outlet, and despite his mental faltering the night of the health director's killing, his thoughts slipping over his gray matter like wet feet on a slick floor, he had once again gained control. He was in command. A man whose mission was close to reaching its pinnacle.

Darwin checked his heart-rate monitor. Seventy-five percent of maximum. Wiping sweat from his face with the back of his hand (less contamination that way), he picked up the pace. As he rounded a bend in the path, a gust of wind nearly stole his breath. He coughed and sputtered, but within seconds he reclaimed his dominance over the environment.

At first, he worried The Voice would punish him for acting impulsively with the director, but once he saw the police and public had finally connected the dots, he praised Darwin for recognizing an opportunity and seizing it.

(*Planning is critical to any mission, but sometimes one must think on his feet and act.*)

The Voice's approval helped elevate Darwin, helped him maintain his ties with the necessary parties without drawing suspicion. Given the pivotal act happening in one week, that interaction remained crucial, and the timing was perfect. All over the country, reports of the serial killer targeting fat people sprouted, and the link to litigation against food industries was thought to be indisputable. The fact the case metamorphosed into the beginnings of a class-action suit drew even more attention to the cause.

What the nurse do-gooder and her lawyer did not understand, however, was the cause was not theirs. The cause was Darwin's, and soon, that cause would be televised for all.

The manifesto was ready. Short and succinct as all messages should be. Such was Darwin's discipline.

"Utopia is a hard-fought destination. The disciplined will survive. The weak will perish. Only then can we reclaim our country where only the fittest can thrive. Join me, my brothers and sisters. Follow my lead. Take action into your own disciplined hands. Together we will rid our country of the obese, ignorant masses."

Despite his exertion, Darwin recited that part of his *magnum opus* aloud, his choppy, breathy words carried away by the wind.

Another check of the monitor. Eighty-three percent. Limbs flying, arms pumping, his pace accelerated more. He was invincible. Nothing could stop him.

In one week, the boy and his accomplices would meet with the Dr. John team. Darwin had gleaned the information from their loose tongues. His presence would surprise them, but they would not turn him away. He had a vested interest, after all. Prior to and during the pre-taping on Friday, he would scope out the premises, find the security weaknesses, learn what he would be up against. The Voice would guide him.

On Saturday, during the taping in front of a live audience, albeit one located in another building, he would kill the boy.

The boy had to go first. Depending on events, it might be the only shot Darwin would get. He hated having to use a gun. His knife had served him well. Anyone could fire a gun, but there were logistics to consider.

Then, if fate was on his side (*and why wouldn't it be?*), he would kill the nurse, end her blaming ways once and for all.

And then the mother.

Followed by the lawyer.

For a moment, confusion seized him. His pace slowed, and his feet faltered. He nearly stumbled on the dirt path.

(*Focus, Darwin. They are all enemies. No matter that the nurse and lawyer are fit and strong. No matter that the mother has shed her pounds of gluttony. They have chosen their side. They have supported the weak. Their deaths will serve as a lesson to all.*)

Darwin nodded, regaining his speed, though a check of the heart-rate monitor showed an extra mile of running would be required as punishment for his temporary weakness.

(*You will be a hero. Maybe even a martyr. You know it may come to that. After next week, your life will change, no longer being the one you know.*)

Again Darwin nodded.

He understood.

As all masters do.

35

____

JEREMY

In one of his fat-clinic sessions with Dr. Green, the psychologist had told Jeremy everybody differed in their food response to stress. Some people stuffed their faces, while others forgot to eat. Dr. Green also told Jeremy to quit saying fat clinic. "You need to respect yourself. When you do, others will too."

Jeremy was pretty sure he'd never command respect, and he was damn sure he'd never forget to eat. Especially with so much going on. Lately the world felt like a giant pinball machine, his fat body bumping and flipping from one life turd to the next.

Oops, make that my overweight *body.*

Although he'd known the Dr. John Show would arrive, the idea of appearing before millions of people hadn't sunk in. At least not until he found himself in an airplane, thousands of feet in the air, on the Wednesday afternoon before the taping.

He looked out the tiny airplane window. His first time flying. He should be excited, especially since he was escaping Calvin, though thankfully the bully hadn't repeated his threat with the knife.

Probably doesn't want his own ass in the limelight.

Jeremy had never traveled farther than Philadelphia, and that was years ago when his grandmother had been alive and GI Dick hadn't yet mutated into a rabid housecat with a bad back.

A part of him looked forward to the experience. Maybe he'd find a

Native American souvenir shop. Buy a dream catcher or a medicine bag like the one Kajika wore on his hip.

But despite Jeremy's mild anticipation, he was also anxious. More than a simple case of nerves, he felt an ill-defined darkness, a black cloud swirling within his body, the clinging vapors immune to his puny inhaler.

Something bad's gonna happen.

In the cramped airplane seat, he shifted his weight, his knees banging the closed tray table for the umpteenth time.

An irritated face shot up from the seat in front of him. "Can you please stop doing that?"

Jeremy murmured an apology.

Sandwiched between his mother and Sue, he couldn't get comfortable. Both women had raised their armrests, a silent act of solidarity on his behalf, but he still felt trapped.

Connie placed a hand on his restless thigh. "You okay, sweetie?"

Jeremy simply nodded. What else could he do? His mother wasn't the one who'd suffered pre-boarding glares from other fliers, each passenger no doubt praying to be seated far from the overweight kid, preferring the screaming toddler instead. The flight attendant's provision of a seatbelt extender had been the final humiliation.

"What time is Sammy getting in tomorrow?" Connie leaned forward to make eye contact with Sue.

"Late afternoon. He couldn't get away earlier, but I thought we could spend the time sightseeing."

The plan was to meet the Dr. John team on Friday to prepare for Saturday's taping. That left Thursday's schedule free. Jeremy wondered if he should have mentioned the powwow after all.

Nah. They'd think it was stupid.

"By the way, Jonathan is coming too." When Sue shared the news, her expression suggested she'd spied something unpleasant on the plexiglass window. "Guess he changed his mind and wanted to tag along."

"I see you like my boss as much as I do."

Sue flipped through an inflight magazine. "I just wish he was more supportive of our cause."

Learning of Jonathan's tag-along only magnified Jeremy's discomfort. At least George hadn't come. Although preferable to Rex, George and Jeremy weren't exactly best friends. Jeremy found the guy stiff and uptight, and sometimes indifferent to Connie's needs. Dick, on the other hand, seemed to think George was his latest brother-in-arms.

Jeremy had to give the statistician credit though. The dude wouldn't take no for an answer. As a result, he managed to get Dick as far as a nearby shooting range, where the two had fired guns and compared aims and probably slapped each other's asses in the process. Of course, GI Dick had required a dose of Jack Daniel's before getting into George's vehicle, and when he returned, his sweaty corpus quivered like a blob of gray jelly. George succeeded where everyone else had failed, however, and if Jeremy hadn't seen it with his own eyes, he would never have believed it. Nor would any of those therapists GI Dick had refused to visit over the years.

More seat shifting. Another tray-table bang. Ongoing swirling thoughts.

"Don't worry. Not much longer," Sue said, giving him a supportive smile. "Either for the plane ride or the Dr. John hoopla. And when we get home, let's re-examine your weight-loss goals. I worry I've let you down in that department."

Sue's smile faded, and she looked past Jeremy through the smudged window. Then she returned to her reading, the inflight magazine having been replaced by a public health journal.

Jeremy stole a glance at the warrior woman. Horizontal creases lined her forehead while a paradoxically slack jaw bore signs of fatigue. If he hadn't known better, he'd think the fighter had been replaced by a pacifist.

Then again, finding her boss dead must have been brutal. Especially with his guts hanging out. Then the job suspension. Plus, Connie had told Jeremy that Sue's husband had sent their daughter away, and in a hushed voice, his mother added that Al himself might follow.

Jeremy decided he wasn't the only one bouncing around life's giant pinball turds.

At least she has balls. Unlike you, you big pussy.

He hadn't forgiven himself for allowing Tito to take the heat over the Facebook prank. At the thought, the black cloud inside him tightened its grip even more. He missed Tito. Other than brief interactions at school, they had little contact over the previous eleven days.

Tito had promised Jeremy it would blow over. "Be strong, my man." Then, as if completely confident in their reunion, Tito had abruptly changed topic and asked Jeremy if he'd heard the latest school gossip. "You know Mr. Pottage, your math teacher from last year?"

Jeremy had almost swallowed the gum he was chewing.

Oh, yeah, I know the guy.

"Apparently some kids accused him of inappropriate behavior. The school fired Pottage, and the cops are investigating. How gross is that?"

The gum had wadded up in Jeremy's cheek like a cement boulder. Thinking about the exchange still gave him the willies. He'd dodged a bullet. A fat, creepy bullet.

Moving the only part of his body he could without disrupting those around him, he rested his head against the airplane seat. He should have told someone. Helped the accusers out. Strengthened the kids' allegations. But instead he had stared at Tito in mock disbelief, pretending to laugh at the molester jokes that followed.

As usual, he did nothing.

With thoughts of lawsuits, live audiences, pedophiles, and fat killers cycling through his brain, Jeremy prayed the thunderous hum of the engines would lull him into unconsciousness.

But his black cloud only tightened.

The next day Jeremy, Connie, and Sue went sightseeing through historic downtown Dallas, everything within walking distance from their hotel. Given the upcoming interview, the three tourists were subdued. Still, Sue being Sue, the nurse clutched her guidebook and enlightened the group with travel trivia.

Jeremy struggled to focus. Not only anxious for the upcoming taping, having third and fourth thoughts on top of his second, he was tired, his sleep disrupted by the sonorous breathing of an adjacent hotel guest. If the walls had been any thinner, Jeremy would have smelled the guy's breath.

A geometric glass prism of a building caught his eye, its collection of squares, rectangles, and triangles reflecting the sun. When Sue saw his interest, she whipped open her shiny guidebook and spouted off facts about Fountain Place. Within moments, Jeremy tuned her out and instead cast his gaze on a big globe covered in chicken wire atop a tall pylon, or at least that was what it looked like to him. Ever the efficient one, the warrior woman flipped a few more pages and informed her tiny tour group about the Reunion Tower. More white noise for Jeremy.

During a stroll along the red bricks of Pacific Avenue, his interest once again piqued as he cast his gaze upon a mouth-watering attraction. A huge spaghetti restaurant.

After submitting his lunch request and listening to an onslaught of reasons why the restaurant wasn't the best nutritional choice, Sue surprised him by consenting, but only if he agreed to go the Holocaust Museum first.

"Deal," Jeremy said.

They had already visited the Sixth Floor Museum and saw the spot from which John F. Kennedy was shot. Jeremy could tolerate one more museum. Certainly better than the boring art center he once visited on a sixth-grade field trip.

Inside the Holocaust Museum, an oppressive silence enveloped them. Juxtaposed among the pleasant interior of carpeted floors and a wood-paneled roof, images of horror abounded, beginning with an enormous black and white photograph hanging near the entrance. A wagon full of corpses. Limbs, heads, and groins conglomerated into a hideous mass.

Jeremy's mouth lost all moisture, his mind all self-pity, and for the next thirty minutes, his gut all hunger.

Covering a large space near the back was a brick-colored boxcar, once used to transport Jews to their death. Through his museum audio set, Jeremy learned that as many as one hundred people had been crammed into the boxcar, the Nazis contracting with the railroad company for a per-person fee. Children under four were free. With no food and little water to sustain them, a trip that should have taken hours often lasted days. Many arrived as corpses.

Sue's play-by-play narration on the downtown streets had halted inside the museum. Jeremy noted her off by herself, staring at a display long after visitors around her had departed. He approached her once, wanting to ask a question, but when he saw her swat away a tear, he turned back.

On the way out, they spoke to an old man whose entire family had been killed in the Holocaust. He'd written a book which was available for purchase. Sue fished inside her purse. Jeremy could barely meet the man's gaze.

What must he think of me?

So fat. Never knowing a minute of true horror, while the Holocaust survivor had endured a lifetime of it. But the man smiled at Jeremy and gave him a free copy of the book.

"So we never forget," he said.

As they were about to exit the museum, Sue approached Jeremy and hugged him. To his surprise, he let her. She pulled away and gripped his shoulders. "If these people had to suffer such horror, if that man survived what he did, the least you and I can do is stand up for what we believe."

Then she hugged him again, and together they exited the museum, Connie wiping her eyes behind them.

Bellies full and legs tired, the three tourists toddled back to the Glenwood Hotel at eight thirty and climbed four flights of stairs to their rooms, the elevator off-limits per the warrior's insistence. Stairs didn't scare Jeremy anymore though. He hadn't lost much weight, but he'd built up endurance over the past several weeks.

The hotel's hallways carried an old-fashioned vibe with speckled brown carpet, velvety wallpaper, and regularly spaced gold sconces that offered the dimmest of illumination. Even earlier during the day, Jeremy was surprised by the darkness. He worried he'd spy two bloody dead girls awaiting his return, like the ones he'd seen in an old horror movie.

Sue's room came first, and as Connie said good night, Sue asked if she could speak to her for a moment. "Just some additional details for tomorrow. No need to bore Jeremy."

Jeremy shrugged and lumbered to room 408 half a hallway down, keeping an eye out for the hand-holding sisters. Tired from the day, he wanted nothing more than to plop on the bed and play his hand-held game. *No, scratch that.* He wanted nothing more than to raid the vending machine for some candy, and then plop on the bed and play his electronic game.

Using the key card, he opened the door to his and Connie's room and switched on the light, its brightness as poor as the hallway's. Both beds had been neatly made in their absence, but sadly, no chocolate in sight.

Jeremy pulled his wallet from his back pocket and checked its contents. One hundred and twenty-seven dollars. Dollars earned from snow shoveling, lawn mowing and, more recently, dog walking.

Thank God for the Duongs.

The two one-dollar bills would net him two candy bars. As if on cue, his mouth watered, but his mind played good angel to his taste buds' bad and immediately conjured the chunk of lasagna he'd devoured earlier that day, not to mention the mounds of garlic toast. Good angel then played hardball and tossed in images of the Holocaust Museum, flush with starving, half-dead men, women, and children.

Jeremy replaced his wallet. Before he could change his mind, he switched into workout clothes and put his sneakers back on. The hotel had a gym. He would use it. He might only last ten minutes on the treadmill, but he would use it. Make Fat Slayer Shelly proud. No more excuses.

Grabbing his key card, he slipped out of the room, feeling more in control than he ever remembered. He decided that moment was *his* moment. Didn't everybody have one? The moment they finally got their act together?

The warrior woman was right. *We can do this*, he thought, filled with a determination as foreign to him as his newfound sense of control.

Walking back toward the stairwell, an energy in his step that wasn't there minutes before, he neared Sue's room. The door was slightly ajar. He was about to knock to inform Connie and Sue of his whereabouts, mindful of the smug grin on his face but unable to squash it, when he heard his mother's raised voice. Curious, he put an ear to the door without pushing it open.

"That can't be right." Connie's voice was a strained cry.

"I'm sorry. I should have told you sooner, but so much has been going on. I was going to wait until after the taping, but I decided that wasn't fair." Sue's tone sounded pained.

"Are you sure it was him?"

"He identified himself as Terry Harjo. Said he wanted to speak to me about something. I never phoned him back, even though he called a couple more times."

Harjo? Jeremy thought. That was his father's last name, but his dad's first name was Clayton. Was Terry a relation?

Jeremy's pulse quickened, and sweat beads broke out on his forehead, all without the aid of a treadmill. What was the warrior woman talking about?

"But I don't understand," Connie said. "Terry's in prison."

"Not anymore. He's been released." Sue lowered her voice, and Jeremy thought he heard shame. "I had Al look into it."

"And you didn't tell me? Oh my God, what am I going to do?"

"Connie, please—"

"Don't you understand? Jeremy thinks his father is dead. How do I tell him I've lied to him all these years? How do I tell him Terry was not the man I pretended he was, but instead, a violent drug addict who almost killed a man? I didn't even tell Jeremy his father's real name, and I certainly never told Terry I was pregnant. Why would he call? Oh my God, do you think he saw us on TV and recognized himself in Jeremy?"

"Let's not jump to any conclusions. Let's..."

That was all Jeremy heard. He stumbled backward, the black cloud squeezing his throat and chest. On reflex, he dug into his pocket, but his hand came out empty-handed, the inhaler still in the hotel room.

He retreated to room 408, first with slow, backward steps and then with forward hustling, all thoughts of new habits and turning points spiraling down the cerebral toilet.

When he reached his door, he leaned against its support, stunned, like a man who'd learned his wife was an alien and his son was a daughter.

My father is alive. All these years I thought he was dead, but he's alive.

Jeremy fumbled with the key card and struggled to slip the plastic into the narrow slot. He couldn't face Connie. Not then. He needed time to think.

Too much. Everything. Just too much. The show. The lawsuit. The media. Calvin. Mr. Pottage. Losing Tito as a friend.

And now this.

He had to leave. Had to get out of there. But he'd wait until early morning. He'd end up lost if he took off at night, and he wouldn't get much of a head start if they came looking for him.

He stuffed his duffel bag with everything he'd need, working at a furious pace, wanting to be feigning sleep by the time Connie returned. With a grimace, he realized his phone's battery was nearly dead. He yanked the charge cord out of his bag and plugged the cheap mobile into an outlet by the desk, across from his mom's bed. He would need a full charge.

Thanks to Tito, he knew exactly where he would go.

Without changing into his sleep clothes — they would only slow him down in the morning — he climbed into the bed closest to the door and turned off the bedside lamp.

Moisture bathed his cheeks, a mixture of tears and sweat, a product of anger and fear.

She lied to me. All these years she lied.

36

SUE

Sue rolled a purple, plum-scented deodorant stick under each arm. She replaced the cap, paused, and then reopened the applicator to apply a second coat. She would need it.

"God, even your antiperspirant is colored," Kayla would say.

Thinking of her daughter dropped an anchor on Sue's chest.

Not today, she told herself.

Although she had spoken to reporters, the public, and large audiences in the past, never would her reach be as great as with the television show. With nerves on the verge of fraying, she hoped her sanity would hold on for a few more days. Even the endless Juney Andrews media blitz had been survivable, though each cry of, "What gives you the right to take someone's child away?" had chewed off a chunk of her soul.

Fog misted the bathroom mirror, the result of a long, hot shower. The fan was useless, nothing but a transient *pffft* sound whenever Sue flicked the switch, but fifteen seconds with the blow dryer did the trick, and soon an enlarging circle of visible mirror emerged. Enough space to apply makeup.

Thirty-nine percent. That was how many people were on their side or undecided, at least in the latest poll, but Sue was confident she could gain more supporters. Viewed by millions, the Dr. John Show would provide a huge push to persuade consumers to take action against the food they were fed, the junk they were sold, the garbage they were served.

The show would air in eleven days, after Thanksgiving. Dr. John didn't usually tape on Saturdays, but he'd rushed their appearance given the hot-topic issue. He'd said the Monday after Thanksgiving, a gluttonous holiday, would be the perfect opportunity to make their point.

A make-or-break moment. Soon Sue's tagline would either be national hero or global pariah.

Inspecting the finished results, she smacked her rose-colored lips, slid into a similarly shaded blazer, adjusted her patterned blouse, and smoothed her dark pants. Then she fiddled with her row of earrings, tightening the clutch of a tiny diamond stud, a Mother's Day gift from Al and Kayla three years prior. Back when her daughter didn't hate her. Back when her husband hadn't threatened divorce. Back when her boss was alive.

Don't go there.

She exited the bathroom. She could handle being a pariah. She'd been one before and she would be one again. As long as change came about, she would weather the backlash.

A glance at her watch (*"God, Mom, nobody wears a watch anymore, that's what phones are for"*) suggested she had time for the continental breakfast before meeting Connie, Jeremy, and Sammy at nine fifteen, at which time a Dr. John representative would pick them up and escort them to the studio for show prep. Taping would be the following day.

Seeing Connie again would require a proper breakfast and a dose of caffeine. After the night before, Sue knew she had let the woman down.

Grabbing the key card from the wobbly desk, a folded-up newspaper under the front leg not doing its job, Sue's plans for breakfast were hijacked by her ringing mobile. She checked the display.

Connie.

Sue answered but after a few seconds, said, "Slow down, honey. I didn't catch that. Jeremy's where?"

"He's gone. I woke up at seven forty — had my ear plugs in — and he wasn't in bed. Not in the shower, but his phone was charging so maybe down for breakfast? And then I saw a note on the dresser by the TV, said he needed to get away, needed to think."

Connie paused for a breath, and Sue seized the moment. "I'm sure he's having breakfast. Did you check?" Although Sue admired Connie for the changes she'd made, she sometimes wondered about the woman's thought processes.

"I've been all over the hotel. Checked the lobby, the dining room, the pool, even the exercise room. No Jeremy. So I called my dad to make sure Jeremy hadn't phoned him. He didn't answer, maybe in the bathroom, so I left a message to call me. And then I showered, you know, so I'd be ready in time, hoping Jeremy would be back when I finished, but still no Jeremy. And then I saw..." Connie hiccuped a sob.

"What. You saw what?"

"His duffel bag was gone."

"You didn't notice that right away?" Sue's body heat rose in irritation and fear.

"I know, I know, but his phone was charging on the desk. He wouldn't leave the hotel without his phone. It doesn't make sense, I don't understand. The team will be here soon. I don't—"

"I'll be right over."

Before heading to Connie's room, Sue called Sammy. She reached voicemail and left a message to come to the Glenwood Hotel, room 408, immediately. "We might have a little problem." Then, not sure if she'd get a chance to return before heading outside, she grabbed a sweater and bolted out the door.

Once in Connie's room, Sue listened to everything all over again, Connie looking even more frantic than she'd sounded on the phone. Still, her pink dress was pressed and her hair brushed smoothly, and Sue couldn't help but picture the positive response Connie would receive from the Dr. John viewing audience.

Everyone loves a pretty blonde, she thought, a little shamefully.

Putting an arm around Connie, Sue guided her to one of the unmade beds. Despite their request of non-smoking rooms, old cigarette fumes scented the air, Connie's floral perfume doing little to mask the smell.

"What should we do?" the anxious mother asked. "I don't know what to do, should we call the police? I think we should."

Connie picked up the phone. Sue calmly replaced it.

"Let's think for a moment. Did Jeremy say anything to you last night? Give you any indication that appearing on the show was too overwhelming? Did you ... did you tell him about..."

"About his father being alive? Absolutely not." Connie stood, then sat back down. Twisting about, she looked like a flustered piglet trying to escape its pen. "I didn't even talk to him. When I got back to the room, he was already in bed. I figured he was worn out from all the sightseeing."

A knock at the door made them both jump. Sue prayed it would be Jeremy, but when she answered, she found Sammy instead.

"That was quick."

"My hotel is only two blocks away. You can't tell someone there might be a little problem and not expect them to come scurrying over." Sammy glanced at Connie, still sitting on the bed. The woman rubbed her arms as if the room were an igloo rather than the stuffy incubator it was. Sue saw Sammy's face go from irritation to alarm. "What's up?"

Before sharing the news, Sue directed Connie to go search all the relevant places in the hotel again. Like a flash of light, Connie was gone, leaving Sue to explain the situation to Sammy, including Jeremy's father being alive. The lawyer sighed so loudly his coffee breath warmed Sue's face. She took a step back. At least someone had gotten their morning cup of java.

"I wish you'd told me about Terry Harjo sooner. About a week and a half ago, maybe two, Janine mentioned a man came into the office. He didn't leave a name or the reason why he stopped by, which Janine thought was kind of suspicious. He said he would try later, but he never did. Maybe it was Jeremy's father. Dammit."

Sammy stomped around the room, going from corner to corner, lifting bed covers, moving furniture away from the wall, checking under beds. He stood up, face flushed, hair in a rare ruffled state. Sue wasn't sure what he intended to find, but she kept quiet.

"Does Connie have any idea where he might have gone?" Sammy asked. "You know her, she doesn't always get her facts straight. Do you think Jeremy forgot his phone was charging? Why wouldn't he take it?" Sammy checked his watch. (*See, Kayla darling, some people do still wear watches.*) "It's almost nine. The Dr. John rep will be here soon."

They stood in silence, both of them glancing around the room, as if a three-hundred-pound teenage boy would suddenly appear. When the hotel room's phone rang, Sue whisked up the receiver before it could shrill a second time. "Oh, hello. Sorry. This isn't a good time. We're in the process of looking for a missing boy."

Connie burst back into the room. Sue murmured a quick goodbye and hung up the phone.

"Any luck?" Sue and Sammy asked in unison.

Connie shook her head and closed her eyes. When she opened them, tears dotted her lashes. "Why would he take his bag? Why would he go? Shouldn't we call the police?" She was quiet for a moment, as if considering the options.

While Sammy assured her calling the police was not necessary, not until they sorted things out, Connie plopped down on the bed nearest the door and buried her head in her hands. Sue doubted the woman was even listening to the lawyer.

"Oh no. Oh no, oh no, oh no..." she said, each *no* growing in intensity.

Startled by Connie's escalating panic, Sue and Sammy again spoke in unison. "What's wrong?"

Connie glanced up, her wide eyes moist and streaked with mascara. "You don't think ... what if he ... oh, God, do you think he heard us talking about Terry?"

Sue started to object, but then, as the possibility of Connie's question registered, she grasped the back of the desk chair and swiveled it toward her, sinking into its rigid support. Was it possible? Had he heard them through the door? Unlikely, but...

Sammy broke Sue's thoughts demanding an explanation. Sue relayed the previous night's exchange between Connie and her.

For a few moments, nothing but silence filled the air, Sammy taking a seat on the bed opposite Connie. Finally, a hacking cough from the other side of the thin wall roused them to action.

Sue straightened. She studied her sensible black pumps. Had they pushed Jeremy too far?

"Sammy," she said, standing up, assuming her take-charge voice. "You head down to the lobby in case the Dr. John rep is already here. Connie, you and I will call the police."

The woman moaned. "Oh, God, my baby. Do you think he's okay? If this is because of Terry, I'll never forgive myself. What kind of mother am I?"

Sue indicated with a look that Sammy should go. He protested the need to call the police, but she shooed him away. Although he worried about Jeremy's well-being, Sue suspected he also worried about the negative publicity a missing poster child would create.

At Connie's side, Sue put an arm around the distraught mother.

Having had a daughter recently disappear for a tryst with an outlawed boyfriend, Sue understood the woman's anguish.

"Don't worry, honey, we'll find him. He can't have been gone long. It'll probably turn out to be nothing, and in an hour we'll be having a good laugh." She rubbed Connie's back, soothing the woman's distress. "Now, let me call the police. It's Murphy's Law, right? As soon as I call them, Jeremy will turn up."

As Sue's shaky hand clutched the hotel phone, she prayed Mr. Murphy would intervene.

37

DARWIN

"I seek you who share my disgust — the strong, the disciplined, the like-minded. I seek you to follow my lead, to rid this country of the mindless, chewing animals who fill our hospitals and burden our bank accounts."

In the musty hotel room, Darwin's enunciation was flawless, his delivery sharp. He had recited the manifesto in its entirety so many times, he hardly needed the physical papers.

But was it all for naught?

With trembling fingers, he removed his reading glasses and aligned the manifesto's unstapled pages. A gold paper clip affixed them together, but the edges seemed off. Darwin removed the clip and straightened the sheets once more. Still they appeared out of sync. He realigned them over and over again.

Missing? How can the whale boy be missing?

"Think. Think of a solution."

Darwin's head shot up. His gaze scanned the room, the papers going limp in his hand. Had he spoken aloud? Or was that The Voice? Differentiating was becoming more difficult. Then again, did it matter?

He is I and I am he and together we are one.

Back to the manifesto. With the discipline only he possessed, he affixed the paper clip one last time and tucked the brief into his satchel, assuring himself the pages were straight. He had to move on.

He could not let the road bump deter him. He would overcome, just as he always did.

With a rental car and binoculars, he had scoured the Dr. John site the night before, a large lot surrounded by an iron fence with one central gate manned by a guard. That security booth was the only obstacle blocking Darwin's entry, but he could easily gain access if he drove with the others, assuming they allowed him to tag along. And why wouldn't they?

But that was before the boy had disappeared.

While the show taped in the studio — a white, ranch-style home on the property — the audience watched from a red barn about twelve-hundred feet away. Back in Cleveland, Darwin had viewed a few episodes of the show as part of his research. Senseless sheep looking to a senseless leader.

What Darwin didn't know, though, was how many security guards were inside the complex.

Does it matter anymore? Without the boy, the plan is moot. I have failed. My words will not be heard.

Pain blasted Darwin's skull. He fell to the chair.

(This is our moment. You will not fail.)

The Voice's tone was tepid, but Darwin knew from experience how quickly his flame could burn. As penance, Darwin ignored the cerebral ache and dropped into a set of triceps dips on the chair, the muscles of his upper arms firing.

"Flaccid gluttons take heed," he recited, his breaths smooth despite the exertion. "Your days are numbered. Change your ways before it's too late."

Like ribbons of silk, the words flowed from his lips. His confidence returned. The ache in his brain lessened.

Spreading out a towel he'd brought from home, he flipped to a prone position on the floor and cranked out one hundred push-ups.

He would find a way. Even if it placed greater risk on his own being. His life was forever changed anyway. Over the past few weeks, his job had grown tenuous, the urges and obsessions proving harder to hide, but after the world saw his face, he hoped to remain an underground leader in the mission, directing his followers while hiding.

But with the boy missing — as the phone call minutes earlier had suggested — too many questions remained. Would Darwin end up a martyr?

He shifted to his back for abdominal crunches, the growing heat in his body failing to reverse the chill of uncertainty.

If death was his fate, so be it. Was he not ready for his struggle to end?

(*Weakness, Darwin, weakness.*)

Pain again, but more stabbing and intense than before. Darwin bit back a moan and had to cease his calisthenics to clutch his throbbing skull.

As quickly as the pain had come, it subsided.

Of course. So simple.

Darwin bolted up. He would get the boy back. He would go to the nurse, go to the mother, and he would get the boy back.

He need only dangle the one thing the whale cherished most.

For what boy, other than Darwin himself, did not love and treasure his mother?

38

To Jeremy, driving north on Route 75 in Texas didn't look a whole lot different from driving in Ohio. Strip malls, chain restaurants, discount superstores, and residential areas, all repeating at regular intervals. The more upscale the homes, the more upscale the shopping and dining. Nothing new there. Maybe fewer trees, a little more dust and junk yards, and a couple more farms speckled with tractors and grazing cows.

A greasy palm print on the bus window clouded his right visual field. Spotting yet another crop of restaurants through the smudge, he decided the biggest difference between Texas and Ohio was the impressive number of barbecue restaurants in the Lone Star State.

Pushing away the image of sticky, dripping, barbecued ribs, his highly skilled salivary glands already on the case, Jeremy replayed his abrupt departure from the hotel.

Hard to believe he'd done it, slipping out at six a.m., his mother oblivious in her silent world of ear plugs and white noise. For Jeremy, sleep had proved elusive, even more so than the night before. On the few occasions he'd been able to drift off, distorted dreams of a drug-addled Kajika beating another man had jarred him awake. The images were so strong, Jeremy almost smelled the chemicals oozing from Kajika's pores. His Kajika. His shaman. But instead of a noble healer, the man was violent and cruel, braided ponytail flapping in sync with malicious laughter.

How could his mother have lied to him all those years?

The new day with its bright sunshine had done little to quell the shock of his father being alive. Where was Terry Harjo? Did he look like Jeremy? Was he fat? Was he still a drug addict?

Everything seemed surreal, and though Jeremy had snuck out that morning, he could barely remember performing the act, as if his body had been on autopilot, but like the idiot he was, he'd forgotten his phone. Left it charging on the desk across the room, thinking only of a quick departure to avoid detection. Cheap phone or not, he'd lost his easiest means of communication.

No chickening out now.

Thanks to the maps and bus schedule Tito had printed out in his room when the two of them discussed Jeremy attending the powwow in Dorner, Jeremy easily found the bus station, not far from the hotel. A scary place best forgotten, but other than staring at the blubber kid boarding the bus, no one had bothered him, each seedy-looking individual tied up in his or her own miserable affairs.

Jarring Jeremy to attention, the bus heaved to a stop, its engine belching.

"Sherman Denison," the stout bus driver barked. "Five-minute stop."

A gangly woman hustled three even ganglier children off the bus, somehow managing to hold three spindly arms to avoid any runaways. The youngest shouted, "I have ta pee, Momma, I have ta pee."

A couple others departed, but whether gone for good, Jeremy didn't know. Few open seats remained, and he prayed the one next to him would stay unoccupied, his duffel bag resting on the thin cushion in hopes of deterring any takers.

Through the window, he watched a shaggy-haired man light up a cigarette and a hurried woman wolf down a breakfast burrito. His stomach panged in both hunger and grief.

How could she lie?

He had no choice but to bolt. Had no idea what to say to his mother. Worse, he couldn't handle Sue's sympathy. Or her insistence they must carry on. "Can't back down now," he could hear the warrior woman say.

Everything came down to the cause. It was all about getting publicity. As if Jeremy could go on national television like nothing had happened. He wiped his eyes and sniffed, wishing he had a tissue so he could blow the snot instead of sucking it up and sniffling, pissing off the dude across from him.

The mother and her scrawny ducklings reboarded, as did one of the other guys who had gotten off, his arms stocked with a big bag of chips and a bottle of soda. Jeremy wondered if he should have done the same, but he had to conserve his money. The bus ticket had cost thirty-four dollars. For once his gut would have to wait.

As the driver was about to close the door, one hand on the lever, the other running through his greasy hair, a voice bellowed, "Hold on."

Crap.

Jeremy shifted his bag to cover more of the empty aisle seat.

Please don't sit by me, please don't sit by me, please don't sit...

The mental plea tapered off. Stepping onto the bus was a large Native American man, not only in height but in muscular bulk. An expansive chest stretched the confines of a black western-style shirt, its red yoke and cuffs embroidered with decorative spurs and saddles. Framing a lined face, weathered perhaps from days in the sun but still remarkably handsome, was a thatch of silver hair, extending to the man's shoulders. All in all, a far cry from Jeremy's flabby pastiness and bird-nest mane.

The colossal man scanned the available rows. He bypassed an old lady, maybe because she was a potential chatterbox or because of her proximity to the gaggle of children. Next, with hands touching the backs of each seat he passed, he ruled out a rumpled, hunched-over guy. Given the one-hundred-proof fumes radiating from the bum, Jeremy wasn't surprised.

That left two remaining seats. One by a normal-weight dude, asleep, no chance of being a talker, and one next to Jeremy, the fat, space-invading kid.

The man's gaze fell on Jeremy, who, up to that point, was unable to tear his own gaze away. An intensity in the stranger's dark eyes made Jeremy catch his breath.

The new passenger sidestepped the sleeper and approached Jeremy's row. "This seat taken?" he asked.

Like a mute dunce, Jeremy shook his head. He swatted his duffel bag onto the floor and shoved it under the seat, leaving even less room for his barrel calves.

"Dan Folsom," the man said, smiling, reaching out a hand, not seeming to mind Jeremy's thighs spilling over onto his seat.

They shook, and before Jeremy could stop himself, he responded, "Jeremy Harjo," dropping his surname as suddenly as his mother had dropped the news of his father.

"Harjo, huh? You from around here?" Mr. Folsom's eyes narrowed.

"Nah. Just visiting. I'm from Ohio."

"Whoa. Long way from home."

"You headed to Dorner too? Are you from there?" Jeremy was surprised by his conversational boldness.

Mr. Folsom nodded. "Yep. Member of the Choctaw Tribal Council. Also run a casino. Met up with some other casino managers in Denison last night."

Though the man's sentences were short, his face was expressive. He looked younger than the gray hair would suggest. Jeremy tried to act chill, but at times, his mouth hung open and he had to remind himself to close his jaw.

While Jeremy's new seatmate talked about his casino, a big-haired woman two rows in front of them answered her ringing phone and proceeded to carry on a loud conversation while chomping her gum. Mr. Folsom winked at Jeremy. "Buses. Lots of fun, aren't they?"

When Jeremy asked why he hadn't driven to his meeting, Mr. Folsom lifted a large hand and pointed to some sort of warehouse on Jeremy's right. Through the palm smudge, Jeremy could see dark smoke billowing from its stack. "There's enough pollution in this world without me contributing to it. Use my own vehicle only when necessary. Not that the bus is very green, but at least it moves us around in bulk."

"That's noble of you."

Much like the air around the warehouse, Mr. Folsom's expression clouded. "Wouldn't say that if you knew my other reason." He paused and reached for a piece of gum from the pocket underneath the shirt's red yoke. Gray fuzz drifted onto his blue jeans, and he brushed it away with a swipe of his hand. Glancing at the gum-chomping phone-talker in front of them, he offered Jeremy a stick. "If you can't beat 'em, join 'em."

Without even glancing at the flavor, gaze still stuck on his seatmate, Jeremy accepted the gum and popped it into his mouth. Hungrily — a different kind of hunger from what he was used to — he waited for the man to continue.

"Years ago, I paralyzed a man from the waist down. Rammed my truck right into his Chevy. I was drunk. Drunk as the cliché of a drunken Indian. The guy was a friend. Still is, though I'm not sure why. Guess he's the forgiving sort. When I do power up my vehicle now, it's often to help Whitehorn get where he needs to go."

"That's kind of you," Jeremy said, the gum eliminating his stupid jaw dropping.

"Kind, nothing. A man has to take responsibility for his actions. Life's all about choices. We make 'em every day. We gravitate to the easy ones though. Easy ones like drinking yourself shit-faced and getting behind the wheel. It takes a real man to make the hard choices. The ones that deprive us of the things we want. Like liquor."

Like food.

Mr. Folsom chewed his gum and contemplated a field of horses on the left. At that angle, Jeremy could only see his cheek and ear. "Haven't touched a drop since. That's a choice I make every day. And believe me, it's a hard one."

Silence fell between them, and just when Jeremy worried their conversation had ended, Mr. Folsom faced him again. "Life is circular. Everything we do has consequences. That phone call that woman is taking? She's disrupting those around her. That gum wrapper?" Folsom pointed to Jeremy's plump fist, the balled-up paper still in it. "A tree had to die. My driving drunk? A man lost the use of his legs."

The gum became an intrusive tumor lodged against Jeremy's back molar. "Smart way to think," he said, cursing himself for sounding so dumb.

Mr. Folsom slapped his left thigh, making Jeremy jump. "Okay, Jeremy Harjo, you know about me. What about you? Why Dorner?"

Jeremy tongued the wad of gum to the side of his cheek. "The powwow. I'm going to the powwow."

"By yourself?" Mr. Folsom's silver hair parted down the center, and without bangs to hide his forehead, his eyebrows shot up or down, depending on his expression. At that moment, they knotted together in suspicion. "How old are you?"

"Seventeen." As soon as the lie flew from his mouth, Jeremy felt shame. He stared at his cramped knees.

Everything we do has consequences.

"I'm visiting Dallas with my mom. She wanted the day to sightsee and shop, so she let me go to the powwow." Jeremy peered up at Mr. Folsom, the man's eyebrows back to neutral on his somber face.

Then, as they crossed over the Red River bordering Texas and Oklahoma and without understanding why, Jeremy blew like an over-pumped tire and spilled his entire story. His true age of fifteen. *War of the Wilderness*. Kajika. His never having been on a reservation before, let alone having met any Native Americans. Sue. The fat clinic. The lawsuit. The media attention. The Dr. John show. His dad, who he'd learned was alive after thinking he was dead. His mom's lie.

Like stinging lava, the words poured out, and what should have taken hours to cover took minutes. Mr. Folsom merely nodded, no judgment, no questions, just nodded. The only piece Jeremy omitted was the fact he'd taken off without permission.

When Jeremy concluded his pent-up tale, Mr. Folsom tugged at his red cuffs and said, "Sounds like you're a man with a lot of responsibilities. Tough choices, huh? Some already made, others left to make."

Mr. Folsom stared out the window at the approaching town, and Jeremy's gaze followed. In the distance, on the side of the road, a gray coyote trotted up a hill. Jeremy had a sudden urge to join the solitary animal.

As the bus made its way to the station, each turn pitching Jeremy sideways and bumping his soft flesh against Mr. Folsom's solid frame, his seatmate smiled. Crooked teeth did little to detract from his appeal. "Well, it just so happens my family's bigger than a small town. Most will be at the powwow. Some participating, others watching. Me, I'll be all over. Join us. Plenty of folks will want to talk your Ohioan ear off. Answer any questions you have. I need to run some errands first, then we'll head over there together." Giving Jeremy a laser-beam stare from underneath raised eyebrows, he added, "I suspect your mom would appreciate that, don't you?"

Jeremy swallowed, but luckily not the gum. He nodded.

The bus came to a stop at seven minutes past ten, only two minutes behind schedule. Mr. Folsom spread his arms, and his face lit up.

"Welcome to the reservation, Jeremy Harjo."

39

SUE

Sue had read many novels in her lifetime. She'd watched numerous television shows and enjoyed countless movies. But throughout all that fiction, she encountered few story lines that could compete with the strange realities she confronted daily: being a key player in the removal of an obese child from the home, seeking a court order to ensure an HIV-positive man's compliance, seeing the health director's eviscerated intestines clumped inside a pizza box.

And that was only in the past year.

So she'd assumed she was immune to bizarre situations. She was wrong.

Congregated in a tobacco-free hotel room stinking of cigarette smoke, used bed sheets, and a fusion of sandalwood cologne and floral perfume were two police officers, a lawyer, a distraught mother, an assistant television producer, and a celebrity psychologist.

Fiction paled in comparison.

So much had happened in the last hour, Sue's head felt like a spinning centrifuge. Dawn, Dr. John's assistant — or assistant producer; Sue hadn't caught the job description any better than she'd caught the diminutive woman's last name — showed up in the lobby shortly after nine. When Sammy explained the missing-Jeremy situation, Dawn had immediately called Dr. John who, in addition to Sue, telephoned the police and showed up fifteen minutes after the uniformed officers. They had all gathered in Connie's hotel room.

Connie and Sue huddled together on one bed, the gold bedspread haphazardly pulled up in attempted tidiness, while the two uniformed police officers sat on the other one. Dawn occupied the desk chair by the window, her bobbed hair the color of dark chocolate, while Dr. John and Sammy leaned against the desk and the dresser respectively.

After asking the usual questions of Connie, including a physical description of Jeremy, his likes, dislikes, where he might have gone, and whether he'd ever taken off before, Officer Schaefer, a middle-age blond woman with a faint pink scar traveling from lip to chin went straight for the weak spot: "Was your son a willing participant on this show?"

Officer Delgado, fiftyish, full head of hair, and more starstruck than his partner, must have seen both Sue and Dr. John tense. "What my partner means is, was he nervous about going on? Maybe he got cold feet?"

Before Connie or Sue could answer, Dr. John stepped forward. Average height with a mild paunch, his full locks rivaled Delgado's, only instead of jet-black, they were honey-brown. In a Texas twang he said, "Believe me, we vet our guests carefully. I have spoken to Jeremy on two occasions by phone, and if upon meeting him today — assuming I do meet him — I have any concerns about his readiness, I won't put him on. I've told him as much."

"Oh, sure, sure, we're not implying anything." Officer Delgado waved both hands as if shooing away a fly.

Dr. John stepped back. His haste to be the first to answer questions was wearing on Sue's already untethered nerves, nerves she vowed to keep hidden from Connie who manifested enough anxiety to fill the hotel pool.

Connie shook her head. "The show isn't why he left. I think he overheard something terrible. Something from the one person who's supposed to have his back."

Connie's face crumpled, and Sue slung an arm around her, just as she had off and on throughout the morning. For Sue, support was the easiest way to maintain control. No time to be weak when one has to be strong.

Officer Schaefer asked for clarification, and Sue explained the conversation about Terry Harjo.

"Don't worry, Connie," Dr. John said. "We'll keep that off the record. I imagine news like that would set Jeremy's world more off kilter than a Tilt-A-Whirl."

Though said with sensitivity, the remark reduced Connie to tears. Dawn jumped off her seat, disappeared into the bathroom, and returned with a wad of rough, institution-brand tissues.

The police wrapped up after Officer Schaefer suggested Jeremy was likely another teenager blowing off steam. Although the note indicated he took off willingly, the policewoman offered to spread the word to help find him. Sue wondered how much Dr. John's presence influenced the offer. It wasn't as if the police didn't have enough to worry about. Tracking down fifteen-year-olds who took off to think on their own was probably not high on their list.

After the two officers left, the room fell quiet. Despite the parted curtains, little sunlight streamed in thanks to a neighboring building, and the two dim-watted lamps did little to brighten the space. Outside the door, maids conversed in Spanish, and a vacuum hummed somewhere down the hall.

Drying her eyes, Connie looked up. "I'm sorry for this mess." She glanced at Dr. John. "I still can't believe you're here. You must think we're crazy."

Dr. John sank to the bed the officers had vacated and leaned forward to grab Connie's hands. "Of course I'd be here. I'm a father, first and foremost. The important thing now is to find Jeremy. We'll help you do that." The psychologist paused and added, "I know this is difficult for you, but would you mind if I sent over one of my cameramen for a bit of footage?"

Like a mother hawk, Sue tensed. She didn't know whether it was the honey locks or the Texas twang, but something about Dr. John made her struggle to accept his sincerity.

The television host must have sensed her ire. "I don't want to take advantage of your pain. I'm not that guy. But I think any reactions involving the lawsuit, including Jeremy's disappearance, will only serve to improve public support on your behalf."

Sue's posture relaxed, and she raised an eyebrow. "So you agree the litigation has merit? You're not simply the vehicle bringing the subject to light?"

Dr. John leaned back and stretched his legs, his spotless cowboy boots landing between Sue's and Connie's feet. He grabbed at his midline and squeezed a roll of flesh through his green sweater. "Of course I think it's got merit, and any conversation we generate on the issue is a plus. That includes Jeremy's struggles, both physical and emotional. So what do you say?"

"I'm not..." Connie rubbed the front of her neck, leaving red marks on the skin. "I just want to find Jeremy. I don't know how good I'd be on camera right now. I'm a mess. I just ... oh, God, I don't know." Connie squeezed the wadded tissues in her hands and gave Sue a pleading look.

Sue stood and straightened her shoulders. "Okay, listen. Connie's exhausted, and she and I haven't had time to brainstorm on our own about where Jeremy might be or why he left. Give us an hour or two alone." She turned to Dawn. "If you want to help, you and Sammy can canvas the neighborhood. Look in restaurants, shops. Oh, especially any Native American themed shops. He took a real interest in those yesterday."

Sue shifted to Dr. John who, judging by the look on his face, wasn't used to taking direction. "If you want to get the search on camera, that's up to you. Sammy? Maybe you can touch base with the police periodically and let me know if you learn anything." Back to the psychologist. "I'll call Dawn in an hour or two, and we'll see where we're at then. Agreed?"

Sue allowed little time to assess their level of agreement before she hustled them to the door. When only she and Connie remained, Connie gave a small smile. "Wow. You and Dr. John together should make for an interesting hour of TV."

"I suspect my daughter would agree." Retaking her spot next to Connie, Sue patted the woman's knee. "Don't worry, we'll find him. I feel it in my bones, and they are rarely wrong."

"I hope that's true, because I think he heard every word we said about Terry." Connie repositioned herself and leaned back against the headboard. Her pink dress had become wrinkled and dotted with tear stains. "I wish I could have been a better mother. I was always so busy, you know? I had to make money."

"Of course you did. You've done the best you could with what you were given."

Connie continued, as if she hadn't heard Sue. "It's not easy without a degree. I was going to be a nurse. I told you that, right? But then I got pregnant. God, one stupid night, but don't get me wrong, I wouldn't trade Jeremy for the world."

"Of course not."

"Pregnant at eighteen. So I thought I'd go to school later when Jeremy was older. Oh, man he was a sweet boy. Always has been. But then my mom got sick and my dad injured his back at work. Then his panic attacks started, and after my mom died, my dad's social phobia got so bad he couldn't leave the house. And, well, before I knew it, five years passed and here I am. No better of a mom. Don't even know where my kid is. God, what must he think of me?"

Sue offered reassurances where needed, reminding Connie of her recent impressive health improvements and her advancement of a cause to help others do the same.

After several more minutes, a knock on the door silenced them.

Sue frowned. "Wow, that was quick. Are they back so soon?"

Connie had already bolted up off the bed. "Maybe it's Jeremy."

She ran to the door, ramming the adjacent sliding closet in her excitement. The wood panels wobbled and banged on their rollers. When she flung open room 408, both she and Sue saw George in the hallway. Connie's mask of confusion shifted to relief, and she rushed forward to hug him.

"Oh, thank God you're here."

Never one for public displays of affection, at least from what Sue could tell given she'd never seen him demonstrative with Connie, George stiffened, his expression as unreadable as ever.

Terrific. One more person to deal with, Sue thought.

Then she brought a hand to her mouth. She'd forgotten to tell Connie about George's phone call earlier that morning.

Hoping to hide her irritation, she stood and said to George, "We're in a bit of a situation. I didn't know you were in Dallas. You should've told me on the phone. Why are you here?"

George said nothing, his angular face and strong jawline as handsome as ever. Methodically, he removed himself from Connie's clutch, stepped into the room, and closed the door behind him. He clicked the deadbolt in place and secured the chain lock. Although Connie seemed pleased to see him, George's presence perplexed Sue.

Why was he there?

Why wasn't he speaking?

Something wasn't right.

40

———

DARWIN

The weak are so trusting. See how she looks at you?

Those idiot eyes, gazing at him, wondering, questioning, and yet still she pawed at him. Nothing would please him more than to chop off those groping hands and shove them down her throat, muzzling that grating whine once and for all.

But the sheep had proved useful. Weeks back in the conference room, when Darwin had seen her and her greasy son pouring over the legal information the nurse had provided, he surmised their intentions. Such was his astuteness. The Voice had rejoiced in the timing. How well suited the litigious sheep were to the mission. Like the final pieces to a puzzle.

In the hotel room, he realized the woman was speaking. He blinked. Both of the sheep were looking at him, the mother with concern, the nurse with suspicion. He had to maintain discipline.

"George, are you okay? George?"

The mother's hand once again found his, and with the other one, she stroked his shoulder. Shaking himself free of her talons, he grabbed her arm and squeezed.

"George, you're hurting me."

"It's Darwin. George is in the past."

"Come on, George, what's going on?" The nurse stepped forward, attempting to free the pink sheep from his grasp.

Darwin knew how to put women like her in their place. Reaching behind his back with his right arm, he whipped out a gun, a gun the mother would recognize if she looked closely enough. Too bad he'd had to knife the ex-soldier to get it. Out of all of them, he was the most tolerable.

Both mother and nurse froze, but Darwin suspected the crazy RN would require more than the threat of a Beretta to keep her down.

"Oh, for God's sake, George, this is crazy. You—"

With weapon in hand, Darwin rammed the back of his fist against the nurse's forever yakking jaw, sending her reeling against the bed closest to the door. Her scrunched face and look of shock made Darwin want to smile. The mother shrieked, and her hands flew to her mouth, but given her weakness, that pathetic outburst was the extent of her interference.

With discipline and control, Darwin spoke. Or maybe it was The Voice. For the most part, they had become one and the same. George had evaporated.

For the best, Darwin thought. George might have been unable to commit to the final task. Early on, befriending the pudgy mother for the good of the mission, not to mention being in the same room as her son, took every ounce of discipline, but like a master might a servant, George had developed a fondness for the woman, especially after she'd shed her chub. Not love or lust, to be sure. Sex had never transpired, the act so unclean it wasn't worth doing, but there were times the woman had amused George.

But not Darwin. He did, however, value the liberal details she shared. The dates of the Dr. John Show, the times, the hotel room number.

Stupid, helpful little sheep.

"Here's what's going to happen." Like a lecturer brandishing a laser pointer, Darwin waved the gun around. "You'll follow me to my hotel room, quietly. Bring your purses and a sweater."

Pulling herself up on the bed, the nurse rubbed her jaw. Uncertainty and fear replaced the judgment in her eyes, a transformation Darwin found enormously pleasing.

Still, as expected, she could not keep her mouth shut, and the tone that followed seemed directed to a child. "Please, George, what's wrong. You—"

He strode closer with the gun. "Darwin. I told you, George is gone."

"Okay, D-d-darwin. I don't understand what's going on, I wish you'd let me help you. The police know where we are. They're looking for Jeremy, and Sammy and Dr. John will be back any minute."

Darwin itched to pull the trigger. Better yet, pluck out his knife and slice off her tongue. But he still needed the woman, so he silenced her with words instead, words he knew the puritan nurse would abhor.

"Know what, Susie Q? How about for once in your fucking life you shut your goddamn mouth? Bet those sanctimonious lips have never tasted your husband's cock, have they? Poor guy. Gets all their bad and none of their good."

Judging by the RN's horrified eyes and twisted mouth, Darwin knew he'd struck gold.

(*Well done, Darwin. Each situation requires a new adaptation.*)

Continuing in a steady voice, he said, "Collect your things and follow me to my room. If you think I'm bluffing and won't kill you, you're wrong. Soon you'll discover my capabilities. Fail to cooperate, and you'll taste a bullet."

Darwin indicated the nurse rise and join him, and after she grabbed her purse and a brightly striped sweater, he seized her arm. He motioned the weeping mother to do the same, but when her pained gaze met his, he faltered. For the briefest moment, his brain hiccuped confusion.

"George is gone. There's only the mission. Let nothing else concern you."

His face twitched in spasm. Had he spoken aloud? Or was that The Voice? It didn't matter.

He is I and I am he and together we are one.

Guiding two compliant sheep up a deserted hotel stairwell to the sixth floor proved effortless for a wolf like Darwin, especially after he'd threatened to "pay a visit" to the nurse's daughter if the women didn't comply. So did binding their arms and legs with duct tape to the two chairs in his hotel room, one from the desk and the other an uphol-stered chair he'd pulled away from the back corner. Though its wooden legs and arm rests were stouter, the furniture still suited his purpose, just as he knew it would. A leader plans everything to the last detail. Only the undisciplined err.

He plied each of their mouths with tape as well. The whole process required mere minutes, the only resistance being complaining and negativity from the nurse.

"This will never work. It's absurd," she blurted before he muzzled her lips with silver binding.

Returning to the know-it-all's weakness, he said, "Remember your daughter. Such a shame it would be to kill her. With her discipline and self-deprivation, she could be one of my followers." Darwin pushed his face inches from the nurse's and lowered his voice. "But if you fight me, I will kill her. No second thoughts."

Wide eyes, a wrinkled brow, and a moan were all that followed. Once again, he knew he'd put a septic finger in the woman's wound.

Retreating to the bathroom, he performed two hand scrubs with a surgeon's meticulousness. After drying his skin with a towel from home, he returned to the sheep and relayed the plan. Upon confirming their understanding to behave, he ripped the tape from the nurse's mouth, put the gun to her head, and retrieved the cell phone from her ugly, polka-dot purse.

He would have preferred the mother make the calls, less chance of acting up, but her whimpering and crying made her an unusable resource, and the more he pointed the handgun to induce compliance, the more she whimpered.

The nurse it would be.

Officer Delgado was first, Darwin having found the cop's card inside the giant bag along with the cell phone. As Darwin held the mobile to her ear, aware of its contamination, the meddlesome RN did such a fine job of lying about the boy's return and calling off the police assistance Darwin rewarded her with the promise of leaving her daughter alive if she continued to play along.

Next up was the Dr. John Show twat he had seen scurrying through the lobby earlier, talking to the lawyer. Neither of them had seen him.

A disciplined leader made no mistakes.

During the phone call to the assistant, the nurse performed less well, faltering in her efforts to convince the idiot woman of their false plans. As such, Darwin was forced to grab the phone and replant the mouth tape.

Closing his eyes, he channeled his discipline.

(*You can do this.*)

Voice cordial, green eyes blinking back open, Darwin said, "Hi, Dawn is it? This is George Koster, Connie's boyfriend. I joined the family a short time ago." He assured the woman all was well and that they'd be at the studio by four o'clock that afternoon, once they had time to regroup and let Jeremy collect himself. Darwin would have liked more time to find the boy but chose that hour to avoid rousing suspicion.

After more chitchat that made Darwin want to crush the woman's skull, the assistant dunce finally disconnected.

Next, he found the lawyer's number on the nurse's phone and sent a text message summarizing what he'd told Dr. John's assistant. The lawyer immediately responded, fussing about needing more time, blah, blah, blah. Darwin simply texted back that the issue was settled, exactly the message Mr. Sanchez would expect from the opinionated hag.

Fighting the urge to rewash his hands, Darwin checked the bedside clock. Over four hours remained before the scheduled rendezvous. Although not what Darwin had planned, a true master adapted when necessary.

The women's gazes followed him everywhere, one dripping tears, the other shooting sparks. He crouched in front of the spark thrower, tugging the tape around her legs to test its hold.

"Almost done," he said, sitting back on his heels, the bulging pockets of his army-green cargo pants bunching up around his hips. "Now we need to call the fat boy and tell him if he doesn't return soon, his nice mommy will be dead."

Both women glanced at each other and then ignited into writhing, moaning lumps, shaking their heads as if on fire. Caught off guard, Darwin stumbled backward before scrambling to an upright position. Looking at the mother, clearly desperate to speak, he reminded her what would happen if she screamed. He ripped the tape from her mouth.

The pink sheep gulped and sucked air as if she'd been deprived of oxygen, the skin around her lips red and irritated. Her words tumbled out. "Jeremy forgot his phone. We don't know where he is. There's no way to reach him."

Darwin stiffened, Sue's phone clenched in one fist, gun in the other. George tried to surface. The Voice was silent.

Focus, Darwin told himself. He shook his head a few times, blinked, and banged his temple with the hand gripping the phone.

He could not lose face. He was still in control.

Slapping the tape back over the mother's mouth, fury flooded his bloodstream. He pressed the pistol hard against her skull. Though her fearful whimpering gave him solace, a line of sweat trickled down his forehead, and his voice shook when he spoke. "You better pray he calls you before four o'clock."

Adjusting the clean sheet he'd brought from home to cover the contaminated bedspread, he sank down on the mattress. An invisible weight compressed his chest and strained his breathing.

He had planned. He had adapted. He had displayed extraordinary discipline.

And he had been crippled by a fat teenage nothing.

His rage would know no boundaries.

41

In the Dorner Event Center foyer, Jeremy's chest thumped in time to the rhythmic drumming surging from the main auditorium. *Ba dum, ba dum, ba dum.* Thudding, pounding, throbbing so intense, it felt as though his heart would burst from its ribcage and join the source of the beat.

Sound, sight, smell, touch. All his senses came alive in the jaw-dropping surroundings. Judging by the grilled scents teasing his nostrils, taste would soon follow. Barely ten feet into the building and already performers whizzed by in a flurry of Native American garb. Browns, oranges, reds, yellows, purples, turquoise. Beaded head bands dashed in every direction, along with fringe-swaying dresses, leather breechcloths, and feathered headdresses and bustles so enormous Jeremy marveled at their ability to stay put. Clothing and fabrics he'd seen in *War of the Wilderness.* Clothing Kajika collected ascending the levels.

It's all here.

On living, breathing people.

Jeremy could hardly believe he was part of it.

Telling himself to chill, he realized Mr. Folsom, or Dan as the man had insisted Jeremy call him, was handing him something. Jeremy clamped his jaw shut and swallowed a pool of collected saliva.

Dan laughed, though not in a mean way. Each time the main

entrance door opened, his silver hair lifted in the cool breeze. "Here's your ticket stub, in case you step out for a while."

Hoping he didn't look as ignorant as he felt, Jeremy said, "Thank you, but you didn't have to pay for me. I have money."

Dan put a hand on Jeremy's back and guided him toward the main auditorium. "It's a privilege to treat my new Ohioan friend. Besides, you'll need your money." Dan waved his free arm toward the aisles of tables and bookshelves lining the front hall where vendors sold their wares. Every available space contained books, T-shirts, dream catchers, toys, jewelry, knives, costumes, head gear, animal figurines, musical instruments, or other Native American memorabilia. Already Jeremy felt their pull.

Dan laughed again as he nudged Jeremy along. "Don't worry. Plenty of time to look around in between competitions. I wanna introduce you to my family."

Inside the auditorium, blue bleachers flanked three of the four walls, many already filled with powwow participants and observers. Padded folding chairs, at least eight rows deep, lined the floor for additional seating. Blankets and snacks kept the audience comfortable for what Dan said would be hours of dance competitions. All around, in various stages of preparation, participants readied for their performances. As Jeremy followed Dan, he watched a woman expertly apply streaks of face makeup to a man already topped with a black-feathered headdress.

On the large center floor was the source of the thumping. A group of men, mostly older, formed a circle and drummed as a group. Many wore Western shirts and jeans. Around them, dressed in more traditional costumes, male dancers bobbed up and down, shaking gourd rattles and jingling bells attached by colorful bands to their knees.

"They're warming things up," Dan said. "Wait 'til the competitions begin at noon. Think you'll enjoy those."

Behind the performance area, against the lone bleacher-free wall, a small stage allowed announcers a platform from which to narrate the events of the Fifteenth Annual Dorner Powwow.

"There they are," Dan said, leading Jeremy to a group of people gathered halfway up the first set of bleachers. As the two men climbed the wide steps, a throng of children bouncing to the drumming rhythm waved to Dan and grinned.

As Jeremy always did, he became conscious of his appearance, but after scanning a room full of fat and thin, it seemed no one paid any attention.

Dan's family was also a mix of shapes and sizes. His wife, Shawna, a tall woman with short hair and a strong jaw line, greeted Jeremy warmly. In addition, he met Dan's brothers, sisters, sons, cousins, nieces, and nephews. Names were tossed out but quickly lost. Lastly he met Dan's niece, Tammy, about Jeremy's age and equally overweight. Dan asked her to stick by Jeremy's side and help him understand the events. If the girl with the long braid, crimson blouse, and jeans was put out by the request, she didn't show it. After helping Jeremy store his duffel bag under a spare seat, the two headed off to the food court.

"The competition's about to start, and if we don't grab something now, the lines will be huge," Tammy said.

As they left, Dan took his wife to the side. They were deep in discussion, and Jeremy saw Shawna look his way. Although he couldn't hear their conversation, he suspected he knew the topic.

Guilt flooded him, and despite the excitement of the powwow, for the thousandth time, he pictured his worried mother. He'd call her. Maybe after the first couple competitions. But he was hurt and angry, and though he hated to admit it, he wanted her to feel pain too.

Besides, he was at a for-real powwow with for-real Native Americans. Sue, Connie, and Sammy were far away. The Dr. John Show was on another planet. The killer was in another galaxy altogether.

The food court comprised a smaller room off the main auditorium. The intoxicating scents of chili, burritos, pizza, Philly cheese steak, kettle corn, and cinnamon rolls dialed up Jeremy's taste buds to high alert. It dawned on him he had not thought of food since having met Dan. He had gone several hours without eating and was none the worse. How many times had he stuffed himself without actually feeling hunger?

Bypassing the burrito, the pizza, and the humongous brownie begging for his attention, he opted for a small cup of chili, a turkey wrap, and a bottle of flavored water. His choices weren't merely an attempt to please the Fat Slayers. Rather, for the first time in a long time, maybe ever, he was more interested in his surroundings than his food.

Back in the bleachers, Tammy and Jeremy dug into their lunches. In between bites, Tammy reviewed the program with Jeremy.

"The competition's divided by categories of dress and age group."

With a napkin, she wiped ketchup from her chin and took another bite of her burger before continuing. "There'll be traditional, straight, grass, fancy, chicken, and then shawl for women. The costumes will be less confusing once you see them in action."

A few minutes later, the first competition began. Men's Fancy Dance. Jeremy's heart lifted to the heightened drumbeat, and the pleasant chest thumping returned, both from anticipation and sound waves. Musical tones and tinctures from unidentifiable instruments joined the drumming, followed by chanting and singing. An infectious, rhythmic blend of melodious but differentiated sounds filled Jeremy with an indescribable joy.

Men in vibrant feathered headdresses and bustles shimmied and bobbed, spun and twirled, jumped and leaped. Their hands gripped wands thick with streamers that whipped and twisted until Jeremy could no longer tell where costume ended and streamer began. Up and down from knees to feet they hopped and whirled, movements frenzied and hectic and pulsating with energy.

Jeremy forgot all about his turkey wrap, sliding the plate underneath the seat. His thighs thundered in rhythm against the chair, and his head bobbed in time. He longed to be out there. Longed to be amid those men, men who commandeered their strong bodies into physical feats of which Jeremy could only dream.

At that moment, his scale didn't matter. Never had he felt so alive. All around him the crowd bounced and bobbed, as if one heartbeat, synchronized in time and space, sustained them all.

After the first competition, he tore himself away to scour the vendors' wares. No matter the cost, he would leave with a memento, something by which to remember the day.

Around the tables he strolled, sometimes having to turn sideways to squeeze his body through. He scanned the jewelry and found a turquoise earring and necklace set for only eight dollars. The earrings would look great on his mom, and the big, splashy necklace would be perfect for Sue.

Carrying his purchase in a small brown bag, he examined the other tables, passing over those with books and videos and lingering on the displays with dream catchers, knives, and tomahawks. He was about to buy a brown and black dream catcher to hang over his bed when the most stupendous sight on a table in the corner caught his eye. He hustled to it, desperate to claim the object before anyone else.

Front and center on the table preened a leather quiver, three arrows with stone tips, and a bow.

Just like Kajika's.

Well, not quite.

Whereas Kajika's bow was sleek and shiny, its grip adorned with gold and ivory, the bow Jeremy held was small with wooden limbs. The bow string was strong though and the arrows sharp.

A Native American man with sinewy arms and ropy hands sauntered over to him. "Smart boy. That there is a functional unit. It's smaller, just under three feet long, but in the old days, most tribes used a short, stout bow like this. Won't shoot as far as the big ones, but believe you me, those arrowheads will get the job done."

"How much?" Jeremy asked, already sold.

Fifty dollars later Jeremy was the proud owner of his own bow and arrows. The man had packaged it in a long cardboard box with a sturdy handle, and as Jeremy carried his weapon away, he ran into Dan.

After sharing his find, Dan asked, "Know how to shoot that thing?"

Jeremy studied the black scuff marks on the floor and shook his head. He felt his face burn.

"Well then, what do you say I teach you?"

Although Jeremy thought witnessing a powwow competition was the best experience of his life, he soon found another to top it. For thirty minutes, in an open field behind the event center where no one would feel the arrow's sting, Jeremy shot his bow and arrows, perfecting his technique through Dan's patient teaching. A small crowd of children gathered — Dan making sure they kept a safe distance from harm — and with each arrow's release they clapped and cheered. Their cries of support bolstered Jeremy's confidence, and soon his aim was spot on.

"Jeremy, you're a natural," Dan said, his voice booming.

The kids retrieved the arrows and praised Jeremy's skill, filling him with an unfamiliar pride.

Finally, Dan indicated they should get back. Jeremy packaged up the bow and arrows. At that moment, he couldn't have felt better if he was one hundred and seventy pounds of pure muscle.

Before reaching the event center, Dan steered Jeremy to a vacant picnic table surrounded by recently trimmed grass, evidenced by the sweet aroma and loose blades.

"I wish I could stay here forever," Jeremy said, rubbing his hands over the box, still disbelieving its contents and the skill with which he had wielded them. The only two things he'd ever been good at were video games and eating.

Dan shook his head. "Novelty is always exciting, but when novelty wears off, problems return. Life on a reservation is hard. This here?" Dan waved his hands toward the main building. "The costumes, the rituals, the culture? That's just a celebration. That's not real life. You know that. Real life is full of pain and hurt. It's full of people who want to harm you for no reason except they can. It's full of temptations and sins."

Jeremy kicked loose grass with his dirty sneaker. "I guess."

"Do you know what the measure of a man is?"

Jeremy thought for a moment and shrugged, foot still kicking and forming a pile of cut blades by his shoe.

"The measure of a man is how well he stands up to life's shit. How well he fights it. How well he avoids its addictive temptations. And it's how well he treats his fellow brothers and sisters." Dan paused for a moment, and then, in a quiet voice, added, "And mothers."

At the mention of his mother, Jeremy's chest tightened, not in a frantic-inhaler way, but in an I-hope-I-don't-cry way.

"A measure of a man is also his honesty. Tell me, son, does your mom know you're here?"

Jeremy's eyes watered. He shook his head.

"Thought as much." Dan pulled a phone from his shirt pocket. "Probably about time you call her."

Jeremy agreed.

Five minutes later, Jeremy was back at Dan's side, legs weak and trembling, face pale. Dan must have assumed Jeremy's demeanor was from fear of punishment, because as he drove Jeremy to the bus stop, buying the return ticket to Dallas for him and helping him board the one-thirty-five bus about to leave, he reassured Jeremy.

"Your mom will forgive you. Moms are good about that." He handed Jeremy his business card and, with a pen from his pocket, added his personal cell number as well. "You call me anytime. It was a pleasure meeting you, Jeremy Harjo. I hope our paths cross again."

Jeremy thanked the man, unable to hold back his tears any longer. Dan gave him a quick hug and told him not to worry.

"Let your spirit guide you, Jeremy."

Jeremy nodded and climbed onboard, taking a seat in the back. His duffel bag — which Jeremy had retrieved from the event center — and bow-and-arrow box were by his side. As he waited for the bus to pull out, body shaking and mouth awash in coppery fear, he had a sudden thought to pull the clothes from his duffel bag and stuff the bow and arrows inside. He then replaced the clothes around the weapon along with the earrings and necklace he'd purchased for Connie and Sue. The bag was plenty big, having accommodated his mother's yoga mat on the trip over and having few clothes to fill it.

Leaning back in the seat, he closed his eyes.

Dan had been right about one thing. Jeremy was worried about punishment, but it wasn't punishment from his mom. It was punishment *for* his mom.

Because a man named Darwin said he had her. A man who threatened to kill her if Jeremy wasn't back on the four-oh-five bus.

"If you tell anyone, if you call the police or alert anyone at all, I'll shoot your mother dead," the strangely familiar voice had said.

Dan hadn't realized how spot on he was: Jeremy would discover his own measure, all right. Sooner than he thought.

42

SUE

Once the cleaning staff finished for the day, hotels approximated ghost towns in the afternoon. Quiet halls, an occasional toilet flush from a bordering room, the hum of the furnace or fan kicking in.

And the hushed mutterings of an unstable man.

George (*Darwin?*) paced the small space, first passing Connie who was tied to the desk chair and closest to the hotel door, then weaving between the two neatly made double beds, and finally wandering past Sue to peek between the drawn curtains. Snippets about "discipline" and "adaptation" occasionally leaked from his pressed lips, along with words about "the mission."

For the most part, however, George was pensive and quiet, excluding his body, which perpetually moved. More than once, he'd dropped to the floor between the beds and performed push-ups and sit-ups, but only after covering the grimy carpet with a towel.

A little after two o'clock, a chirp from one of the two cell phones lying on the desk made the three of them jump. Sue recognized the text alert as her own, an annoying crescendo, decrescendo warbling that per Kayla should be put out of its misery once and for all. Was her daughter okay? Surely George was bluffing about killing her. Could he really do such a thing?

The statistician grabbed her phone with its rainbow-colored case and read the text. His lips pulled into a sneer. After returning the cell to the desktop, he dispensed several pumps of the hand sanitizer he had planted on the nightstand.

Sue wondered about the text. Kayla? Al? Both were still hostile toward her, Kayla over being cut off from her boyfriend and getting yanked to her aunt's, and Al over the throngs of press inhabiting the Fort's front yard. Nothing like the death of a public health director and the suspension of a "lawsuit-hungry" nurse to give the reporters a nonstop rush. The journalists had found no shortage of disgruntled mouthpieces to interview over the previous two weeks. Sue supposed her enemies couldn't wait to call the media to share their views.

According to Tucker Andrews, "Sue Fort has put her nose in too many people's business. Took my daughter away, she did, and at what cost? Her boss's life."

Brent Johnson, charged with harassment and accosting Sue in the parking lot and still a person of interest in the murder of Dr. Chen, had told whichever reporters would listen, "That suspension was nothing more than a hand slap. The woman deserves to be arrested for crimes against the public. She's ruined my life."

Mark Swanson, father of Jeremy's bully, had chimed in a few days before as well. "Sue Fort always needs to be in control. It's her way or the highway. She's way out of line to sue those industries."

Sue refocused her scattered thoughts. She watched George pace the small room and heard him counting steps. The ache in her jaw where he'd struck her had subsided, though her shock at his action had not. Glancing at Connie, she hoped to reassure the terrified woman everything would be all right.

But would it?

George had snapped. Although always a bit strange and not the friendliest employee, Sue never would have guessed him capable of abducting and restraining his co-worker and girlfriend. Being a germaphobic, introverted fitness buff did not make one a psycho. For the millionth time, she wondered about his intent.

Outside the door a man's voice startled them, causing George to halt mid-step. A woman's laugh followed, but the two voices tapered off as they passed down the hall. In their wake, a whiff of fried food seeped into the room, and Sue imagined their arms heaped with takeout boxes from the Glenmore Grill on the ground floor.

Her stomach cried out for a bite, but a second chirping alert from her phone masked the intestinal growling. George checked the cell again. Another sneer. More hand sanitizer.

Must be Sammy, Sue thought. She snorted air through her nose. *This is crazy.*

Moaning, she tried to get George's attention, his concentration back on his sit-ups. She shook back and forth in her chair.

When he didn't respond, only muttering numbers as he counted his reps, she tensed her muscles and rocked the chair until one of its stout legs lifted. Then she thumped back down on the carpet.

Enough was enough. She was sore, hungry, and she had to pee.

Ignoring Connie's pleading look, Sue kept up the thudding racket.

Finally George stood, studied her with eyes that seemed elsewhere, then blinked and growled. "Stop that or I'll hit you again."

Sue paused but quickly resumed her moaning, trying to signal she had something to say.

George tightened his jaw and stepped forward. "If I remove the tape, you better not scream. Don't think I won't hurt you."

Given his menacing gaze, Sue planned to comply. It wasn't her she was worried about.

Kayla.

The tape ripped from her mouth except for a small segment at the corner where George let the strip dangle. Taking two deep breaths, she expanded her seemingly air-starved lungs. "George, this is crazy. Talk to us. Maybe we can help."

Leaning in closer, George assumed his newly adopted low, eerie voice. "George is gone. Darwin's here. Call me by the wrong name again, and you'll regret it."

"Okay, fine, Darwin. Please, we're hungry and we have to use the bathroom."

Connie nodded in vigorous agreement. Pale streaks lined her face, the tears having washed away her bronzer.

Sue rushed on. "Those texts. Were they from Sammy? You know he'll come looking for us when we don't respond."

"Will he? Or will he figure Sue is just being Sue and will get back to him when she damn well pleases? No one knows I'm here, Susie Q. And no one knows you're on the sixth floor." George sank back on one of the beds, a rare rest in his perpetual motion. "People like you? You think you're strong, but you're weak. You blame others for your own deficiencies."

Sue's bladder pressed against her pubic bone. Anger and frustration mounted, and before she could stop herself, she erupted. "Oh, for crying out loud, Geor — Darwin, this is crazy. A gun? You? Release us now, or I'll scream and thrash until I get someone in here."

Like sand art, George's face shifted from sinister to absolute blankness. Sue found the new expression far more terrifying. Unreadable, he stood and hovered above her, hands compressing her pinned arms, the weight of his body behind them. It seemed eons before he spoke again, and when he did, that weirdly controlled voice, different from the panicked tone he'd used upon learning Jeremy didn't have his phone and more frightening than his mutterings, frosted her insides. "Crazy? Oh, Susie Q, you haven't seen crazy yet."

He smashed the tape back over her lips, and before she saw it coming, he whacked her in the face with such force she nearly toppled back in the sturdy chair, its front legs lifting up and then thudding back down. She bit the tip of her tongue, and the pain was so intense, she momentarily forgot about the sting on her cheek from his open-hand blow.

Occluded mouth or not, she was stunned into silence. Was this the same George who ran her statistics? Made her pie charts? Ate her heart-healthy granola?

Not possible.

Connie's crying intensified, but despite Sue's pain, both physical and emotional, she refused to cry. She'd already betrayed herself by cowering to Brent Johnson.

George resumed pacing, as if nothing had happened. "I'll tell you what's crazy, Susie Q. Crazy is disgusting sheep stuffing themselves until they explode and then bitching about it and blaming somebody else. Just like your fat son." George pointed at Connie, and her whimpering heightened yet again. Sue worried if the woman didn't get a hold of herself, she'd choke on her own secretions.

Still focused on Connie, George squatted in front of her. He spoke with a cruel laugh. "You thought a man like me would want you? So desperate for attention, you were. Lapped up any tiny crumb I gave you. Pathetic."

George stood and checked the time. "Not much longer now. Soon we'll meet your son. Your fat little piggy who you stuffed until he oinked and squeaked. I know all about mothers like you. You disgust me."

Sue half expected George to spit on Connie, but instead he turned his back on them.

"Thanks to me, this country will see what happens to fat piggies. Like my boss did. And Talia, Miss Fat Witch. And soon you too."

At that point, George started reciting phrases about sheep and wolves, leaders and followers, weakness and discipline, but Sue barely heard. Her belly cramped in fear, and her throat constricted, as if all oxygen had been sucked out of the room.

George killed Dr. Chen? Gutted that poor man and eviscerated him like some animal being rendered for sausage? It wasn't possible. And Talia? Wasn't she a secretary in the stats department? Sue had rarely crossed paths with the woman, her interactions always with George, but she had heard something about an employee suffering a heart attack.

Nothing made sense. George was delusional. No way he could have committed such heinous acts. She refused to believe it.

Because if she did, their fate was already sealed.

43

———

DARWIN

*L*ook how they fear me, even the strong one. Look at her try to decide whether I'm telling the truth.

(*The time is near.*)

They would leave in less than an hour to retrieve the piggy sheep from the bus stop. From there they would drive to the Dr. John studio.

"You're finally here," the short twat would say.

Once inside, Darwin would take command. They would film him reciting his manifesto, though not in front of a live audience as he'd hoped. Holding off until the taping the next day was no longer an option.

Adaptation.

And if the end came to Darwin and the footage never shown? Didn't matter.

(*Because you planned. You foresaw obstacles.*)

Yes. In the form of a mailed copy of his manifesto to the big-nosed reporter prior to leaving the airport. Even if he died a martyr, his words would be heard.

Darwin paced. So much energy. No need to sit.

He glanced at the clock and blinked to process the numbers. Had ten minutes passed so quickly?

"Those who are weak must not survive. Whether or not I succumb, you will carry on what I have started. Only through fear will sheep take responsibility for their gluttonous ways."

The words would flow smoothly. Soon his purpose would be known, his acts carried on by the like-minded.

He walked to the window and peered out between the germ-ridden drapes. Graffiti tainted the building opposite the hotel, squiggles of red, blue, and white in disordered groupings, their meaning unclear. Leaning in and looking to the side, he could make out a fast-food joint next to the building, only half of its sign visible, the same yellow color as the rolls of fat filling the rounded sheep who dined there.

He closed the curtains, once again relying on the two dim lamps for illumination. No need for lightness. Soon their world would be dark.

Fifteen more minutes had passed. How was that possible?

A noise distracted him, much like a mosquito buzzing around his head. The nurse. She was rocking and moaning in her chair again. Given the women's contortions and leg squeezing, he supposed a bathroom break could not be avoided. The last thing he wanted was for them to piss themselves. Such proximity to human waste would tax even his strongest discipline.

If I let you relieve yourself, you must try nothing, or I swear you'll regret it.

When neither woman responded, Darwin realized he had not spoken aloud. He tried again, and both women nodded in agreement.

The mother was easy. After releasing her adhesive binds and nearly retching while listening to her void, not daring to close the door, Darwin made her wipe her tear-streaked face in anticipation of their departure. Then he allowed her a drink of water. The blond sheep gulped three glasses so hungrily, liquid trickled down her chin and splashed her pink dress. Darwin's revulsion intensified. As he moved to re-cover her mouth, she squeaked, "Are you going to kill my Jeremy?"

Darwin smacked the tape back in place, making sure its hold wasn't weakened by the water. He dragged the mother back to the desk chair and retaped her limbs.

See how the sheep lets me control her?

Next was the nurse. Darwin hesitated, feeling more reservation with her, but he could not allow her to piss herself and soil the room. Standing behind her, he clamped a hand on her forehead, her hair short and coarse like a man's. He pressed the back of her head against his abdomen to warn her once again of the consequences should she fight. "Remember your lovely daughter."

The nurse nodded. He cut her tape and led her to the bathroom as he had with the mother. Watching her relieve herself embarrassed him. Without warning, George resurfaced, and images of grant-writing statistics flitted across Darwin's mind.

Darwin shoved the statistician aside.

She is no longer your colleague.

After the know-it-all finished, Darwin allowed her a drink, gun pressed close to her head as she greedily swallowed the water. After retaping her mouth and grabbing her arm, he prided himself on keeping her controlled. She was a tall woman and physically strong, he would give her that.

But before they cleared the bathroom, the high-and-mighty nurse grabbed the drinking glass and used it to take a swing at Darwin's head. Had he not ducked back in time, the thick tumbler would have done far more damage than the small thump he received. As he reached for the nurse's still armed fist, fury fueling his moves, the petulant sheep kicked his shin and tried to elbow him in the eye.

Despite her strength, she was no match for him. He seethed and flushed in rage, and unable to maintain his emotional control, he yanked the nurse out of the bathroom and cracked the side of her skull with the gun. A sickening crunch of metal against bone echoed within the quiet room. A wave of heightened whimpering erupted from the mother, blessedly muted beneath her occlusive tape.

The rebellious nurse collapsed to the floor, blood oozing from her scalp.

Darwin kicked at her with his foot. His mouth went dry, and he longed for a drink of his own.

What have I done? She's no good to me unconscious.

Breathing heavily, he zeroed in on the clock. Almost time.

(Calm. Find your discipline. That's what sets you apart from the others.)

Darwin swiped the back of his gun-free hand against his lips and ran his fingers through his dark hair. The Voice still guided.

While dragging the nurse back to the chair, Darwin heard the belligerent mouth moan, and he sighed in relief. Struggling under her statuesque frame, he propped her back up in the chair and re-secured her limbs with a fresh round of tape. He would have to cut the binds again soon. In a short time they would descend the stairs to the side entrance, beyond which his rental was parked.

Needing a moment to collect himself, he wet a washcloth in the bathroom. Returning to the nurse's side, he applied pressure to the trickle of blood matting her hair, even though the act disgusted him. The bleeding was superficial, and he was able to clean the site along with the drops of blood on her face and red blazer, but a lump was forming beneath her scalp. He hoped the Dr. John team wouldn't notice. In the meantime, he kept watching her for wakefulness, his skin prickling in apprehension and anger over her vile attempt to thwart him.

Finally, the wayward sheep opened her eyes. She blinked. She scanned the room as if trying to remember her place in it. After spotting Darwin and the pistol, a lone tear fell from her eye.

Darwin smiled.

He had won.

44

———————

JEREMY

Jeremy had no idea what kind of hell awaited him. Last to file off the bus, his rear end banged the door's release handle, making it buzz in reverberation until the grim-lipped driver stilled it, her disapproving gaze not lost on him.

Departing passengers climbed into waiting vehicles. Some entered the station, maybe to pee or grab a soda. Jeremy was tempted to do the same, not because he had a full bladder or craved a drink, but because he longed to put off an encounter he didn't yet understand.

He hovered outside the bus, not sure where to go. The usual city sounds of traffic, horns, and diesel engines greeted him, and a bank sign across the street told him it was seven minutes past four. The air was cool but not uncomfortable. A scrawny woman with scraggly hair and a drugged-out look darted past, ramming Jeremy's bag. "Sorry," she mumbled, not bothering to turn around.

He gripped the duffel bag to his side. Having seen no need for the empty bow-and-arrows box, he'd left it on the bus.

"Jeremy."

His mother's voice. Off to the left.

In a small parking area, he saw George standing outside of a dark SUV, the only other vehicle a white Honda four spaces away. Connie's head poked through the rear window.

Oh, thank God.

George waved Jeremy over. Confused and cautious, Jeremy shuffled forward and heaved himself into the front passenger seat as instructed. He found Sue behind the wheel, an apologetic expression on her face and a clotted lump on the side of her head. Stupidly, he wondered what scared him more, her wound or her driving around Dallas.

Behind Sue sat George, spine forward, body rigid. Connie trembled next to him.

"Oh, Jeremy, I'm so sorry." His mother, wide-eyed and tear-streaked, leaned forward as if wanting to hug him. George forced her back, bouncing her head off the headrest.

Scared, Jeremy shifted his heft to reach and grab his mother's hand, forgetting all about his anger and hurt over her lie. He saw the duct tape around her wrists and looked at George in horror. The man responded by ramming a gun against Connie's head.

This can't be happening, Jeremy thought. "Wh-what's going on?"

"Don't you worry, Eating Bull. You'll find out soon enough." George shifted the handgun to the back of Sue's head and instructed her to drive. "Take the exact route we discussed, understand?"

Sue nodded, and despite the gun kissing her scalp, her ready compliance terrified Jeremy. That was not the warrior woman he knew. Inside, his guts bubbled and churned as if he'd purchased that soda after all.

"Give me your wrists," George ordered Jeremy as Sue pulled out of the lot. From George's left hand dangled a lengthy strip of duct tape.

Hands shaking, Jeremy pushed the bag down between his legs. At three feet long and stuffed with a similarly sized bow, the task wasn't easy, and the duffel jutted up between his spread thighs.

Against his better judgment but guided by the roving gun, he held out his hands, allowing George to lean forward and duct tape his wrists together.

"A nice long strip for you, butter boy."

Jeremy saw his mother wince, but then, as if for Jeremy's sake, she attempted a smile. A red, dotty rash circled her lips, as if someone had ripped off a bandage.

"Okay, whale boy, this is how it's going down. You're going to sit there, shut up, and cooperate. If you don't, your mother will die. It's that simple. As if..."

George's tone went from eerily controlled to incoherent rambling, and his eyes grew vacant, frightening Jeremy even more. The pistol caught his attention, particularly the initials scarred into the metal barrel: **R.B.**

Before Jeremy could stop himself, he blurted, "Is that my grandpa's gun?"

George blinked, awareness resurfacing. He nodded for several seconds before speaking. "Thanks to the element of surprise, not to mention my skill, the old bastard didn't even put up a fight."

Connie stared at George, open-mouthed. "Did you ... did you kill my father?"

"Told you I was capable of anything." He raised his voice. "Tell him, Susie Q. Tell the fat porker I'm capable of anything."

"Yes," was the warrior's subdued response.

A new wave of fear engulfed Jeremy. His mouth dried up, while his skin grew moist and clammy. Had George really killed his grandfather?

He's lying. Just trying to scare me.

For the next few horrifying minutes, Jeremy listened as George's monotonous tone listed off the murders he had committed, starting with Sue's boss and ending with a "fat sheep at a gas station."

"A fat-ass like you. Hogging my space, contaminating my air, soiling me with his diabetic flesh. And yet *I* have to pay for his health care." George's pitch rose, and he launched back into spacey mutterings.

George a killer? Because people are fat?

No matter how many times the thought pinged around his brain, Jeremy couldn't grasp it. Nor the idea of his grandpa being dead.

GI Dick? No way.

Controlled George resurfaced from his rambling and reached into the side pocket of his cargo pants. He plucked out a phone sheathed in a rainbow-striped case. Had to be Sue's.

After pulling up a contact, George told them he was texting the assistant they were on their way. "Remember, Eating Bull, no heroics." Then the psycho laughed. "But what's a fat pussy like you going to do?"

George was right. He wasn't Kajika. Or Dan. Or even Tito. He was yellow-bellied Jeremy.

"Almost there, Susie Q. Good girl. See? You *can* let someone else tell you what to do."

In a kind, almost childlike tone, Sue said, "Please, Darwin, it's not too late."

Darwin? Who the hell's Darwin?

"I can stop the car and let you out. No one will have to know it went this far."

"Shut up, you controlling witch!" George's face ballooned into a twisted, purple beet, and all three captives jumped.

They drove the rest of the way in silence, Jeremy staring out the window, his body rigid and tense. City morphed into country. To the right, fields of long grass. To the left, a well-kept trailer park.

Sue signaled and took the next exit. It led to a winding road, where a sign indicated the Dr. John studio complex was up ahead. One mile to go, though one mile to what, Jeremy had no idea.

As they entered the complex and approached a white security booth, George cut Jeremy's wrist binds with a switchblade. Sue decelerated the SUV to a crawl, and George issued a final warning to comply. To reiterate the point, he tickled Connie's side with the gun barrel. No one laughed.

Inside the small booth, a graying guard with a starched shirt emblazoned with the Dr. John Show logo greeted them. Ear buds burrowed into his ears, and he whipped them out, a flush reddening his cheeks.

"Oh, sorry. Distracted by my podcast. Not much else to do at this hour. What can I do you for?"

Before Sue could answer as George had instructed, the guard peered into the car and recognized both Sue and Jeremy. "Oh, welcome. Dr. John is expecting you. I'll let them know you're on your way. Drive about a quarter mile and turn left. You'll see the studio on the right. Farther ahead is the barn for the audience, but of course, that's empty now. Tomorrow though, well, you'll be a star." The guard winked at Sue and added, "And for the record, I think it's great what you're doing."

Sue offered a weak smile and drove off before the guard could say anything more. She followed the path as directed, her jaw sagging and her eyes sad.

A quarter mile later they were at a white, single-level home with plush landscaping, scattered flower beds, and a pond in back. Three ducks floated on the portion visible to the upcoming guests, the water rippling and shimmering in the setting sun. A small porch ran the length of the home, centered by four stairs leading from a stone walkway to an ornate front door.

Dr. John already waited at the entrance, still a good distance from their vehicle in the U-shaped driveway. To Jeremy, he looked like he did on TV, only instead of a suit, he wore jeans and a hunter-green sweater over a checkered, collared shirt. His light brown hair lifted in the wind, giving him a movie-star quality despite the rounded belly. Behind him, Jeremy saw a woman peeking over his shoulder. He assumed that was Dawn, a producer he'd spoken with on the phone a couple weeks back.

The psychologist waved at them, and when George rolled down the window, warning those in the car to silence with GI Dick's gun, Dr. John called out, "Come on in. It's only me, Dawn, and Monty, my cameraman. We didn't want to overwhelm Jeremy. We know it's been a tough day."

Dr. John's smile was as genuine as George's was spooky. To nobody in particular, their captor mumbled, "And what the wolf wants to know, the sheep delivers."

George shifted his gaze to each of them in turn. "Fatso, you'll go first, then Susie Q, Mama, and me. Follow my orders, and everything will go according to plan."

Before opening any car doors, George ripped off another piece of tape, handed it to Jeremy, and tilted his head toward Sue. "Wrap her wrists together tightly."

Jeremy once again did as he was told, hating himself for doing so. George then took two sweaters lying on the back seat — a white one Jeremy identified as his mother's and a colorful, striped one — and flung them over the women's bound hands to hide the tape. When he finally gave Jeremy the go, Jeremy stepped out of the SUV on legs more wobbly than the disgusting flan dessert Sue had eaten at the restaurant the night before.

Was that only last night?

With trembling arms and moist eyes, he reached inside the vehicle for his bag but stiffened when George said, "You won't need that, Eating Bull."

"Um, I have diaries of my weight loss and stuff. Dr. John wanted to see them." The swiftness with which the lie came both relieved and impressed him.

George stared, face impassive. "Whatever. Just get going."

Like children on a field trip, they formed a single-file line and marched toward the stairs.

George can't do anything with three other people in the house, can he?

Then again, the guy had killed people in sick, twisted ways because they were fat. No telling what he would do. He'd said if they followed his orders though, everything would go according to plan.

But what exactly was that plan?

45

———————

SUE

As a child, Sue had loved hopscotch. A skip of a rock and a hop. Crossing Dr. John's long stone pathway, each plate a different gray hue, the game surfaced in her mind. Unfortunately, George had a different game planned, one whose objective he alone understood.

Did he kill Connie's dad? Will he hurt my Kayla? Al?

Sue shuddered, her head throbbing from both physical and mental pain and her body shaky. Thank God she'd been able to drive. She prayed the injury was a simple concussion and nothing more serious. She had to remain sharp. Had to try and keep her mouth shut no matter how difficult it proved. After George's murderous confessions, all doubts of bluffing were gone. If they played along though, maybe they'd be okay.

Oh, dear God, please let us be okay.

Dr. John held the beveled glass door open for his approaching guests. His face was tanned and his expression welcoming, though his gaze was focused solely on Jeremy, the leader of their single-file pack.

Sue's sweater draped her wrists and hands, the colorful fabric flapping in the breeze but not betraying the silver tape underneath. Inside her blazer, she shivered. She watched Jeremy take slow, unsure strides, duffel bag ramming his right thigh. He gazed periodically over his shoulder at Connie who walked behind Sue. Bringing up the rear was George, likely pressing his gun into the small of Connie's back.

"Welcome, welcome," Dr. John said when they finally reached the porch. He extended his hand to Jeremy in greeting.

Dawn peered over the psychologist's right shoulder, and a young cameraman with a bald pate stood to the host's left, recording their entry.

"Don't worry about Monty here." Dr. John waved dismissively. "Just because we're taping doesn't mean we'll use everything we record."

Jeremy shook Dr. John's hand and nodded in response. The boy's expression emanated more emotion than Sue had yet seen from him. Too bad that emotion was fear.

After a brief nod to the rest of them, Dr. John put his arm around Jeremy and led him inside. Monty followed behind with the camera. The psychologist's focus remained on Jeremy. He hardly acknowledged the rest of them, probably trying to put the boy at ease.

Darwin's right arm still pressed against Connie's back, as if in loving support, which was how it would appear to Dawn from the front. He smiled as the assistant made small talk, but Sue knew the slightest provocation could set him off. For the past several hours, she'd seen the man go from calm and controlled, to vacant muttering space cadet, to enraged psychopath.

Don't do anything stupid, she told herself, blinking, her vision blurred since the skull-crushing blow.

The group followed Dr. John and his team through a wide foyer into an expansive studio-lit room with ocean-blue walls and white wainscoting. Crown molding of a similar wood ran the length of the ceiling.

Blue, the color of calm.

Not today, Sue thought.

A large leather couch rested a few feet in front of the back wall, where an arched doorway on the left opened into a peach-colored kitchen. Another arched door on the right led to a hallway which Sue suspected housed bedrooms, though what purpose they served in the make-shift studio, she didn't know. A matching leather loveseat and two brown checkered chairs aligned perpendicularly to the sofa on either side, allowing all parties to face each other.

Guests not held at gun point, that is.

Sue felt a golf-ball sized knot in her throat. If anything happened to Jeremy or his mother, could she ever forgive herself?

Monty, still filming, backed up to the arched doorway leading to the kitchen. Dr. John turned and faced his guests. Fanning his arms out, he invited everyone to take a seat. "Wherever you're comfortable."

A fraction of a second later, a shriek split the air. "He's got a gun!" Dawn cried, hands waving and eyes widening.

For a moment, time seemed to stand still, confusion on Dr. John and Monty's faces. Then George raised the gun into full view and ordered everyone to the couch. "Not you, Monty. You stay there and keep taping."

Dr. John's expression went from surprise to anger. "What in the hell is going on here?" The television host made a move toward George.

"Stop or I'll put a bullet in her head." George's words were flat but specific. The gun's barrel rested against Connie's skull. What little composure the woman had managed to find crumbled. Her face melted into fear and fatigue, and a series of sobs bubbled from her lips.

Dr. John froze but then took another tentative step forward. Sue shook her head forcefully. She wanted to tell the psychologist that George meant what he said, but no words came out. *A first, for sure,* her husband would say.

"Trust me. I'll blow her brains out. You think you can get the gun? Maybe. But she'll be dead first."

George's threat had the intended effect, and Dr. John stopped advancing, but Sue could see the wheels churning in his mind. Wondering how he could get his security's attention, no doubt. Sue wondered if there was anyone else besides the booth guard. Probably not, given the hour.

After weighing his response, everyone else rooted to their spots on the cushy carpet, Dr. John said, "Listen, I'm more confused than a chicken in a pig pen, but let's take it nice and slow. You tell us what it is that you want, and I'll do my best to make it happen."

"Now you're talking, Doc." George looked at Monty, the camera still raised in the man's trembling hands, his distressed, dark eyes hovering above the viewfinder. "You keep taping. Talk about a juicy show, right?"

George's thin-lipped grimace reminded Sue of a horror-movie monster. She wondered if they could overtake him. Six to one.

But at what price? Whose price?

"As for the rest of you, get over on the couch. Now." George retrieved the roll of duct tape from his left pocket, gun still in his right hand against Connie's head. When no one moved, he shouted, "Sit the fuck down!"

To Sue it seemed even the giant mirror above the fireplace shook at George's intensity. Dr. John and Dawn scurried to the sofa, and Connie and Sue followed, their sweaters still dangling from their bound wrists. The four fit on the large piece of furniture without difficulty.

Jeremy moved closer to the couch but stood looking helpless as to where he should go. George handed him the tape and commanded him to bind Dr. John and Dawn's wrists behind their backs, starting with the host. Jeremy took the tape, hands visibly shaking, and moved behind the couch where he dropped his bag and followed George's instructions.

While he taped Dawn's wrists, George making sure of his compliance, Sue saw Monty shift in her peripheral vision and start to lower the recorder. She wondered if the cameraman was contemplating overtaking George while he was distracted by Jeremy's task. The terrified part of her hoped he did, but the sensible part hoped he didn't.

Monty must have thought his odds were good, because he dropped the camera and charged toward George.

But George was too quick. He saw the cameraman and swung the gun in his direction, halting Monty in his tracks. At the same time, Dr. John bolted up, and before Sue even processed what she was doing, she burst up as well.

Three against one.

A gunshot popped and echoed in the spacious room. Dr. John cried out, blood darkening the thigh of his jeans. Sue rushed to the psychologist, but George punched her aside. She fell backward and landed hard on her tailbone in front of the couch. With bound wrists and blurred vision from a new rush of pain and vertigo, attempts at righting herself failed, and she plopped back down against the sofa's leather folds.

In her dizzy fugue, she heard Connie crying and Dawn yelling. "Please, you have to let me help him. He's bleeding."

Sue blinked, trying to clear the mental fog, wondering how much damage the earlier blow had done to her head. Once again she tried to pull herself up onto the couch.

Jeremy? Where is Jeremy? Are you okay?

She heard George order everyone back on the sofa. She finally managed to get there on her own.

"Keep taping, keep taping," George hollered at Monty. "Everybody shut up. If you don't want anyone else to get hurt, just shut up. It's time to…"

George trailed off, and his gaze shifted to the wall beyond their heads. He mumbled something incoherent but startled back to attention when Dr. John's phone rang.

"That's probably my security guard wondering if everything's okay. You best get out of here if you don't want to be discovered."

Was Dr. John right? Had the security guard heard the gun shot? Over his podcast?

Sue tried to focus her mind, tried to will reasonable thought through the disorientation of pain, fear, and despair.

The look on George's face told her he wasn't worried about Dr. John's warning. Or at least Darwin wasn't, given his was the expression her deranged colleague wore.

Blood saturated the left thigh of Dr. John's jeans. Sue knew she needed to apply pressure to the wound but was relieved the bullet entry was far from the femoral artery. She bit down on her lower lip, trying to remain calm. For the first time since George had abducted them, she believed she would not survive the night.

So many deaths already. All on me.

Sweat dotted George's handsome face, but if he was nervous, his steady grip on the pistol didn't betray him. He moved closer to Dr. John, seated on the end of the couch nearest the kitchen. "If you or anyone else tries that again, I'll kill you, but if you cooperate and your man keeps taping, we can accomplish what I came here for." George gave another one of his eerie smiles. "I promise, you'll have one hell of a show on your hands. Help me spread my word, and none of your team has to die."

Sue wondered if what George said was true. Would he really let them go? If so, what was his point? Reading his so-called manifesto on camera? Then why did he need Jeremy and Connie? Or her?

Oh, dear God, please don't let him hurt Jeremy. That boy doesn't deserve this.

She thought about Sammy. He had to be going crazy, wondering why they hadn't called or texted. Her phone had gone off repeatedly in George's pocket, though he'd switched it to vibrate, silencing its annoying chirp once and for all.

Just like he might silence them.

Thoughts of her family weighted her already heavy heart, and she almost joined Connie in tears, but she had to stay strong. Weakness would accomplish nothing.

Dr. John's phone rang again. Sue glanced at him. His face was pale, and his demeanor had weakened. No longer was he telling George what to do.

George straightened, stepped back, and looked to each of them in turn, first Dr. John, then Dawn, followed by Connie and Sue. Then he settled his narrowed gaze on Jeremy. His hand tightened around the gun, and he reached for something in his back pocket.

"The time has come, sheep. Time for Darwin to make history."

46

DARWIN

A mind could play tricks. Over the years Darwin had learned that. Sometimes, after hours in the cold basement closet, a young George would daydream. He would conjure a world of playmates, laughing fathers, and smiling mothers. Thin, smiling mothers wearing white summer dresses with cherries on the hems. Little George had liked cherries. He liked the sweet red juice. But now George was gone, and red blood had replaced cherry nectar. Sweet red blood had crowned Darwin king.

Survival of the fittest.

(*You're so close. Don't lose focus.*)

Standing in the center of the room, the studio lights illuminating his perfection, Darwin pulled the manifesto from his back pocket and gripped the pages in his hands. Not that he would need them. The sentences were a part of him, as vital to his existence as his heart and lungs. He homed his gaze on Jeremy. Another vital part of his existence.

Not anticipating the sheeps' revolt had been a mistake. Like the nurse, the doctor considered himself a wolf. Darwin had squelched their resistance, but at what cost? Had the slovenly guard heard the gunshot? Doubtful, given his absence.

Still, events had not proceeded orderly.

(*Focus. Order has been restored.*)

The Voice was right. The doctor lay back against the sofa, bloodied leg but bloodless face. Weak and powerless. A Texas sheep.

(*You are the master. Recite your words to the world.*)

Darwin cleared his throat. He ordered the cameraman to tape his address. Noting Monty's strong arms and thin frame, he added, "Obey and you may one day be among the disciplined few."

Monty said nothing but maintained the camera on Darwin as commanded.

Lifting his face to the recording device, Darwin began his recitation, speaking with a confidence only those of his caliber possessed. Sensing time was running out, he started halfway down the page, but despite the urgency to finish before further interruption, he could not deny his pride at having reached the mission's pinnacle.

"America, you are a laughingstock," he began. "Nothing but gluttonous fools stuffing their empty heads and massive bellies. I, Darwin, the leader of this movement, a movement made necessary by the mindless, masticating sheep of this land, refuse to be mocked by association. The time has come to seize control. Government restrictions will fail. Motivational pep talks will fail. Litigation will fail. Only fear will succeed, threat of immediate death by my hands or those of my disciples. With my knife, the pathetic, mouth-stuffing sheep will curb their gluttonous acts. But despite my strength, I cannot act alone. I need the likeminded, the disciplined, the strong to stand alongside me. Survival of the fittest."

Darwin paused for effect, reveling in the faces of respect and awe before him.

Four sheep on the sofa, clinging to my words. One fat sheep behind them. A likeminded follower recording my brilliance.

The mission was proceeding perfectly. Control and order had been restored, and Darwin's grip on the Beretta remained strong.

He continued. "Brothers, sharpen your knives. Sisters, gather your guns. There is work to be done. Through fear, we will reclaim our country, one gluttonous sheep at a time."

(*Look how they shrink before your gun. Look how they hang on your every word.*)

On and on the words flowed until, with The Voice's encouragement, Darwin delivered his last lines, gaze unwavering from the camera. "To clarify my intent, I offer a sacrifice. A sacrifice for you, America. A symbol of what's to come."

Darwin paused one final time, redirecting his gaze on Jeremy. As always, his stomach heaved in disgust at the fat blob, its round face pink and moist. The boy's trembling hands gripped his mother's shoulders, one frightened sheep clinging to another.

Before Darwin could stop it, an image of young George flashed in his brain. A grade-school boy, fat and fatherless, lonely and sad.

(*We're so close. Discipline, Darwin. There is too much at stake.*)

Darwin blinked the image away. *Yes, much at stake. The time has come.*

Bolstered, he finished his recitation. "America. I give you the poster boy of fat, a boy who blames the world for his morbid obesity. For you—"

"Please, George, stop. This is insane."

The mother's plea caught Darwin by surprise. He had not expected protest from her, weak as she was. He shifted the gun toward her head and watched as the whale's hands dug deeper into his mother's shoulders, his face suggesting he would soon soil his pants.

Then, shockingly, the boy spoke up. "Don't you dare hurt my mom." His voice cracked, and a tear trickled down his doughy, flushed cheek.

Darwin laughed. "Is that the best you've got? Once a pussy, always a pussy, I suppose. But no more. Today you will be a martyr."

More pleas from the mother, cries from the nurse, grumbling from the doctor. Darwin ignored them all. Such was his discipline.

"Monty, be sure and get this now," he ordered.

George raised the handgun, aimed it at the boy's heart, a fat-heavy heart destined to tick a short life even without Darwin's intervention.

"For you, America, a sacrifice. A new direction for a lost herd. I give to you: Eating Bull."

As Darwin's finger stroked the trigger, the mother sheep screamed and bolted from the couch. She swung at Darwin with her bound wrists, but like the doctor and nurse, she was no match for his speed and agility. He kicked her and sent her flying back toward the sofa, where she collided with the nurse who had also risen. Their presumptuousness both amused and irritated him, and as he was about to reverse his order and kill them first, the doctor too weak to interfere and his bound assistant too occupied with trying to help him, Monty lowered the camera. Before the cameraman could betray Darwin again, a voice from behind startled them all.

"Everything okay in here, Doc? You didn't answer your—"

(*Hurry, Darwin. You must hurry.*)

Darwin swung around. The guard stood in the doorway of the large room, eyes wide and hand fumbling for the gun perched upon his hip, but the sheep was not quick enough. Darwin fired. A crack boomed within the stunned room. The bullet pierced the man's left chest, and given the Beretta's smaller caliber ammunition, Darwin was pleased with his aim. One shot to the heart was all it took, even with the gun's inferior lethality. Tan shirt became red.

Just like cherry juice.

The ineffective security sheep clutched his chest in shock, and then, as if remembering his own weapon, he reached for his gun once again. He never got past the holster belt. He collapsed to the ground, bubbling a few final hiccups before falling silent.

For a moment Darwin blinked in confusion, but The Voice came to his rescue.

(Quick. Get his gun. Then get the boy or it will be too late.)

Darwin sprang for the security guard's gun and shoved it into the thigh pocket of his cargo pants. Then he whipped his body back toward the sofa where the weeping, screaming, and fumbling sheep awaited their destiny. He had to finish. Time for the boy. He had to get the boy.

But when Darwin looked behind the couch, the boy was gone.

47

JEREMY

If someone had told Jeremy that by the end of the day, he'd be scurrying along the floor like a crab, huffing, puffing, and dragging his fat rolls and duffel bag across Dr. John's kitchen linoleum, he would have thought the person insane. Yet there he was doing it, clueless as to his next move.

After George had shot the guard, something in Jeremy snapped, and before he knew what he was doing, he dived to the floor and set off for the nearby kitchen. A result of gut instinct or shock, he had no idea. All he knew was a theoretical escape window had opened and he prayed he'd fit through it. Someone had to act.

Once out of view of the living room, he heaved himself to his feet and contemplated his next move. Lemon-scented chrome appliances and white cupboards surrounded him. Sweat dripped off his face and plopped to the floor. Everything was sharp and clear, as if viewed through a high-powered lens.

He spotted another arched doorway in the back. With duffel bag slung over his shoulder and slamming against his hip, he ran through it, ending up in a rose-colored dining room. From there he reached the hallway he'd seen earlier when he entered the home. One big connecting square. Three bedrooms lined the hallway, the first two nearby, the last one farther away. He resisted looking over his shoulder for George and ignored the cries and chaos coming from the living room. His only focus was reaching the far bedroom on the right.

The measure of a man is how well he can stand up to life's shit. How well he can fight it.

Dan's words echoed in Jeremy's brain as he huffed into the bedroom, its hunting-themed décor eerily appropriate for a kid about to discover his measure.

Jeremy plopped the duffel bag on a wide daybed, its down comforter dotted with deer and rifles. He grasped at the bag's zipper, but his trembling fingers fumbled and slipped over the metal aperture. His lungs wheezed, and his airway felt two inches too narrow, but there was no time for a puff from his inhaler.

"Connie, don't."

Jeremy heard the warrior woman's warning from down the hall, and the thought of George hurting Connie fueled Jeremy's anger and made his sausage fingers comply. Despite the sweat dampening his palms, he yanked out the bow along with two arrows, tucking the spare into the back waist of his sweatpants. With an energy he'd never known, he grasped the bow with his left hand, knuckles blanched from the pressure, and loaded an arrow into the arrow rest with his right. Raising that arm, he pulled the hemp-fiber bowstring back until it was taut and tight, hungry to release its weapon.

Sweat dripped into his eyes, but he puffed the droplets away with rapid, wheezing breaths.

Scuffling and screams nearby. Were the others putting up a fight? Could they restrain George, allowing Jeremy to trade bow and arrow for asthma inhaler?

A gun shot popped, and Jeremy's bowels cramped in fear. Something thumped against the wall. Cries followed, a blend of male and female pitches.

Please don't let my mom be dead. Please oh please oh please...

He heard his mother shout, "Jeremy, get out! He's coming for you."

He sagged in relief at his mother's voice, but footsteps in the hall near the first bedroom made him quickly tighten his grip on the weapon.

"He's coming. Jeremy, he's coming." The warning emanated from Sue, though it sounded weak.

Did George shoot the warrior woman?

A wave of nausea washed over Jeremy, and he fought the urge to vomit. His heart thumped in his chest.

"Come on out, Eating Bull. If not, Mommy's gonna swallow a bullet." George sounded crazed, and Jeremy imagined the pistol pressed against his mother's head. The guy already shot two (*three?*) people. What was to keep him from shooting Connie as well?

Stomach acid splashed and burned his throat.

"Jeremy, get out! George, please don't."

His mother's sobs nearly eroded Jeremy's resolve. What made him think he could take the guy? He stole a glance at the bedroom window and hesitated, wondering if he'd fit through its frame. He shook his head and turned back to the doorway.

I have to do this.

Footsteps in the second bedroom. A closet opening and closing.

The measure of a man is how well he can stand up to life's shit. How well he can fight it.

Jeremy tightened his grip on the bow and pulled the arrow back even more, wiping sweat away from his face with his right shoulder. He took a deep, wheezy breath and stepped into the hallway.

Exiting the second bedroom were George (*or Darwin, or whoever the hell he was*) and Connie, a gun against her head as Jeremy had feared. His mother's eyes flashed pure panic, and Jeremy knew that a natural or not, he was not a good enough archer to avoid hitting her.

When George spotted Jeremy and the weapon in his hands, the psycho's surprise made him halt, allowing Connie the opening she needed to wriggle from his grasp, clearing the way for Jeremy.

Without thought or pause or second-guessing, Jeremy let the arrow fly. The tip found its target, but George had shifted his body to regain hold of Connie, and only his left arm was pierced.

George howled and stared at the arrow sticking out of his upper arm. At first stunned, his face soon blazed livid. Connie once again freed herself, but George seemed not to notice. Instead, his concentration was on Jeremy.

Not bothering to remove the embedded arrow, George raised the gun in his right hand. "You're dead, fat-ass."

Jeremy fumbled to load the spare arrow, his mind focused on nothing else, not even the firing of George's gun, which echoed through the hall and released the scent of gunpowder at the same time

Jeremy shifted his body and the second arrow took flight. The stone tip pierced the left side of George's chest.

The wacko who was once his mom's boyfriend fell backward, psychosis and craze replaced by confusion and uncertainty.

"Survival of the fittest," Jeremy mumbled.

But something felt wrong. He couldn't breathe. He felt weak. Really weak. As though he might faint.

Connie came running down the hall, followed by a shell-shocked Dawn and a bleeding, limping Sue.

He wanted to tell the warrior woman he was relieved to see her alive, but when he tried to speak, nothing came. Around him mouths moved, faces blurred, and gazes slid to his belly.

Jeremy looked down. He saw a blood stain on the left side of his T-shirt. *Hey, it looks like Texas,* he thought before grayness clouded his vision. Like a cool sheet on a hot body, he floated to the soft carpet. Never had he felt so light. So weightless and thin.

The last words Jeremy heard were the warrior woman demanding to know if Monty had called 9-1-1 and ordering Dawn to get something to cut their tape.

Jeremy smiled in his new darkness.

Even with a bullet in her, the woman was bossy.

48

———

SUE

No, *no, no, don't you dare die, Jeremy.*
Dropping to the floor with bound wrists and a bullet in her hip wasn't easy, but through gritted teeth and a yelp, Sue managed to get there. "Connie, we need to apply pressure until I can assess the wound."

The mother, bent over her son, didn't seem to hear, just kept kissing Jeremy's head, her taped hands as useless as Sue's. "Jeremy, oh Jeremy, wake up, sweetie. Please. Oh God oh God oh God oh—"

"Connie." Sue's tone was sharp and clipped and accomplished the desired goal. Connie lifted herself off her son's torso, tears once again streaking her face which had long since been cleansed of makeup. Jeremy's blood stained her pink dress.

"Dawn, I need something to cut this tape. Now." Sue's command bellowed down the hall, and until her request was granted, she planted bound hands onto the left side of Jeremy's abdomen where the majority of blood pooled. She needed to remove his shirt and see where the bullet hit.

In the meantime, her right hip burned and throbbed. The injury forced full extension of her limb, while her left leg crouched at Jeremy's side, as if she were merely stretching her thigh muscle rather than tending to the shooting of a fifteen-year-old boy.

Given the lack of significant bleeding, she suspected her own bullet had landed superficially in her hip muscle, a hip with the right amount of cushion, according to Al.

Where are those scissors? Or a knife. Anything.

Sue hoped Monty was okay. The two of them had charged George when he pursued Jeremy, netting Monty a hard tackle and a head thump on the granite counter and Sue a poorly aimed gunshot. Though not knocked out, Monty had lain there stunned. Hopefully, he'd recovered enough to call 9-1-1.

Where on earth did the bow and arrows come from?

"Here, I found these." A breathless Dawn hustled down the hallway and dropped to her knees. With kitchen shears, she cut Sue's duct tape and then started on Connie's. "Sorry it took so long. Monty didn't come to right away, and I needed him to cut my own binds. And Dr. John, well, he doesn't look so good. I'm just so—"

"Did you call 9-1-1? And get me some towels for the wound." Sue wasted no time and started cutting away Jeremy's shirt.

"Monty did. He's staying with Dr. John. He's—"

"Back up. Please. Both of you. I need room."

Dawn took off back down the hallway, and Connie pulled away from Jeremy, her face drawn and anxious.

Sue found Jeremy's carotid pulse. A strong heartbeat drummed against her fingers, and she closed her eyes in relief. Remembering Jeremy's ashen face from his clinic blood draw, she realized the sight of his own blood had probably contributed to his collapse. The boy's eyelids fluttered open, and for a moment he looked at Sue. Then he closed them again.

Sue pulled off her blazer, the blouse underneath sticking uncomfortably to her skin after a day of high-octane perspiration. The maneuver blasted a lightning bolt of pain through her hip and thigh, and she nearly bit her tongue from the spasm. Her body heat skyrocketed, and her heartbeat thumped in her ears, suggesting she might join Jeremy in his blackout. When the pain's intensity weakened, she wiped Jeremy's wound with her blazer and inspected the injury.

"Is it okay? Will my Jeremy be okay?"

Sue nodded at Connie, not trusting her emotions enough to speak. The bullet had entered the left outer abdomen and appeared to exit laterally through the soft tissue. From its position, Sue assumed it missed the spleen along with the other internal organs. For once, Jeremy might be grateful for his own extra cushion.

The blood flow diminished, but she maintained pressure none-theless, praying the ambulance would arrive.

Jeremy's eyelids fluttered open again.

"Jeremy? Can you hear me?" Sue asked.

The teenager blinked, then nodded. He raised his head a bit and looked at his belly. The shredded, bloody T-shirt splayed open, revealing white mounds of flesh streaked with congealing blood. His eyes rolled back, and Sue worried he'd faint again.

"Jeremy. Stay with us. You're okay. You're going to be okay."

"Oh, my baby. Did you hear that? You'll be okay, sweetie."

Jeremy's eyes fought to stay open. He offered a small smile to Connie. Then he rolled his head toward Sue and croaked, "Did I get the crazy bastard?"

Sue barked out a laugh. "Yes, honey, you did." Her expression quickly sobered. "I'm so sorry. Sorry I got you into this."

Jeremy shook his head and tried to prop himself up. His strength encouraged Sue that the wound was even more superficial than she'd thought, but she gently pushed him back down, not wanting his abdominal pressure increased. "Stay down. You'll risk more bleeding."

"Not your fault," Jeremy said, complying, his words escaping in a wheezy rush. "Dude was insane. By globbing him onto us, you prob-ably stopped worse from happening."

He batted at something on his right side, and when he mumbled for his inhaler, Connie retrieved it from his pocket. After two puffs assisted by his mother, Jeremy fell silent and Sue could feel his muscles relax.

When he looked her way again, she said, "I appreciate you trying to make me feel better, but it's still on me."

"Least you had the guts to do something," he said.

Smoothing back Jeremy's sweaty, clumped hair, Sue smiled and shushed him. "There are all kinds of bravery in this world, my friend, but unexpected acts from the quietest among us are the bravest of all."

With that, she bent down and kissed his doughy cheek.

———

After Sue showed Connie how to maintain pressure over Jeremy's wound, she called out to make sure Dr. John was okay. He insisted she tend to Jeremy and not worry about his "tough Texan ass." Then it was time to face what she dreaded.

George.

Although convinced he was dead, it was her duty as a nurse to confirm. If not, he too would need attention.

As much as she hated to give it.

The touching interaction with Jeremy had taxed her heart, and she wanted nothing more than to be back with her family, away from the nightmare. Despite Jeremy's reassurances, Sue knew the recent horrors were on her.

Down the hallway she heard Dawn say, "Are you sure you should be taping this?"

"Hell if I know. Haven't exactly experienced shit like this before. The doc asked me to do it."

Monty sounded as uncertain and frightened as the rest of them, but Sue barely registered their conversation. Instead, she called for Dawn to help her, while the faint sound of sirens materialized.

With Dawn's assistance, Sue scooted backward on the cream carpeting, ignoring the explosive pain in her hip and the blood trail she left behind. As disturbing as the task was, she had to confirm George was dead.

Two fingers to the carotid artery served up the answer. No pulse. Although relieved, Sue also felt a hollow sadness. How long had the man been hearing voices, for surely that must have been the case? Were there signs she'd overlooked, so busy with her own life and responsibilities? Can people ever truly know those around them?

With enough blame on her plate to feed Cleveland, Sue studied George's face. Gone were the seething gaze and sneering mouth. In their place, surprise and confusion. Had he, too, wondered what had led him to his final act?

Goodbye, George Koster. I pray you finally find peace.

Sue dragged her heavy, increasingly numb extremity to the living room to check on Dr. John. Maybe Jeremy was right. Maybe the heinous murders George had committed weren't her fault. But his hurting Jeremy? That was on her, and she'd have to carry that burden for the rest of her life.

But live she would. Jeremy too. And despite the day's horrific events — or maybe because of them — they would get their message out. The right message. Not George's messed-up delusions.

His deranged scheme only magnified her belief: society, not individuals alone, needed to solve the country's weight problem. Name calling, finger pointing, and righteous superiority were not the way to invoke change. Everybody had a part to play.

Despite a bloodied and wounded hip, despite a sweet teenage boy who almost died, despite a family ready to disown her, Sue believed that as strongly as ever.

With the sirens growing louder, she planted herself in front of a weak but conscious Dr. John.

Would I do it all again?

Seeing that Dawn had adequately tended to the psychologist, Sue sank back against the base of the bloodied couch, too weak to mount its skewed cushions and pillows. She closed her eyes in exhaustion, breath relaxing when the siren blares reached the home, and pondered her own question.

Maybe she'd pay more attention to those she brought on board. Make sure they were fully invested, rather than twisting their wants to fit hers. Maybe she would better prepare her own family.

But social justice was in her blood.

The day I stop caring is the day I stop living.

Paramedics burst through the door, Dawn guiding them to the wounded, Monty capturing it all on film. Sammy and the police were right behind them. Sue supposed the lawyer had tried to call Dr. John, and when no one returned any of his calls, including her, he drove out to the ranch in exasperation and fear.

Would I do it again?

Sue grimaced.

She'd known the answer before she even asked.

EPILOGUE
JEREMY

Five months later

J eremy jogged down a residential street near his house. Spring air cooled the sweat on his face, and his heart thudded energetically against his ribs.

Can't believe I haven't needed my inhaler yet.

With arms pumping at his sides and sneakers pounding the pavement, his mind wandered back to the past several months.

If it was attention Sue and Sammy had wanted, they got it. A madman trying to kill a fat kid on camera tended to snare the public eye, especially when said kid was suing the food industry. According to George's manifesto, which he'd mailed to Tony Farr, the *Cleveland Times* reporter and Connie's new boyfriend, the plan was to kill the "litigious sheep" in front of the Dr. John live-audience taping, but thanks to Jeremy's flight to the powwow the day before, George had been forced to improvise.

Jeremy had learned about George's descent into madness from the news. Tales of the statistician sprouted in every media venue, but he also gleaned bits from Sue, like how the police found evidence of self-injury in the guy's condo as well as hundreds of jigsaw puzzles, some completed and some still in boxes, and enough workout equipment to fill a small gym. Nothing but health food, either. Stories of self-starvation, physical extremes, and pinched nipples and scrota abounded. How people had deduced the nipple and scrotal torture, Jeremy didn't know, nor did he want to find out. He'd had enough of George-slash-Darwin to last five lifetimes.

The attention had elevated Sue and Sammy's lawsuit to new heights, resulting in recruitment of an army of eager plaintiffs in a huge multi-state, class-action lawsuit, allowing Jeremy and Connie to opt out. Even Juney Andrews's family leaped on board, the formerly threatening father doing a one-eighty on his feelings for Sue. Together they used Juney's trying ordeal and her controversial removal from the home to fuel their cause. Although the litigation was still in its infancy and no food manufacturer or restaurant had discussed settlement, according to Sue, success was only a matter of time.

Jeremy had his doubts about that. More people than not thought the litigation was stupid. He gave the warrior woman credit though. At least the country was engaged, and some who previously blamed the obese alone for their weight had started to withdraw their skinny pointing fingers.

To Jeremy, the issue lay somewhere in between. No one forced the food in his mouth. No one told him to play video games instead of sweat through one of Fat Slayer Shelly's workouts. On the other hand, Burgers and Buns stacked the odds against him, and if what Sue said about the food industries was correct, that they spent lots of money to find the perfect combination of ingredients to make him keep stuffing his pie-hole, weren't they at fault too? At least in part?

Jeremy decided the issue was for Sue to deal with. He was focused on losing weight, which meant he still saw the warrior woman at the weight management clinic and occasionally for dinner at her house. She was as bossy as ever and just as tough. She told Jeremy that once she'd convinced the police to relinquish her surgically removed bullet after their investigation, she kept it in a spice jar on her office desk. "To remind me that social justice can never be silenced."

Jeremy checked his pedometer. *Over a mile already.* He kept jogging, his thoughts distracting him from the physical exertion.

Though Sue never stopped fighting, the warrior woman seemed happy. She was back at the health department doing work she loved and was thrilled with the center's new permanent director. "A boss who can tolerate my efficient personality," she'd said. The Fort family was back together as well, though the last Jeremy heard, Kayla still picked at her food.

Wish I had that problem, he thought. Then he felt bad for thinking it. Kayla was seeing a therapist. He shouldn't make light. *Same problem as me, just different ends of the spectrum.*

Sue's cop husband, Al, was glad there were other plaintiffs to take the spotlight off his wife. The litigation still didn't sit well with him, but over dinner one night he'd shrugged and told Jeremy, "If a bullet won't stop her, why should I?"

Sadly, GI Dick hadn't been so lucky. According to the autopsy report, George had slit the ex-soldier's throat, most likely to get the old guy's gun and keep him from calling the police. Jeremy's grandfather had not left his chair nor put up a fight, leading the medical examiner to conclude the man was either napping or caught unawares. Tony had found GI Dick the next day when he'd stopped by to see if the guy knew why Connie and Sue weren't answering Tony's text messages.

Jeremy's stride faltered. His eyes stung, though not from sweat alone. Despite his grandpa being a grade-A jerk, Jeremy grieved over the man's cruel death. No one deserved that.

Jeremy's own bullet was a through-and-through. A fat tissue fly-by, he liked to say. When the kids at school asked for details, patting his back and crowding around him, he omitted the part where he fainted at the sight of his own blood.

Starting the last six blocks of his jog (*one and a half miles so far — yes!*), Jeremy continued with mental distraction.

His life had been nonstop changes and challenges since Dallas. He'd forgiven his mother for lying about his father all those years, especially after he met Terry Harjo back in December. Terry had recognized Connie on television and saw his own face in Jeremy's. After what happened to Jeremy in Dallas, he contacted Sue again.

Jeremy would like to say he and his father had immediately bonded, but life wasn't a movie. Getting to know a father previously believed dead took time. Terry laid it all out for Jeremy. Told him not to be angry at Connie for lying. He was an ugly, drug-addled man in his youth who did ugly things as a result.

"Ain't no excuse, but it is what it is. All I can do now is show you I'm a changed man. If you'll let me, that is."

In the diner where he and Terry met, a lump of swallowed broccoli had lodged in Jeremy's throat. "My mom never told me anything."

"I'm not surprised. Your mom has a pure heart. Just like you, from what I hear." Terry smiled, his teeth stained and chipped. "She wouldn't want you thinking your dad was an addicted asshole, but the fact she gave you Harjo for a middle name shows she wanted you to have at least some link to your heritage."

Jeremy looked at his father and saw his own expressions on the man's roundish face. Though stocky like Jeremy, Terry packed far more muscle, probably a remnant of prison weightlifting. Their hair colors differed too, Connie's blonde diffusing Terry's jet black. "Do you still drink or do drugs?" Jeremy asked.

"Nothing, I swear. Got clean in prison and haven't touched it since. I understand if you never want to see me again, but I had to lay things out as they happened, start us from a place of honesty. Where you want it to go from here is up to you."

Jeremy thought about it for weeks. Then, with Connie's blessing, because he wouldn't have done it otherwise, he called his father. Terry had found a job as a dishwasher as well as a decent place to live. He said he'd like to move back to Muscogee territory, maybe get a job at a casino if they'd allow it with his one-eighth blood, but he wasn't sure he could leave until his probation was over. He pointed out he wanted to be on solid footing with Jeremy first though.

After their subsequent meetings, Jeremy figured they might work things out. Having another guy to talk to was a relief, especially someone who didn't belittle him like GI Dick had. He and Terry even talked about going to the Dorner Powwow the following fall, where Jeremy could introduce Terry to Dan Folsom.

Jeremy missed Dan. E-mails and phone calls kept them in communication, Dan voicing his pride over what Jeremy had done. "You're a natural warrior, Jeremy Harjo Barton. One that keeps the peace but defends himself and others when necessary."

Jeremy had practically burst upon hearing those words, and although he knew it was wrong, he wished Dan were his father instead.

But again, life was what it was, and Jeremy's finally seemed to be headed down the right path, especially with the warrior woman and the Fat Slayers' help. Dr. Green's, too, since Jeremy had started opening up to the weight management psychologist. Food, George, the shootings, GI Dick's death and Jeremy's response to it — they pretty much discussed everything. Jeremy felt lighter in body and spirit as a result. Pizza, hamburgers, and candy still beckoned, no lie, but their cries grew softer as the pounds fell off, fifty in total so far.

Another pedometer check. Two miles. Winded but not wheezy, Jeremy slowed to a fast walk. He'd met his goal.

Wait till I tell Shelly.

Since he'd mastered Fat Slayer Shelly's circuit workout, she was creating new goals for him each visit. The more he exercised, the less he hated it. He still used a controller inhaler for his asthma, but he hadn't used the rescue inhaler in weeks. The gray gunk around his neck from too much insulin in his blood had faded, and he was off the medication.

His improved health meant he didn't go to the emergency room anymore, but Dr. Sneeker had contacted Jeremy after the Dallas fiasco, and since then, the two played *War of the Wilderness* together online. Even though the doctor sucked and kept getting his avatar killed, Jeremy still had fun.

Jeremy rounded the block and headed for home, heart rate back to normal after his cool-down.

Next week I'll try for two and a half miles.

Dr. John had kept his word. Didn't bring up anything about Jeremy's dad when they finally taped the show for real. Then again, with the attempted murders, the television psychologist had plenty of fodder to fill half a dozen broadcasts or more.

Although Jeremy had feared the worst, his appearance on the Dr. John Show made him a celebrity at school. In a good way. Instead of Eating Bull, everyone called him Sitting Bull, a label spat out by the media after Jeremy's victory over George Koster, whose name was close to George Custer, the general defeated by Sitting Bull at Little Bighorn. Wrong tribe or not, Jeremy kind of liked it.

Instead of taunts, the kids at school asked for details about George, the bow and arrows, and how it all went down. They even fist bumped Jeremy on his leaner look, and though he still had a good eighty or ninety pounds to go and every day was a struggle, for the first time, he felt like he could do it. Besides, Tito had become the third Fat Slayer. No way was he going to let Jeremy backslide. Jeremy was back in Lacey's good graces as well. He hardly dared hope where that might lead.

Mr. and Mrs. Harris allowed Tito to hang with him again. Jeremy held no grudge. They just wanted their boy safe. Although they banned Tito from Facebook, their son discovered Twitter instead. He tweeted about Jeremy's weight-loss progress and said the account was getting lots of followers.

Jeremy mounted the five steps to his front door, the stupid frame still banging every time it closed. He could smell Connie's grilled lemon chicken, and his mouth watered in anticipation.

As he sprinted upstairs to shower, lighter in every sense of the word, grinning at the bow and arrows displayed in a glass case on his wall but sad his grandfather never got to see them, he thought about the best outcome of all: Calvin no longer bullied him. Well, he still ridiculed Jeremy from time to time, but Jeremy's new friends either ignored the red-headed pimple or told him to shut up. Even if they didn't spring to Jeremy's defense, it wouldn't bother him. He no longer found Calvin a threat. Jeremy had learned to fight back. He learned his true capabilities.

He found his measure as a man.

The End

AUTHOR'S NOTE

Although *Eating Bull* borrows from current events, the book is fiction. Other than Cleveland geography, most places are imaginary, including the Cuyahoga County Public Health Center, Mason High School, the unnamed children's hospital, Burgers and Buns, and other restaurants, hotels, fitness gyms, and stores. Furthermore, Dorner, Oklahoma is a fictional town as is its fictional powwow, though its creation stems from Durant, Oklahoma and its annual Choctaw Casino Resort Powwow, which is a wonderful experience if one's ever that way. Other fictional creations include restaurant alliances, Bilko's Snacks, Brover's Industries, the *Cleveland Times* newspaper, *U.S. Life Magazine*, *The Friday Inquirer*, and the online game *War of the Wilderness*.

Every public health department functions differently. Most do not have weight-management clinics, although many have specialty clinics for women and children, travel, tuberculosis, and others. But as with all fiction, some license is necessary to power the story. Furthermore, it is not my intent to villainize food industries alone, and unlike Sue I don't really believe lawsuits are the way to go. Many companies have started to improve the products they sell. Additionally, cities are working toward better built environments, including Cleveland which has put several initiatives into place. Rather, what I hope to highlight is the multiple determinants behind a complex problem like obesity, including individuals, families and social structures, communities, food and geographic environments, institutions, and policies. Public health practitioners understand real change can only occur when interventions target all levels, not just the individual alone. Although this novel takes place before the Affordable Care Act went into effect, passage of the healthcare law may improve things as well.

For readers who would like more information on the addictive qualities of fat, sugar, and salt, two excellent resources are: *Salt Sugar Fat* by Michael Moss (Random House) and *The End of Overeating, Taking Control of the Insatiable American Appetite* by David A. Kessler, MD (Rodale). The 2014 documentary, *Fed Up*, produced by Katie Couric and Laurie David, also highlights the food industry's role in obesity, particularly its effect on children.

Writing *Eating Bull* was difficult at times. I don't like fat-bashing, and I believe the media incorrectly finds overweight people one of the last acceptable bastions of politically incorrect humor. One need only watch television and movies to see that. But I do believe in engaging people in dialogue to improve not only our nation's health, but that of our children's, since they must shoulder the consequences of our actions. Though I would use different language to address the issue than Darwin, and even Jeremy who frequently denigrates himself, I hope through fiction I can invoke thoughtful reflection.

ACKNOWLEDGMENTS

Many thanks to Kevin, Lori, Mike, Alec, John, Elyse, and Marc for reading the book in its earlier stages and offering feedback. Thank you as well to Maddie, Dianne, and Frederick. Time is precious, and you giving me yours is greatly appreciated. The same goes for my social media friends without whom I would not have made it this far. Your support on Twitter, Facebook, my blog, and elsewhere means the world to me. Also thank you to my editor, Rebecca Dickson, and her team for giving my manuscript objective eyes. Furthermore, I want to thank Lance Buckley (Lance Buckley Design) for his eye-catching cover art and Science Thrillers Media for getting my book out there. And finally, a big thank you to my family members on both sides of the aisle for your support, and to my husband and sons for continuing to put up with my writing hibernation. I couldn't do it without you.

ABOUT THE AUTHOR

Carrie Rubin is a physician-turned-novelist who writes genre-bending medical thrillers. She also has a cozy mystery, *The Cruise Ship Lost My Daughter*, published under the pen name Morgan Mayer. She is a member of the International Thriller Writers association and lives in Northeast Ohio.

To hear about upcoming releases, you can subscribe to her infrequent newsletter or visit:

www.carrierubin.com

ALSO BY CARRIE RUBIN

The Bone Hunger

The Bone Curse

The Seneca Scourge

Pen name Morgan Mayer:

The Cruise Ship Lost My Daughter